# The
# First
# Vet

## LINDA CHAMBERLAIN

ISBN:1503038602
ISBN-13: 9781503038608

# DEDICATION

This book is dedicated to Patrick, Amber and Max – it couldn't
be for anyone else, now could it?

# AUTHOR'S NOTE

Two hundred years ago horses were vital to the British economy. They were as important as oil is today. But until the opening of the veterinary college in 1792 there was no one to help if they were sick or injured other than untrained farriers who sometimes butchered them. There were complaints in Parliament that more horses died at home from ignorance than on battlefields. Bracy Clark was one of the college's first pupils; he led in the first horse to its infirmary. This story is inspired by his writing and his lifetime battle against animal cruelty.

# ACKNOWLEDGMENTS

My thanks to the British Library and the librarians at the Royal
Veterinary College for their help with this work.

Also to Will Jessel for the stunning cover photograph, Ben
Catchpole for cover design and last, but certainly not least, my
editor Liz Bailey. Thanks to all of you.

# CHAPTER 1

*Camden, near London, 1794*

Someone had to challenge the man. The governors, the other students – none of them listened to me but Professor Coleman would have to if I could bring myself to accuse him. I couldn't prove he was corrupt, he was too clever for that, but I followed him once, I saw him put the money into his own pocket.

The wind carried my voice as I rehearsed what I would say to the man who ran this place with an iron fist. The short journey from the veterinary college to his house was made difficult by the clouds obscuring the moon and I stumbled on the uneven ground. I stopped and steadied my breathing. I walked on, with more care this time.

I turned into St Pancras Way, saw the house and knew I couldn't waver. I would have to speak my mind but how to dress it up without offence? Perhaps, it didn't matter. I had nothing to lose. Every day there were rumours of bankruptcy and I feared having to return to my brother's with no qualifications and little hope. And to think, I'd given up a promising career in surgery to be here.

My hand gripped the knocker hard but I had to clear my throat when I asked the maid for Professor Coleman. She showed me to his sitting room and I was welcomed by its overwhelming heat and his very broad smile.

He shook my hand with such warmth and yet he must have been dismayed to see me. We were hardly friends. 'Clark, my dear boy! What an unexpected pleasure,' he said with far more charm than necessary. His damp hand was withdrawn from mine with such speed that I knew he was apprehensive. 'Do come in. Such a fearful night, is it not?'

'Thank you. Indeed...indeed it is.' I joined him where he stood by the fire. He was a man of medium height but I dwarfed him and he took a step back. 'You must have known…expected me, surely. Professor...I hope you don't mind my catching up with you in this way only you've cancelled so many appointments, I began to fear you were avoiding me.'

'Oh, tut, tut, why would I make such an effort?' he sighed, leaning on the mantel and examining his long fingers. 'I would first have to notice you, would I not? Come now, I'm teasing but of course it's an honour to see any of my students at this late hour and my door is always open. I hadn't thought to extend the privilege to my home...but why not?' His eyes took their time assessing me, taking in my disordered hair, my unpolished boots and my carelessly tied neck cloth. 'Are those top boots? For the evening?' He shook his head wearily and exhaled. 'Oh, never mind, I digress.'

'Professor! What do my boots matter...when you...? Oh, you preside over the college, sir, and you must know that today something happened that concerns me greatly.' The smile hadn't shifted and he waited as I calmed my irritation. 'Well, I was told not to order any more copper of sulphate for the dispensary. I could hardly believe it. There must be a mistake.'

He coughed to cover his amusement but I could see his look of relief that I had called about something as insignificant as a shortage of medicines.

'Really? How distressing,' he said, happily. 'Give me a

note about that tomorrow and I will look into it. So diligent...but I can assure you tomorrow will be early enough.'

'It keeps happening, sir. We can't treat our patients without the medicines we need. It never used to be like this. I ran that dispensary after Monsieur St Bel died and I made sure we never ran out.'

'Indeed,' he said, one eye quivering at my mention of his predecessor, a Frenchman who was as skilled at the veterinary arts as Coleman was ignorant.

'Surely the college has enough money to buy something so essential and what if one of the horses were to die as a result of this ridiculous policy.' I stopped pacing and rejoined him by the fire. 'These medicines are not expensive.'

'Not expensive!' he cried, then moderated his voice. 'If you had to buy them from your own pocket you would know they were and you wouldn't want students wasting them all the time. But if Mr Clark requires me to investigate he must give me a list. Tomorrow. Surely, you didn't venture out on a night like tonight just to tell me this.'

'The wind is blustery, nothing more. You will look into it, then?'

'I have said so. The dispensary will be stocked with the essentials.'

Ah, the essentials. He'd made me an empty promise and we would be fighting over the meaning of that word until I graduated but I had to let it go for now. I had something far more serious on my mind - if only I could find another word for corruption, one that didn't sound so dishonest.

'There is another thing, Professor.'

'You relieve my mind.'

No, there was no other way of saying it, so instead I asked him, 'Is it true that we are to give up the lease on the fields? Quite an extraordinary thing for a veterinary college to have no pasture for the horses in its care. It seems we are soon to be a laughing stock.'

He was brushing at specks of ash on his sleeve and paused only for a moment. I was skirting around the issue that plagued me but I surprised him and he exhaled slowly as if he was preparing to walk in tight boots.

'Where did you hear such a thing?' he asked. 'Rumours run through the college quicker than dysentery, do they not?'

'It's true, then?'

'No, the governors have to look at all the options and it won't be up to me in any event. But why should a young man like you worry about some fields? Why can't you be like the others and find distraction in the nearest tavern?'

He was laughing in that indulgent way he had but there was nothing kind about the suggestion. The college was run like a monastery and the hours and the rules were so strict that two students had already been thrown out. Doubtless he hoped I would obligingly get myself drunk and then expelled.

With his short, dark hair and pale face, the Professor looked older than his years but he was in his prime, young to take charge of the college. I was twenty three but the gulf between us was greater than years. I knew little of his background beyond his medical training but the luxury of the room only confirmed my suspicions. Goodness, we were cut from different cloth.

The carpet beneath my feet was thick and luxurious - deep enough to hide a thousand lies. From the dim light of the candles I could see the room was elegant. No draught ruffled the sweeping velvet drapes, no chill hung about the room which was such a contrast to our Spartan conditions at the college. A fine painting of a race horse hung above the fireplace and reminded me of the reason for my visit. How pathetic I was. How far short I had fallen from the challenge of my imaginings. The lines I had rehearsed lodged in my throat and the pause was awkward. He wouldn't tolerate me in his sitting room for long and I had to keep him talking. About anything. Until the moment was right. Oh, if only I had proof.

'I have no interest in the tavern and you know it.' I closed my eyes. I couldn't get angry. 'Sir, we shouldn't be in this mess, facing closure. Not with so many new students. You say it's only rumours but, if we are thinking of giving up the fields, it appears to be true.'

'Nonsense,' he bit out, still restrained. 'The college won't close. The government will back us; they have to.'

My hands clenched. 'We shouldn't have to grovel to the politicians not when we have such an income. It's shameful. We have hundreds of subscribers paying us to treat their horses and all your new recruits. Damn it, where are the fees going to, Professor?'

There! I'd said it. And now I only needed to look at his face to find the truth. And yet he was smiling. Not a happy smile, of course, more the weary look you'd give an irritating child you weren't ready to smack. There was a vein on one of his temples that stood out in moments of tension and even in this light I could see it.

'What are you implying?' he hissed, before glancing over his shoulder. 'The fees are not your concern. Stick to your studies, Clark. I gave you all an essay on the respiratory system to write and it won't do to get behind, you know.'

'It's written.'

I wouldn't be diverted and waited, watching him. He knew what I was suggesting even though I'd stopped short of accusing him.

'How dare you ask me about the fees in this way?' he said quietly. Had I not been standing so close, I wouldn't have heard.

'It's my duty to do so.'

'Your duty is to pass your exams and get the hell out of this college. Something you should do with ease. From the moment I was appointed, you've been trouble.'

He was remembering the time he examined the wrong leg on a lame horse. It's more easily done than you might think but I pointed it out in front of the others and he's never forgiven me.

'Professor, I know I irritate you but I demand that you give me some explanation for the plight this college is in. You owe me that at least.'

'You demand?' he said, staring at me. 'An interesting

choice of words.'

'I apologise,' I said, meeting his gaze but knowing it would be unwise to antagonise him further. There were months of studying with the man ahead of me and he was very powerfully connected. 'I would be grateful if you could explain. I gave up a lot to be here, as you know.'

'Very well,' he said, coldly taking his time, assessing whether I was worth the effort.. 'It's simple enough, after all. Have you never before realised that the founders and your very dear Frenchman didn't raise enough money? They were lamentably short if they were to build a college worthy of the name.

'The new infirmary was devilishly expensive and there was no way the student fees would pay for it. Fortunately, our income has increased considerably. So, Mr Clark, you should be thanking me for saving the place but instead you dare to come here making snide accusations.'

For a minute he made me doubt myself. Was I so influenced by my distaste of him that I saw wrongdoing where there was none? Perhaps I was being foolish but I knew in my heart how false he was. That pulse on his right temple told me how anxious I was making him and there was something else bothering me. His avaricious look every time he made a new recruit.

'If you have saved the college I would indeed thank you. But the rumours haven't ceased and we all know you are appealing to the Prime Minister for funds. I am only asking what any member of the government might query.'

A sudden rustling sound and a slight cough drew my attention to the other side of the room which was swathed in shadows. The noise came from somewhere beyond a small sofa where the Professor must have been looking at some papers, now forgotten.

It seemed we were not alone. All this time someone had been listening. No wonder the Professor was speaking in whispers but she must have heard me accuse him. For God's sake, I'd been loud enough.

# CHAPTER 2

I shouldn't have felt embarrassed but I did. I had come so close to losing my temper and I had accused a very eminent man of something highly unsavoury, implied it at least. In front of a witness. Who on earth was she?

Not surprisingly the Professor didn't share my look of dismay - he'd known she was there but how had I missed her? I must have been so consumed with anger and now I felt all the numbing awkwardness of bursting in on their intimate evening. The Professor was guilty of all sorts of crimes but I'd never suspected he kept a woman with him here. Perhaps, she didn't live at the house and only visited occasionally. Did the governors know? Would they care?

He lit more candles from the flames in the grate giving me a chance to see her properly for the first time. Her hair was brown and glossy. I make her sound like a horse but she wasn't; she was enough to make any man forget what was right. She was very lovely and my face coloured when I saw she was wearing what looked to be silk. How did he dare dress her so finely?

She sat back, perfectly at home and rested her chin in one hand as if she was giving something serious consideration.

'You seem to forget,' she said with surprising assurance

for someone who had been discovered alone with an unmarried man, 'that it's quite usual for the head of any educational establishment to take a percentage of the fees. He would only take what is fair and he would never do anything wrong, you know.'

She looked at each of us in turn, the picture of innocence, waiting for a response. She'd said it as lightly as you'd talk about the weather and yet she'd confirmed my worst fears. Her lover, I assumed that was their relationship, was bleeding the college like a surgeon with leeches to feed. I had yet to find out how much he was taking but perhaps the man would oblige me.

'Professor?' I said.

The Professor's eyes were closed and his skin took on a sickly pallor. He recovered himself quickly though and assumed an air of ease as he pushed at the logs in the fire with his foot risking embers that danced around him.

'Don't meddle, if you please,' he told her with ill disguised annoyance. 'I have told you before.'

'I'm sorry, Edward, I didn't think I was,' she said with a tilt of her chin. 'There is nothing wrong with my memory. I only mentioned it because...'

'Enough. You have said enough.'

I thought I had interrupted a cosy evening and yet there was an atmosphere between these two that was tense. I began to wish that I had never come but no, it was worth every bit of this discomfort.

'Forgive me,' I said, enjoying that it was my turn to smile. 'I thought you were alone, sir. Perhaps you would rather leave this interesting discussion for another time...at the college...or...'

'No, there is nothing to discuss. All my dealings with the college are open and honest but they are not your concern. And yet you dare to bring this to my home.'

'I must apologise for that, Professor. I had no idea you had company.'

I turned to leave but was stopped by the man's cold

charm. 'Politeness, dear boy?' he groaned, theatrically. 'A little late perhaps but your manners could be important when setting up your practice. I, for one, will certainly miss your entertaining opinions when you leave since you have such a turn for melodrama. Now that you've recovered yourself, you must allow me to introduce you both.'

That shocked me. What possible motive could he have for keeping me here? He must wish to smooth this over, turn it into a social call and yet I had no idea what would I say to her. My family were Quakers, my upbringing was strict but even my mother would never have shunned such a woman. I would somehow have to understand but it saddened me to see her here – with him.

'Christina,' the Professor drawled, 'allow me to introduce Mr Bracy Clark who started at the college before my time.' I focused on one of the oil paintings. A hunting scene, I think. 'He famously led in the college's first horse last year and it will surely give him a place in the history books but, naturally, we may add modesty to his many qualities. He rarely mentions it.'

'Indeed, Edward. I remember hearing of it.' How sweet she sounded. She even made his name brim with kindness.

'Clark, allow me to introduce my sister, who will be residing with me. I fear you may have shocked her with your rather foolish outburst.'

Sister! I was too slow to hide my look of surprise and could see the likeness now as her hand touched one perfect ringlet that tumbled over her shoulder. And her dress. It might have been silk but it was modest. I met so few women at the college, you see, our lives were very confined.

I bowed, finding as much relief in the formality as the avowed relationship. 'Miss Coleman. Such a pleasure.'

She nodded and seemed puzzled by my beaming smile that might have betrayed my dreadful thoughts. She turned to her brother with a mischievous dance of her eyebrows.

'Shocked? Oh, Edward, what nonsense. I was only a little startled as I have never heard anyone speak to you like that before. My brother tells me he's enormously popular at the college, sir, but of course it's a worrying time so I suppose that might account for it.'

I apologised again for disturbing them but she cut me off with an airy wave of one hand. 'So, you were one of the first here, Mr Clark? That was quite a risk.'

'Really? Why do you say that, ma'am?'

'Well.' She gave the matter some thought. 'The place wasn't finished. There was no infirmary, no stables and nowhere for your lessons. I don't know how you managed and there was only that rather odd Frenchman in charge, so it's a wonder the place ever managed to open.'

She was right although I hadn't cared at the time. 'It didn't seem like a risk even though Monsieur St Bel had to teach us from this very house. It was his then, you see. But he was such a good teacher, the college was his vision and it was an honour to know him.'

'Oh, I see. You must miss him; it was very sad about his death. At the college, too. And it took so long to find someone to replace him. It must be a relief to have my brother looking after you, whatever his faults, and of course the college was in great danger of closing before he was appointed.'

'Oh, that wretched émigré, his very name tires me,' sighed the Professor. 'There are more of them in London than there are blackberries but they have very different standards to us, you know. My dear, you should have seen the state of this house when I arrived. You would not have wanted to unpack your trunk. It's so amusing that people call them leaders of fashion!'

It wasn't the first time I'd heard him dismissive of St Bel like this. The Professor might mock but the French were far ahead of us having opened their first veterinary school thirty years ago. Without St Bel's vast knowledge we would have remained a country dependant on the blundering farriers to doctor our animals. People were so suspicious of science, laughed when they heard it might be applied to the horse and I despaired that Coleman would do nothing to dispel such ignorance. Now he wanted to drive St Bel's memory into the grave with him.

While he regaled us with the poor state of the house, its threadbare rugs and pervading smell of damp, I searched for the brother's likeness in Miss Coleman's face, the mocking twist of his lips. She was younger than him and wasn't burdened by the same, square bone structure that gave the Professor his prominent jaw. They shared the dark polish of mahogany rather than pine, a chiselled dip to the nose but features that were refined on a woman seemed pinched on a man, as if the mouth had no room to relax. Miss Coleman was soft and smiling and had more power to throw me off course.

'I'm surprised you know all this,' I said to her, once the Professor had exhausted his complaints. 'Surely, it's of no interest and...'

'Oh, it is,' she interrupted, regarding me beneath suddenly frowning brows. 'Did you assume I would take no interest in my brother's work? I do, I'm afraid, although Edward says my scientific curiosity is dreadfully unnatural. You men think to have the only inquiring minds. What do you leave for us? Home and hearth are rather limiting, you know.'

'If you haven't a wish for it, I suppose,' I said, as pleasantly as I could. 'But you mistake me, I was only surprised because we've never met and yet you know something of me.'

A faint smile dimpled her cheeks. 'Mostly from what Edward has told me. But you're a scientist. Don't you think there is so much more to the world than domestic concerns?' Then she whispered, 'I apologise, I should really keep my views to myself.'

'It would certainly make a change, Christina,' the brother said, through tight lips. 'You are shockingly outlandish and Mr Clark didn't come to hear all this nonsense.'

'No, he came to give you a dressing down and was talking as though the problems are your fault which anyone can see is quite ridiculous.' Her eyes were wide with life, willing me to share this happy line in banter. 'I'm doing an excellent job of distracting him.'

11

'I don't seek for him to be diverted, my child. I have already put his comments from my mind. His visit does not concern me in the least.'

I didn't believe a word but the sister's lively conversation had taken the venom from my tongue. I wanted to ask how he paid for his comfortable lifestyle but it was foolish to accuse him in his own sitting room, in front of his innocent sister.

Or was she? There was no awkwardness about her, only assurance, and she was peering at me intently. There was a smile, it was warmer than the Professor's disdainful smirk but it could have been equally false.

'Concerned? No, why should you be, Edward?' she said. 'Although, it's strange to see Mr Clark a little lost for words. Ever since he noticed me sitting here he has become unsure of himself. Why is that, I wonder? Did you not want a witness to your slander, sir?'

# CHAPTER 3

I wasn't ready for that and neither was the Professor who turned to her sharply with a look of disapproval.

'Christina, how many times must I tell you?' he said. 'We have left this subject behind.'

'I have said no slander, ma'am,' I replied, ignoring the Professor's remark. 'My awkwardness was...well, it was merely a misunderstanding.' I could hardly explain that I'd mistaken her for the man's fancy piece.

'Perhaps I misheard. I thought you were implying that my brother was taking too much money from the college.'

'Forgive me, but this house is the only part of the college that seems amply provided for and now the governors are going cap in hand to the government. Every day there are rumours that we might close.'

'There is nothing cap in hand about our approach,' the Professor insisted, his voice rising with annoyance. 'The country needs horses and so of course it needs vets. There were complaints in Parliament only the other day about how many horses were dying – more at home through lack of care than there ever was in the wars. Let our MPs put their money where their mouths are. No, Christina, don't try to interrupt.'

She moderated her voice to a determined whisper. 'But

you haven't refuted him. Not properly. And he certainly hasn't apologised.'

'I did rebuff him but you rarely listen. Clark, my sister won't be happy unless I call you out or some such foolery but we will leave duelling to our idle aristocrats. Don't forget he is young, his foolish notions are best ignored and he did apologise for bringing all this to my home when he knows it should be saved for the college. If I remember rightly, we were going to ring for tea.'

I glimpsed the frown he sent her before he turned to me. 'Don't forget,' he said. 'The war with France will make us secure especially if it is a long one. One doesn't like to profit from such things but where will the cavalry regiments be without horses, eh?'

'On foot, I would imagine.'

'Yes, very witty,' he said, indulgent once more. 'I'll put one of my students in every regiment and for that the government will be happy to pay me. The college will be safe. Indeed, it will thrive.'

'But you hope to train them in three months! I don't call that safe, Professor. I will have had three years training by the time I've finished. It's madness to shorten the course.'

'There's no choice and they will be better than the farriers. The governors approve, you know. You are wasting your breath, I'm afraid, and my time, but I am at your disposal.'

Every hair on his head was arranged with precision. His face was lean, almost cadaverous with the fire throwing shadows of distortion, and the nose was long and angular. His waistcoat was covered in flowers and his neck cloth bore the intricacies of a puzzle. Vanity – that's what I was dealing with. He was seeking glory and position but the good of the horse meant little to him.

Miss Coleman got up to call a servant and took slow steps as if her leg had gone to sleep from sitting too long.

'Oh, do sit down,' her brother tutted, just loudly enough for me to hear. 'I'll do it.'

'I am perfectly capable of...'

'Of course. But it is quite unnecessary.'

'Anyway, I didn't want you to fight him,' she mumbled, resuming her seat. 'But I can't believe you let him speak to you like that.'

'Leave it be.'

He said something else I was unable to hear and she seemed satisfied. A flustered servant arrived and Miss Coleman asked for tea. Later, she was smiling and in command of her temper once more. She passed me a cup and added some sugar to her own drink with some delicate silver tongs. I was admiring the china, possibly Wedgwood, and began to see the funny side of the situation. I was taking tea with the man I thought corrupt and I was making polite conversation with his sister. I leant back, with my legs crossed at the ankles. My top boots were something a gentleman might wear for a ride on his horse and were in want of polish and my hair was long, tied back in a braid that was working loose. I cared little for appearances but for once would have appreciated some elegance. Everything about me was too big and solid – my neck, my jaw, even my nose could be described as strong.

Miss Coleman sat on the edge of her seat and glanced at my large hands cradling the delicate cup. 'Mr Clark, are you the student who wrote about the famous race horse?'

'I am, if you mean Eclipse. You must have been reading the Professor's files because I can't picture him telling you about *that.*'

'Yes, they fascinate me, I'm afraid.' She seemed pleased to find a safe subject. 'Edward hates the servants moving his papers and so I like to tidy his study. The post mortem was rather controversial, if I remember. Didn't the Frenchman carry it out?'

The Professor sighed. 'Only because there was no one else. He botched it, of course.'

I kept a lid on my irritation. 'He did not botch it, sir. I was there and it was conducted very properly. It was a great privilege to write up Monsieur St Bel's findings for him. My friend, Edmund Bond, was given the skeleton.'

'Was he really?' Miss Coleman gasped. 'What a prize. There was nothing about that in your work.' She turned to her brother who seemed bemused. 'I have to read some to know where it should be put away.'

He grunted.

'I'm glad you found it interesting,' I said. 'I recorded his career and the findings of the post mortem because so many people wanted to know why he was so fast. Monsieur St Bel was successful in that endeavour, Professor.'

The man shrugged. 'Was he really?'

Miss Coleman faced me as if we were the only people in the room. 'I wish I had read more. The cause of death was of less interest then?'

She cast a sly look at her brother who was examining the ornaments on the mantelpiece. He held a delicate figurine in the palm of his hand and was wholly occupied by its smooth finish.

'Christina,' he said quietly, without shifting his gaze. 'I hope you aren't going to give us details of that horse's demise. Not many people will tolerate your interest, or rather your obsession, in matters that are not in your sphere.'

'Oh, fiddle!' she said. 'We all know he suffered from gripes, poor animal. Now, Mr Clark will find a cure for such things with your help, Edward. Do tell me more.' Her eyes widened happily, I almost believed her sincere.

'Certainly, if your brother doesn't mind.'

'Oh, he only gets moody if I rattle on,' she laughed. 'He doesn't think a lady should discuss medical procedures.' And then she whispered quite audibly, 'It's terribly unseemly.'

'I doubt you would have found the post mortem to your taste. Even Henry, my brother, was taken ill at the sight of it.'

'He shouldn't have gone if he hadn't the stomach for it. He'd have been in the way. Edward says the same of me. He won't let me watch you at the college. As if *I* would swoon.'

The Professor rubbed his forehead wearily. 'What would people say if I let you go to a post mortem? What a spectacle that would be. You want to be the talk of the neighbourhood but I'm sure you will be *noticed* without my help. Yes, you might remain on your feet but you would distract my students. It is not going to happen.'

'Distract? Oh, I doubt it,' she countered. 'Besides, I'm just as capable of scientific endeavour and your students would hardly be talking to me while they are cutting up a dead horse. Really, Edward, are you suggesting they would flirt with me? That would be a first and, anyway, we would be above such silliness. Oh, it would be wonderful to understand the workings of an animal's body, to find out why he had died and then use the knowledge on those still alive.'

Women who were interested in science were regarded as such oddities but I'd always imagined they would be prim, starchy creatures. This one seemed to revel in her brother's disapproval and was checking me for similar signs of disgust. But no. If my eyes dilated it was for quite another reason.

'The college is no place for someone of your...your nature,' her brother said. 'You must leave it for those who are more able and give up this tendency to court favour with everybody. I don't know what you hope to achieve by it.'

She reddened and was flustered until her shoulders rose with strength. 'Mr Clark, I do apologise for reading your file but when papers are left open – well, anyway, I only read the smallest bit so I don't see how anyone could object. Don't worry, he doesn't mean it.'

I told her not to give it another thought but the Professor's sour words puzzled me. From under my brows I saw him staring at her with distaste. That he should view me with hostility came as no surprise. I had often seen what lay beneath his charming exterior but many of my fellow students took him at face value. The figurine the Professor had been cradling was returned to the mantelpiece, its head was broken.

'I trust it wasn't...I hope it wasn't too boring,' I said, averting my eyes from her brother.

His brooding presence grew out of proportion to his slim frame and I could sense the power that drove him. I desperately wanted to keep her talking.

'Oh, no, it wasn't at all. So, why was Eclipse so fast?' she asked, throwing me a sweet look of expectation.

'It was his heart, ma'am.'

'In what way?'

'Well, it was so big.'

The Professor shook his head. 'I expect it was but why would we discuss such a thing so soon after dinner? Is it only me or is it terribly stuffy in here? I can't bear an overheated room and if only people would get a bit more fresh air into their lungs there wouldn't be the health problems there are today. As a surgeon I often found that an open window was more effective than a dose of medicine but what patient would pay our fee if we cured them so easily, eh?' He chuckled and got up to pull aside the drapes and open a window, taking deep draughts of cold air. 'I might have told you about one of my patients when I was in practice with a very troublesome respiratory disorder who I was able to help with this method. It is no different with the horse.'

Miss Coleman nodded at him briefly, before returning her attention to me. 'Do go on,' she said, quietly. 'This is so fascinating.'

I drew closer to her. 'His heart was far heavier than average. So, naturally he could run with very little effort. I was too young to see him race but they say he galloped with his nose trailing on the ground. Mr Stubbs's portrait doesn't show that, naturally. He was very beautiful even on the dissecting table. A light sorrel colour with a very impressive head.'

'He sounds like he was a difficult ride. I pity the poor jockey. How did he manage?'

'John Oakley never got out his whip, so they say, he just had to stay on but that must have been a challenge with such a head carriage. The horse was never beaten and he made the rest of the field look like donkeys.'

She laughed and even her brother gave a glimmer of a smile. 'No wonder he had to retire. How ironic,' she said.

'Yes, a victim of his own success. No one would bet

against a certain winner and so his racing career was short but sweet, his future was at stud.'

'And that's where we shall leave him,' the Professor said when he saw her animated face. 'Christina, I have never appreciated such discussions and I had hoped that in this, at least, you might heed me. We will maintain a semblance of decorum, if you please.' Then he muttered, 'Surely, there must be some femininity in you somewhere.'

'Yes, it was careless of me to smile,' she agreed. 'I must be such a trial but please don't look so concerned. You know I wouldn't dream of enquiring any further.'

Her brother eyed me with irritation as if I should know that mention of a stallion at stud was not to be endured. Miss Coleman's lips trembled and her eyes were watering with suppressed amusement. She looked at me from under her lashes and I had to stare at the floor. My mouth was also quivering.

'That's enough,' he told her.

'Oh, absolutely.'

I ignored the man's warning.

'He was a remarkable animal though, sir. In his lifetime he sired more than three hundred winners. And countless others, probably. That's some achievement, you must admit.'

'Undoubtedly but...'

'Do you know, he was so popular that a special carriage was made for him? He was pulled around the country by two enormous drays so that he could visit the mares of his acquaintance and still remain lively enough for the job at hand.'

'Clark! Please!' Professor Coleman had turned white and his eyes darted towards his sister who was beautifully spellbound.

'And the stud fee. You will never guess how much.'

'We have no interest in...'

'I'll tell you then, shall I? Fifty guineas.'

I felt a sense of achievement at Miss Coleman's snort of astonishment. She blushed to the roots of her glossy hair and could only look at me for a moment before she had to turn away. Perhaps she was embarrassed but I thought she was laughing. For some reason I didn't care although I knew this sort of thing wasn't discussed in mixed company. It was like a shared confidence, something deliciously forbidden as if we were wayward children up to some devilment. Perhaps I was being silly and boyish, seeking to defy the Professor in any way I could but I sensed she wanted to join in the prank. Her face was outwardly calm but her eyes told me everything.

'That's an awful lot of money, Professor,' I continued. 'When you think that a lot of the horses in our stables might not be worth that much.'

My words were aimed at the Professor but I was watching his sister and barely noticed his look of thunder. I shook her hand before I left shortly after. It was soft and warm but her guard was back, loyalty had reclaimed her. I bowed and would have gone but her brother demanded my attention.

'Do me the honour of coming to my consulting room. Tomorrow. After the morning lecture,' he said, coldly. 'Don't be late.'

Perhaps I would be castigated for discussing stallions with his sister but then realised my mistake. He might have something to say to her on that subject but with me the stakes were higher. My accusations were not forgotten.

# CHAPTER 4

'Where have you been, Bracy?' Edmund Bond breathed a sigh
of relief and stopped still. 'It's getting late, you know. I've been
looking for you everywhere.'

'Have you? I'm sorry.'

'You might have said you were going out, I'd have
come with you. I haven't escaped this place for a month and
here you are sneaking out on your own to have a good time.'

He had a fist full of papers and a book under one arm
which he tossed onto a side table as I joined him in the
college's dimly lit corridor. His fair hair was cut short and he
was dressed conservatively with buff pantaloons and plain,
dark waistcoat and coat – a picture of efficiency with his fists
settled on his hips waiting for my explanation.

'Where can the swotty little sod be?' he said, laughing. 'I
was about to check the stables but Fred's just come from there
and he hadn't seen you either. You've not been to the Inn,
surely?'

I ran a hand through my disordered hair, found the
braid that held it back and stuck it in my pocket. 'Not an
outing of pleasure, I'm afraid. I went to see the Professor.'

'Of course you did. Seeing as you two are such friends.'

'No, really. I did.'

'Oh. That was quite an honour and while you were there no doubt you had a little chat about what the hell he's up to because there's talk of us having to give up the lease on the fields. Did you know that?'

'Yes, but I've still no idea if it's going to happen.'

'Did he invite you?'

'Of course not. I turned up unannounced.'

'What for? Oh, no. You tackled him, didn't you? Did you...did you really accuse him?'

'I'm not sure. Oh, goodness, I can't remember what I said but I think I levelled pretty much everything at his door. Edmund, he's taking a cut of the fees.'

'He told you this, did he?'

'No, of course not. But his sister did, much to his embarrassment.'

'Really?' He stared at me, unable to credit the news. 'So you were right. Damn the man. He'll ruin the college but, Bracy, the governors must have agreed this. Unless he's taking more than he should. Come on, we don't want to be overheard. The kitchen is empty.'

He led me to the end of the corridor, grabbed a pewter candle holder from a side table and pushed me into the warm room that smelled of the watery, mutton stew we had eaten for dinner. Shining copper pots and pans filled the shelves and plates had been left to dry on a wooden rack. The only noise was the rattling of the sash in the wind. We sat on the massive pine table that had been scrubbed with a solution of vinegar after the servants had cleared up. If the cook saw us using her facilities as a seat she'd have our hides but we felt safe knowing she had left for the night.

'I challenged him about the fees and we argued for a bit,' I confessed. 'Then he introduced his sister who let slip that he takes a cut. She said it was customary.'

'I didn't know he had a sister,' Edmund replied. 'He's kept her well hidden. You shouldn't have challenged him on your own like that. You must be mad.'

'I had to. He's already made the college a laughing stock

by shortening the course. He only cares about getting rich.'

Edmund's face was pale. 'Did you accuse him of corruption? Stealing?'

'No, I didn't go that far. He'll have me out of here if he can.'

'I bet he will, the rogue. I wish you'd spoken to me before you rushed off, full of spleen. Oh, my God. What have you done?'

'I'll find out soon enough. He wants to see me tomorrow. You know he hates the lot of us. Oh, I know he's always friendly, that's his way. But, deep down, we're a problem for a man with such an open palm. He only wants his new students; he gets good money from them for much less work.'

'True. There's no more money to be made out of the likes of you and me.'

'The governors daren't challenge him. They're so frightened because they've no one else unless they look to France and that can't happen thanks to the war.'

'They would have to replace him if you can show he's as corrupt as you think he is.'

'But how can I prove it? I can't break into his study and look at the accounts and I doubt they would tell the truth.' I paused and then laughed. 'Or should I simply ask to see them, as if I have the right?'

'Did you really think you'd be able to stop him by confronting him? Where's your common sense? Yes, you'd have been better off breaking in and sneaking a look at the accounts. Now, he'll try and ruin you as well as the college. I wish you had thought this through.'

I leapt from the table and opened the door of the pantry. I had an appetite for bread, cheese too, if there was any. Edmund joined me, holding the tallow candle aloft and pushing me to one side as he spied the bread in a wooden bin.

'You're always hungry,' he said.

'Not when I'm asleep…and I'll sleep better once I've got this inside me.'

We found cheese under a crockery dome. It was dried but tasted good and we consumed it quickly knowing we were running out of time before bed. The college was in Camden, far from the fleshpots of London, and was run on strict lines. We had to be in bed by eleven, up first thing and were not allowed to indulge in strong drink or associate with the servants. Two students had already been thrown out for devoting too much time to the nearest inn and its skittle ground. A petition hadn't saved them and there had been no relaxation of the rules. It irked me that there could be no association with any of the domestic staff and yet it was acceptable to be ignorant of the workings of the horse. I was one of the few who could cope uncomplaining with the rules. My sins were a precocious knowledge but I was learning to hide that.

Our feet echoed on the grey, stone floor as we headed to our rooms and I told Edmund more about Coleman's sister. 'I thought she was some fancy piece at first. Not that she looked like that but I didn't know what to think.'

Edmund laughed, shielding the candle from draughts. 'What a life, stuck with the Professor every night. Can't we befriend her? Was she pretty?'

'I can't remember what she looked like. She might have had brown hair...but why should we get to know her?'

'Must I really spell it out? Well, she might tell you how much he takes out of the fees. Plus, you said she tidies his study so she might have access to the accounts. You could do with a glimpse at them and I thought she might like to hand them over to you. Of course, you'd have to make her sweet on you but I think you are capable of the sacrifice. There again, you've had too many years with your head in a book for most women's taste. Brown hair? Is that all you can say?'

I laughed emptily. She wasn't beautiful in a conventional way because she had a very animated face. Yes, her eyebrows were very mobile and her chin seemed to have quite a defiant tilt. And her lips. I can picture her lips because they were unusually large. What you would call a big smile. She had quite a pleasing figure, too. When she perched on the edge of the sofa, listening to me so intently, I was momentarily put off my stride but Edmund wouldn't be interested in hearing about that.

'I think you would call it brown but I might be wrong. How would I make her sweet on me when I'll probably never see her again? Besides, I couldn't do anything so unscrupulous. You shouldn't even suggest it.'

'I think you'll find I wasn't serious...but why wouldn't you see her again? If she's living with Professor Coleman we are bound to see her. Apart from some cows and a few farmers, society is rather limited here unless you count the smallpox hospital.'

Our cramped rooms, which overlooked the stable yard, led off a long corridor with a sitting room at the far end. Fred Cherry, another student, was sitting on a stool near the fire and looked up when we opened the door. I closed the curtains and sat down, tugging at my boots which were muddy and damp.

'What on earth is that smell?' Edmund said. 'Fred! Were you on duty tonight? You're meant to treat the horses not bring them inside with you.'

Fred rubbed his stained pantaloons which were causing the problem and sniffed his hands. 'What are you talking about? I've washed. Since when did you worry about such things? We work with horses so don't be surprised if we all smell like a stable.' He had a thick crop of unruly, dark hair and the wiry physique of a jockey. His father bred fine, blood animals and he had lived with horses all his life. 'Not suffering the same problem after your hard day in the dispensary, then?'

'You mock but I was rushed off my feet making worm balls. I can still smell the linseed,' Edmund said, coming to sit opposite him.

'You'll need to make more of them tomorrow,' I said. 'That bay mare is in urgent need by the look of her.'

'Yes, sort her out, would you?' Fred muttered. 'She's making a mess of my clothes as well as her stall.'

'Bracy's on duty tomorrow. He'll make them,' Edmund

said. 'He runs that dispensary better than any of us. By the way, we're getting low on alum in powder. I wanted to make some lineament but couldn't. Are we allowed to order some more?'

I doubted it but then the door bounced against the wall and our conversation was halted by the arrival of another student. William Sewell walked in looking too exquisite for such quarters. In spite of all our outdoor work his skin was reminiscent of a jug of milk and he surveyed the room as if he expected heads to turn.

'Does no one think of anything else?' he sighed, adjusting his shirt points which formed a stiff frame for his face. 'I despair. Really I do.' He gathered up his sketches from a small table he had been working on and examined one with approval. He was no scholar but a great favourite of the Professor's. 'Mmmm…I like that, even if I say so myself.' He put the sketch down and returned his attention to us. 'As I was saying, how would any of you fare in the polite - um, world? I can just imagine dear Fred being introduced to a lady of quality. He'd scratch his head. No he'd sniff his, you know, armpit, and wonder why her ivory fan had turned limp. Bracy is hardly any better.'

'Why?' I said, laughing. 'I've never had any complaints about my conversation.'

'You surprise me. You're always on about the horse. Or ailments, something like that.'

'It's my major concern while I'm here; I'm perfectly able to discuss other things.'

Fred yawned and stretched. 'So can I. Anyway, what's wrong with checking your armpit? How else does a man know when he's in need of soap and water? You might have caught me doing it but that doesn't mean I would in front of your mother.'

'Oh delightful! Dear Fred, you are so droll. But your prospects would be greatly improved if you tidied your appearance.' William's face was full of derision. 'Bracy, those clothes are large. Edmund, that snuff-coloured coat is dull and Fred has no sense, no style at all. His neck cloth has been worn for days and it wasn't tied well in the first place.' He struggled out of his own coat with some difficulty, groaning with frustration, thanks to the tightness of its fit. 'Professor Coleman says my own turnout is - oh, goodness, that's it - and, you know, it doesn't take an enormous effort.'

He put the coat carefully on the back of a chair. William admired a dandified style and often copied the Professor's elegant touches - his fob watch, and his snuff box. He was wearing perfume which was a new innovation.

'The man shouldn't be worried about the clothes we wear,' I said. 'No one would expect a vet to be dressed fashionably. Oh, I know you manage but I don't know why you bother. He's letting any old tradesman come here and they don't aspire to the polite world, not that the haut ton would have them.'

'I hadn't thought of that,' he said. 'Anyway, there's another reason for making a little more effort with your rig out. An addition to Professor Coleman's household. You might see her occasionally although whether you will be um - whether you will meet her, as I did, is a moot point bearing in mind all those problems I mentioned earlier.'

Fred was feeling the lack of female company and lifted his head swiftly from his hand. 'Who are you talking about? A woman?'

'Indeed, a young woman. Didn't I just say? The Professor's sister. Charming but sadly she'll say whatever comes into her head. She fancies herself intelligent which would be amusing but she's quite a responsibility, unless... No, I can't see in what way anyone can help him with Miss Coleman.'

'I met her tonight,' I said. 'I can see why you might have a problem but there is nothing wrong with a woman being intelligent.'

'You met her! Well, you should have said, instead of being so secretive, keeping quiet all the time.' William's eyes darted about the room. 'You'll have noticed how lively she is and in her situation that isn't always a good thing. Not that the

Professor made any complaint, such a remarkable man.'

Fred had thrown sleep to the corners of his mind. 'I didn't know Coleman had a sister. What does she look like?'

'She looks...well, I don't know. Like the Professor, I fancy, not that he's - well, not very - but they look very much like brother and sister, you know. Her face is quite lovely, which makes one feel all the more pity for her. She's been living with some aunt but now the old lady has died and, since both their parents are dead, she's going to be residing with him. I couldn't discuss it with him, awkward business, doubt he had much choice. Where else could a woman like that go?'

'Why would we feel sorry for her,' muttered Fred. 'That's taking it a bit far, isn't it? I know the Professor rattles on with his odd sayings but he knows an awful lot of people and that could be useful for a sister. She'll meet all sorts of eminent surgeons. Even the Duke of Northumberland visits his house, they're great friends.'

He got off the stool and was furiously pulling off his clothes and examining them.

'Fred, what are you doing?' I asked.

'I want a clean neck cloth for tomorrow. He's right, look at this, I'm a disgrace.'

It was hardly surprising, I suppose, that a group of single, young men should strut and ruffle their feathers at the mention of a woman coming amongst them.

'Come on, out with it,' I asked William. 'What's the matter with her?'

A look of distaste marred William's pale features. 'She fights it, that's the trouble. At least, that's the impression I got. She even insists on riding, don't you know? That blood animal in our stables. Nice looking animal, bright chestnut. At least, I think it was chestnut. What she's thinking of I don't - mind you, I hear she's perfectly able to handle it. Hardly bears thinking about, does it?'

'I'm still not with you, my friend,' I said, picturing the lively woman who had eyed me with such hostility but then laughed so delightfully.

'You've not seen it? Oh, dear. It's so obvious if you see her - well, walking. Such an embarrassment for the Professor and of course it means she'll have little chance of - who in their right mind would marry her? No wonder she shows such an unhealthy interest in the sciences and she's even read that dreadful book by Mary Wollstonecraft about women. It's hardly the thing but the Professor is very tolerant.'

He looked at the blank faces around him and sighed. 'The woman is a cripple.'

# CHAPTER 5

Oh, how I came to hate that word. It was so laden with restrictions and it hardly described the woman I had met in the Professor's sitting room that night. She was so lively. I remembered her eyes dancing with mischief and how she talked to me in a way no woman had done before. She was interested in things that were important and she was no meek creature either. It was obvious she fought to get her own way in spite of her domineering brother.

My first impression of her had swollen like a sponge in water. I hadn't thought her beautiful but then I had been blinded by my fury with the Professor. So, she wasn't conventionally pretty, her features were strong, her lips rather full and her whole demeanour showed that she had to fight for life's every inch. The tilt of her chin was enough to show her resolution. I had seen no evidence of her lying on a couch or carrying a stick. She rode a horse. She was fine. Yes, she had walked a little stiffly. I thought she had been sat still for too long but that hardly made her a cripple.

'How can you be sure?' I snapped at William.

'Don't be cross with me, Bracy,' he said. 'I didn't do anything to her. She walks very strangely, that's all. It's almost like there is one leg different, shorter than the other. There was a boy in my village like that and he got teased, quite mercilessly, not that I said anything about that to the Professor. Really, I didn't know where to look when she started walking. I must say, I'd rather she had stayed sitting down and do you know, I think the Professor agrees with me.

'He was telling me how she persuaded him to buy that horse from Tattersalls. Definitely a chestnut, now I come to think of it because he said something about it. Of course, he regrets buying the animal because he can hardly tell her not to ride it. He could, I suppose. Oh, she must look ridiculous on horseback.'

'What makes you say that?' I asked.

'It stands to reason. If she walks like that she'll be a bit of a sight on the back of a horse. Well, I can't picture it.' He laughed and a look of revulsion marred his soppy features. 'I don't even want to picture it! He should have got her a...a mule. Let's hope she keeps the thing in walk, eh?'

'You are mistaken,' I said. 'Her leg, if it is lame, might hardly be noticeable on horseback.'

Fred shrugged and put his neck cloth back on. 'You had me interested for a minute there, William. I might make this neck cloth last another few days in that case. Isn't that typical? We get within a furlong of a woman and what happens? She turns out to have one bloody leg.'

They laughed and William did an impression of her stumbling walk until he fell into one of the chairs. It was impossible for me to laugh, they were being so childish. William, who was tall and as tender as a sapling, wriggled around in the seat, groaning and even Edmund was smiling at his ridiculous performance. He saw my face and the smile was wiped from his own.

'I think you must be exaggerating,' he said, one brow arched at me in question.

'I tell you, I'm not,' William cried. 'Oh my God, how on earth does she get on a horse, let alone ride it? Someone would have to lift her on. It doesn't bear thinking about. I would be so embarrassed if she asked me for help. Professor Coleman must know how it's done, he's very kind, but how? Two hands? A leg up? No, I know – I would have to throw her on. That's it. Do you think someone leads her? Waste of a good horse, if you ask me.'

I had heard enough. 'She'd hardly come to you for advice, William. I've never seen you on a horse.'

'I'm not much of a rider, it's true, but if I was I wouldn't be wriggling about like she must. I could be quite good if I put my mind to it. Sadly, I'm much too busy to become proficient. I've still got that essay on the respiratory system to finish. I'm dashed if I can read the notes I made but it doesn't matter, I can remember most of what he said.'

I had the impression there was more to William's lack of riding than he made out. He wouldn't have lacked the opportunities when he was growing up but he handled the animals in our infirmary with nervous apprehension.

'I'd be happy to teach you to ride,' I said. 'There are plenty of animals here that need exercising. You could come out with me tomorrow if you like. We have time after lunch before the next lecture.'

'No, no, I thank you. I must study. Did I not mention - the Professor is looking for an assistant? He's hinted that I would make the ideal candidate but I must get to grips with all this anatomy. The thought of lecturing is rather frightening but I don't see why I couldn't do it. Oh, I wouldn't teach you lot, I'd never be able to concentrate if you were crowding the lecture room but the new students. I'd be good enough for them, wouldn't I? The Professor thinks so anyway and that's all that matters, to my mind.'

'Write it down first then they'll make sense of what you're saying,' Fred muttered. 'I might apply for the post myself. I know anatomy far better than you, plus I can handle the horses so why shouldn't I? I suppose I'll have to brush up on toad eating the Professor but it would be worth it. Did he say whether there's much of a salary?'

Edmund applauded the challenger heartily and I was grateful for his intervention although it meant he had seen through my thinly disguised interest in Christina Coleman. I sat in one of the chairs and picked up a book I had been reading earlier, letting them fight over the merits of the two candidates. I turned the pages but had trouble remembering where I had left off. I looked at one page three times before realising I had read it earlier.

The pair of them fighting over Coleman's job sickened me. I thought neither of them worthy even though Fred was my friend and had a lifetime's experience with horses. William's mockery didn't surprise me but Fred was a better man than that. How could he talk so heartlessly about a woman who was so disadvantaged? How could he laugh?

Oh, he hadn't said much but his attitude was so acceptable that no one would challenge him for it. I might have smiled at William's antics myself had I not met the woman earlier. Don't we all scorn people who can't achieve what we manage with so little effort and yet by rights we should admire their struggle? Even I, occupying this moral high ground, was conscious of warring emotions inside me. I felt defensive of Miss Coleman, I had an urge to protect her from their disparaging remarks but I had to acknowledge that she had disappointed me. Like Fred, I could bemoan that I was within a furlong of a woman of interest only to find she wasn't what she first seemed.

At least she hadn't seen my regret. It lurked somewhere between me and a book that was making my eyes glaze over. For many minutes I refused to accept William's portrayal. She wasn't that bad. I had seen with my own eyes as she got up slowly from the sofa. Ah, yes, then the Professor had intervened. He stopped her even though there was no great difficulty and no stumble. Oh, my God she could laugh, too. She loved my story about the stallion even though her brother was outraged. So what if she limped, I wanted to talk to her again. I didn't care, it took nothing from her. It was such a shame. The poor woman, to have a face that could entice only to have it marred by an ugly walk. I felt her loss and for some reason it felt like my loss too. I had no right to the feeling and nothing to mourn but it sat inside me like a poor dinner.

'You've read that page, Bracy. Come on, out with it.'

Edmund sat opposite me. The noise in the room had dissipated. Fred and William had gone off to bed.

'What do you mean?'

'You were fine two hours ago. You were Bracy Clark, angry young student, seeking to avenge the vile and greedy professor. Something - or someone - has happened in between. I've known you too long to pretend nothing is up.'

'Of course I haven't changed. A lot has happened tonight. This business with Professor Coleman is occupying me, that is all.'

My friend drew his chair closer to the fire and shook his fair head sternly. 'That won't do, not for me. You had better tell me about the man's sister. We don't have secrets, you and I.'

We did but he was ignorant of it. My thoughts turned to the post mortem of the illustrious horse, Eclipse. Edmund had done most of the physical work that day and we were both spattered with blood and dirt by the end it but he was the one who wielded the knife under St Bel's expert direction.

'We do, Ed. There is something I've kept from you for quite a while.'

'What! Surely not.'

'I've never told you because it sounds so petty.'

'Well, tell me now. Get it off your chest.'

'You have Eclipse's skeleton. I've envied you ever since.'

Edmund laughed and nodded his head in despair. 'What a funny fellow you are. I tell you what; I will bequeath it to you. One day it will be yours.'

'No don't talk like that, you will make me maudlin.'

'Very well, we will leave it that I am looking after the old boy for you. I suspect his bones will be on this earth far longer than ours. Now, tell me about this woman who's touched your upper works or some other bit of you.'

'You're not going to be crude, are you?'

'Only if you keep quiet.'

So I told him what he wanted to hear, keeping back

what I didn't want to tell him, what I wasn't sure of.

Even to my own ears I sounded confused. I was upset and annoyed. I was upset with Miss Coleman for disappointing me but then I also felt guilty. She had enough to cope with in life without adding my emotions to the equation.

'Do you know, Ed, I think he might be cruel to her,' I said, remembering how coldly her brother spoke to her.

'That's rather melodramatic, Bracy. Didn't you say she was finely dressed? And don't forget he's bought her a rather nice horse. I would say he sounds like an indulgent brother if anything and you might be letting your distaste for the man influence you.'

'You're probably right. I'm probably imagining it. The trouble is we fell out early on in our relationship and neither of us has been able to forgive. I will try harder, I promise. I might need to tomorrow.'

# CHAPTER 6

Damn it. I was too old to be kept waiting in the Professor's consulting room like a naughty school boy. He was hoping to torment me with worry while he interviewed yet another new recruit.

My brother, Henry, had warned me there might come a day when I would regret giving up my surgeon's apprenticeship. In spite of the dressing down I was anticipating the only regret I felt was over the Frenchman's death and the appointment of his ridiculous replacement. If only St Bel hadn't died. A futile thought, I know, but one that plagued me each time I sat in the college's newly opened lecture room. The Frenchman never saw it for he died eight months after we opened and now Professor Edward Coleman presided. The two men couldn't have been more different. St Bel was knowledgeable but burdened by his émigré status – a man who lived in an alien country while war was brewing with his own. He feared spies at every corner and sometimes suspected his pupils were eavesdropping and plotting against him.

Coleman, on the other hand, came to us boasting of his ignorance but swelling with confidence. I handled him badly from the start. The trouble was he knew nothing about the horse's anatomy or its ailments and thought he could apply what he knew of human diseases to this new branch of science. I couldn't help knowing more than him. Was I supposed to hide my knowledge to spare the man's feelings? What folly it was for the governors to appoint him. He was charming, he was well connected but he would undo the profession.

The consulting room was the Professor's domain, neat and precise. There were no papers on the mahogany desk. Quills and ink were artfully arranged; books lined one wall, matched into colours with a section for green ones and another for red and so on. William Buchan's leather bound work on domestic medicine was rubbing shoulders with a guide to the Lake District so it would be a miracle if the man ever found anything.

I yawned and fiddled with the quills, testing them for sharpness. There was a good supply of ink but no paper lying around so I couldn't idle the time with writing. The Professor's hat on the coat stand proved a bit of a temptation. I looked in the glass hanging on the wall. People said my hair was chestnut but, to me, it was thick and the colour of mud. The hat fitted me quite well but my hair would need a cut if I was to carry off the elegant look. The Professor's cane, with an engraved silver top, found its way under my arm.

'Clark!' I drawled. 'Your relentless questions are tedious and keeping me awake. You are the most troublesome guest.'

The Professor's thin lips would appear more dangerous when delivering such a dismissal. Trying it again, I hardened my face until I had it just right but realised I was wasting an opportunity. I opened the door. The porter's lodge was empty and beyond was the lecture room where a group of students was gathered. A horse was being led out the creaking, wicket gate - one of our patients bound for home. It was Thursday, so a lot would be collected today unless they hadn't made a recovery or were bound for the dissecting table. Closing the door, I leant back against its hard surface. Somewhere in this room might be the college accounts. I had five minutes, maybe more. Surely, I would hear someone coming across those flagstones and have enough time to hide my tracks.

I started with the shelves but wasn't diverted for long. I sat behind the desk on a leather bound chair and put the hat and cane to one side. The top drawer was locked but the one underneath slid open without a noise. Paper, more quills, some letters. The next drawer was more interesting and had a lists of students, proposed changes to the rules, minutes of the governors' meetings.

There was a noise outside, a voice which gave me enough warning to close the drawers and lean back in the chair. My heart was leaping about but my breathing was measured enough although I'd rather not face the Professor while lounging on the wrong side of the desk. To rush to the other side risked an appearance of guilt.

The door opened and I saw dark blue velvet brushing the floor and a pair of soft, laced up riding boots. The lady wearing them gasped at the sight of me and shut the door quietly.

'Mr Clark!' she said, with grim disapproval. 'What are you doing there?'

'Ah, Miss Coleman. You're late.'

I remained still, as though I belonged there and put my feet up on the desk for good measure.

'What are you talking about, sir?' She seemed flustered but uncertain, may be laughter and annoyance were at odds within her.

'Oblige me with good punctuality in future; you know I don't like to be kept waiting.'

Her mouth dropped, forming a perfect, soundless pout. She looked around. She even glanced at the door to ensure it was closed. 'Does Edward know you can do his voice?'

I leapt up, wanting to narrow the distance between us. I walked about the room and came to a stop just behind her, close enough to breathe in the freshly-washed smell of her. Soap. Expensive soap.

'Not unless you say something, Miss Coleman. I would be frightfully grateful if you didn't tell him.'

'You are being ridiculous.' She turned to me over her

shoulder. 'What are you doing here?'

'Waiting. I told you that.'

There was no sign of the Professor from the window. My hands rested on the window ledge and with one finger I surreptitiously slid open the catch. I had made no plans to break into the consulting room but, should I wish to, it was now a little easier.

I yawned. 'Are those papers for me to sign, my dear? Just put them over there. I'll look at them next year. I have a lame horse to examine but damned if I know which leg is troubling the animal.'

She laughed but then bit down on the sound. 'If he knew you did this you would be in such trouble. He hates people laughing at him. I wish you wouldn't, it's not respectful. And hardly fair. He would have no trouble knowing which leg was lame.'

She blushed and I remembered William's unkind comments about her disability, realising that the mention of lameness might trouble her. It was too late, I would ignore the issue but how on earth could a woman who walked so stiffly, manage on a horse? I could see the awkwardness in her movement more clearly now that I was looking for it and, although it wasn't as marked as William made out, it was apparent. And now I was as curious as William was scathing. How would she stay on? And if she took a fall there might be a risk of serious injury. I was shocked that the Professor allowed her such freedom, it was hardly in character and the horse looked a handful even for a good rider.

'Are you sure he'd get it right, Miss Coleman? He might advocate checking the horse's mouth, you know? But tell me, what are you doing here? I have an appointment, you see. With your brother. I wasn't expecting you although of course it gives me immense pleasure to see you again so soon.'

'How kind you are,' she said, matching my tone. 'More pleasure than seeing him. Yes, I don't doubt you. If you are in difficulties with him, you only have yourself to blame. All those things you said last night are not his fault.' She looked to the door again as if she feared him overhearing. 'The college was without a professor for months until he was appointed. If it was going to close, it would have done then. He saved it, Mr Clark, and please believe me that he will make it secure. He has so many plans but I mustn't speak out of turn. There's nothing he hates more.'

'I'm sure you are right, he brings out the worst in me. Here, won't you sit down? Let me take those papers for you.'

She sat down and sighed. 'You talked as though he was dishonest. I know you only hinted at it but your inference was quite clear. Mr Clark, I think you should apologise to him, you have quite misunderstood him. And make it profuse is my advice. Believe me, it works every time, I should know.'

I shrugged and cast a quick glance at the papers she gave me before I put them on the desk and resumed my place of power on the Professor's seat that was measurably larger than her own.

'Perhaps I will. But it will be difficult and even harder for him to believe me sincere.'

'Can you do any other voices?' she asked, after a pause.

'Miss Coleman! You really shouldn't - I'd rather you didn't - um, encourage me. The consequences, nay, even the results, of doing so, ma'am, are very grave. Of course, if I keep this neck cloth nicely starched and in enough knots to cover half my chin no one will notice what I get up to. At least, they won't notice my lack of um, that some of my words are…well, missing.'

'Oh, heavens! Is that Mr Sewell?'

I felt pleased, although it could hardly be anyone else. 'I'm still working on that one. It's difficult in that he copies your brother's weariness to such a degree that the two have a tendency to blend if I'm not careful. There are subtle differences, naturally. William doesn't share your brother's intelligence and he talks in so many directions at the same time that much of what he says comes out as a muddle.'

'You're very good at it. I'm so glad I'm a woman. At least, you won't dare to make fun of me in the same way.'

I couldn't keep my eyes off her but I felt like a child curiously investigating his father's snuff box, attracted by the exquisitely decorated lid, longing to sample something frowned upon. So it was with Christina Coleman. Nothing would so infuriate her dreadful brother more than to see a growing intimacy between us. Perhaps he would forbid such a thing but she appeared to be a match for him, she had enough spirit.

It was so different seeing her without him in the room. Their similarities didn't disgust me and my enmity was forgotten. I had an urge to touch her, take a pinch of her and breathe in deeply. The desk between us was fortunately situated; I wanted to leap over it but knew I wouldn't. She laughed, so my thoughts must have been well hidden, she wasn't uncomfortable.

'I'm rather glad you're a woman, too,' I said. 'But why would I mock you? Surely, you are perfect just as you are.'

'Perfect?' She hesitated, searching for signs of derision. 'Well, I suppose I am most days, naturally.'

I laughed. 'Me too. We have so much in common. Quite astonishing. What else do you think we might share?' She straightened her back as though about to leave and I felt an urge to stop her and hold onto the moment. 'Tell me about your horse. I've seen her of course but...'

'You want me to tell you about Firefly? Now? Mr Clark, you must know my brother is seriously displeased with you. After all the things you said to him you shouldn't really be surprised but you don't seem in the least worried. Why do you wish to chat to me about my horse? Perhaps you are not taking your situation very seriously.'

'I take it she's rather fast. She certainly looks it.'

'Since you're terribly good at mimicry you'd do well to adopt a conciliatory tone with Edward. Hide your lack of respect; it doesn't help you in the least. He's doing his best, works all the hours God sends and for that he deserves some recognition, even from you.' I nodded and she appeared to accept that was all the acknowledgement her brother would get. 'Yes, she's very fast. I've not had her very long but she's very responsive. Do you know, just the lightest touch will control her and riding her is like floating across the ground. She's the best.'

'Liberating, isn't it? To ride an animal like that?'

'Why, yes! Is that what you feel?'

'Of course. Doesn't everyone?'

'I don't know. I've never spoken to anyone about it. I thought it was just…'

'What? Just you?' I sighed, feeling a quiver of impatience. 'Because you don't walk as well as some people? It might mean your experience is heightened, I suppose. In which case you are more blessed than the rest of us. Your pleasure is twice as intense, wouldn't you say?'

'Perhaps it's more.'

'I envy you.'

'Don't be silly,' she said quickly, sliding one hand on her leg as if she would smooth away the pain of it. 'I can't think of anyone who would care to be in my shoes. They are not always very comfortable.'

'I'm sorry,' I said, knowing it sounded rather empty.

'There's no need. It's not your fault.'

'You should ride every day, it must be beneficial.'

'Thank you. I will do.' She sounded haughty and one dark eyebrow seemed to query my right to advise. 'Mr Clark, you must think of your future and stop this idle nonsense with me.'

'Idle? Oh, come now, that suggests a waste of time and it was never that. So, you think my punishment will be severe. You're probably right. But I don't feel as though I'm waiting for my executioner although if I was a condemned man this would be the perfect final half hour.'

'Now you are being very foolish,' she said, getting up with alacrity. She stood unsteadily with her hand on the back of the chair and her voice faltered. 'Are you flirting with me?'

'Quite possibly. Yes, I suppose I am. Do you mind?'

'For pity's sake, why?' she said, bemused.

'Why not?' I said, sliding from behind the desk and

coming to stand near her. Her hand gripped the chair and then she peered at me, as if she would delve inside for the truth. 'No, don't hide behind that lame old excuse. Anyone who looks further than your smile should be cast aside.'

'Oh, please!'

'I'm serious. Why would anyone want more than an intelligent, beautiful woman?'

'I'm hardly that and people do want more. Always.'

She might have muttered something about two legs but I wasn't sure because the door opened and I realised that flagstones gave insufficient warning especially when I was so painfully distracted.

# CHAPTER 7

I stepped away from her guiltily as the Professor walked in. His silence seemed studied, as if he wanted to make us ill at ease. His elegant clothes must have been lightly scented for the perfume filled the room, obscuring the freshness of his sister. He walked behind his desk and slowly picked up his hat and cane putting them on the stand with a look of accusation.

Miss Coleman's nostrils quivered and one eyebrow arched delightfully. She might have been laughing although there were no external signs and I smiled at her when the Professor turned his back. My answer was another quarter inch of height from the eyebrow and the same degree of lift from the shoulder. She wasn't risking a smile.

'Good day, Professor,' I said. 'Very interesting lecture this morning.'

I decided to take Miss Coleman's advice and flatter the man. The respiratory system was the Professor's one area of expertise, he returned to it often and it might help to show some enthusiasm.

'I'm glad you thought so. Thank you for my papers, Christina. Surely, you are not going to ride in this weather?'

'Certainly, you wouldn't want the horse getting over fresh,' she said, peering out the window and laughing. 'I'll probably go this afternoon; perhaps the wind will have dropped by then. There's no need to worry, Edward. I haven't yet been blown off the saddle.' Then she muttered, 'I haven't shrunk after getting wet, either.'

'Where will you be going? Through the fields again rather than visiting, I hope?' She nodded and he sighed. 'Oh…very well. I'll ask the stableman to have her ready if you insist.'

He nodded his dismissal and I opened the door for her. At a wave of the Professor's hand I sat on the chair Miss Coleman had used. I may have looked wistful for the Professor's smile was particularly tight this morning. Somewhere inside his head was the truth and those rigid muscles had to do daily battle to keep it locked up safe. A moment's relaxation or a genuine smile might see him revealing his true nature and that would never do. He sorted through the papers his sister had brought him, again I was made to wait but not for long this time.

'Annoying me is some sort of game for you, isn't it? I must tell you I find it rather tiresome.'

'What do you mean, Professor?'

'It's a charming thought but she won't help you. She despises you and you have no chance of unsettling her loyalty to me if that is your aim.' He grunted softly and let out a breath. 'Strange, isn't it? That a man of your infuriating honesty should be quite so devious. I hadn't thought you capable of such a thing.'

'What makes you think I was paying empty compliments, sir?' I should have been uncomfortable. No man wants a flirtation interrupted or mocked and I didn't appreciate being the butt of the Professor's humour.

'I believe your description was quite floral. Calling her beautiful. Yes, and intelligent. I can only assume you've been reading too many novels. Don't involve her in this little battle between us; it would not be worth the excitement. You are right about one thing. She is too clever to think you sincere.'

'I thought I was merely stating facts, Professor. It must

be hard for a brother to notice that a sister is beautiful. Growing up together, I suppose you must stop seeing the other person. I only have a brother and I must say I don't find him in the least attractive although I've been told he's quite a handsome man. But it's impossible for me to see it.'

'Don't talk nonsense. You cannot be in earnest. You! Flirting with my sister!'

'I think I was merely paying your sister a compliment. It's a commonplace activity. Is there something wrong in that?'

'It would be amusing to see you continuing with this course but I would advise against it.' He took a breath and let his shoulders relax. 'I won't allow it.'

'Even if I was sincere?'

'Particularly in that case. I have no desire to see her played with in this way, do you hear me?'

What was wrong with this over protective brother? Did neither of them see how lovely she was? Not in a conventional way and yes, her intelligence would be a barrier for some people who might be shocked at her interest in science. I might be maligning her but I was sure she played up her fascination merely to cover her disability. The Professor thought I was toying with her, even Edmund had suggested it but I despised deceit. I could only toy where I wanted to play although annoying Professor Coleman was added spice.

I couldn't sit in a room with Christina Coleman and not be drawn to her. I wanted to pick up her hair, to see for myself if it was as soft as it appeared and whether the curls would wrap around my fingers. I'd told her she was beautiful because she was so unaware of it. It mattered to me that for all her confidence she doubted herself as a woman. She didn't know her own worth, she rode a horse but still hid behind her lame leg, blaming it for all the things she feared she couldn't do. She had to know the truth. Had it sounded laughable? Insincere? Yes, I'd wanted to touch her. I'd have kissed her given enough time and a better location. And a bit of encouragement.

The Professor hesitated and fiddled with one of the quills. There was an awkward silence while he appeared to come to some decision. Then he rubbed his brow with one hand as if it ached.

'Christina is not like other women, Clark. She walks with great difficulty, she tires easily and I have the devil's own job to stop her from exhausting herself.'

'I sympathise.'

I was also spellbound. I had never seen this honest, open side of the man. That he should confide in me of all people was quite shocking since we were hardly on good terms. He must have been brimming with anxiety.

'She is quite wilful,' he explained. 'She even insists on riding every day saying it's good for her. I ask you, how can all that jolting on the back of a horse help a limb that's already in such a mess? She doesn't care what the weather is doing, she'll even go out in the rain and it's my opinion that the damp won't help her either. She won't listen to the doctors and she won't pay me any heed. Naturally, with a leg like that she knows her limitations socially. Her expectations are not high, that much is obvious. And to hear you meddling with her.'

'Meddling?'

'A distressing word, I agree. You are trying to goad me but it is my burden to care for her and I will do so to the best of my ability. It's unlikely she will marry. Who would want…? Well, enough of that. Suffice to say I don't want someone like you making my job even more troublesome than it is. Do I make myself clear?'

'Perfectly. She sounds as though she is very difficult to manage.'

'Difficult! She certainly is.'

'Then another solution occurs to me. Stop trying.'

'Clark! Have you not been heeding me? I am her brother, her elder brother. There is no one else who will care for her.'

'You make her sound quite helpless. Surely, she's not.'

'Have you seen her walk?' I nodded my head. 'Believe me, a flight of stairs is a serious obstacle for her.'

'But not impossible.'

'True but to see her making the attempt is quite unpleasant. She used to run about when she was a girl in the most awkward, ridiculous fashion. Thankfully, she's thought better of doing so. I should be grateful for that, I suppose. When you think there are so many things she could be doing, sewing and flowers, things that women do. They should be enough to satisfy her.'

'But she rides. That's remarkable, surely.'

'Is that what you would call it?' He brushed his sleeve thoughtfully. 'Must I be more explicit? I should never have bought her the wretched animal but the cob was getting old and I was persuaded, thanks to her persistence. She knows just how to get what she wants, in fact I'd say she uses her disability to very good purpose and yet it's hardly seemly for her to be careering about the countryside on her own. It's hardly the thing for a woman, even a woman without Christina's difficulties. Sometimes, I honestly think she has no self consciousness at all. She gads about as though no one worries about her infirmity. Who wants to see such a thing? It upsets people, they don't know where to look but she doesn't care.'

'You'd rather she stayed at home? Hidden.'

'How charmingly you put it. I wouldn't be so blunt. It may surprise you to hear that I'm not heartless but having such a sister doesn't help a man in my position, she should be aware of that. I can't understand how she can carry on as if there's nothing wrong with her. She could at least be less conspicuous. If she stayed at home a bit more no one would notice that there was something wrong with her. This way, there won't be a man or woman within ten miles of here who won't know her.' He took a breath and spoke in an undertone. 'She's only been here a few days and she already visits Mrs Wrench. Can you credit it? A woman who runs the Elephant and Castle Inn! Yes, I'd rather she curtailed some of her activities.'

'It must be difficult for both of you. Perhaps you should let her care for herself a little more. She's not helpless. I expect there's a lot she could do only you've become so accustomed to thinking and acting for her that it's become a habit. But, you'll find, that the more she takes on for herself the better she will be.'

'Oh, enough of this,' he said. 'Thinking about it fatigues me and I didn't ask for this discussion. No doubt, you were trying to divert me.'

I was about to protest for the discussion surprised me too and was of his own instigation but he held up one hand to stop me. Miss Coleman must have been a grave concern for him to talk to me about it but I was left with a feeling of disquiet. I tried to imagine what it must be like for her to live not only with a disability but also with her brother's doubts and restraint. It must undermine her, surely, and yet she appeared so lively. She knew how to navigate around the man, had even convinced him against his better judgement to get the horse she wanted.

I had learnt more about the Professor in those few moments than I had in all the time he had been at the college. I felt for him, he seemed weighed down by his responsibilities but I felt even more for his sister who was a nuisance and an embarrassment. He didn't use those words but he would have done anything to tuck her away out of sight as if she was hindering his advancement in society. She was a burden thanks to one injured leg and yet I couldn't see much wrong. So what if she limped? Why would anyone feel anything but pride in her achievements? The woman got on a horse! Perhaps they kept to a sedate walk but she was brave to do even that much.

Then I remembered that horse of hers. It was not the sort to amble along and she'd said it was fast. I was determined to see her ride and wondered how I could contrive it.

'Believe me, Professor, I wouldn't use your sister to rile you. If I have anything to say, I would say it to your face. You must know that much of me.'

'Indeed. But I also know how much trouble you've been. You are always asking questions. No, it's more than that. You are always challenging.'

'I find it a useful way to learn.'

'Then you should have learnt a lot by now. This latest outburst was unforgivable. Your tone was full of innuendo and although you stopped short of it, you were accusing me of dishonesty.'

'I should apologise,' I said, conscious of my insincerity. 'It was said in such a hurry.'

'Always so polite. It's a wonder that you never had the courtesy to get drunk since it would have pleased me immensely.'

'I have no inclination to do so. Besides, it's against the rules.'

'Quite. How convenient had you flouted them. No matter. I have made allowances for your age. You are naturally hot headed even though you are diligent and in view of your excellent record I have decided not to tell the governors of your scurrilous allegations.'

A convenient decision. One that didn't surprise me. His hard eyes never left my face as he delivered the blow.

'One of us must quit the college,' he said.

He sat back in his chair, his hands steepled beneath his chin and his eyes fell into slits. He was wearing a black coat, tightly fitted to his lean frame and a brilliant white shirt - well suited to the day's business.

'I beg your pardon, sir?'

'You heard me.'

Still I hesitated. One of us might be leaving sooner than expected. I didn't imagine it would be the Professor who didn't look on the verge of resignation. Did he mean this? I could hardly believe it.

'Well, I'm not a betting man,' I said. 'Are you hoping I will oblige you and leave quietly?'

'I have no expectations in that direction. I'm not a fool and you are not the sort who will go anywhere without a great noise. But you seek to undermine me and this I will not tolerate. There isn't room here for both of us.'

'And what do you propose, Professor Coleman?'

'You are bright. You know everything there is to know about the horse so you can take your exams early.'

'What?'

'I have no doubt you will pass. With honours. You will be qualified and you can set up your worthy practice. You have nothing to gain by staying.'

'And you have everything to lose.'

'What is that supposed to mean?'

'You said yourself that I undermine you.'

'You seek to do so but you won't succeed.'

'And because of that you will have me removed.'

'I'm not removing you and there will be no stain on your character. Far from it. I am recognising your great achievement. I'm allowing the country to benefit from your expertise. Clark, this country needs vets. Badly. I want you out there practicing. There is nothing more for you to gain by staying here. You should see this as an opportunity.'

'And are the others to benefit from this great chance?'

'Why not?' The Professor paused and smiled thoughtfully. 'Yes, indeed. Anyone who's ready to sit the exams will have the opportunity to do so. You can take them this summer. You will be tested by two very eminent surgeons.'

'Surgeons!'

'They seem the most appropriate.'

'I'm surprised you are not going to ask Mr Cross, the knackerman, to perform the task.'

I laughed emptily but the Professor was like flint. I stood up hurriedly. My stomach felt hollow and words were difficult.

'Don't bother taking any of your little complaints to the governors. They will approve my idea.'

'I expect...yes of course. We shall see.'

I had little hope of being heard. They would want the accommodation for more students. Ones who will pay for a three-month training course and a piece of paper qualifying them as vets. I felt like a candle that had been snuffed before it had burnt down.

51

# CHAPTER 8

The small dining room had a full complement of clattering plates, noisy students and the smell of soup. It was always this way at lunchtime. Sometimes the racket made conversation difficult but we weren't allowed to take food to the sitting room so we jostled for space here.

'We should do it tonight, Bracy,' said Edmund, who hadn't recovered from the shock of my news. He was fidgeting with his spoon and hadn't started on his lunch.

'Definitely,' Fred agreed, through a mouthful of bread. He swallowed and shook his unkempt hair. 'And don't look so innocent. You didn't unlock that sash for nothing and it will take you too long to get anywhere with the lady.' He turned to Edmund and winked. 'Bracy knows his way round a cadaver horse but the flesh and blood of a living woman has stumped him.'

'That's not fair,' I protested, foolishly rising to the bait. 'I've only met her twice.'

'Enough time for any decent man. You prefer a fetlock to a nicely turned ankle, that's your trouble, my friend. You should enjoy a sample one of these days. It would do you the world of good.'

Edmund snorted and seemed to forget his worries over

the exams. 'There haven't been any shapely ankles on the dissecting table since we've been here. We should complain.' He sighed and watched as food was brought to the neighbouring table by one of the servants. 'This place is worse than a monastery, at least monks don't have to look at women bringing them food and clearing their plates. Damn it, have you seen that new girl? That one, over there.'

He nodded towards a woman whose dark hair was peeping beneath her white cap. Fred groaned and said he had.

'Is she new?' I asked, peering at her.

They both laughed. 'You see what I mean?' Fred muttered. 'The poor girl is seriously lacking fetlocks for Bracy's taste. You should have given me the job with Miss Coleman but my talents have been overlooked once more. I say we go for it tonight. All you have to do is give me a leg up and I'll be through that window.'

'No, Fred. You have too much to lose. I'll do it myself since I know my way around without a light.' I pushed away my empty bowl. 'Be my lookout. That will be enough.'

We occupied one end of a long refectory table. The Professor was at the other end of the room, not eating but talking to a group of students. We crouched over our food and our heads came close, like animals at a trough.

'You'll get stuck in that window, a big fellow like you,' Fred insisted, running a finger under his neck cloth as though it was bothering him. 'Leave it to me, I'm more agile.'

We would have carried on arguing but Edmund stilled us with a heave from his boot under the table. We were getting too loud or the noise in the room was diminishing at the wrong moment.

William Sewell sat at our table and nodded haughtily when a servant gave him a bowl of soup. He looked into its watery depths and his nose creased. 'I hope I'm not interrupting anything. Oh dear, this soup is tepid. You seemed like…like conspirators. What are you up to?'

'Is there any more, Annie?' Fred whispered, his eyebrows dancing, ignoring William's pique of disapproval.

The girl mouthed that she'd check and rushed away before he could reach out with one hand.

'You're not meant to talk to the domestic servants, Mr Cherry,' William said, pulling up his shirt sleeves with dainty affectation. 'You should be aloof but you persist with this thing and it's a familiarity. If the Professor…'

'Oh, do shut up, William. I wasn't talking to her, much as I would like to. I was asking for some more food. There's no rule against that as far as I remember. If you ever get in a position of power, William, do us all a favour and get the rules changed. Why shouldn't we talk to the servants and what's wrong with taking food to our rooms?'

'It's good to have the distinctions. And you obviously have been too familiar - you know her name.'

'That proves nothing,' I said. 'Fred Cherry calls all the dark haired girls Annie. The fair ones are usually Nancy, if I remember. I don't know how he gets away with it and it doesn't seem to get him very far. Ah, but I lie. She's bringing him another bowl. You lucky man.'

I leant back in the chair and looked at the new girl in her plain serge gown. Her sleeves were pushed up to her elbows and her face was hot from rushing around. She was round and honest looking and seemingly aware of our scrutiny but she'd lose her place if she was caught being too friendly. I took the bowl from her, passed it to Fred and asked for another for myself.

'Thanks, Annie,' Fred said.

'It's Nancy, sir,' she said, winking at him.

She asked William if he wanted more bread but he waved her away and didn't pause in his careful sipping of his soup.

Finally, he dabbed his mouth with a napkin. 'I suppose you know it's an important day. For all of us.' I thought he might be talking about the exams and wondered whether he knew or would be taking up his hoped-for appointment on the strength of them. 'They are compiling our case to the government. I was privileged, very much so actually, to see a draft copy and I have to say Professor Coleman has an excellent way with words. You see, I hadn't considered that our little veterinary college was potentially important to the nation.'

'Had you not?' I said. 'You only have to realise how vital the horse is to the economy to know that veterinary science is worthy of investment.'

'Exactly!'

'There are commercial reasons for backing this college. It's quite ridiculous that we are so forward with every other scientific interest but this one.'

'Did you help him write it?' William asked.

'No, I didn't. Then there's the moral issue. We use these horses. It's only right that we care for them. Instead, we shorten their lives. That's something we have to correct. We need to find out what we are doing wrong.'

'You take on an awful lot, Bracy,' William said, laughing.

'Only because until now we've taken on so little. If you're not eating that bread, pass it over.'

William pushed his plate to me with one finger, watching my enthusiasm for the food with distaste before speaking slowly and carefully. 'It would only require a small exertion from the government to support us, you know. And…this country's commercial interests are managed with dexterity and a success that command the admiration of the civilised world.'

He said this speech with much concentration, his eyes looking inwards, searching for the right words of Professor Coleman's to quote.

'Quite,' I said. 'I can picture you lecturing already.'

'Dear, dear, I'm to try it - with the new students. I anticipate…well, I hope to become the Professor's apprentice. It's a little nerve wracking for me. The responsibility, you see. I never expected to be so honoured, or chosen, but he thinks I'm ready enough. I've decided how I shall manage, though. If anyone doesn't follow me, I will say it all again. Then no one will have any cause to grumble. What do you think, Bracy?'

'I think you will earn your place in the history books, William.'

'Indeed. History. I'd like that. By the way, I hear you're riding that hunter this afternoon. Won't one of the grooms take it out?'

'Professor Coleman doesn't trust a groom to assess his soundness,' I explained. 'Plus, he stumbles and then runs off. One way of getting rid of me, I suppose.'

Edmund ran a hand through his neat, fair hair and got up from the table, beckoning me with one eyebrow. 'I'll come and see you off. Are you coming, Fred?'

Once we were in the corridor we could speak freely and wasted no time making a rendezvous for later that night, one I was beginning to regret. They weren't letting me back out.

'Listen, Bracy, you might pass those exams easily but the rest of us will bloody struggle. He's wrapped it up nice and neat but effectively he will be getting rid of us,' said Edmund.

'I have no idea if he can make the rest of you sit them early,' I said.

'We'll know soon enough,' said Fred. 'But our chance is tonight. We need to find something incriminating, then we'll take it to one of the governors. Yes, Granville Penn. He's an honest man; he'll do something about it. If they're not careful they'll have Coleman at the helm for decades.'

'I shudder at the thought,' I said.

'I'll get that locked drawer open. That's where the havey cavey stuff will be.'

'Fred!'

'Don't start again, Bracy. Have you seen your shoulders lately?'

'Yes, and I've measured them against that window. I'll fit.'

Fred laughed. 'But I'll fit better.'

'Come on, you two. Why don't you pick straws for it?' said Edmund. 'I hope you've got a good story in case you're caught.'

'I have,' I said. 'I left some papers there this morning. I

needed them back.'

'In the middle of the night?'

'It's the best I can think of. He thinks I'm always studying so at least it's believable.'

'Whatever happens, you mustn't get caught.'

# CHAPTER 9

It wasn't believable for a minute and if I was caught in the Professor's consulting room at midnight I'd be out of the college in an instant. I wouldn't be taking my exams and my chances of practicing would be destroyed. Was it worth the risk just to prove Edward Coleman was putting his own financial interests before anything else? I doubted it was but dislike of the man was making me reckless.

Talking made us late reaching the stable yard with its warm, animal smell and soft buzz of activity. Quite a few stalls were empty, their occupants having gone home and new patients were not due until tomorrow.

I wasn't surprised to see Miss Coleman there but puzzled when she approached William who was wiping his hands on a roll of cloth. I nodded to her but she might not have noticed me for she seemed focused on him for some reason. The bay hunter was tied up near the mounting block and although he was already saddled I wanted to check his feet before setting off. I kept myself busy while I listened to them.

William's frown lifted and he gave her an elegant bow. 'Miss Coleman. How delightful. I take it, you are riding, today? Yes, quite so – it is a perfect day for it, even if a little windy.'

He was elegantly dressed as usual in buff pantaloons and

a neatly folded neck cloth set off with a pearl pin. His blue coat was tightly fitted but his shining boots were spattered with dust.

'I ride every day, Mr Sewell,' she said, beaming. 'Is my brother such a hard task master that you never get the time?'

'I have much to occupy me - if I'm to be so honoured. I must study, you know. But I don't complain. I leave riding for more physical creatures.'

I resisted the temptation to look up, he was talking about me and I didn't want to hinder their conversation. William led the way into the stables and gave orders for her mare to be brought outside.

'Hurry up, now. Don't keep her waiting,' he told one of the grooms.

The horse was led into the sunshine, her coat glistening like a polished conker. Miss Coleman stroked the soft neck and checked the girths.

'By the way, Mr Sewell, I wonder if you could do something for me.'

She smiled at him hesitantly, a trace of invitation in her eyes. William seemed alarmed, his face reddened and his mouth chewed silent words.

'Yes, of course. Um…anything to oblige. You must need a leg up. Let me call one of the grooms.'

He couldn't look at her, he was so embarrassed and was about to run into the stables for assistance. What a graceless idiot. I would have helped her myself but was loathe to add to the drama since he was making such a cake of himself. Besides, Miss Coleman had the situation well in hand although her lips were tightening.

'No. I wasn't going to trouble you with anything so unpalatable, Mr Sewell,' she said, taking a deep breath. 'I'm perfectly able to use the mounting block like anyone else. If I needed help I would ask for it.'

She led the mare to the block. Her steps were slow and uneven. I was shielded by my own horse but she must have known we were all scrutinising her with some morbid fascination. There must have been about six of us on the yard, students and grooms, but none of us were sure whether to offer assistance.

William averted his eyes but managed to hold her horse with a limp grip. Then she eased herself onto the saddle as if she'd been doing so unaided all her life and took up her reins as the mare danced on the spot. There was an air of relief about her so perhaps it hadn't been as easy as it seemed.

Looking down on William, she said, 'There's a horse at the Elephant and Castle Inn that's lame. If you have time, would you be so kind as to have a look at him for me. I would have asked my brother but I know he will be too busy.'

'You want me to…to look at it?'

'Only if you have the time.'

'As a favour?'

'Well, I would be very grateful but I suspect Mr Wrench would pay you, he's very fond of that animal according to his wife. I saw her on my way here. She said Mr Wrench relies on the horse and he's terribly worried about it. Naturally, I thought of you. I hope you don't mind having a quick look.'

'But, Miss Coleman, I'm not…able. Besides, I don't think…'

'Well, you will be more qualified than any farrier in the country. That must count for something. I'm only asking you to look at the horse, not to treat him in any way you don't feel able to. Mr Wrench wants to take him to the forge in the village and we all know how horrific that can be. I thought you might regard it as an opportunity.'

'Indeed - most kind of you. But if something were to go wrong. Oh dear, did the Professor suggest you speak to me?'

'No, I haven't spoken to him. I haven't had the chance but…'

'Miss Coleman, without guidance, I'm not sure. He allows us to treat the animals here under the strictest supervision and we are very grateful for the help. Without it – oh, dear, how would I manage? An honour to be asked, of course.'

'Well, some of the new students have been trying to help so I thought you might…'

'Have they? I'm not sure they should…and you thought to ask me?' He moved closer to her and spoke more quietly. 'Want to help the Professor in any way I can. His assistant - hope to be, at least. So, you see, rather awkward. The studying leaves me very little time.'

'I see.'

'I suspect Mrs Wrench is trying to take advantage of you. Well, of course you have a kind nature. You should tell her about becoming one of our members. Then they would get veterinary care for their animal.'

Miss Coleman looked more annoyed than defeated. 'I'm sure you are quite right. I shouldn't have mentioned it. Good day.'

Her mare moved sideways forcing William to take hurried steps to keep out the way as she headed for College Lane. I decided to follow her but gave her a few minutes start. I didn't want to be obvious. It took me longer than expected to catch up with her as she was not keeping to a sedate walk. Her mare turned when I came up behind her and gave my mount a rumbled greeting. Miss Coleman gasped in surprise.

'For pity's sake! What are you doing?' she cried. 'Are you trying to make me fall off?'

I eased the hunter towards the mare and let the two get acquainted.

'Miss Coleman,' I said, bowing my head. 'I apologise but there was no choice and, besides, I could see you were ready for anything as soon as you rode out of the college gates. I wasn't attempting to unseat you, as you well know.'

She shielded her eyes from the sun and seemed puzzled; her grip on the reins tightened. 'Mr Clark, have you been watching me?'

'Not for its own sake, ma'am, but I have been following you. I wanted to talk to you.'

Her face reddened. 'Well, you should have spoken earlier. You saw me at the college but you ignored me for some reason and now I find you chasing after me like a highwayman. It's funny but you look like a highwayman in those dark clothes. You only need a mask and a pistol. What if my horse had swerved? I must say I find your behaviour most strange.'

I moved my horse alongside hers and whispered. 'She didn't swerve, she knew I was behind you even if you didn't but I'm sorry if I alarmed you. I thought, under the circumstances, it would be better if we were not overheard.'

That gave her a jolt. She had no idea what I was talking about. The prospect of a private conversation made her eyes narrow. She fiddled with her gloves and looked as if she might canter off given enough provocation. She wore a neat hat and the sun was picking out lighter shades of chestnut in her dark hair which escaped down her back. She looked at me intently and took a deep breath.

'You asked the wrong student,' I explained.

She looked up at me, squinting because the sun was low, as realisation dawned. Her smile was tinged with relief but would have found no answering glimmer in mine. I was still smarting from my meeting with her brother.

'Did I?'

'The excellent Mr Sewell is not the man for you on this occasion. He'll give you good advice on tying a neck cloth. Indeed, he might be quite expert on your own clothes.' I looked at her riding habit, noting the softness of the cloth. 'Yes, he'd tell you whether it's the latest style but I wouldn't tax him with anything more demanding.'

'That's not very charitable, sir,' she said, masking her amusement.

I shrugged. 'No, it's not, is it? You'll have to forgive me. I'm not feeling very charitable today and he is the last person who will take liberties with the rules. I, on the other hand, have no hope of advancement at your brother's hands and so I'm perfectly willing to take a look at this horse of yours if you'll lead the way.'

'Would you, really?' she said, ignoring my mention of her brother. 'But I don't think it's urgent, she certainly didn't say it was. It's at the Inn, only a stone's throw from the college, you must know the way and you only have to tell Mr Wrench that I sent you.' My face must have been stony because she carried on explaining. 'Mrs Wrench said its foot was hot and now her husband's talking of seeing the farrier. I thought someone here might have a look at it seeing as they are almost our neighbours but Mr Sewell didn't think Edward would like it.'

'He wouldn't.'

'Oh,' she hesitated. 'But, I would hate to get you into trouble, Mr Clark.'

'Strictly speaking, I mustn't use or sell any of the college medicines outside. Whoever drew up the rules before the Professor joined us was probably worried about corruption but that doesn't mean I can't look at it, wouldn't you think?'

My laugh had a bitter quality and I looked past her to the college where sounds of activity carried in the breeze. Horses were neighing in alarm and John Bale, the head stableman, could be heard issuing instructions to the grooms.

'We'll take the chance, shall we?' I said. 'But I would suggest it's dealt with now before the animal is harmed. There's no knowing what the farrier might do to it. Sadly, they don't stop at fitting shoes and I would hate Mr Wrench's horse to be butchered by one of their home-spun operations.' I looked at her with a challenge. 'Shall we go?'

'You want me to go with you?'

I moved my horse around her, circling until she could look at me without the sun getting in her eyes. 'Yes, of course.'

'But why?'

'Because I know you want to come.'

'Do I? And how do you know that?'

'You told me yourself that home and hearth are too confining so naturally you want to come. This is the perfect opportunity. You are hungry to know more and why shouldn't I take you?'

'And why do you want to take me?'

'Do you want to know all my reasons, Miss Coleman?'

'Yes, it would be strange if you didn't tell me.'

'I would like the pleasure of your company.'

'Oh,' she said, startled at my frankness.

Our eyes locked and she couldn't pull away even though her face reddened. She seemed confused but there was no hesitation in me. Flirtation could have been a new arena for her but since I had decided it was time for her to experience it, I carried on.

I took a breath to stop myself rushing. 'I would like your company and you want to come. That should be enough; the rest will sort itself out if it wants to. Or, I could pretend that I need you for protection since your brother might be angry if he finds out. Yes, we'll settle for that, shall we? I'm taking a risk and you can help minimise it.'

'Mr Clark, you are being flippant.'

'In what way?'

'Saying you would like my company to save you from Edward.'

'Indeed, I am in earnest. He listens to you, does he not, and you would make a very good case on my behalf. And now I come to think of it, your company would be a fair exchange for seeing to Mr Wrench's horse. You don't expect me to attend it for nothing, do you?'

'I didn't think I was to be part of the bargain,' she laughed. 'I'm sure Mr Wrench will pay you if that is what you are worried about.'

'No, you are not part of the bargain and I am not worried about payment but will you not come with me? It would brighten my day.' I smiled at her flustered face. 'I'll let you watch.'

# CHAPTER 10

I turned my horse towards the Inn and finally she fell in beside me as though it was the most natural thing in the world.

'Miss Coleman, you are truly an unusual woman.'

A smile creased her face. 'If you mean that for a compliment let me tell you that I don't want to be. You can have no idea how much I would love to be like everyone else. There is little pleasure in being so different, you know. I just want people to be natural with me, I don't want to embarrass them but I can't seem to help it.'

'I understand, believe me, but I wasn't talking about physical differences.'

'What then?'

'You think more deeply than most people.'

'Perhaps. Or it could be that I am more nosey than is usual. I always wanted to know how everything works, what people think and why they do what they do. That's why you don't like Mr Sewell very much. You think he has little thought beyond his stylish outfits.'

'I never said I didn't like him.'

'You didn't have to.'

We found the Inn yard quiet, being too early for much trade. A servant was sitting on a step chewing a piece of hay and didn't acknowledge our arrival, a group of chickens scratched in the dirt and were better hosts since one squawked, possibly in welcome.

I leapt off my horse before coming to Miss Coleman's side. 'There will be a mounting block somewhere but I can't see it,' I said, offering to help her down.

Accepting help seemed to annoy her but most women would need help dismounting thanks to the side saddle and elegancies of a riding habit. I suppose there was something rather intimate about the whole thing. There was no avoiding my hands on her waist as I steadied her, no escaping the proximity of an embrace. My face was so close she must have felt my breath on her forehead. My eyes bore into hers, saw how green they were, how her eyebrows darted into her hair when she was puzzled. There was a dimple, more of a crease that lit up her face when she smiled and enveloped me in warmth.

'You're fine,' I assured her.

Her hand was in mine and I could feel her hesitation. Did she always feel this way when she returned to the ground? I wanted to ask but didn't want the interference of words. Her hold on me tightened for a moment and she took a first step.

'Yes, I am,' she said, realising it was true. Her feet looked steady. 'Shall I hold the horses while you go and find Mr Wrench?'

A sash window was thrown up and Mrs Wrench's head burst out. 'Miss Coleman, is that you?'

'Yes, indeed,' she replied, waving. 'I've brought Mr Clark to see the lame horse.'

The landlady scanned the yard from her high vantage point. 'I told him you was an angel. Now, where is that man? Joshua!' she shouted, ringing a bell.

She couldn't see the waiter on his step or how he levered himself up with an effort that would have suited a man twice his age. He wandered onto the yard and peered at her.

'Don't just stand there gawping at me, Joshua. Go and fetch Mr Wrench, and where's the groom when he's needed?'

She shut the window but it was possible to hear her sing-song voice as it followed her body's progress through the Inn. She must have found Mr Wrench in the tap room for we could hear her bemoaning the fact that he was washing the glasses when there was a wench who was paid to help.

Mr Wrench was as thin as his wife was round. His black hair was an inadequate covering but he had a red, shining face that lit like a beacon when he saw us.

'Miss Coleman. Sir. I can't thank you enough. Now, let me take those two horses for you. My groom will house them for us. Why don't you be comfortable in the parlour, miss? Mrs Wrench will bring you something, that's for sure.'

'I'd rather watch, if you don't mind,' Miss Coleman said, following us to the stables and ignoring the landlord's start of surprise. 'I don't often get the chance and I'm curious what could be wrong.'

He laughed and scratched his head giving her a strange look. 'It might not be very nice. There's nowhere for a lady to sit, you see, and it might be more comfortable for you inside.' Then he added what he seemed to think might be the winning argument. 'Mrs Wrench will be expecting you.'

He looked to me for approval but I had made the promise to let her watch and ignored him. Within minutes her presence was forgotten, I had a knife out of my pocket and was cleaning the lame foot and prodding its sole. The sight of the knife alarmed Mr Wrench who was mouthing a silent prayer.

'I thought you were going to use science,' he said, as though it was something mysterious and dangerous.

'I am.'

'Is it safe? I'll not have witchcraft here, you see.'

I stood up straight and folded my arms. 'I will use my medical training on your horse rather than spells which I have no knowledge of. There is no danger unless to myself if I am clumsy. I suspect this is nothing more than an abscess which I will drain without injuring your poor boy. Could I have a bucket of water, Mr Wrench? And a cloth or a brush?'

Mr Wrench ran about as though the dappled grey gelding was about to foal. He gave instructions to the groom to bring towels and asked me if the water should be hot.

'No, cold but clean will be fine.'

'Is it serious? He can't walk, sir. Nor put it down on the ground.'

Tears pricked his anxious eyes. The animal looked equally strained as if days of discomfort were ahead.

'No, it's not serious if my diagnosis is right but you'll need to keep it clean and if you can make a hot bran poultice he'll be fine within a few days.'

Mr Wrench pulled a handkerchief from his pocket and blew his nose. Once I was done, relief overpowered him and he threw a thin arm around me fondly, listening to my instructions.

Clouds were gathering and forcing the temperature to plummet by the time we left the Inn. Miss Coleman halted her mare at the edge of a promising hay field and watched a pair of rabbits scampering in alarm at our approach. She turned to thank me and praised my work, expecting our ways to part.

'I wish they were all that simple,' I said. 'It was very superficial so it will heal very quickly.'

'You were very good with that horse. Why didn't you let Mr Wrench pay you?'

'I'm hoping for free ale for the rest of my stay.'

She shook her head and laughed. Instead of parting, we fell into an easy walk alongside the field, barely noticing the route and oblivious of the time. The sun was fading and a playful breeze tossed the clouds as if warning them not to give us any rain. The ground was soft without being muddy which any rider will know is perfect if you want to test out all the paces.

'What's the matter with the horse you're riding?' she asked.

I looked down at the bay as I had the task of checking

the animal's conformation. 'He stumbles and doesn't pick his feet up. I must confess I haven't been concentrating on him. He's said to be a daisy cutter and although that doesn't sound the most serious condition it can be alarming if your mount falls over as this one has been known to. The Professor has put Grasshopper shoes on him to see if they make a difference.'

'How exciting, he's hoping to patent that shoe,' she cried, joyfully. She watched my horse pick its way carefully, she examined each footfall. 'You must tell Edward that they work. I haven't seen him stumble once. Has he?'

'No, I confess he hasn't but his stride seems shortened. I'd like to see what he's like if we put the speed up although there is a risk he will try and run off.' I smiled at her and nodded to the side of the field. 'Shall we?'

I let her canter ahead knowing the bay was no match for her mare, its legs were sluggish, its feet were awkward in spite of the warnings I'd received about him bolting. I watched her in awe since her difficulties on her own feet disappeared on the back of a horse, it was like a cure. So many riders carried themselves with such a stiff back that they bounced about with no softness or give. She had a spring to her body which absorbed the animal's movements and she had such confidence that she would ride with one hand, guiding with a touch of the rein on the animal's neck.

I watched her race to the end of the field with her dark curls bobbing and beating time against her shoulders. Her joy filled me and lifted my own worries. She didn't cry or shout out but I knew she wanted to. There was something childlike about her, perhaps some vital experience had been denied her and she was now fulfilling it like a canary released from a cage. Clods of earth flew up from the mare's hooves and made her seem like a hazy dream dipping in and out of focus. She was rushing away from me but I could see her face as though it was next to me.

I knew I would kiss her, if not today then soon. I thought we both knew it would happen. It didn't seem right to plan such a thing but I could picture leaning down from a horse, holding her chin and tasting her while she was full of confidence. She was different when she was riding and I knew it would be better then. She was trotting back to me now and I realised what it was that changed her.

Power. It filled her body and soul. Without a horse she was too aware of her body and its limitations, if she could just ignore the problem she could almost make it go away. At least, she could shrink it to its right proportion. She tried to make up for her body's lack with sharp conversation, her intelligence and her interest in science but on horseback she didn't need to. She was free.

I'd wanted to kiss her when I'd helped her dismount at the Inn yard. Holding her for longer than I needed was all I could do with the servant lazily watching us. So instead, I breathed in the scent of her and watched her thoughts tumble in her eyes. That's when I knew that I wasn't alone with this urge. She felt it too. That's why she'd smiled and let me touch her and steady her.

She was getting close enough now to share a smile. What would the Professor say if he could witness such a conspiracy? She wasn't intimidated by her brother in spite of the threat that seemed to simmer beneath his surface but she was young and her life was in his hands. Out here, in the fields, I felt we were safe from him. Oh, but I could see no way forward, no future. I could only think of the present which was brimming with euphoria.

'Miss Coleman, you did that beautifully,' I said as she rode to meet me. 'I'm sorry we couldn't join you.'

She was breathless and her face heated as she patted Firefly on the neck. 'Did you see how she almost glides across the ground, she's so light. I think she must be the best horse I've ever ridden. She's so fast. That was wonderful. What was the matter with your boy? Couldn't he do it?'

'He might need longer to get used to these shoes, I'm not sure. At least he didn't fall over, for that I'm thankful. Where are you riding to?'

'Not far. I'll explore a few more hay fields because I

want to know the way to Kentish Town. Another time I want to visit my friend, Suzanna Goodall. Her father is the attorney there. Do you know him?'

'I have met him but not his daughter. Are you the same age?'

'Yes, we were at school together. We both finished when we were fourteen and we kept in touch when I went to stay with my aunt. She died, you know. That's why I came to live here with Edward. There was nowhere else for me to go.'

She laughed and she didn't seem to find it painful or difficult to talk about. I asked whether she had been close to her aunt and about her parents. She talked quite happily about them and her brother who must have been ten years her senior.

'You won't always live with your brother, though, will you? Are you so attached?'

'Where else will I go? Of course, Edward will probably marry soon.'

'Really? I hadn't heard.'

'That's because I haven't arranged it yet! He needs a wife and lots of daughters and I suppose I might be quite a useful aunt. Suzanna will know someone, she might even be suitable herself which would be even better than a stranger. I wonder if…oh, listen to me. They've never shown the least interest in each other but I'm sure whoever I find for him won't have me thrown out on the streets.'

I was dismayed that she could accept such a life lived through other people when she could have one of her own if she would only take the step without fear of stumbling.

'Why do you look at me like that, Mr Clark? Did I say something funny? I don't see why Edward shouldn't marry. Even though you find him a difficult man, women say he's rather interesting.'

'I wasn't thinking of Professor Coleman. Forgive me but his future happiness is not my concern.'

'No, of course it's of no interest to you but you were giving me such a black look that I was wondering whether to be frightened of you.'

'Were you now? Somehow, I don't believe you but I'm surprised you've mapped out such a dull future for yourself. Will you really accept the role of usefulness in your brother's household, when you should be loved in your own?'

We were riding slowly again, Miss Coleman leading the way along Crooked Lane, a narrow path that would take us to a bridge over the Fleet River. She was laughing at me and I must have sounded pompous rather than lover like. I had talked in the abstract to avoid sounding as though I was declaring myself. Mostly, I wanted her to aspire to everything life could give her. I wasn't offering myself since I wasn't confident of my reception let alone aware of my intentions.

'Mr Clark, I accept what has happened to me,' she said, touching her right leg absently as though it was her heart. 'I'm not going to make my life miserable by pining for something I can't have. It's very easy for you to say all these things but I won't allow you to stir up some ridiculous desire in me. One that no one can satisfy. Why shouldn't I enjoy my brother's children? I will be perfectly happy, I assure you.'

I reached across and picked up a lock of her hair, marvelling at its softness. 'You are beautiful and intelligent, you should have more. I don't...I don't understand why you can't see it.'

I wanted to convince her but didn't know the words. Her face clouded. I could see her doubts but I wanted to find the power I'd seen as she flew across the field. The horses, as if sensing their riders were distracted, ambled to a halt and I trailed one finger down her cheek and found the back of her neck. Her eyes lowered as I gently pulled her towards me.

'Don't,' she whispered.

'What are you frightened of?' I said, stroking her face with my thumb.

There was resistance in her. Her back had lost its spring and she sat alert so that I knew I had alarmed her.

'I don't know how,' she said.

She bit out the words and I sensed it had cost her much

to make such a confession.

'Don't worry, neither do I.'

# CHAPTER 11

We moved on peacefully but I felt strangely tongue tied. I held her hand and smiled, expecting her to be a little perturbed as we neared the college. She wasn't. She smiled back and I dropped her hand reluctantly even though the stable yard was deserted.

'You don't need to wait with me, Mr Clark. One of the grooms might lead me home on the horse and then bring her back.'

'They are notably absent though,' I said. I tied up my horse and turned, ready to help her down. 'Or would you rather me lead you back.'

She spoke tightly, the sounds muffled, as she considered her imminent return to the ground. 'My right leg gets stiff; it might even buckle unless I loosen it up. I need a little time before I get off.'

Ignoring me, she took her leg in both hands, lifted it free of the saddle and stayed there turning her foot until she was sure of its strength.

'Are you ready? Just tell me what you want me to do. You don't need to feel embarrassed.'

'I'm not,' she snapped. 'Don't be ridiculous.'

'Hardly. I'm trying to be helpful but you're biting my ear off.'

'It's only that I prefer to do things for myself,' she explained.

It appeared the last thing she wanted was my understanding. Perhaps it was too close to pity for her liking and irked her. She had got off with my help at the Inn and hadn't made such a fuss. Perhaps, I should never have kissed her because now she seemed conscious of me in a way she hadn't before. Ah, but I didn't regret it. I hadn't expected it to feel as it had. So natural but so consuming. And so hard to stop. I thought it would quench that feeling inside me but, instead of satisfying, it had added more intimate thoughts for me to deal with. It had changed something between us and I hadn't expected that either. Now, I knew a part of her that didn't need words of explanation. It was as if we were now inextricably linked or I could see into her thoughts. I had never understood possessiveness before but I felt its grip on me now. How was that possible from one kiss?

I was holding Firefly's bridle and rubbing the mare's ears until her head lowered in ecstasy. She wasn't tired but the ride had given her almost as much contentment as it afforded her rider and she was happy to linger, getting to know a new acquaintance.

I gauged the belligerence that danced across Miss Coleman's face. 'I can understand that but you have a side saddle and a riding habit to contend with. I think you'll find that it's quite customary for a man to help a lady off her horse and wouldn't be considered over interference. Neither would it be unseemly but, if you prefer, I could lead you over to the mounting block and you could slide off quite neatly.'

She gathered up the reins and would have ridden Firefly the few yards but the mare was ignoring her instructions and traitorously offering the underside of her neck to my ministrations.

'Come on, you daft thing,' I said, leading the mare.

Miss Coleman coloured, knowing I wasn't talking to the horse. The head stableman, John Bale, came hurrying to the yard accompanied by a worried frown on his lined face.

'I'm sorry, Miss Coleman. I didn't know you was here,' he cried, as she got safely to the ground.

He took the mare from me. 'Make sure she's rubbed down properly, John, and stick the bay in his stall. I'll need to check his feet again.'

'There's another one for you to see, sir. That sorrel mare of Mr Granville Penn's seems to be getting worse.'

Granville Penn was one of our governors and had been central to the establishment of the college. His horse was in our stables with an intermittent digestive upset and had the status of special guest.

I turned to Miss Coleman hurriedly. 'Can you wait five minutes? I will escort you home but I need to make sure this isn't the gripes. She hasn't been well for days and I'm worried we're not getting the better of it.'

'Why should I leave just as things are getting interesting?' she cried. 'And anyway, I don't need your help getting home, Mr Clark. I'm perfectly capable of finding my own way.'

I barely heard her and strode into the stables. I wanted to examine the mare before it got dark. Gripes could be fatal and I didn't want to miss any of the signs. I took one look at the patient languishing in a cold sweat and gave orders for her to be covered in blankets and brought outside. I put my ear to her sides and observed her dilated nostrils.

'She's in pain but we might catch it early enough,' I said. 'We'll see if she'll take a little gripe mixture in some warm bran. Failing that I'll have to get a drench down her.'

One of the grooms brought a bottle which I inspected. I recognised the handwriting and gave it back. I had little confidence in William Sewell's abilities and wanted the batch I had made myself. 'Go to the dispensary. Edmund Bond will know what to give you. Quickly!'

I adjusted the blankets and put my hand on the animal's shoulder, pleased that she was warmer.

'Will she be alright?' Miss Coleman was behind me, watching me examine the mare.

'It's too early to say,' I said, without turning around. 'I will be less worried if she eats something. I'm sorry, I thought you had gone home.'

'Perhaps, I could help.'

'It could get rather ugly,' I sighed. 'Your brother would not thank me if I let you stay.'

'He won't know.'

'He knows everything and I'm warning you, this could be an unpleasant place to be for the next half hour.' I felt irritable but spoke gently, much as I would to a nervous animal. 'I fear you won't like it.'

I shouldn't have said it. Telling Christina Coleman that she wouldn't cope was a sure way of getting her to stay. Her brown curls were disordered from her ride, there were splashes of mud on her face and she was glowing with eager vitality. Left to myself I would let her stay but the stable hands would consider it strange and Professor Coleman would no doubt add it to my list of crimes.

'Miss Coleman, I'm in enough trouble without this.'

She stood facing me with her hands on her hips. 'Do you think I've never seen a horse with stomach pains before? I've ridden since I was a child and I've nursed them many times. I can assure you, I will neither get in the way, nor will I get distressed.'

'I'm sure you won't but, while you might have nursed a few sick ponies, I doubt you've seen many die. Gripes can kill and if this gets worse no one here will have time to look after you. Neither will I be doing the gentlemanly thing and escorting you home. It would be best if you went now while there's light enough to see.'

'Mr Clark, I don't need looking after. And I'm staying.'

'Damned idiotic.'

'I beg your pardon.'

'I said…oh, you heard me…and be warned, the language could get far worse than that. If this mare goes down, writhing in pain, those lads will be cursing her to get up; they'll need to if we're to save her.'

There was a stubborn set to her jaw but I shrugged my shoulders, accepting defeat but inwardly smiling. I should never have taken her with me to the Inn, not that I regretted it for one minute. I admired her spirit and hoped it would be enough but, if she was staying, she'd have work to do.

'Very well,' I said. 'Perhaps you would be good enough to make sure they're getting the warm bran ready.'

I put my ear to the mare's sides again, listening carefully for the noises of her stomach. The more activity I heard the happier I would be. Miss Coleman darted off to the stables to chivvy one of the boys who was preparing some feed. By the time it was ready I had approved a new bottle of gripe mixture and was tempting the animal to take it from my hand.

'What's in it?' she asked.

I offered her a smell. 'Oil of peppermint, among other things. It's very good for the digestive system. If I could get her to relax, we'll be half way there.'

The mare took a few tentative licks from the bucket and then head butted it away irritably. She pawed the ground and lurched forward as if she could escape the pain of her heaving sides.

John Bale spoke urgently. 'Don't let her roll, sir. She's going to get worse before she gets better is my guess.'

'She'll not get better unless I can get her to take this. I'll put it in a drench, I've got to get it down her throat,' I said.

I handed John the horse and took Miss Coleman by the shoulders, pushing her to one side of the yard. 'Keep clear of her,' I warned. 'She'll not know where she's putting her feet.'

The mare was walked across the yard in fits and starts, helped by the cajoling of John and two stable lads. She was bathed in sweat but we kept her covered to stop chills. Twice the animal threw herself to the ground, bringing down one of the lads and narrowly missing the burly stableman at her head. The pain came in waves but we got the medicine into her during the lulls. We held her head up before she could spit it out and by the time I'd done it three times her attempts to roll on the ground were lessening.

'Come on, Mrs Penn. We'll not be losing you, we've our good name to think of,' John said, as he walked her round. He wiped his hot face with a cloth and patted the mare as though she'd won a race.

The stable lads, brothers in their early teens, cheered at the sight of her and Miss Coleman's jaw dropped in surprise.

'Too soon,' I warned. 'She's not out of danger yet.'

We kept walking her until I lost track of the time and the sun began to dip behind the trees. It felt peaceful, the mare was relaxed and the birds were greeting the news with a bedtime song. I was examining her when John whispered in my ear.

'Shall I be taking the lady back, then?'

I glanced over my shoulder to the mounting block where Miss Coleman was sitting. She looked frozen, the wind had strengthened and I could see the hunch of her shoulders against the chill air. 'No, I'd best do that myself. I'll be as quick as I can. Keep this one moving for a while and see if she'll eat some of the bran. She'll need watching all night.'

Christina stood when I approached. 'You don't have to take me, you know. I can see you're reluctant to leave. It's only a two-minute walk.'

'Really? It takes me five. Come on.'

'It's kind of you.'

'Not really. I'm only escorting you to get myself in your brother's good books.'

'I don't believe you, you're funning me,' she said, giving me an arch look, not knowing whether to laugh.

'We're not the best of friends, as you know. Being kind to you might be the only thing between me and ruin.'

We headed to the lane that would take us to the Professor's house, a three-storey building in St Pancras Way. The wind persisted and was getting colder with the diminishing daylight. I eased my pace to match her slower one. I thought she was uncomfortable, perhaps the cold had stiffened her and she walked as though it required her concentration. I took off my coat and put it around her shoulders.

'Thank you. Oh, it's so warm.'

'Chasing an animal with gripes is hot work,' I said.

I had had such mixed feelings towards her when we first met, all of them coloured by my antipathy for her brother. The more time I spent with her, the less confused I became. She didn't look for sympathy and she didn't hesitate to speak her mind. She challenged me again about my attack on her brother and urged me to apologise for the sake of the college. I didn't like to tell her that he'd already thought of a convenient way of hastening my departure.

'I have no wish to harm the veterinary college,' I said. 'But I shouldn't speak to you of this, it's not right.'

'Oh, nonsense. Why shouldn't you? Are you afraid I might tell tales?'

'No…but I wouldn't want to turn you against your brother. He must be important to you and well…you have to live with him. I don't wish to create distrust between you.'

'How arrogant you are!' she said. 'Really, you couldn't turn me against him. With all that nonsense you came out with? Why, that's laughable. I shall tell my brother about Mrs Penn, though. It might help you although I fear it might remind him that you are ready to leave here. It's quite obvious that you will make an excellent vet, Mr Clark.'

I thanked her, ignoring the sting in the compliment's tail since I might find out sooner than expected thanks to the exams.

'Are you worried?' she said, softly.

'About leaving the college?'

'No, about Mrs Penn.'

She stumbled on the rough terrain and I took her arm, drawing it through my own and feeling the coldness of her hand. 'Yes, there's reason to be, I fear. Stomach ache. It's can be a killer for a horse and yet such a simple thing in a human.'

'Why is it so serious?'

I laughed, doubting whether I should give her details. It seemed so easy to write about such things, I could discuss it with my fellow students without any discomfort but no woman would want to be told the answer. Would she? Christina Coleman was nestled close to my side and looking at me with undisguised curiosity.

'They can't vomit,' I said, watching her reaction. 'If they over eat, say, they can get blocked. If they roll on the ground from the pain they can twist the gut. That's why it's so important to keep them moving and stop them going down.'

'I see. How obvious once you know.'

'I'm of the opinion that the key lies in our feeding of them. They are grazers, after all, and should only eat in small amounts at a time. There is so much to learn that I'm not sure I will ever know it all. When you tell your brother about this mare you might bear that in mind and not sing my praises too much. It's too early for me to leave here.'

'Well, you have a few more months. It will be enough, surely?'

'No, I don't. I'm to take the exams early. Some of the others, too. Your brother conveniently thinks I'm ready.'

'Oh, I'm sorry, I didn't know.' She paused and then smiled. 'Everything will be fine, though. Please, don't worry. I know you will be one of the most famous vets in the world! Now, there's a challenge for you to live up to.'

She made me laugh and forget my worries. We carried on in comfortable silence with her hand still curled in the crook of my arm. Professor Coleman was rushing down the steps of the house, his greatcoat wrapped around him carelessly. He pursed his lips as his sister withdrew her hand and put more distance between us.

'Ah, Christina,' he said. 'I was about to come looking for you. It's getting dark but I see Mr Clark has you in hand. How thoughtful.'

She took off my coat and handed it to me without a glance. 'Yes, very kind. Thank you, Mr Clark. He insisted on escorting me although I said I could manage quite easily.'

'I'm sure he did but then he is a young man who always does the correct thing. On the surface, at least. Of course, it gives him the opportunity for his favourite sport. Perhaps, you didn't know, my dear, what a sportsman he is. Had you read the files more thoroughly you would know this. Cricket. Riding. He excels at all the disciplines.'

He laughed quietly but I didn't know whether to join him. He was playing with words but his meaning was hidden. His sister was equally in the dark and, since she looked puzzled more than worried, it relieved me that she wasn't intimidated. At least he was no tyrant.

'How interesting, Edward,' she said. 'I would have been back earlier but one of the horses had an attack of the gripes.'

'I see,' he said, turning to me. 'Why was I not informed?'

'I was coming to tell you now, sir,' I said. 'It's Granville Penn's mare. She's been brewing this for days. We managed to get some gripe mixture into her and she seems out of immediate danger. She's being walked and kept warm.'

'So, you thought to come and tell me of this emergency with all haste.'

'Yes, of course.'

'It's remarkable how calmly you brought me this news. I'm full of admiration that you managed to saunter so slowly with my sister with this on your mind. Yes, I can see you must have been torn between your duty to get to me quickly and your desire to linger. On this occasion desire came first. At last – we have Bracy Clark neglecting his duty. How very interesting, if only out of academic interest in view of our discussion this morning.'

'I couldn't come sooner, or spare one of the lads. We were too busy with the mare, Professor.'

'I understand perfectly and of course it was impossible for you to run since you were impeded with Miss Coleman.' He turned to his sister having removed his thin veneer of affability. 'Do you remember my telling you, Christina, that you would distract my students?'

'I was not doing so, Edward. I kept out of the way...'

'No, don't interrupt me, if you please. Even with your very obvious limitations you have managed to achieve what no tavern wench has managed. This worthy individual barely leaves his desk. There is always a book in his hand and never the smell of alcohol on his breath. Believe me, I have wished for it on many occasions. And now, he has left a sick horse in order to walk with you so courteously.

'On the other hand, I might be overestimating your remarkable powers. His sweet words are probably aimed at me, my dear. Ah, but you're intelligent and will have worked that much out. Let's face it, why would they be anything else? Don't look so puzzled. Has he not been complimenting you once more? It is such good sport, is it not, Mr Clark?'

'You mistake the matter, Professor. I have never confused compliments with sport in the way you imply. I approach both disciplines with honesty.'

I sent Miss Coleman a glance, warning her to keep quiet about our ride together. He didn't need to know about that - I wasn't sure which of us would be in the greatest spot of bother. The Professor was guilty of many things including cruelty if he was to imply that no man would bother with his sister on her own account. She wasn't keeping up for once. She looked confused. Oh, God I couldn't let him spell it out for her.

'Sir, I must get back to the horse with your permission.' I eased myself into my coat and hoped my departure would be enough to stop him. 'There's always a danger that mare will go down again and I would rather keep a watch over her myself for a while.'

Miss Coleman wasn't listening to me but was staring at her brother. Her cheeks carried two spots of red and her lips were compressed tight. They appeared to be locked in conflict while I was a mere observer.

'It is Granville Penn's horse, after all,' I continued. 'And it's always wise to be extra cautious. I've a mind to make up a stronger gripe mixture if you are agreeable.'

I wanted to leave and began to back away.

'Edward. What are you trying to say?' she cried.

Her brother made a noise like a set of bellows. 'Don't let him use you, my dear. All his flattery means nothing; you must not listen to it.'

Like all good bellows, they merely fan the flames and Miss Coleman looked ready to ignite. 'But you were implying more than that, weren't you?' she said. 'You act as though no one might be interested in me. As though it's impossible. Do you think I am unaware of my situation? There is no need for you to rub it in. Mr Clark has kindly walked me home, nothing more, and you have given us this ridiculous display as your thanks.'

That was a bit of a leveller. The Professor was about to say more but Miss Coleman had begun her awkward walk to the house. She looked uncomfortable and although it must have been difficult, she was stomping. He glared at me before dashing after her and lending his support as she climbed the few steps to their front door.

# CHAPTER 12

Mrs Penn got through the night without another attack but I was worried about her and had no thoughts of breaking into the Professor's consulting room. I was examining her the next morning when I saw him hurrying to the stable yard, adjusting his hat. The sun was midway in a cloudless sky and the promise of heat created swarms of flies which the horses endured with lazy nodding and swishing.

'Just one moment, if you don't mind,' he called out, tucking his cane under his arm.

He seemed pleased to see so many students on duty including some of his raw recruits who were following me like a shoal of fish. He greeted us all individually, proud that he could remember our names and a little of our history. Our contretemps in St Pancras Way seemed forgotten, and wasn't even mentioned last night when he came to check on the mare. He took the bowl from me and sniffed the gripe mixture without comment.

'It will be useful for you to observe me on my rounds, gentlemen. I might need to make adjustments to our treatment.' He patted the mare robustly on the neck. 'This old girl has had a severe case of worms and a touch of gripes. She's over the worst. See how placid she is? Her temperature is normal and there's no evidence of pain.'

The Professor lifted the blanket from her back and felt her sides. 'This won't be necessary, Clark,' he said, handing me the bowl.

'But, Professor, she's not out of danger.'

'You surprise me. I thought I had made my diagnosis quite clear.' The Professor's smile was aimed at inducing silence. 'Follow me, everyone.'

'I tell you, sir, I'm very worried about her. Her sides are very tight and I fear she's only placid because she's exhausted. I can ease her pain for a short while but we can't get it gone for good.'

He had taken a few strides towards the stables before halting and peering at his feet. When he turned, the smile was back and he folded his arms. He scanned the crowd of students as though they were his audience at a play.

'I have always admired your diligence. No doubt you will make an excellent vet but you will be a poor one since all your profits will be poured down the mouth of some healthy animal which has nothing ailing it. Let's look again, shall we, since Mr Clark requires it.' He folded the blanket onto the horse's rump exposing her damp coat. With his cane he pointed at her sides. 'Please try to distinguish the difference between a hot animal and a sick one. Are her sides heaving with pain? No, they are not. She is still. She is perfectly sound and will no doubt outlive me. What are the symptoms of gripes? Quickly, can anyone tell me?'

William answered him. 'Pain…oh, and rolling on the ground. Sometimes the horse will kick at its own stomach. Yes, that's it - and paw the ground.'

'Excellent. We have none of that before us unless we turn our attention to Clark himself.'

The Professor laughed, gloating when amusement spread. He took one final look at the mare and tossed the blanket in my direction but I let it fall to the ground. I stood, staring at him, hardly noticing that Fred had picked it up and put it on a low wall.

Coleman led his students towards the stable building, taking measured strides and ignoring my shocked face. The warm, moist smell of the stable greeted us and the Professor scanned the stalls. He used his cane to illustrate his instructions, a tap of a cobweb sent a lad hurrying for a besom and a raised eyebrow was enough to open more windows.

The stables were the best I'd ever seen and the Professor insisted they were kept spotless. They were set on a gradient to afford maximum drainage, the cobbles were swept until they shone and the solid, wooden partitions between the stalls were topped with rails so the horses could see each other but not fight. The hay racks were solid, made from wrought iron while wooden pegs on one wall stored halters and bridles. The equine propensity to defecate was a constant battleground and one that made the Professor talk warmly of his days as a surgeon. He sighed and beckoned to Edmund.

'Get one of the lads to see to this, please,' he said, with his customary urbanity.

Then he wanted a closer look at his patients, calling on us to lead out the animals in turn so he could inspect their hurts and evaluate their improvement. He worked methodically, speaking clearly and simply about strains, bruises and how to draw out infection using a bran poultice. I was distracted and could hardly listen. The humiliation was familiar but my worry about the sorrel mare wouldn't go away and I kept looking at her through the door.

He was coming to the end of his inspection and called on one of his new pupils, Eric Kettell, to pick up the foot of a grey Hanoverian. It was a challenging task for the former tailor but more easily achieved than a page of writing.

The Professor pointed at the horse's shoe with his cane. 'This horse drags his feet; and is intermittently lame with no apparent cause but here is our culprit. This heavy shoe. Take him to the forge. Let's see what our new Grasshoppers can do for him.'

William Sewell, who was at the front of the crowd, seconded the suggestion. 'Ah, yes! The Grasshopper. So revolutionary, if I may say so, and, of course, it makes so much sense to have a lighter, neater shoe. Have you patented it yet, sir?'

'I have. I am rather pleased with it. Very soon, we'll have all the horses fitted with them as soon as they come here.'

'What a good name you will make for us, Professor. And to have thought of it is…well, most remarkable.'

'Thank you, Sewell. Lead the horse outside, Kettell.'

The heat of the college's own forge spilt into the outside air like a boiler and carried the sounds of hammering metal onto metal. A skylight pierced the warm gloom inside where George Whelan was crouched over a massive anvil set onto a wooden block. He looked up as the party approached and nodded to the Professor, then stretched his back as though it might need a turn in the fire to have its kinks knocked out. His hands reached for his hips as he assessed the horse walking towards him.

'What a tumble down fellow. Grasshoppers for him, sir?'

The Professor nodded and gave me a curt dismissal. I had seen enough horses shod in my time and didn't relish another lecture in favour of the Professor's new shoe, especially one backed up by William's praises. It was nauseating to see him flattering a path into the Professor's esteem with so little substance beyond smooth words.

I was sent back with Fred and Edmund to finish the tasks from the rounds. There were poultices to apply and an ugly gash that needed dressing again. The yard was being swept by a stable lad as though it was the hallway to a grand house.

Fred spat out a piece of hay he was chewing and turned to the sorrel mare. 'I'll put her back, shall I? At least she looks like she'll survive.'

'Not until I've finished giving her another dose,' I muttered. 'The Professor's diagnosis is driven by the accounts and his desire for a new wardrobe.' I assumed a mantle of fatigue and said: 'I have a delightful waistcoat in mind, I must afford it somehow, gentlemen, and these horses have no need of expensive medicines. Have I told you about the patient I once cured of influenza by blowing on him?'

Fred laughed but looked around in case any of the grooms were within earshot. It was becoming common knowledge that I mimicked the Professor and it was high time I stopped doing performances in our sitting room. They were getting too popular.

We finished after more than an hour, helping each other by working in a team when we felt need of advice or if a horse was difficult and had to be held. We were confident with the animals and, I think, proficient with their treatments. Fred's diminutive hands could apply a dressing quicker than anyone and he'd joke that he'd learnt the art at his father's breast.

I smiled as a chestnut head with its familiar white blaze nudged me in the ribs. 'Hello, Firefly. It's good to see a horse that isn't ill,' I said, rubbing the animal's ears until her head lolled in stupefaction.

There were a handful of animals kept by the college including the Professor's own mount and a heavy horse used to pull a cart. The rest were patients.

'It's a very nice horse.' Edmund paused and studied me. 'Do you know, I think you must follow my first suggestion?'

I was conscious of a guilty twinge. 'What was that?'

'Miss Coleman,' he said. 'You were going to make her fall for you, remember? It shouldn't be difficult seeing as you are such a handsome fellow and she must be the loneliest female this side of London. I'd say any of us could do it. We've got to find a way of getting our paths to cross.'

'That's not going to happen.' Fred scratched his head and yawned. 'Better to break into his consulting room, if you ask me. There's no way the Professor's sister is going to hand you the accounts. Why should she? I saw her riding the mare yesterday, you know. I thought she looked normal. I suppose she would on a horse and I didn't see her walk. William says...'

'To hell with what William says,' I said, cutting him off angrily.

Fred turned to me but I ignored him and was rinsing my

hands in a bucket of water. Edmund was smiling and answered Fred's questioning look with one raised brow.

'What are you looking like that for?' I asked as I dried my hands.

'I've never seen you lose your temper before,' Fred explained.

I sighed. 'She is normal. It's only other people's narrow mindedness that makes her different.'

'But isn't she a cripple, then?'

'She has one leg that appears to give her trouble. It's probably painful but she barely mentions it. William has a brain that isn't fully functioning but it won't hinder his advancement. Do you understand what I'm saying, Fred? She's no less a person for having an injury or for walking with an uneven gait and it angers me to see someone accept half a life. I suspect Christina Coleman is so accustomed to society's attitude that she accepts it without complaint. She probably has very little ambition and will waste her life keeping house for that brother of hers.'

I tossed a cloth back onto a peg and had to retrieve it when it fell to the floor.

'No, the Professor won't keep her,' Fred snorted. 'He'll marry her off to someone like William. You and I might think she may never marry but you forget how powerful her brother is. He'll find someone to take her on and who better than that half wit?'

We approached the stone archway that formed the main college entrance where a group of students was gathered around a woman selling nuts and oranges from a basket. Fred was hurrying towards her, interested in something she had to offer, and didn't see my look of thunder.

Edmund did and put a restraining hand on my arm. 'Leave it, Bracy. He doesn't realise.'

# CHAPTER 13

The day, which began early and would finish late, was too promising to lose a horse. The sun rise owed more to water colours than oils. The different shades seeped and bled together and, as the sun made its steady ascent, steaming mist lifted from the fields to reveal grass that was pricking with life. It would be a warm day, the wind was gently stirring and the Fleet River wound its way to London as though hurrying was for another season.

As students, we enjoyed far more personal space than the average servant and were rarely woken before six when it was time to get up. The thin curtains were no defence against light so the room was filling with shadows which soon would give way to colour and form. I woke quickly when the call came, already out of bed when I saw who was shaking my shoulder.

'What is it, John?' I asked.

'Mrs Penn, sir. She's gone down and can't get up.'

John Bale was a highly competent stableman, if anyone could get a sick horse to its feet it was him. The man's agitated frown hurried me into my clothes and I went to wake Edmund, knowing I might need help.

'Has anyone sent for Professor Coleman?'

'Yes, sir. He's been sent for but…'

'I know but I'm sure he will want to supervise this if it's as bad as you say.'

'Oh, it's bad alright. It's like she's finished.'

At the stable yard we were greeted by whinnies of hungry approval by those well enough to know it was breakfast time but our concern was monopolised by the sight that met our eyes in one of the stalls. The sorrel mare that I had battled with only two days before was wedged against one wall, a look of exhaustion masking her fine breeding. Her coat was slick with sweat and her eyes were dull and listless.

'She's given up,' said Edmund. 'We'll not save her.'

'Has she been rolling?' I asked John, ignoring Ed's acceptance of defeat.

'No, sir,' the stableman replied. 'She's collapsed but she hasn't got the energy for rolling, it seems to me. We've got to get her up if we can, no horse can stay down like that.'

He was right. A horse that was too weak to stand up wouldn't survive long, its body wouldn't function. 'Come on then,' I said. 'Ed, help me get her off her side. Come on, girl, let's go.'

I pushed at her neck so there was just enough room between the mare and the wall for me to squeeze into. Edmund attempted the same manoeuvre at the other end until we were able to push against her.

We started shouting, pushing and coaxing. At one point Edmund leapt clear when her body tipped towards him. The animal was like a dead weight, impossible to move. Our faces were hot and our voices rasping. We sat back on our haunches while the stableman watched in growing dismay.

'Did you try the whip on her, John?' I asked.

'Useless.'

I got up and fetched the long whip that was propped in one corner of the stables. I cracked it on the wooden partitions; hollering and making the other animals stir in alarm. Then I approached the mare, slapping the whip on the walls as I got closer. She turned her neck, her eyes locked with mine. I had her.

'John, quickly. Go to her head, push on her neck where I was,' I said.

I whipped the ground, close to her tail and just missed her legs. The three of us were shouting and coaxing. She groaned and flung her front legs from under her. And there she stopped. Half way.

'Be careful, don't let her crush you if she lays down on her side again, sir,' said John. 'Put some straw down the side of her. That'll support her.'

I started whipping again, lashing the walls to warn her there was a worse fate than the pain she was in and making sure my voice mirrored the threat.

'Come on,' I shouted. 'You can do it.'

The mare's breathing was rapid but something stirred in her as if she would make one last effort to please or escape the danger of us men. There was a grunt of effort and Edmund leapt out the way just as her back legs scrabbled to get purchase on the floor. And then she was up, standing on shaking legs, not looking at her rescuers and impervious to the praise we gave her.

I gave a sigh of relief and wiped my brow. Edmund leant against the wall to get his breath back and John muttered that he never thought to see her stand again.

'What do we do now? She looks awful,' said Edmund.

He turned at the sound of booted feet on the cobbles. Professor Coleman walked into the stables, a smile of greeting on his face.

'I thought you'd want me to alert you, Professor,' John said, apologetically. 'But we've got her up as you can see.'

'You did very right, John. Good morning Clark. Bond. I see you've been busy. Let's have a look at her outside where the light is better, if you please.'

The Professor was immaculately dressed as usual. His black coat was beautifully tailored, his waistcoat was colourful and his boots had the gloss of a healthy horse. The only sign that he had rushed was a carelessly tied neck cloth and the absence of his customary cane. He took one look at the mare and nodded his head, his eyes shutting as though they might keep him from the animal's reproach.

'What medicine has she had?' he asked.

'Nothing, sir. Not since you came on the rounds yesterday,' I said, omitting to mention the extra dose I gave her.

'Quite right. It wouldn't have made any difference. We'll not get the better of this, gentlemen. I have little hope, I'm afraid. Keep her out here; prevent her from going down and rolling if you can. Walk her and keep an eye on her. Clark, when did you last check her?'

'Just before retiring last night.'

'And how was she then?'

'Tired. Rather dull but not in pain.'

'Didn't you think she would need checking again in the night? That's the second time you have neglected this case.'

That made me flinch but I met the Professor squarely. 'I object to that, sir. I asked John to set a watch on her and I was to be called as soon as she showed any sign of distress. He came to me at five. That is not neglect. My only mistake was in not challenging your diagnosis that she was out of danger and didn't need any more gripe mixture.'

'You knew full well there was a risk of relapse. It is the nature of gripes and I have told you so on many occasions. I am seriously displeased.'

Just then the mare groaned, as if she was tired of the raised voices, and sank to the ground. Her sides were heaving and her legs thrashed, forcing us to give her a wide berth.

The next few hours were painful for all concerned. We got her up but her attempts to throw herself down became more frequent. The Professor took his leave eventually, saying there was little hope and nothing more to be done since the gripe mixture appeared ineffectual. Edmund and I stayed with her, forcing medicine down her, taking it in turns to walk and sooth until she went down for the final time.

'No,' I cried out when her legs stopped twitching. 'She can't go. Not like this.'

Ed and John held me; they tried to pull me away.

'She's gone, sir. There's nothing more we can do,' John said. 'She's not in pain now.'

'What did I do wrong? Surely...I can't believe it...'

I crouched down and stroked her ears, conscious that it was my apology. Mrs Penn had been one of my patients and I had failed her miserably thanks to my ignorance. I aspired to be a vet but couldn't even cure a case of gripes. I don't know how long I sat near her. I wasn't ready to part from her because walking away would have been acceptance. Her damp body lay inert on the yard, robbed of elegance by a swollen stomach. I should have ignored the Professor, given her gripe mixture through the night. Its effect was so limited; surely, there must be something more powerful to give an animal that was in that much pain. I was useless against such a powerful adversary as Death. I had so much to learn.

Edmund whispered that he would send one of the lads to notify the Professor. 'It's not your fault, Bracy. I think she only stayed alive as long as she did to oblige you.'

I grunted and looked at my friend's ashen face. 'She was my responsibility. Mine! I let her down. There must have been something I could have done.'

'More mixture? It can only do so much, you know.'

'It might have helped but he'd have blamed me for overdosing her. Sometimes I think he doesn't care. That mixture of his has very little effect so why doesn't he try something else? I tell you, he's not interested unless as he can sell it and pocket the money.'

Edmund put his hand on my shoulder and squeezed. 'Steady on. He did care and he would have stayed with us if he could have.'

I shrugged and took one last look at the mare who was destined for the dissecting table. 'Not enough.'

# CHAPTER 14

I didn't ride for days, may be weeks, after that. There would be other lost patients but this was my first and she was so tied up in my battle with Professor Coleman that I would probably never forget her. Surprisingly, he had enough sensitivity to keep me away from the post mortem. In my unkind moments I thought his motivation may have been self preservation. A dozen students, may be more, heard him mock me. How confident he had been that she would outlive him. He never acknowledged he was wrong. That was never his style. At least he stopped blaming me for her death. His sister was a great comfort, although he was blissfully unaware of it. She told me I would learn from her death, it would help others in the future. I thought of the useless gripe mixture we had at our disposal and thought it unlikely - unless I could come up with something better.

The loss of Mrs Penn had one other consequence. We hadn't the heart to break into the Professor's consulting room. The exams were looming and that distracted us. Plotting Coleman's downfall was insufficient to take me from my studies. His sister held more lure. Eventually, I contrived to start riding with her again. I had two free hours from my studies after lunch and I took any of our patients that needed exercise to aid their recovery. I never set out with her and we always returned separately. There was little point arousing suspicion and I didn't need her brother warning me off. The Professor was overjoyed at my industry and asked me to keep monitoring the effectiveness of his Grasshopper shoes. I can't say I was impressed with them although I restrained my criticism. So far, I hadn't ridden an animal that was happy beyond a steady trot but since many had come to us lame it was difficult to assess them. I was young; I had other things on my mind and had no inkling of the trouble the wretched things would cause.

Instead, my eyes were fixed on a trim, blue figure waiting for me in a gateway. She was laughing, one hand was resting on her thigh and the other held the reins lightly.

'Mr Clark, are you riding my way?' she called out as I approached.

'I am indeed.'

'How strange! What a coincidence.'

'Yes, isn't it?' I hadn't seen her for days and was unsure of my reception. 'Do you mind?'

She looked at me boldly and she was smiling. She didn't mind at all but might be searching for some way of admitting the fact without appearing too acquiescent. She took up the reins and circled around my horse until I had the feeling we were in a sale ring and she was deciding whether or not to bid.

'Why would I mind?' she said. 'It's not for me to stop you riding any place you like. Which way are you going?'

Ah, she had me there. I had no idea of the route she was taking but hadn't expected her to tease. There was a playful light in her eyes which warmed me and made me bold.

'It won't matter,' I said.

'Surely, you must have a preference.'

She laughed and set off up the lane, turning her head to see if I was following. I was. I must have looked the devoted slave. I had no will of my own, no direction in mind, only the urge to be with her picking up crumbs of attention she might bestow. The sun was high but there was a light breeze which kept us from getting hot. The trees were in full leaf now, their colours fresh and vigorous and the ground still soft from the spring rains. I pushed my horse into trot and placed him alongside hers. The path narrowed and our legs touched. I apologised but she ignored me.

'Your mare is well named,' I said. 'Firefly. I'd hazard a guess that her best pace is canter.'

'You'd be wrong, the gallop is better, by far.'

She knew no restraint on the horse and I was impressed each time I saw her. 'You look as though you've known each other for years. She's got just the right amount of blood horse in her. Good bone. Lovely conformation. Quite, quite stunning. The way she moves is so elegant. The perfect horse for a lady.'

I looked from the mare to Miss Coleman's face and paused. She turned away from me as though I had stung her. You see, it was impossible to reconcile this rider with the woman William had the gall to describe as a cripple. Her hips swayed in time with the mare, her hands were the lightest I had seen and her back flexed with ease as she ducked under the trees. There was nothing she couldn't do on a horse. Christ, she could even kiss until I was simmering with heat. So, why shouldn't I call her horse elegant? Did it remind her of her own inadequacies? I hadn't thought of the way she walked or how it must hinder her confidence. How stupid of me.

'I'm sorry, have I offended you?' I asked.

She didn't answer. I knew I had pained her. I suppose riding was her one chance of freedom when she forgot the compromise of her life, enjoyed the speed, the grace that a horse lent her unless someone like me reminded her of it.

I underestimated her, it seemed, for she bounced back in that quirky way of hers. 'Don't be silly. You can't offend me by praising my horse. It's just that...'

'Go on.'

'Sometimes I wish life was like this all the time. I should live on a horse, really. As soon as I get off I'm like a fish that's been thrown out of the sea. I'm squirming around in the most ridiculous way, putting in lots of effort but not getting very far.' Then her voice changed and she became angry. 'It's so frustrating. I used to be able to run, if you could call it that but I don't even think I can do that anymore. Why, I can hardly get out of a chair with any speed. I can sit there looking like a woman, demure and elegant, but it's an illusion. I'm a mere oil painting compared to the real thing.'

'Do you define a woman by her ability to run, then? Surely not. How many women run beyond their girlhoods? Miss Coleman, you are very hard on yourself and take too narrow a view. Now it is you who is being silly.'

Her eyes snapped at me. 'I'm not silly, you silly man.' She shut her eyes and took a deep breath. 'But I do get rather cross. I'm sorry. Talk to me about something else. My brother told me you are a Quaker.'

'Did he now?' I said, turning to her in surprise. 'Well, my parents were Quakers and I went to a Quaker school. The upbringing never leaves you.'

'What does it mean?'

'Do you mean, what are our beliefs?' She nodded, looking thoughtful. 'That's the thing, there isn't anything strictly speaking. We believe there is God in everybody. And so there are no priests, no ritual and no church. Just a meeting room for the Friends.'

'Why is there no clergy?' she asked, quite shocked at such an omission.

'Because a priest would only come between a believer and God. We are all equal, wouldn't you agree? No one has that superiority over another man and so anyone can speak.'

'Even women and children?' she laughed.

I nodded. 'Yes, of course.'

'Is it true that you oppose war?'

'Utterly and absolutely.'

'Was it difficult being brought up like that?'

I stopped to look at a stream that meandered between the trees. In the distance, a buzzard was circling without troubling its wings.

'Not at all. It meant we were a little different and that's not easy when you're young, sometimes I saw it as a blessing but at others it was a burden. It gives me a perspective on life, though. I'm so used to it but sometimes it's a problem for other people.'

'What sort of perspective?' she said, bringing her horse next to mine.

'That we have a purpose, that we have something to accomplish on this earth and should leave it a better place. You see, what a person does is far more important than what they say. Sometimes it's too much to live up to. I more often think I'll never achieve anything.'

'Of course you will,' she laughed. 'I wonder what my purpose must be. Sometimes my silly, little life has no greater goal than walking up the stairs without stumbling. So, tell me, Mr Clark, what is it that you hope to give to the world? Is there going to be a great work that you will leave behind for future generations to marvel at? Perhaps you will write something very clever and that will be your legacy.'

'I'm sorry, I'm being horribly earnest,' I said.

'Nonsense. Please don't think I was mocking you when you have every right to be earnest. What more worthy endeavour can there be than to become a veterinarian? I envy you and wish I had a purpose. My life seems to be an existence and nothing more. You are very lucky.'

'Well, don't envy me. I have no more idea what my purpose is than you do. I just feel that everyone has something to achieve. One day it might be clear to me.' I looked up at the sky and felt easier. 'It might be better to be one of those buzzards. What nobler existence can there be?'

'To rule the skies and frighten everything below!' she cried. 'I don't believe you aspire to any such thing. Don't worry. One day you will have a very successful practice and everyone will be seeking your advice. You will have more patients than you can cope with, their owners will be singing your praises and you will get very rich, I'm sure of it.'

I was surprised she had so misunderstood me. 'Miss

Coleman, financial reward has never been my motivation. I don't seek a rich practice. Indeed, I need very little.'

'Of course, I didn't think. How foolish of me. You are certainly unusual, Mr Clark. What man setting out in the world will proclaim to a woman that he's not seeking to make his fortune?'

'Not many, I agree. But I wasn't talking to you as a woman, at least, not in the way you're suggesting.'

'Then, what?' she asked, as a blush crept under her skin.

'More of an equal. A friend.'

She shrugged her shoulders and appeared amused. 'That will be interesting. And such a rocky beginning to our friendship with your allegations against my brother.' I waved that aside. It wasn't something we could talk about. She continued, 'As for being equals? How strange to even consider it. I can't imagine any man seeing *me* in such a light. What woman expects to be treated in such a way? You will be telling me next that Mary Wollstonecraft's ideas will catch on. Have you read her book?'

'I have. It is very interesting.'

'*A Vindication of the Rights of Woman*, I think it's called but really, is there any wife on earth who thinks herself equal to her husband? It's rather an amusing thought.'

'Is it? And yet you told me yourself there was more to life than domestic concerns.'

'Oh, yes, but that's different. I get bored, you see.'

'I've grown up with the idea of equality so it seems the most natural thing in the world to me.'

'Friends and equals?' She turned to me with one eyebrow twitching. 'You make it sound very dry. How does kissing come into it, then? Or was that not part of your plan when you arranged to accidentally meet me this afternoon?'

There was a pause and then I broke into a bout of laughter that in some measure hid my embarrassment. It wasn't surprising that she should see through me but that she should acknowledge it was mortifying.

'Do you want me to kiss you?'

101

'That's for you to find out, I think.'

'I wouldn't like to impose. I thought you might like to give me a hint. Some sort of signal.'

'What! You want me to pout my lips? Make my eyelids dance or something?'

'Perhaps. Or something more subtle.'

'I'm afraid I don't know how to be subtle. It's just that if you are going to kiss me I wish you would get on with it. We've been riding now for at least half an hour and you have been so horribly polite that I don't know what to think. You've never been polite before and I find that the uncertainty is quite terrifying. Of course, you might not want to repeat the experience but if that were the case why would you follow me? Unless, it really was accidental and not by design. In which case - well, I don't know how you can get out of it now without offending me. I will understand if you'd rather not but…'

I slid off my horse and tied him to a tree. I came to her side and offered her my arms. Her monologue ceased and she looked unsure.

'You want me to get off?'

'Yes, come on. I dare you.'

There was little hesitation, she leapt into my arms and I held her close, kissing the side of her face. 'There, I've hooked you, my petit poisson.'

'I only look like a fish when I move,' she laughed.

'You'd better stay where you are then.'

I kissed her and found my appetite swelling. I thought it might diminish, that I might be able to satisfy my craving for her by sampling her lips but I was wrong. We were both panting but one of us groaned. It must have been me because her body tensed and withdrew. Her face was full of surprise. At least there was no sign of recoil and she didn't let go of my waist. Her hands were like tiny sources of heat that burned through my shirt.

'Enough?' I asked her.

Ah, how that look of disappointment delighted me. I had never experienced such desire before, never held it nor fed it with this teasing dance. I wanted to up the tempo and pulled her closer, returning to her lips and then her neck when she moved away.

'Bracy, you will stop when I ask, won't you?' she said, breathlessly.

'I promise. Kiss me.'

I would have promised her anything. I was raging and hardly heard her. My hands were in her hair, her beautiful hair, making it tumble, free of pins, down her back. How long it was. So thick. And then she was kissing me back. Letting my tongue find hers. I felt as if I was running down a steep hill. I could have stopped but everything was against me. Gravity. The tiredness in my legs. The knowledge that she would be mine if only I kept up this relentless descent. I had an overwhelming urge to lay down with her. Images that would have shocked her took the strength from my legs and quickened my breathing. I needed her to stop me but I was touching her breasts and then searching for a way among the soft folds of her clothes. Finding her thighs.

Her body was pressed to mine but I was desperately trying to find a way of making us closer. I was pulling her towards me, anxious and rushed. Was I really trying to join us together? How foolish I was. How overwhelmed. I would have carried on, driven like a madman and ruining our lives but from somewhere a doubt surfaced. Moving away from her brought a welcome drop in temperature. We looked at each other, not in horror, but with some sort of trepidation. That each of us could create such a loss of control in the other. There might have been blame, too. She must have blamed me for going so far. Was she angry? I wished she had stopped me. I shouldn't have lifted her riding habit like that and then I was remembering the feel of her, the silkiness of her bottom and the desire in me rekindled. She was rearranging her clothes and seemed shaken. I apologised.

She raised one eyebrow, she was quite coquettish. 'Why are you apologising? Do you regret that?'

'Of course I regret it, how can you ask me? I never

should have done such a thing. Never. I'm sorry. I quite forgot myself.'

'Perhaps you should do so more often.' She was composed again, more so than I was. Her clothes were as neat as she could make them although her hair was in disarray. She could have just got out of bed, by the look of her.

'I only meant to kiss you,' I whispered.

'And now you wish you hadn't?'

'No, I'm not sorry for that.'

'What then?'

'I shouldn't have touched you like that.'

'But I wanted you to.' She watched me pace about, trying to still my agitation. 'Why won't you look at me? It was nice and now you are ashamed. Did I do something wrong?'

She closed the gap between us and soon her head was resting on my chest and my arms were around her. My hands were firmly on her shoulders, I wouldn't allow them to move an inch. There would be no resumption.

'My darling, it wouldn't have stopped there. We were playing with fire.'

'Not fire, Bracy. I think you were playing with something else entirely. You hands were stroking my…'

'Don't remind me. Hush.'

I was kissing the side of her face but I made sure not to open my mouth. I didn't want to start tasting her again.

'Would you have seduced me? Is that what would have happened?'

'Yes, perhaps. Lord knows, I certainly wanted to if I could have.'

'Me! You would have seduced me. Here.' She started laughing but I couldn't understand her merriment. I was anticipating her disgust or her fear. She was thrilled. Her arms, which were surprisingly muscular, filled with energy and began to vibrate. And her face was glowing with vitality. 'Until the other day I had never been kissed. Not like that anyway. You do it with your mouth open, don't you? And today. Your tongue. And you kept doing it. On and on.'

'Miss Coleman, I got carried away.'

'But I liked it.' She wasn't shouting but she was crying out loudly. With some joy. 'You can hardly put your tongue in my mouth and call me Miss Coleman. I think you had better call me Christina. At least you must when we go riding. Will you try and seduce me again tomorrow?'

How she could make it sound so innocent was beyond me. I was shocked and she folded her arms and smiled. She looked so lovely. Her hair was curly and tangled and her cheeks were feverish. There was no question that she was very womanly but it was possible to see the child she had been. It was her foundation and it hadn't been tutored or spoilt.

'Of course not,' I said.

'But you don't find me repulsive. You want to seduce me but you think you shouldn't. Is that it?'

'Christina, I want to court you…not take you on the ground.'

'Take me?'

'Make love to you. Swap your virginity for mine. Deflower you. Us. And no, I don't find you repulsive. You are beautiful. Wonderful. I want to cherish you, not treat you like this. Grabbing and mauling you in such a hurry.'

'Oh! Is that what would have happened?'

'Exactly. Now do you understand?'

'I thought seduction was something else.'

She turned away from me and went to fetch her mare who was cropping the shoots of grass by the bank of the stream. She moved quite easily, the limp was barely noticeable and she sounded self conscious as she talked to the horse. I had finally dented her enthusiasm for love making. She was uninhibited and unaware. I realised no one had bothered to warn her to be careful of men, no one thought she would marry and, until now, no one had awakened her desires. How trusting she was. How easy to take advantage of her. What a risk the Professor was taking. To leave her in such ignorance assuming no one would find her attractive. That everyone would be put off by her limp. What fools, if they were?

# CHAPTER 15

She was in no hurry and chatted away with little self consciousness but I had a lecture to return to and didn't want either of us to be missed. She started explaining how her brother helped her onto the horse when they didn't have a mounting block by making a cup with his hands for her good leg.

'We usually get it right by the third attempt,' she said, happily. 'Do you mind?'

'Not at all,' I said, kissing her on the nose.

I gripped her lightly around the waist and tossed her into the saddle. I was considerably taller than her brother and wasn't above the desire to show off my physical strength. It was beneath me but I wanted to impress her. I was successful judging by her open mouth and look of surprise. I could feel her eyes upon me as I fetched my own mount and her little *thank you* was breathless.

'Bracy, can I ask you something?' she said as we turned for home.

I nodded in spite of my discomfort.

'Should I feel ashamed? It's just that you do so am I meant to? I can't really ask Edward, he rushes out of the room if I mention anything about what happens between men and women.'

'You've done nothing to be ashamed of but, you're

right, it's not something you would discuss with your brother.'

'Then why are you ashamed? It can't be wrong when it made me feel so lovely. I don't understand why you look so wretched. Look at your miserable face. And you didn't go too far anyway. You stopped as you promised you would. You didn't take me on the ground…and I didn't take you. So what's the problem?'

She said this almost theatrically as if I was exaggerating the difficulties I had placed us in. I had awakened desires in a woman who was vulnerable and she hadn't the understanding to be angry with me. Much as I would love to court her, marriage for me was a long-term goal and not an immediate concern. I had exams to pass, a practice to set up, I had nowhere to put a wife.

'I might have ruined you and that's why I'm ashamed. Our activities…well, yes, they were very pleasurable…'

'There, you see, you enjoyed it too. It was glorious; I've never felt like that before. I must see if I can find some literature about it because I think our blood was rushing about. I had some of the most wonderful sensations and I knew you felt the same because you were quite out of breath. For once, I was like a normal woman, don't you see? No one will tell me these things but that's what normal people feel all the time. So, why shouldn't I?'

'You should. When you are married. And you mustn't find some literature about it; that would be quite improper.'

I didn't like the thought of her marrying. I felt greedy for her and possessive no doubt brought on by indulging this passion I had for her. Only a few days ago I had been able to talk to her with a clear head but it seems I crushed that ability when I delved so far into her clothing. In spite of my words I was already regretting my high moral stance. I wanted more of her. It was highly likely that I would follow her riding again and although I wouldn't attempt to seduce her there was a good chance that she wouldn't share my reservations.

Crooked Lane with its twists and turns had fields either side and straggly hedgerows which seemed too suffocated to provide much shelter. There were men working in one of the fields, leading a horse pulling a cart laden with hay so I would have preferred a better screen than the hedge afforded. Christina waved to them and I remembered the Professor's dismay that everyone appeared to know her.

'I can't ignore them,' she said to me quietly. 'They supply the college with hay.'

'We should have separated earlier,' I said.

'Good afternoon, miss,' the driver called out. 'It's good to see you with some company. Safer for you, to my mind.'

He nodded to me with approval and I waved back. I recognised him and knew he farmed the land to the east of us but couldn't remember his name.

Christina stopped at a gap in the hedge. 'How is Mrs Dalton today?' she called.

Apparently, Mrs Dalton was much better and there had been no need to call out the doctor which was a blessing because they could ill afford it after another bad harvest. Mr Dalton wanted to know how Miss Coleman was doing, whether her brother was well and how that fine horse was behaving.

'I nearly fell into the hay stack when I saw how fast she was going the other day. I don't know how you manage to stay on her. It's a marvel, that it is,' he said.

I didn't want to be unsociable but time was pressing, I needed to be back and I could hardly leave her there alone.

'Christina, we must be going,' I said, quietly.

She waved goodbye to the men and sighed. 'The weather hasn't been kind, you know. It's made it very difficult for all the farmers. Mr Dalton fusses over me, I'm sorry. Edward hates it. He thinks he's the only one who's allowed to do it. They mean well but sometimes I wish they wouldn't bother. You don't worry about me, do you? On a horse, I mean.'

She was laughing as though her spirit was irrepressible and the sound banished any thoughts of concern. Yes, she could fall off but so could anyone. Riding a horse came with an element of risk, the unexpected could happen, mistakes could be made but there was nothing to say she was in more danger because of her disability. She rode exceptionally well; the horse was fast but sensible so why shouldn't she enjoy it? It seemed to me that she was liberated and made able bodied by the horse.

But to say I didn't worry about her made it sound as though I didn't care. I was fast realising that I did. And with caring came an element of fear. Of what, I asked myself? Losing someone who was precious? Not wanting to see them hurt? All of those things were reasonable. What Professor Coleman was guilty of, to my mind, was taking concern a step further. Creating limitations and dependency.

'I don't worry about you riding,' I said. 'You do it so much better than most people I know. But…'

'Ah, I knew there would be one of those. Go on.'

The path widened and I rode alongside her. I took up a tress of her hair and took out a leaf that had taken up residence. 'I care about you and want you to have a full life. If anything I would want you to take more risks.'

'More? That's such a good idea. I've never jumped her, you know. I didn't like to since I ride on my own so much and, to be honest, it wouldn't be easy with a side saddle. But you could teach me, couldn't you?'

I told her I would but made her promise never to do it when she was on her own. If you were going to fall off that would be the time for it. She knew of the perfect place; a woodland where there were some fallen trees that hadn't been cut for timber. She was excited at the prospect of our lesson and made me promise to make a start tomorrow. I didn't know if I would have a horse the Professor wanted me to ride but she insisted there was bound to be, that I should be more positive.

'Bracy, do you know? When I'm on the ground I have one good leg. When I ride I have five of them! No wonder I feel so amazing. God, I love this horse, I would be nothing without her. It's the only time life is like this for me.' She ducked under a branch and let her mare break into a trot. Then she turned to me, a smile breaking into her sun-flushed cheeks and a look of revelation upon her. 'Oh, it's not the only time. Of course. Earlier. That was wonderful too. Not the same. Better. No, different. But it made me free. I think I will have to tell Suzanna. Well, you don't expect me to keep it to myself, I hope?'

It was lovely to have my fumbling efforts so appreciated although to be compared to a ride on a horse struck me as less complimentary. I was torn between warning her to say nothing to her brother and the violent urge to kiss her again, certain that I might need to hone my skills. I couldn't help laughing, especially when there was such wonder on her face.

'You're embarrassed, aren't you?' she said.

'Not at all. You are quite without inhibition, Christina. I could get to like it but it's possible that I never should have told you that story about the stallion. I hold myself responsible for the outcome and your brother was right to censure me.'

I must have been attracted to her even then without knowing it. I wouldn't have told her about Eclipse's work at stud unless I had that devilment in me. Surely, I knew what I was about that night on some level. Teasing and testing her.

'Bracy? I was thinking.'

'Yes.'

'Would it be the same with anyone?'

'What do you mean?'

'What we did. It was physical. Very physical, wouldn't you say? But it felt very emotional. I was wondering if it would be the same whoever I did that with. I can't imagine it, somehow. With you it was wonderful. I don't believe for a minute that you've never done that before. I thought you were very skilled.'

'Thank you, Miss Coleman.' I nodded but didn't answer her.

I was at a loss. I had no idea what she would feel in the arms of another man. My own feelings were becoming more and more apparent. The thought of her with another was sickening.

It might have been a lie but I told it just the same. 'It wouldn't be the same.'

We had only a few more days. Enough time to get to know each other. We were discreet. Well, I was and I managed to persuade her to be as careful. We chose the quietest routes for our rides and never returned together although on one occasion our horses made such a noise about the separation that we were obliged to act as if we had met by chance. I hated the subterfuge but we had no choice as I could hardly pay social calls to the Professor's house. There was a heavy weight of responsibility upon me and each day it seemed our desires might topple it. Had she been brought up like any other genteel, young woman my task might have been easier but she wasn't. She was so exuberant and looked to me for a taste of something she believed her life would deny her. She often used the word seduction, asked whether I had an inclination for it today and laughed when I told her I did not.

She was toying with me, pushing me, all the time making me forget she should be cared for and protected. I took the precaution of keeping her on horseback. The riding lesson I had promised took her mind from the pleasure her body could give. Firefly popped over the logs in the woods like a veteran and I taught Christina to bend to the horse's neck as she took off. She wanted to tackle some of the bigger logs but I managed to dampen her enthusiasm, not certain how easy it would be with a side saddle. Women went hunting so I knew it was possible but Christina's body had its restrictions and it would be senseless to forget them entirely.

Restrictions? It was impossible to see them. She had me building a row of small jumps and she seemed as good as the most able-bodied women of my acquaintance. There was never any trouble controlling the horse. Everything was managed with a light touch and impeccable balance. She dipped her back as I showed her, giving the horse its head with the reins as she stretched and landed.

'That's amazing, it's like flying,' she cried. 'She didn't stop at one of them. That last one must be two foot high and she cleared it so easily. Shall I do it again?'

'One more time, unless you think Firefly has had enough.'

'Don't be silly, she's never tired. She's my legs and makes me walk on air.'

Christina was laughing and elated. She was breathing hard from the exertion and her face was hot but I thought there would be no harm doing more. 'Let her speed up slightly for the last one then. But be ready for it, she might jump it bigger.'

The horse had talent and might throw in a big jump for the sheer hell of it. Caught unawares, a rider could easily be toppled. We were not only running the risk of Christina being injured, we were also in danger of being discovered. How would I explain bringing her home after a fall?

I was beginning to regret this whole escapade. There was no other way to describe it. Here I was encouraging a woman with an injured leg to put her trust in a finely-bred animal with sharp speed and a deft turn. I must have been mad.

'Christina, keep the canter steady,' I cried.

I managed to keep my eyes open as she approached the first of the four. It was tiny and barely an obstacle but Firefly was tossing her head to get on with the job. Christina was struggling to keep her in check.

'Use your seat, talk to her,' I said.

She sat back and used her weight as a brake. I could hear her soothing words as the horse took the next two. Confidence seemed to fill her. Instinct took over. I was horrified but she seemed to let the reins slide through her hands. She gave Firefly her head and let her go for the last three strides to the final jump. Oh, she made it look easy. She turned to me, even from a distance I could see her eyes glisten with emotion. I thought I might go the same way but smiled happily. Then she sank onto the horse's neck as the mare ambled towards me. She wrapped her arms around her and buried her face in her mane. It was a private moment that excluded me. I didn't mind.

Later, when we were heading for home, she turned to me. 'Edward wouldn't like it. We had better not tell him.'

'I wasn't planning on mentioning it,' I laughed. 'He'd be furious if he even knew I met you riding.'

'He would be but he might have to get used to the idea.'

'Christina, are you feeling rebellious?'

'Yes, you see, I've come to the conclusion that you are right. Although, he's usually very kind to me he tries to stop me doing so many things. And it's very subtle. He says that I'm looking tired, he worries that my leg is troubling me more than it was a week ago, he suggests the doctor should visit again or that I should rest…or that he should buy a carriage and I could go for a drive instead of riding. Riding is my one freedom.'

'You are very good at it. You make it look easy,' I said.

'I don't know. The cob we had was a good teacher; he never let me fall off. I could never have learnt on Firefly. Edward has changed lately.'

'In what way?'

'Bracy, I think I'm an embarrassment to him. He finds it hard to look at me and he's getting very impatient. You know how easy it is to try and finish a sentence for someone who stutters. You do it only with the aim of helping or saving them from something that is so much trouble. But of course it's not a help. It's the worst thing in the world. He's like that with me. He wants to do it for me and he gets angry when I try to stop him.'

She was a mix of outrage and upset. She touched her right leg in that absent minded way of hers. This time, she seemed cross with it for troubling her career-minded brother. I didn't think for one minute her handicap would hinder the man's advancement since there was nothing in the way of his charming manner. He never produced any papers, no books were being prepared as you might expect from a professor of such an institution but no one seemed to mind. He was corrupt, I was sure of it but no one seemed to know…or care.

'How can you be an embarrassment? He should be proud of you,' I said.

She was right but I couldn't tell her. Her brother was mortified and shamed that his sister walked with a limp. He would hide her away if he could and if he accumulated enough money he might even be able to. Perhaps he would pay someone to take care of her or house her where his social connections were not affronted by the sight of her. Perhaps she might affect his own marital prospects; the thought of a crippled sister residing with them might put off a well-connected bride. For the first time I realised how precarious her situation was. She was wholly dependent on her brother and, if her chances of marrying were thought slim by everyone I had spoken to, what was her future?

'I've never asked you before, Christina. How did you hurt your leg? Or, were you...'

'No, I wasn't born with it, if that's what you're asking. The simplest of accidents. I was a little girl, only about three, and I...well, it was very stupid of me...I fell out of a window.'

'You are lucky to be alive!'

'Ah, it was on the ground floor and I should have bounced but instead I broke my silly leg and it didn't heal very well.'

'It sounds as though it wasn't set properly or perhaps it was a particularly difficult fracture.'

'I thought you would blame the bone setter. You would have done a much better job of it, I'm sure. Then, of course, I was a very difficult patient so I would have tried even your skills. They found it nearly impossible to keep me still so I suspect I made the problem worse. My brother thinks I'm doing the same thing now. Always gadding about, so he says.'

'Was he unkind to you that day, when I walked home with you? He was so angry that I hated to leave you with him.'

She became flustered and occupied herself with straightening her reins. 'I have never seen him so mean,' she said, eventually.

'What did he say?'

She took a breath while I kept a check on my rising anger. 'Some rather unkind things about you, Bracy.'

I didn't care what he said about me but I suspected he had gone further than usual. 'Tell me.'

'Well, he thinks you are seeking to topple him but I know you wouldn't want to do that. You might not agree with him but you must know he's doing a brilliant job, working all these hours and persuading Mr Pitt to fund the college. I told him so but he wouldn't listen. So, now he's got the idea that I am part of your plan. That you are not interested in me for my own sake. How could you be? What with everything there is about me.'

We were riding side by side down a shady path and I touched her arm, forcing her to stop. 'You must know that's not true.' Her doubtful look made me anxious. 'Look into your heart, Christina. Isn't there a little piece of me in there? That's no lie.'

'Yes, I know you are there but that doesn't mean I know what's in *your* heart. And I can't expect someone with your brilliant future, even Edward says you have one, you know, to…to…saddle himself with someone like me. What he says is true.'

She laughed but she was close to tears. I hated myself almost as much as I detested her brother. He had robbed her of all hope and ambition. He wanted her to live half a life rather than strive for more and risk failure. He disgusted me and I couldn't even credit him with a noble motive. Perhaps he wanted to save her pain and disappointment but I couldn't see it.

The sullen, grey water of the River Fleet kept pace with us and matched my mood. I was no better than Edward Coleman. Perhaps I was worse. To stir up desire and leave it unfulfilled. To give her a hint of love but no promise of a future. What did that make me?

A guilty man.

Weighed down by sadness, we rode in silence. The

Professor could have been sat on a horse between us; such was the barrier of his words. We were far from the college and I was concerned about the bay mare I was riding. She was tiring and so we stopped and tied the horses to the trees, letting them crop the branches and the thin grass.

'We've come too far; you're as tired as my horse?' I said.

For the first time in my hearing she admitted it. So I picked her up and carried her to the shade of an oak. I sat next to her, still uncertain how to convince her that I wasn't such a rogue. First, I had to convince myself.

'I'll be fine soon,' she said. 'We can canter back to St Pancras fields in no time. You won't be late for your lecture, I promise.'

'That doesn't worry me...but he does. These things he's said to you. They are not true. You must know that unless he has so destroyed your confidence. I haven't lied to you and I'm not using you to get at him.'

'I believe you, Bracy, and I told him that even though he was very angry but...' She hesitated and I stroked her cheek, pained that her eyes avoided mine. 'I probably won't marry. That's what he told me. I've always known it. And that's the truth.'

'It's nonsense.'

'Is it?' She turned to me.

She wasn't challenging me but there was a question that sat between us. One that I was in no position to answer. I wasn't ready for marriage. I couldn't support a wife and, much as I wanted to court her, there was little hope I could offer her. My future was uncertain. I, too, was dependant on a brother to establish myself. I had exams to pass, a practice to build and I needed Henry's support to get it off the ground.

'You might meet someone you want to marry. You mustn't let him take that from you.'

'But what if I have met someone?'

'Have you, my darling?'

'Yes,' she whispered. 'But even he doesn't want me.'

I took her in my arms. 'Then he's a mad man.' I kissed

her, long and hard, knowing that passion couldn't lie. 'He does want you, he loves you, but he's not a rich man. Will you wait for him?'

'Of course I will. I'm not going anywhere.'

She laughed and gave me such a wanton look that I couldn't resist kissing more of her. I would have forgotten my lecture had she not reminded me of it later.

# CHAPTER 16

Fred didn't feel ready for the exams and asked me to help. We were in the sitting room with the windows wide open in a vain attempt to cool us down. The heat built intolerably in this room and there was very little breeze stirring the air. Most of the flies were drawn to the stables but we were close by and got our fair share. There were crows gathered by the church yard and pigeons closer to home as well as smaller birds such as thrushes and blackbirds. Fred couldn't focus and I was little better even when I was testing him. He was obsessed.

'We mustn't break in there at night,' he said. 'It would be foolish.'

'I agree.'

'We have to be brazen, Bracy. Oh, that sounds funny, I like that.'

'Fred, pay attention,' I said, resting my notes on my lap. 'You need to know these parts of the leg.'

'I do know them. Don't worry. At least I will when the time comes. Whether the examiner will know the cannon bone from a coronet band though is a moot point. Surgeons! How ridiculous that we will be examined by surgeons. So, I'm thinking we need to get in there in broad daylight. We just walk in when the coast is clear. One of us keeps an eye on the door and the other searches. Simple as that.'

'And if we are caught?'

We had the room to ourselves apart from a servant who was sweeping the dark wooden floor. The room was bereft of any adornment and no amount of cleaning and tidying would make it sumptuous. The fire hadn't been lit for the last few weeks but the smell of wood smoke lingered, trapped by the furniture and the hearth rug.

Fred sighed and stretched in his high backed chair. 'Nothing could be simpler. If we are found in the Professor's room, we pretend we are waiting for him. We wanted to discuss the exams or something. It will be a lot easier than explaining why we've climbed through the window at midnight when we should be in bed.'

'No, there would be no getting out of that one. I'm so glad we didn't do it. It would have been madness.'

'So, are you with me?' Thankfully, he spoke quietly.

The cleaning woman was enveloped in a cloud of dust and noise but loyalty to the Professor reached into all the corners of his domain and I wouldn't want to be overheard.

'I suppose. But you know there's a locked drawer. That's where the accounts will be,' I whispered.

'We might find the key. It's worth a try. We might be lucky; the books could be sitting open on his desk.'

'The Professor is meeting the governors this afternoon. They will be doing a tour of the infirmary and the stables. It would be perfect timing.'

'Excellent.'

And so, once again I found myself sitting on the Professor's ample leather chair while I looked through his correspondence. It was dull work. Bills, minutes of the governors' meetings – all were neatly kept but not incriminating. Fred stood guard at the door, holding it slightly open so he could see the porter's lodge and beyond. The Professor was no writer; that much was clear to me. My futile search for the accounts was distracted by his awkward attempt to pen an article about the respiratory system. Why, the poor man, who spoke so well, lost all elegance on paper. I had never seen so much crossing out, so many dreadful and confused phrases. With so little skill on the page I thought it doubtful he would ever publish a paper on the veterinary care of the horse. What a failure, what an omission that would be.

Fred ran a hand through his thick, untamed hair and toyed with the door handle. His light, little feet tapped out an irritable rhythm on the floor. 'What is it? Tell me, man,' he said.

'You won't believe it. Such nonsense,' I laughed.

He shut the door and came to look over my shoulder. 'Is this the Professor's work? No wonder he wants William for his assistant. No danger of being outshone. Yes, they will make a pretty pair.'

'I never thought William corrupt, though. Not like this one,' I said.

'Ah, but he's young. And he's certainly corruptible.'

I sighed. Fred was right. The future of our profession was in their hands unless we could find a way of ousting them. We read a bit further, letting our dismay grow with the turning of the pages.

'This isn't getting us very far,' Fred muttered. 'It's not what we came for. Let me look at that locked drawer. You watch the door, you're too slow here.'

He pushed me out the way and rattled the drawer as if impatience would open it. I opened the door a crack and signalled with my hand at the sound of voices. A horse being led out the wicket gate was playing up. The gate was dragging on the ground, frightening the animal and causing it to rear.

'It's alright. They won't be coming this way. Hurry up, Fred. This is making me nervous.'

'Patience. Don't rush me.'

He turned his attention away from the locked drawer and pulled out some papers from a cupboard behind the desk. He was quiet for so long that his soft whistle of exclamation made me jump. He put everything away apart from one piece of paper.

'Listen to this,' he said. 'This is perfect.'

'A letter?'

'Yes, from a Mr William Pontifax. Name mean anything to you?'

'No, not at all.'

'He's one of our subscribers. He had a chestnut, blood stallion here, oh, let me see…about two months ago.' Fred turned the letter over and whistled once more.

'Come on, what does he say?' I couldn't leave my post but wanted to snatch the letter from Fred's hand.

'The man's threatening Coleman with legal action. Come on, we better get out of here. I think we need to keep this,' he said, tucking the letter into his pocket.

'Fred, read it to me first. Come on, we've got time. I might have to make a copy.'

'No, we need the original, my friend. We must make sure the governors know of this because it's my guess he's trying to cover it up. Mr Pontifax blames the college for the loss of his valuable stallion. He says it came here with a mild lameness and within two weeks was crippled thanks to the treatment he received. The Professor stuck Grasshopper shoes on him and sent him home. The man writes – *he never walked again without pain or misery. He was destroyed.*'

'And he's suing? I don't blame him but why haven't we heard about this?'

'Was there anything in the minutes of the governors' meetings?'

'Nothing. Surely, this will open their eyes and he'll have to tell them if there's to be a court case. I hate to say this, Fred, but this could help us. We need something that will dent his confidence. Something that will stop him. All we have to do is make sure the governors know of it.'

I was so intent upon Fred's revelations that I had neglected the door and rushed to my post once more. We decided to keep the letter as I was anxious to get the address of the aggrieved Mr Pontifax. Before we could leave I heard approaching footsteps, shut the door and leant back against the

121

wall.

'Someone's coming!'

Fred tucked the evidence in his pocket and sat in the Professor's chair. His smile was positively smug but didn't put me at ease. I pulled away from the wall as the door opened and a familiar dark head and appealing eyes found mine. She was in my arms in seconds. I hadn't meant to fold her so tight and instinctively shut the door on the outside world. She was saying my name, she sounded anxious and it worried me but then her lips began a feverish search. I had declared my love to her and, even though we were shy and secretive, I cared little that Fred was being treated to this display.

My body was blocking her view so she couldn't see him, sitting like a child monarch on her brother's seat. Her eyes were shut so there was nothing to check her spontaneous outburst, only what little control I could summon. Once I had kissed her thoroughly.

'Oh, Bracy, you can't ride with me. Mr Dalton must have said something to him. He's being awful about it. Hateful.'

I feared this might happen. It was only a matter of time before we were found out. We always rode at about the same time and, although we were careful, we rode through working farms. There was hay to harvest, animals to herd and fences to mend. We met people, sometimes we spoke and it wasn't only Mr Dalton who said it was good for Christina to have company. But Edward Coleman distrusted my motives and had reacted angrily. He thought I wanted to topple him from power and, although Christina might think it another of his worries, it was the only one that he had right. I would love to see him gone from the veterinary college, exposed and disgraced, but I hadn't stopped for a minute to consider what effect that might have on his sister. The woman I loved.

That letter in Fred's pocket. It wouldn't end the man's career but it might set the governors on the path of inquiry. Surely, they would read it and question what else the Professor was doing wrong. It was a powerful weapon, one I had to use even though it would bring pain. I couldn't spare Edward Coleman but maybe I could protect Christina. She didn't have to know our plans.

'I say, you two,' Fred muttered, laughing. 'Shall I get him dunked in the water trough, ma'am?'

She pulled away from me, mortified, and whispered: 'Oh, my God.'

I squeezed her hand. 'Christina, you must have met Fred Cherry before. He's a friend of mine; you don't have to worry about him. He won't say anything.'

He was perfectly capable of gossiping to every student here but since I was so much bigger than him I thought intimidation might keep him quiet. I gave him a threatening look that Christina couldn't see.

'I didn't know you had been so busy, Bracy,' he said. His lack of diplomacy struck me as odd. 'Or so successful!' He was grinning and winking at me like a monkey at a fair. 'You could have saved us so much trouble if you had only given me a hint.'

How inept he was. William was right when he complained that Fred lacked social graces and it was hardly surprising that Christina was blushing again. I nodded my head to tell him it was time to go, we had the evidence we needed. He was still on the wrong side of the desk.

'What are you doing here, anyway?' Christina asked. 'Edward is seeing the governors and they'll be having dinner later so you won't see him until tomorrow. I hope it's not urgent.'

'Relax then, Bracy. He's not going to catch you red handed,' Fred sighed, with relief. 'Or me.' He patted his pocket and laughed. He sat in the Professor's chair still and whistled. 'I've been dreading him coming in.'

It occurred to me that Fred was under a misapprehension and thought Christina was in my confidence. Our performance might have given such an impression and now he was grinning with satisfaction.

'Well, not dreading exactly, we hoped to catch up with

him here but forgot about his meeting,' I said, sending him a warning look. 'Fred, you need to study. Come on.'

'Red handed?' Christina said, as though she had just caught the nuances of the conversation. 'What are you two up to? Don't leave me out of the picture.'

My alarmed face didn't register with him. His hand was searching in his pocket. Pulling out the letter. Christina snatched it from him and read. Her brow furrowed. Her cheeks became two spots of red, like the wax seal on a letter.

'What does this mean?' she asked when she finished.

The letter was dropped to the desk and Fred scooped it up, folded it and slid it into his inside pocket. 'It means that we've got what we need. He's kept this quiet, you see, but…' Fred finally cottoned on to the fact that the sister was not against the brother and spoke with more uncertainty. 'It's quite possible that…I fear the governors don't know about this. It's probably time they did. It would only be right…I think so, anyway. No?'

'You would expose him? Why? Just because there is one grumbling subscriber. One man who has lost his precious horse when so many have been healed.'

'Christina, that is not the case,' I said. 'So many are being harmed. The Grasshopper shoe is a failure but he doesn't see it. It puts pressure on the hoof walls and…'

Fred huffed. 'He's right, ma'am, but he should spare you the details. Lots of them go home worse than they came. Or they don't go home at all. It's worrying for all of us. But the Professor doesn't see it. He's patented that shoe and he's making a fortune from it. That's all that matters to him, begging your pardon.'

She took a sharp intake of breath and turned to me as though I was a freak show. 'It's true then,' she said.

She was staring at me. Accusing me. Fred answered. 'I'm afraid it is, Miss Coleman. We've known it for ages but didn't know how to prove it. This will help but I doubt it will be enough. I don't suppose you would help us…you see…the accounts must be somewhere…'

'I mean, what Edward said is true. You really want to see him disgraced. You want him out of here.'

'It would be better if he went quietly,' Fred laughed. 'There doesn't have to be any shame involved. You're his sister and it's only natural that you want to defend him.'

She hardly heard him. Her eyes were locked on me. 'You lied to me.'

'No! Well, only about that,' I insisted.

'You were using me.'

'Christina. No.'

'How could you tell such lies?'

'The rest was no lie.'

'You expect me to believe that? You have done a hateful thing. There is guilt all over your rotten face. You spun a little web around me but now I can see you for what you really are. Edward was right all the time but I hadn't believed him. How silly of me. This letter that you so prize will not harm him. How can you both be so foolish? One angry subscriber against so many who are happy. You are wasting your time.' She shot me a venomous look. 'As well as mine.'

'Don't go. You must hear me out. Fred, get out of here, will you?'

He scurried out of the room and shut the door. Christina made as if to follow him but I stayed her with my hand on her shoulder. She peeled it off and dropped it distastefully. She didn't look at me.

'Why would you seek to ruin him?' she asked, quietly. 'I don't understand.'

'I know he's your brother and it must pain you to hear ill of him but what he's doing is terrible.' She sighed and put her hand on the door. 'Please, listen to me. The college is facing bankruptcy while he's getting rich.'

'We are hardly rich,' she said, turning as if she had been stung. 'Why, we hardly ever entertain people for supper and, when we do, we don't have more than three courses. We have a cook and only one maid; that is not high living.'

'He's taking more money than his predecessor.'

125

'Well, he was French and radicals have very low expectations.'

'He was no radical, he was an honest man. Your brother, I'm afraid, is not. He is patenting his horse shoes and medicines and he is selling places on our veterinary course to anyone with the fee. We have linen drapers, paper hangers and tailors signing up – very few are educated and some of them have never sat on a horse. He doesn't scruple because they will never oppose him.'

'Unlike yourself.'

'Yes, we are certainly at odds.'

'And you will do anything, it seems.'

I took her face between my hands and forced her to look at me. 'Never. I never lied to you about what is between us.'

'There is emptiness between us.'

'I love you. Why won't you believe me?'

She freed herself from my hold and stepped back. 'Because you are false.'

# CHAPTER 17

Granville Penn was a founder of the college and was important to all of us. Before our first professor died so suddenly we used to see him here a lot but now that the college was built, his involvement had waned.

I knew him to be a man of influence and desperately wanted to see him. I was loath to put on paper my fears for the college and my doubts about the man at the helm. So, I wrote asking for a meeting. Fred and I were invited to his London house the following Sunday.

I was riddled with doubts but could no more ignore this duty than I could pretend indifference to Christina Coleman. The conflict was painful and, although I didn't expect her to be happy, I hoped she would come to understand. I had no wish to turn her against her brother but how could I make her easy with me if she believed in him? It was impossible to reconcile the situation. As long as she trusted him then I must be viewed as the most despicable creature out to harm his reputation and ruin her by default. If there was some way of protecting her while I exposed him, I would do it. She was no longer talking to me so it was impossible to discuss it with her or work out a strategy.

Our rides together were stopped at the Professor's

intervention but she would have avoided them anyway since that fateful day in his consulting room. I sometimes caught a glimpse of her returning to the stables on Firefly. Yes, they rode in the mornings when she knew I was at lessons. My only connection with her in those days was through the horse. My slavish devotion was reduced to ensuring her mare had enough hay and was not neglected by the busy grooms.

Foolishly, I cherished those quiet minutes running my hand down the mare's fine legs knowing how much mobility they afforded Christina. I knew every sinew, every muscle, tendon and bone while her feet were my close friends. Neat little things they were but now fitted with Grasshopper shoes.

'Am I mad to follow this course?' I asked the horse, who was alone in welcoming my affection. She took another mouthful of hay and checked my pockets for the scrap of bread I had raided from our dining table. 'The honourable course is hellishly painful. Should I abandon it in favour of happiness? Ah, the chance has gone, has it not? Your mistress will not be mine. I'm afraid I have ruined what little hope we had.'

Firefly checked me for signs of further food, took the disappointment well and accepted a rub around her ears. She was an alert little horse and ceased her chewing at some noise from the stable lads at the other end of the building. Then she nudged me none too gently in the ribs to make sure the massage continued.

'So, I must carry on. It will make us all miserable but might save the profession from ruin. It must be my purpose in life. No, I don't believe it either. Did I really say all that twaddle to her? And you heard me, too. Shocking.'

Sunday approached and my apprehension increased. Fred and I cleaned up well. Our clothes were as freshly laundered as we were ourselves. We had permission to visit my family in London and that was our cover. My brother, Henry, and his wife lived in Holborn but our destination was in a more fashionable quarter. St James.

Granville Penn's town house sat amongst the

extravagant homes of the nobility and appeared to glance at them with disapproval. It was an older, lower building than its neighbours, its door was painted black and there were no flambeaux to light the steps at night. The Penns were an old Quaker family with no desire to flaunt wealth. We had that in common and it gave me hope.

A servant ushered us into his study where he sat behind a desk. He was a man in his prime, soberly dressed and with long, dark hair carefully brushed back from his forehead. He seemed so lost in thought that he might have forgotten our appointment although he promised that he remembered us both from his visits to the college. His face was serious and unsmiling; the fingers that reached to us in a handshake were covered in splashes of black ink.

'Forgive me,' he said. 'My thoughts are with the book I'm writing. Geology. Do either of you have an interest, gentlemen?'

Fred looked worried and I expressed some vague knowledge which enabled Penn to explain the book that would be his life's work. I knew enough to be able to question him with a degree of intelligence but I was floundering. I didn't know how to get him onto the topic we were aching to discuss.

'Is that your grandfather, sir?' Fred asked, masking his boredom with geology and its link to spirituality. He got up and gazed, open mouthed, at a portrait on the wall behind the desk.

Granville Penn's likeness to his illustrious grandsire was obvious – the deep set eyes, the heavy brow and the slight, bony jut of the nose. He waved a hand without glancing around. 'That's him. William Penn.'

'Founder of Pennsylvania,' Fred enthused. 'How extraordinary to have part of the New World named after you.'

I feared Fred was steering us further from our purpose but nothing could have concentrated our host more quickly. Talking about his grandfather was dull work. I suppose every visitor asks him the same questions.

'To business, gentlemen,' he said. 'Your letter was quite

mysterious. How can I help you?'

He listened to us for nearly half an hour. He read the letter Fred pulled from his pocket and questioned us carefully from behind his steepled hands. A black-faced clock chimed from the mantel and the sun found a way between the partially drawn curtains to light the room. I was still in the dark with no idea how our allegations were received. We hadn't flinched to tell him every fear and every grumble. We talked about corruption, we accused the Professor of getting rich at the expense of the college and we complained about him shortening the course.

'I hear you - and it saddens me,' he responded at last. 'We had such high hopes. We still do but you must think of the bigger picture. Perhaps it won't always be thus but right now if we are to impress the government we need a lot of veterinary surgeons. Spending two or three years over their education is a luxury we can't afford. You are two of the lucky ones.'

'What about Professor Coleman, sir?' I said. 'Surely, you must see that he's not fit to lead such an institution.'

'Even if you could prove everything you allege there is little that can be done. You were at the college from the beginning and so you know how precarious it was. It nearly closed when my friend, St Bel, died and we can't afford to lose Professor Coleman. There's no one else and he's very careful, you know. You would struggle to prove this against a man who dutifully pays the college for his horses' keep.'

'And the training?' Fred asked.

'Professor Coleman has our support because the college won't survive otherwise. I'm sorry, it's not perfect but it's better than nothing.' He took a turn about the room and looked out the window. 'And we know about Mr Pontifax's complaint. I'm hoping he will think better of pursuing it.'

We had risked so much to hear this and I was at a loss. How could an honourable man take such a position? He was discounting our allegations for the short-term goal of securing support from Mr Pitt. How I hated politicians at that moment including our worthy Prime Minister. Men who were anxious to do the appearance of what was right without worrying about the substance. There was public outcry about the treatment of horses and the large numbers that were dying so young and it made no sense to produce an army of vets who would add to the confusion.

'He's threatening legal action, Mr Penn,' I said in a final attempt to make him see reason. 'Justifiably so.'

'He will be made to see the futility of such a course. Nothing can be gained from an attack on the college. Think what we had before. Do you want to go back to the farriers holding sway, conducting operations? That was barbaric and the college is progress with all its imperfections.

'Gentlemen, I understand your concern but if you want to serve the profession you should study rather than stealing the Professor's letters.' He tossed the paper on his desk in front of Fred who tucked it back into his pocket. 'See that it is returned.'

Another ten minutes and we were dismissed. He was careful to placate us and assured us that our visit would remain private but my heart was heavy. I was bitterly disappointed. Fred was silent while we walked, brooding and aimless. By the time we reached Piccadilly, the pavements were alive with people and carriages crowded the street. A group of barefooted boys were playing at the corner and looked up as we approached, their eyes gleaming at the sight of us. We were hardly men of fashion but our clean trousers and sober coats were elegant enough to make us stand out. We were worth a touch.

I gave them each a penny and coupled it with advice about getting home and eating properly. My urge to be charitable was ingrained, like the dirt behind their ears.

'You should have bought them an eel pie, Bracy. There's no knowing where that money will end up. Someone will have it from them,' Fred said, standing on his toes to see further up the street.

'You're right,' I said, fumbling in my pockets for more coins.

There was a pie shop a few yards further down. The window was up and the pies on the table freshly baked judging by the smell. We turned but the boys had disappeared, swallowed up in the press of people gathered around a woman selling kindling wood.

We had no thoughts about where to go. We wanted to get to Henry's for an early supper and then he was to drive us back to college. For now, we were on the town with time to spare. We found a coffee house a few streets away where for a few pence we could get a pot of tea and some bread and muffins.

'What now?' Fred asked, taking the seat opposite me.

His hair was in a state of negligence but his eyes goggled with eagerness as if I might have answers. The coffee house was brimming with people but we knew no one and were ignored. There was a table of French émigrés speaking in undertones next to us. The news from their country was always worrying and it was impossible not to feel for them. Their talk of the revolution they had escaped made our own concerns seem a minor disturbance on the world stage.

'We could try some of the other governors. Granville Penn's might be a minority view,' I said. 'This is so frustrating. I can't believe he wouldn't do anything. That he will actually leave that man in charge.'

'The trouble is that he's right.'

'In what way?'

'There's no one else so we're stuck with him. One day, I give you my word, Coleman will be brought down. Just think, in a few years we will be among the most experienced vets in the land. Then we will have more influence and will be worthy adversaries,' Fred explained. 'Who cares what a couple of students have to say? I will bring out a newspaper and then, I promise, we will expose him. I will get you to write for it, Bracy. You have such a way with words.'

'I will set it up with you. It will be an honour,' I said, smiling at the thought. 'Perhaps, you are right. We never stop learning and one day our knowledge will be recognised. I can only hope so.'

'Have you given up hope with the lady?'

'Not entirely. But she's not talking to me. I think you would call that a setback.'

'Were you serious about her?' He sounded so surprised, much to my chagrin.

'Yes. Oh, I don't know. Why not?'

'No reason,' he said, the lie written all over his face. 'She's not the class of woman one can play with. If you spend time with her it has to be serious, I suppose. She's not an obvious choice though, is she? If she's not talking to you it might be for the best.'

I had known Fred closely for the last two years and he didn't have to say more for me to know what he was thinking. Christina was not someone a man married. She had trouble walking and although I was willing and able to forget about it no one else did the same. From there it was easy to question how she would cope as a wife and a mother. Would the demands be too much for her?

She told me once she had all the appearance of a normal woman but none of the speed. She couldn't get up without forethought and she couldn't grab a child about to fall. Motherhood might be a trial to her but would she even cope with the pregnancy? I hadn't worried about it simply because I hadn't thought beyond those precious times with her and seeing her on a horse made me think she could do anything. Fred shared the Professor's view that she should deny herself those things and it was the half life she had mapped out for herself until I had upset her thinking. Not for the first time I kicked myself for hinting at the possibility of more. I wanted to release her from the confines of her life to satisfy my own cravings and in doing so had created desires in her she might be unable to fulfil. It was not a noble deed.

# CHAPTER 18

The exams were two weeks away and our time was filled with studies and caring for our patients, leaving little opportunity for me to ride any of them. Our stables were full and the death rate, although not alarming, was enough to ensure we had material for dissection. Mr Cross, the knackerman from Camden, provided us with bodies occasionally and it didn't matter that many were mules. They were cheaper but once opened up, they were much the same.

So many were young. That was the surprising thing. It bothered me terribly that an animal which reached full height by the age of five or six, was often dead soon after when the horse should live to thirty or forty. There was something we were doing that was shortening their lives by a half or even more and, although I tried to engage the Professor in a discussion about it after one of his lectures, he laughed wearily and told me not to worry.

'It will not be part of your examination,' he said. 'You know where the shoe goes by this time; you won't need to know much more.'

He was exaggerating of course and irritated by my wish to arrest the criminal waste of their lives. Christina would have talked to me about it. I missed her and almost asked him how she was but stopped myself in time since it wouldn't help to reveal my interest.

He was in an affable mood that day saying the exams wouldn't trouble me and even asked whether I sought an army appointment. Mr Pitt wanted a vet for as many regiments as possible in exchange for financial support which was forthcoming at last.

I was heartily sick of Mr Pitt and told the Professor of my aim to set up in the city of London where there were enough working horses essential to our economy to keep me in practice for the rest of my days.

'Do you not seek something more exotic than the heavy horse? You could do better - but no matter.'

He sighed and looked at the college building with its high walls and blind arches. It was a plain structure with little ornamentation but Coleman had taken on the pride of ownership. If only he wouldn't fill it with the lowest characters. Following me into the stables, he watched as I checked one or two patients, quizzing me about their treatments and whenever possible making some adjustment to their care.

'What's in that lineament?' he said.

I had run the dispensary single handed after St Bel died and most of the remedies were born of his tuition. 'Sulphate of copper, alum in powder, vinegar and some honey. I heated it and added sulphuric acid when it was nearly cold.'

'Very good. But not too much copper. Is it working?'

'It is much improved, sir.'

He was writing in a notebook so I wouldn't have been surprised if the mixture was patented and put on sale with his name on it but he had another purpose in talking to me and coughed awkwardly.

'This animal, Clark.'

His friendly tone should have alerted me that he wanted something. 'Yes, sir. He's not very popular among the grooms.'

'No, but they are not very good riders. Oblige me by taking him out this afternoon if you can spare the time. As you know, he also has a respiratory problem that has improved thanks to our regime.'

I was agreeable for my own purpose. Christina hadn't ridden this morning and I was desperate to talk to her. We didn't have much longer and, if I could only see her, we might have a chance. She was right. I had been false. I was trying to ruin her brother but I'd failed. She would have to forgive me. I kept my eyes away from her mare, fearful her brother might read my thoughts.

'Very well. I'll gauge his performance for you.'

He was a miserable animal who bit anyone within a yard of his stall and was known to be a difficult ride, having bucked off one of the lads yesterday. By the afternoon I was taking a footpath through the college grounds that led to the bridge over the river. The animal, a black carriage horse, had trotted up without coughing when we tried him in the stable yard so now came the test to see whether he would cope with a half hour ride.

It wasn't raining but there was a heavy cargo of clouds and a blustery wind. The light was dim and the fields wet after yesterday's thunder storm which broke the hot spell of the previous weeks. I was pleased the animal wasn't nervous although he cocked an ear at the water rushing beneath the bridge.

Christina occupied my thoughts so much I barely gave the horse my attention and had to drag my mind back to the Professor's instructions, knowing that I needed to monitor his paces and listen for every whisper of breath.

St Pancras Church was ahead of me and the fields beyond it were green and inviting. The fence around the graveyard was falling down and the grass uncut so that the grave stones mimicked sprouting pieces of rock. What a mess it was in. So many of the grave stones were tipped over that I thought resurrection men must have dug up corpses to rob or sell. Some surgeons were known to pay good money for a regular supply.

I turned away from the sight of such a grim trade and searched the horizon for another horse, one with a rider dressed in blue velvet. I knew she was riding as her mare was not in the stables and I couldn't shake off feelings of unease thanks to that morbid graveyard. My dark thoughts would be lifted by the sight of her and so my eyes scoured the fields hungrily until I spotted movement towards Pancras Wash. It was too far to see if it was a horse and rider, still less if it was a woman dressed as I remembered.

The ground was marshy by the Wash since it flooded so often and it wasn't easy riding even in the summer. Why would she go there? To avoid me? Changing course, I headed that way since it wouldn't matter if my ride was a bit longer than expected.

As I got closer, I couldn't understand why the figure had stopped moving. Perhaps it wasn't a rider. The light was dim, my eyesight was good but my imagination was doing strange things. I'd promised myself some speed on this horse and squeezed through a hedgerow, giving him his head along the side of the field.

'Keep your joy to yourself,' I told the animal at the first sign of his spirited bucking.

I gathered the reins until he was easy with me and then pushed for more speed. I couldn't say why but knew I was in a hurry. Three fields later I was lost. No, I was trapped. The hedge was thicker, the gate that would take me to the Wash was tied up with rope and I was on lower ground and couldn't see evidence of a rider anywhere. Fortunately, my horse sensed the proximity of another animal and called out. He was answered and I couldn't have picked up the location better if I'd had a map reference and a compass. We galloped back down the field to a gap in the hedge. Once through, I saw her.

Her riding habit was like a pool of blue. She lay only a foot away from the horse, slightly on one side with her arms reaching out as if she wanted to pull herself up. She wasn't moving an inch.

'Christina!' I shouted.

I told her I was coming. I even told her to wait for me, again and again, but her silence was frightening. So was the marshy land that separated us. It was like a swamp and I had no idea how deep it was.

She was only twenty yards away on higher, stony ground, but the distance was great thanks to the marsh. I walked my horse up and down, unable to get closer.

'Wake up, damn it. Christina,' I shouted. She didn't move and I couldn't tell if she was even breathing. 'Don't let me be too late.'

I was her only hope. I had to cross that marsh. Had to risk it. I scanned the desolate spot to see if there were drier routes but realised a rider would only find out once committed. I had to chance it since there was no other way but this was best done at speed since a slow walk would see us sinking. Thankfully, my horse willingly picked up a strong trot, goaded by his desire to get to the mare. His hind legs struggled and splashed but the animal was strong and ploughed on. I leapt from his back as soon as we reached her. Her face was so pale. She was unconscious. At least she was alive and for that I whispered a prayer of thanks.

'Come on. Don't do this to me,' I cried, feeling for a pulse at her wrist. 'Miss Coleman! Christina! Please.'

I needed her awake but feared to move her in case she had more serious injuries. I held her hand which was deathly cold. I called her name and batted her face.

'Can you feel your hands, your feet?'

'Don't be…stupid…' she said, groggily. 'Of course I can. I'm not a complete cripple, you know.'

It was such a relief to hear her voice that I laughed. Yes, it was a bump on the head and it hadn't diminished her nasty little tongue one bit.

'You've had a fall. I'm going to examine you and then I've got to get you off this wet ground.'

Christina was still argumentative. 'Fall?' she said. 'Jumped. I jumped off when she went lame. Oh, my head.'

She slumped back onto the ground with a hand clutching the side of her head. There was a swelling above her ear but I was concerned about her legs and crouched down at her feet.

'Can you wriggle this foot?' I said, holding one in my hands.

Her torn clothing told the story. She must have jumped off and her beautiful but voluminous riding habit had caught on the pommel, making her tip and land on her head instead of her feet.

'Of course I can. How did you get here? What are you doing to my leg? I told you I've hurt my head, you silly man.'

'Now, this one,' I told her.

My hand on her knee made her sit up suddenly. Her legs bent, confirming there was no serious injury.

'There's nothing wrong with my leg that wasn't wrong before,' she said. There was a look of pain in her face as she flexed her right limb. 'May be some bruising.'

'Don't try to get up,' I said, taking a look at the side of her head. 'Not yet.'

I lifted her hair as I'd done before but this was no lover's opening move. My hands checked the rest of her head. My body was behind her and I held her to my chest hoping to warm her. She began to shiver so I took off my coat and made her put it on properly.

My own body was hot from the ride and I put my arms around her. She began to relax and her head flopped against me. She might have been delirious but thank goodness she hadn't passed out.

'Christ! How am I going to get you home?'

She touched my arm, squeezed it reassuringly. 'I'm going to walk. Don't be silly; just give me a few more minutes.'

She sounded better than I could have hoped. I tilted her face and found she was smiling. I pulled her closer and lightly kissed the top of her head. It was my only liberty. I heard the sweet sound of her sigh.

She was damp from the wet ground and time was against us. 'Come on. Try to stand,' I said, pulling her slowly to her feet.

I didn't release my hold but let her take a few steps. She

leant against her horse, getting her breath back and holding my coat tightly around her, while I checked the animals. Her horse was sharply lame while my own was breathing hard and covered in sweat. Christina wouldn't be able to ride, she'd never be able to walk either and I was reluctant to leave her while I went for help. A chill was a certainty but it might be the least of her problems.

I wanted to know that Firefly could limp home if she was led from the other horse. Her injuries would have to be checked later, there was little I could do now other than ensure she was willing to move. I undid the black horse's girth and set his saddle onto the path.

The look on Christina's face was incredulous. 'Bracy, what are you doing?'

I was preoccupied but smiled at her use of my name. 'We'll be more comfortable bare back.'

'But the saddle…?'

'Can be collected later. It hardly matters.'

I gathered her up and tossed her onto my horse which was tired enough not to move. Then I detached one of Firefly's reins from the bridle until we had one long rein to lead her and handed it to Christina while I launched myself up behind her.

With one arm around her I held my own reins, took Firefly's from her and urged the sorry party home. I was surprised the injured mare came so easily and I could see Christina thinking the same.

'She knows being left alone is a worse fate. She'll walk because it's her instinct to stay with the herd.'

'Is that why I'm letting you…' she hesitated.

'What? Speak your mind, you know you want to.'

'Is that why I'm allowing a hateful man like you to manhandle me like this?'

'This was the only option I didn't reject. And I promise not to manhandle you too much.'

'What were the others?'

'I could have gone for help. It would have taken at least

half an hour which might have been dangerous in your condition. You could have ridden on your own while I led you but I wouldn't have been able to stop you falling off in a faint. And I wouldn't be able to keep you warm. You see, it's the best way.'

'You make it sound so noble and yet you seem to be enjoying yourself. You are going to be in such trouble if you drop me.'

'How would I manage to do that?'

After a few minutes she answered, 'I think I might fall asleep.'

'Try and stay awake. Talk to me, tell me anything, how you hate me...I don't mind...but I won't ever let you fall. Don't worry.'

She looked sleepy, probably from the blow to her head, and her eyelids were fluttering. Desire may have been lurking in her grey eyes but the hope made me feel guilty, this was hardly the moment and it was more likely she was feeling distaste.

'Why...why did it have to be you?' she groaned. 'Not fair...not really. I won't fall asleep...do you know why?'

'No, go on...tell me.'

'Because I don't trust you.'

I couldn't help laughing. 'Very wise.'

'You are despicable,' she muttered into my chest. Her head was bent and her voice was tight. 'You would probably touch me again.'

'Christina, I was examining you, it's very different.'

'Hateful man.' She rubbed her face into me and sighed as one hand crept around my waist. 'I've missed you.'

I kissed the top of her head and held her closer still. 'And I've missed you, my love.'

I barely took in the details of that ride. Later, I couldn't remember what route we had taken, whether the horses were difficult or what the ground was like. For those few minutes we were alone, being rocked by the rhythm of the horse. She was right, I shouldn't have been enjoying it but, in spite of the worry, I was. I felt so possessive and shouldn't have to give her back, not to a brother whose values were questionable and whose protectiveness was stifling. Perhaps she only accepted my touch, my proximity, because she had no choice but her body was soft and relaxed as it clung to me. By the time we reached College Lane she could have been asleep and I had to break the spell by making her stir.

'Christina. We're back. It's going to be alright.'

She patted my arm but didn't lift her head. 'Such an optimist.'

'Perhaps I am but I'm not a fool. I'll make sure it is. Do you hear me? I won't let anything bad happen. You have to trust me.'

Would she pick up my meaning? She roused. She searched my face but her own was clouded. She had a bump on the side of her head, she was probably in shock and, ridiculously, I was speaking in riddles. Her state of mind might be to my advantage or maybe not. Barriers, awkwardness, anger. All were gone. I wanted to tell her what holding her had done to me, how I felt warm even though I was chilled to the bone and why I was happy even though she was in pain. I was at a loss. How could I feel elation? Caring for her in that brief time had given me such a taste for the role, one I wanted to keep.

It was over almost as quickly as it began. As soon as I turned the horse into the stable yard we were surrounded by people whose words washed over me. She was lifted to the ground, a blanket appeared and I felt…separation. I was hit by cold air, the dampness from her clothes had seeped into my own and I shivered. I slid to the ground and was met by questions.

I could hear Professor Coleman calling her name and yes, I suppose there was anguish, and then there were orders for a horse to be harnessed, people were told to hurry. Soon his hand was on my shoulder pushing me away from the others and demanding answers.

'Why can't you speak, man? What happened?' he said,

exasperation oozing out of him. 'Did you plan to ride with her?'

'She's hurt. Don't trouble yourself with that.'

'I want answers. And by God, I'll have them. How could you let this happen? Both horses are covered in dirt and sweat; you've obviously been going too fast.'

'You need to get her home. She can tell you better than I what happened.'

Edmund threw a blanket over my shoulders. 'Bracy, you're shivering. Here, drink this.'

The tea was hot and sweet. The wind had died down but it was a damp, chilly day with little summer promise. Dark clouds looked to be brewing over St Pancras Church and in the distance there was the sound of thunder and the cry of the rooks.

The Professor stuck to my side. 'And her mare is hideously lame. What foolish games were you playing? Were you racing?'

I didn't bother to answer him. Later, I wondered why I hadn't as it might have saved some trouble but, for now, I was too angered to give the Professor the truth. I wanted to be maligned and wanted no thanks. Let there be a debt.

'You need to get her home, sir,' I said, standing tall. 'She has a blow on the left side of her head that needs checking. She might be concussed but there are no other obvious injuries. Both her legs are fine but possibly bruised and she's chilled. I'm afraid she was on damp ground near Pancras Wash for far too long.'

'What the hell were you gallivanting there for? The most ridiculous, dangerous place to ride. How dare you take her there? She's a cripple, I've told you that.'

'No, she isn't.'

'Just look at what you've done. You've risked her life. We'll be lucky if she ever walks again after this.' He was poking me in the chest. He began to irritate me and I batted his hand away. 'What else have you been doing with her?' he hissed. 'Her clothing is torn.'

'Yes, but that was hardly my fault. I found her like that.'

'Are you sure about that?'

'I am. I'm also sure she will walk again. She'll ride again, too. This mustn't stop her. Accidents happen; they are one of the risks of living.'

The subject of our discussion took swaying steps towards us. She was still pale. No, she was tinged with green and likely to be sick. I was pleased to see she could walk even if she was unsteady and with her usual gait.

'Christina, you shouldn't be hobbling about like this,' the Professor cried. 'Wait in the gig for me.'

'Have you finished this ridiculous performance?' she said under her breath. 'Do you know every groom has stopped work to listen to you both?'

The grooms, as well as a few students, were gathered around the yard, some had the courtesy to return to their tasks. Christina was shaking. I knew because she held my arm for support. She berated her brother but could hardly tell the story of her fall. The effort seemed to draw the last bit of strength from her and I knew she was about to faint. She slumped against me and I took her in my arms. I lifted her into the gig and turned to the Professor.

'She needs to get home. Damn it, you might be no vet but you're a surgeon. She needs hot food, a warm bed and rest…but not a lifetime of restrictions.'

He got up into the gig next to her and I turned away.

# CHAPTER 19

We didn't need the Professor's guidance to know what to do with the two horses. One was lame and needed careful examination. The other was tired after the exertions of our gallop and I hoped rest would be sufficient remedy. Edmund and Fred helped me with Firefly once she had been rubbed down and fed.

'There's heat in both her forefeet,' Fred muttered as he got up. 'And a raised pulse. Feel it.'

I did as he asked. The heat was greater on one foot though and I turned to them in alarm. 'Founder! I can't believe it. This horse was sound. Her feet were good.'

Edmund shook his head in dismay since founder could finish a horse. 'She's well, she's regularly exercised. Surely not. It would be so sudden.'

He examined the mare's feet for himself and nodded his head. We were all shocked and incredulous. You see, founder has been crippling horses for centuries but we understood it so little. I had dissected a few animals with it, including Eclipse, and there was usually an alarming separation between the hoof wall and the sole of the foot. The bone inside would be at the wrong angle but of course it was impossible to see this on a living animal.

'There could be a link with the Professor's shoes,' I

warned. 'Ed, I've been riding these animals and the shoes worry me more and more each time. He's made them so narrow and with that bar down the centre of the foot. How can I explain it? Their feet become heavy. Given a bit more time I suspect they are seriously uncomfortable.'

'Don't say that,' Edmund cried. 'They are on virtually every horse here. It would be such a disgrace.'

'Grasshopper shoes were fitted this week. Today the horse goes lame and there's pain in both fronts. You think it's a coincidence. I say there's a link. This is the cause.'

I pointed at Firefly's feet which were being paddled on the ground. In other words she was resting them in turns because she was in serious pain.

'I don't think the Professor will agree with you, Bracy,' said Fred. 'And you can hardly send the mare to the forge yourself and have the shoes taken off.'

'No, I can't. I don't know what to do.' I was powerless. Oh, the frustration of it. 'Expecting Professor Coleman to cure her would be like asking Mr Cross for help.'

'The knackerman?' Fred asked.

'The very same. Only, Mr Cross has a little more in the way of knowledge. Firefly's chances of survival might be greater with him.'

'I'll speak to the Professor,' Edmund offered. 'Do you really think taking the Grasshoppers off will be enough?'

'No, she'll need time as well. I'll talk to him, Ed. I can just imagine what he will say, though. You overwhelm me, Clark! Your diagnosis is most entertaining; I will give it my serious consideration and might do something about it next year.'

'Well, I'll come with you especially if you feel inclined to mock. An hour ago he was about to throw a punch at your face.'

'He was a trifle disturbed, wasn't he? I expect he's calmed down. I hope so anyway.'

Firefly's ears were back and her nostrils were tight. She seemed more annoyed than pained. She tolerated me stroking her neck but didn't check my pockets in her usual fashion. She shifted her feet relentlessly, like a kitten suckling its mother in ecstasy, but there was no joy in the animal. Ed was beside me.

'If only he didn't have the care of her,' I said.

'Her? Or them?'

'Christina is capable of sticking up for herself. At least, I hope she is. She has a formidable temper; it must run in the family.'

'Was Miss Coleman badly hurt?'

'Chilled to the bone. Concussed but only slightly. Left to her own devices she would be back on a horse within a day or two. What worries me most is how he will use this.'

'What do you mean?'

'It wasn't a serious accident.'

'It could have been very serious had you not found her.'

'True. Oh, I suppose you are right. But he will use it to keep her indoors. That's where he wants her. Safe and out of sight. He's ashamed of her, you know. His attitude disgusts me. I have to get this horse better, don't you see? For her sake.'

Ed ignored the outburst. 'And yet it would be the common view. How many cripples…I mean, people who don't walk so well as you or I, tear about on a horse?'

'How does she manage?' Fred asked when he joined us. 'It's no wonder really that she fell off.'

'She didn't fall. She told me she jumped off because the horse went lame. Her riding habit must have caught on the pommel and tipped her up. Fred, she's a better rider than you.'

'I don't believe you, surely not.'

'I taught her to jump in less than half an hour. She's good, I tell you.'

'If the Professor knew what you've been getting up to he would definitely punch you in the face. Anything else she's learnt from you?'

I smiled but would not be drawn and led Firefly back to her stall. I sent one of the grooms with a message to the Professor about the mare but decided not to give a diagnosis since he was likely to reject it. I returned to the college with serious misgivings and damp clothes. At least I was able to rid myself of the latter.

I didn't hear from Professor Coleman so checked the mare later but found no change. I wanted news of Christina and walked up to St Pancras Way after supper. I hoped her brother might be out and that I would be able to see her, even if it was for two minutes, just to see that she was unhurt.

I rapped the brass knocker. A maid in a black dress told me the Professor was out. She was wide eyed when I asked for Miss Coleman.

'She's in bed, sir. She's had a fall from a horse.'

'I know. I found her. I wanted to know how she was.'

She looked behind her into the dimly lighted hall as if the shadows might be listening. Then she beckoned me in with a dip of her head.

Her hand found my arm. 'Are you Mr Clark?' she whispered.

'Yes, but just tell me how she is. I'll not go until I've found out.'

'She thought you would come. I'm to take you to her. She's upset, sir. She always is after they've had words and he's locked her in.'

'He's locked her in her bedchamber! Has he done this before?'

'I don't know, sir. She's not been with him long. I do wish she wouldn't ride that animal. I always said it was dangerous and now look what's happened. She'll be lucky if he lets her do it again but it's no doubt for the best.'

She took a candle from a small mahogany side table and led me up the stairs. I followed her example of walking on the edge of the treads where the wood made the least complaint. There were sounds of industry from the kitchen, pots being scrubbed and a song being sung, so we would hardly be noticed but I was picking up her air of caution.

We moved swiftly but the less noise we made the more I heard my heart. I hadn't anticipated this invitation and looked behind me to the door at the slightest sound from below. I had been pleased the Professor was out but now I wanted reassurance that he wasn't likely to return soon. Did she really want to see me?

The maid unlocked the door to reveal Christina's room bathed in the light from a candelabra and a roaring fire. It was hot so hardly surprising that she was pinked cheeked. She was wearing a white nightgown embroidered and gathered at the neck and was propped up with pillows. Quilts surrounded her until she appeared to be in a nest.

'Bracy,' she said urgently, holding out her hand.

I rushed to her side, relieved to be forgiven. She had called me a hateful man so I hadn't been sure of her, not until I saw her face. I sat on the bed and cradled her in my arms.

'I'll just be outside, miss,' the maid said, locking the door.

Christina thanked her and then complained. 'Bracy, I'm not an egg. Hold me tighter than that.'

It was easy to oblige her and reassuring to discover she could kiss as well as I remembered.

'Ah, you didn't blunt your tongue in that fall, then. My little love. How is your head?'

'Aching. But don't worry about that. Bracy, he doesn't believe me. He thinks we were out riding together.'

'I know. I should have told him straight away. I don't know why I didn't.'

'He wouldn't have believed you either. How can I make him see sense?' She was trembling slightly, her face was flushed and I asked whether she was chilled. 'No, the doctor's been; I'm only bruised. I'll be up tomorrow if they let me.'

'And your leg?' I asked, holding her away from me in scrutiny.

'Is as thin as a pin.'

Through the covers I touched the leg that dominated her life. She was startled but let me run my hand over it.

'Don't,' she said, a little flustered.

I guessed she was self conscious and smiled at her. 'I came to see how you are and all I can do is caress you. You

149

must think me terrible.' No, she didn't think that. She seemed hot and threw off one of the quilts. 'You are strong, Christina. You could deliver a useful kick if necessary.'

'I'd kick Edward if I thought it would make any difference.'

'I'll talk to him, you must rest.'

'Now you sound like him. Do you know? He accused me of throwing myself at you. He said you would never bother with me unless I had given you the most unspeakable incentive. Bracy, I didn't know what to say. He knows we've been riding together. If he knew what else we've been up to…he would twist it…and spoil it.'

'He'll not find out, sweetheart. Don't get upset.'

'It's easy for you to say but you don't have to live with him.'

'Neither will you. Not for ever.'

'I shall live on my own. Then I won't be a burden for anyone.'

'How will you contrive that, my love?'

'Oh, I don't know. Somehow.'

'I thought you might wait for me. I don't like to ask it of you. I have no right, nothing I can offer you. The hope of a career no one has ever heard of before. A vet for hire. That's what I'll be and the whole world to convince that it's worth paying my fee. I would take you away from here tomorrow but my future could be grim. Henry was right. There would come a day when I regretted giving up my surgeon's apprenticeship.'

'Don't be silly, of course you will succeed. How can you doubt it? Look how full the college's stables are. The country is crying out for vets and people won't be suspicious of them for long.'

'You'll wait then?'

She had no time to answer for there were noises in the hall. Voices. The maid rushed into the room, shut the door and leant back as though she would keep out a storm.

'Oh, miss. He's back. We never expected him so early. Whatever are we to do?'

She was distraught. Of course, she would lose her place if the Professor were to find out about her part in these proceedings. She flitted about the room straightening Christina's brushes, picking up a cloth that had fallen from the wash stand and closing the linen press. She was putting the room to order for an inspection overlooking the fact that there was a greater untidiness at hand. Me.

'Mary, keep still a moment,' Christina whispered. 'He won't come in here for at least half an hour. Could you sneak Mr Clark out the door while he's in his study?'

'But the stairs, miss. Begging your pardon but he's heavy and he makes them creak.'

'I'll climb out the window,' I said.

'Oh, please. No. That ivy is not strong. You will fall,' Christina cried.

'Then I will have to hide and leave later. This cupboard should be big enough.' I looked into it with some disquiet. The upper part of it was fitted with shelves and it wasn't deep. I would need to sit on the floor and hope Mary would be able to shut the door.

She was peering into the hallway, listening.

'He's coming,' she said.

Wisely snuffing some of the candles, she ushered me into the cupboard and pushed the door against my folded legs. It shut but I would only have to take a deep breath and it might bounce open again.

'Mary, you might have swept in here,' I complained lightly. 'If I sneeze, it will be your fault.'

'Bracy, this is no time to tease,' Christina wailed.

Her nervousness was palpable and yet I felt like laughing. How ridiculous it was to be hiding. I could have been a qualified surgeon by now had I kept up my apprenticeship. I would have been calling at the front door, invited into the parlour and offered a glass of Burgundy. Professor Coleman would have greeted me as an honest suitor; I would never have known him for what he is. There would be no enmity. Instead, I was playing in the shadows and behaving like a sneak. My loss of status was very lowering.

'I have some medical training, you know,' I said quietly. 'Couldn't we say I was here in some professional capacity? Were he to open the door I fear I would be somewhat at a disadvantage.'

'No, hush.'

'This is madness.'

Then I could hear her talking to Mary who was adjusting her pillows. She was greeting her brother rather coolly. He was pacing about the room. The door opened and closed. That must have been Mary's exit.

I've been told that eavesdroppers never hear well of themselves. Neither do reluctant ones, as I was to discover. Cramp was making a claim on my left leg and I breathed in and out through my mouth in case my nose betrayed me. Sneezing was a serious possibility.

There was a scrape of a chair, the sound of someone sitting and then an audible sigh from Christina.

'Don't look like that, Edward,' she said. 'I'm not dead. A few bruises. It could have happened to anyone and it's ridiculous for you to be so cross about it. Tomorrow I will be up and about and you won't even remember there ever was an accident.'

'My dear Christina. Always so optimistic. Allow me to say that it won't be as simple as that. It appears that I will have to thank *him* for your safe return. The prospect doesn't please me.'

'So, you believe me now?'

'I have had your story corroborated. It seems his finding you was a coincidence if his friends are to be believed. Why either of you headed to that wet bit of ground is beyond me but I won't trouble you with more questions now, my dear. His finding you seems to be yet another discourtesy. It would give me the greatest pleasure to find some fault with him. It appears the worthy man has no vices. He doesn't drink, he keeps away from the taverns and, apart from his ridiculous performance in your direction, he doesn't appear to have much interest in women.'

'We don't need to talk about him now though, Edward. Such a dull subject and I'm a little tired.'

I wriggled my foot soundlessly and resolved to make her pay for that nasty comment.

'Dull! Indeed. Typical of his kind, I'm afraid.'

'What do you mean? Quakers?'

'People who make a great noise about frugality. They don't understand anyone else's aspirations and they sneer at comfort as though it's excess. He even tried to fix my interest once in a stove he created. Said it used less wood than an open fire. As if such a thing is of interest to me.'

Professor Coleman laughed so much you could be mistaken for thinking he was happy. I remembered that conversation early in our relationship. I still had hopes of winning his approval, showed him my design for a stove but was met with the usual disdain.

'He's not a bad man even if he does prose on a bit.' She was endeavouring to keep her voice low, presumably so I couldn't hear, but I was very much in the room with them. 'Can you not drop this animosity?'

'What an entertaining thought. It would be a terrible mistake though. He's already been to see Granville Penn. Oh, Penn didn't tell me but I worked it out from something he let drop. There was a reserve that wasn't apparent before.' I could hear the Professor get up from his chair and move about the room. 'I know he has shown you some attention and it's gone to your head but you don't admire him, I hope.'

'Well, no…'

He didn't appear to notice her hesitation. I could have sworn she was about to say something nice about me and even though it wouldn't have helped us it might have made my cramped quarters a little less uncomfortable.

'I'm relieved to hear it,' he said.

'How is Firefly? Did you check her, Edward?'

'Ah, the mare.'

His pacing increased. I could feel the movement of the

boards and the anxiety in the room. He came closer to my hiding place and I held my breath knowing we were on the same piece of wood. I worried he might feel my presence through his shoes; he might open the door from some idle curiosity or some instinct that drew him towards me. Then he was gone and I could work my lungs once more. A log was thrown onto the fire; he brushed the dirt from his hands.

'She is alright, I hope. The lameness will get better, won't it?'

'Who knows, my dear? For once, I am in agreement with the worthy Mr Clark. He has diagnosed founder, I'm told. I expected to see him in the dining room; I wonder where he's got to. No matter. That pleasure awaits me tomorrow.'

'Founder! Are you certain? He never said.' She might have given us away but the Professor didn't pick up the remark. 'Oh, my poor horse. That's so serious, so painful.'

'Indeed, the outlook is grim. I fear you may have been riding her rather hard. You are so fond of speed. I have never understood why. Just because you are unable to hurtle about on your own feet doesn't mean you should ask a horse to do it for you...and this is the result. It will teach you to heed my warnings, I suppose.'

'You will do everything for her, won't you? Surely, there must be a cure. This is the veterinary college, if anyone can help her...well...'

She ran out of words. I could hear she was crying. I wanted to silence him. I wanted to go to her. My legs were numb but my anger was moving inside me, growing until the cramped space was unlikely to contain me.

'Of course, we will do all that we can but we can't wreak miracles. With founder the damage can be very deep in the bones and is often fatal.'

There were more sounds of distress. I held my head in my hands. Why did he have to do this to her? I willed him to leave the room, to stop this game.

'Oh, Edward. I didn't mean to hurt her.'

'I know that, my dear. Don't upset yourself. Here, take

my handkerchief. Dry your eyes. The main thing is you are well and with a few days rest you will be able to come downstairs again. It's only a horse, after all.'

The sound of her crying was like a finger plucking the strings of my own emotion. Soon, it was the only noise and I assumed he had left. I waited until I was certain and then opened the door and stretched my legs in front of me until the circulation returned. The soft light of the room made my eyes blink until they landed on the woman prostrate in the bed. Her dark hair was spread across the pillow and her face was red and tearstained.

'Don't listen to him,' I said angrily.

She didn't speak but clutched my hand without looking at me. 'Did he lie then?'

'About the cause. Yes.'

'Oh, nonsense. He wouldn't lie to me about a thing like that. And anyway, what does the cause matter? Founder is very serious. It might kill her.'

'No. I won't let it.'

'Oh, Bracy. How can you heal it?' Her crying eased and she sounded angry.

'The cause does matter. It will point us towards the cure.' I sat on the bed and made her sit up. I wanted her to look at me, to know I was sincere. 'I think it's the shoes. The Grasshoppers. They were fitted about a week ago and it's no surprise to me that she's now lame. There's a link. I just need to prove it.'

'Oh, listen to you. You are trying to blame my brother. How can it be the shoes? Lots of the horses are wearing them but you hate him so much that you're blinded by it.'

'I'm sorry, but no shoe has ever looked like that. So narrow and with that bar down the middle that runs over the frog.' I said, more loudly than I meant to. 'It might be his fault and to hear him blaming you is outrageous.'

'I do ride her fast. He's been telling me not to, you see, and I have ignored him. He's right to tell me off. Please don't go on about the shoes. It's stupid.'

'Christina. I've been riding the animals here. Those shoes of his are making them worse.'

'Oh, enough! We've got to get you out of here. He would go mad if he knew. Do you think you could keep your voice down when you berate him? He's locked the door. You might have to climb down the ivy.'

I trod softly to the door of her room and tried the handle. The door was locked. By the time I returned to her side she was crying again. I held her hands and let her. That horse was special to her; I knew that more than anyone. That horse was her legs.

With Mary's help, I got out the way I had come in. She had a key and waited for the Professor to fall asleep in front of his fire before she came for me. I took off my boots and we crept down. There was less background noise, no work from the kitchen, only the crackle of the fire in his study to hide behind. I was aware of every footfall and each creak on the stairs spoke of my subterfuge. I was relieved to be outside and to hear the bolt slide on the front door. I looked up at the window I knew to be Christina's and laughed at myself. I could hear my older brother and his warnings that one day I would regret my choice of career.

I would write to him and confess he was right for I hated this creeping about. I had lost respectability in favour of an uncertain future. You see, a surgeon has an established profession and the veterinarian sits beside him like a jester next to a king. He has yet to be regarded as something more than a joke and somehow Henry knew it all those years ago when some madness induced him to come with me to the post mortem of Eclipse. I should have felt empty at the loss of my prospects but somehow I was glowing at having gained something finer.

# CHAPTER 20

Firefly was one of many and since she wasn't bleeding or in immediate danger she wasn't given priority treatment. It's likely that the Professor didn't want to favour his own animal in this public arena so I checked her myself first thing in the morning. She was still lame on both fronts but the right was more severely affected and therefore masking the problem with the other. I felt for her pulse below each fetlock and found it tumultuous. The change in her was distressing. The spark had gone from her eyes, her nostrils were tense and her ears were flat. She had no interest in the world.

I gave orders for her to be given a deep bed of straw hoping it would cushion her feet and relieve her discomfort. I'd have taken her to the forge but knew I must wait until I'd spoken to Professor Coleman although there was little hope he would agree with my proposed treatment.

He was on duty from an early hour, brimming with his habitual efficiency and priorities - the cleanliness of the yard and the abundance of fresh air. Dust and cobwebs were not tolerated and neither were droppings which were a constant battle for the stable lads. The Professor took a tour of the stables issuing instructions and checking treatments with his assistant-in-waiting following like a child's kite, jotting down notes.

I was poulticing a grey mare suffering from a violent kick when Coleman approached her stall. He asked me to remove the poultice so he could inspect the wound which had affected the tendon making it swollen.

'I trust you've treated that first, Clark? It needs to be thoroughly cleaned,' he warned. 'When did this injury occur? It doesn't look fresh.'

'She was kicked on Monday and came here yesterday, sir. It's had three days to get worse. I cleaned it and applied sulphate of zinc when she arrived. This morning, I'm doing the same.'

'I've always admired your efficiency. No doubt the animal is relieved to be in your good hands.' His dark eyes mocked as I reapplied the bandage but I disappointed him by not getting the thing tangled. It's easily done especially if the animal decides on a different agenda such as kicking the vet's head.

He sighed as he walked away, signalling me to follow. William was reading from his notes. 'Sulphate of zinc, did you say?'

I nodded.

He was wearing a dark blue coat and pale breeches. Since he was the note taker he managed to keep himself cleaner than the rest of us. He was willowy and taller than Coleman but somehow more diminutive as if his weaker personality pervaded his body.

We walked down the line of stalls collecting students in our wake who were called to hear the Professor's instructions. The horses crunched on their hay, not caring that their fates were soon to be outlined but, in spite of death's hovering presence, this was a peaceful place. The smell of hay and the stamp of dozens of hooves seemed to overturn its constant threat. So many were very ill or injured, so many bore the signs of crippling disease and yet there were no cries of the hospital ward. Our charges bore their ill luck, sometimes their ill treatment, with noble fortitude.

There was enough talk among the students for me to attempt a private word with the Professor. 'May I talk to you about the mare, sir?' I asked.

'Not now, Clark.' He waved a hand in front of his face. A yawn was stifled.

'It can't be left and I think I know what's troubling her. You see, she's got very small feet and…'

'Oh, enough. Did I not make myself clear?'

It was always this way with him. Impossible to talk to unless you were admiring the cut of his coat. 'You did, Professor, but I must insist. It's my belief that she has founder. You know, as well as I, it's a very serious condition and concussion may have played its part. Especially with those shoes. The design is…'

I was going to say flawed but he turned his back on me and spoke to William. I was determined and bided my time. His shoulders were tense; there was a twitch visible beneath one ear so he was not as nonchalant as he made out. I folded my arms and was the picture of patience.

'Professor?' I said quietly when I was unable to wait any longer. 'Please…will you not listen. For her sake?'

There was a pause while he digested that. 'Did I hear you correctly? Her sake?' He turned to his audience and spoke more loudly. 'Gentlemen, it has come to my attention that my sister has become a source of amusement for some of you. Nay, your puzzled faces protest your innocence. She has become something of interest to one of you. I never expected such a thing to happen for a moment and I am vastly disappointed. She is nothing to you, Clark. Please keep your thoughts entirely on the horse while you are here.' There was a glint in his eye when he turned back to me. And a charming smile. We mustn't forget that. 'Your industry overwhelms me but I fear it is misdirected. Rest assured that I examined my sister's horse this morning and have the case well in hand.'

'Sir, with respect, it's my opinion that the shoes may be causing her harm. It would be worth taking them off, giving her some rest and see if we can improve the state of her feet.'

'Is that so?' He nodded his head, laughing lightly. 'Clark, unfortunately I am in your debt. Your…your kindness to my sister was most fortuitous but I hope you won't let my gratitude go to your head. There is nothing wrong with the Grasshopper shoes. Any revolutionary idea has its detractors but let us move on. Now, here is something you would be very unwise to ignore.' He pointed his cane at a young chestnut with a striking flaxen mane and tail. 'Sewell. A tendon injury, is it not?'

'Indeed, sir. I believe. The leg. Possibly the hind. Let me look at my notes. No, it's the back leg and yes, you are right as always. The tendon.'

'Oblige me by arranging for this horse to be taken to the forge for firing.'

Oh, lord. Firing! St Bel had used this treatment and it was much favoured by Professor Coleman. Years later, I came to abhor it but for now my mind was open. The struggle from the horse against his handlers and his vet is never more extreme than when a hot iron is applied to remedy his injured legs. He fights as though his life is under threat and who can blame him for the pain must have been extreme. If the treatment worked I might have been easier but I had seen so many distressed and crippled. An injury to cover lameness, could it ever be anything more?

William saw my face and knew not to ask me to lead the horse. He called to one of the grooms since it was not the vet's job to apply a catalogue of restraints. The fellow grabbed a twitch from one of the pegs on the wall and I wondered if it would be enough. I had never viewed the forge as a place of care. The roar of the fire, the whoosh of the bellows and the constant hammering were at odds with an animal's life and each nail that was driven into the horse's foot was a prick to my conscience.

It was the beginning of a hot day and the big, double doors of the college's own forge were wide open. Smoke boiled out carrying its own distinct smell. The hot coals glowed like a crack in the earth and George Whelan was turning new-made shoes in the heat using a long iron. He was a good smith, calm and steady in his character. His forge was well ordered and he never questioned his place in the hierarchy of the college. If Professor Coleman wanted Grasshopper shoes fixed to the horse's tail he'd have done it if he could. I once tried to discover his opinion on the shoes, freely expressing my own views on their failings but he cut me short with a laugh.

'When you're the Professor yourself, then we'll listen to you,' he said.

He knew his work well and his performance wouldn't be dented by a clutch of students gathered in his domain. He accepted the Professor's instructions with a nod of his head and ushered the horse inside. Professor Coleman made a quick tour of the building; his eyes seemed to be searching for an elusive error.

'Let's see, who have we got?' Whelan said, sizing up the groom. 'Think you can hold him?'

The groom could hardly admit to doubt, waved the twitch he held in his left hand and smiled as though it might be his last. The twitch was a highly effective and harmless restraint. There were two short, wooden poles connected by a strong piece of string a few inches long. The fleshy part of the animal's top lip was grabbed, wrapped in the string which was then twisted until the lip was tightly pinched. No animal would play around when placed at such a disadvantage. The horse ceased his fidgeting in an instant although his eyes continued to roam, ever on the lookout for danger. The handler's confidence grew and indeed we all relaxed once he seemed sure of himself. The horse's memory gave him no cause for alarm; his visits to the forge were for shoeing and wouldn't have caused him any pain.

Whelan plunged a long rod with a flat end in the heart of the forge and folded his arms while it got to temperature. One of his assistants was busy making shoes, shaping the hot metal with mighty blows of a hammer. Sparks danced around him but never seemed to land.

There was time and so I asked the Professor if I could

examine the injured tendon. The horse had walked out of his stall lame and stood in the corner resting the leg.

'Pray do,' he said. 'I would value your opinion.' Surprisingly, he didn't sound sarcastic.

I picked up the horse's leg. I had to hold onto it as he had other ideas, kicking me being one of them. Finally, he relaxed and allowed me to trace every outline of that tendon with a firm touch. It carried the telltale swellings of strain and the application of the slightest pressure drew a corresponding reaction from the animal so I was able to locate the injury.

'Do we know how long he's been rested?' I asked.

'Sewell?' drawled the Professor.

William flipped through his notes. The answer was not to be found whichever way he held the book.

'The injury seems to be fairly recent. There's plenty of heat in the leg, some swelling and more rest may set him right,' I said.

'I'm glad you mentioned heat, my friend,' said the Professor. 'You see, everyone, the application of heat to an injury can accelerate its healing. This is the science behind firing. It may seem barbaric but I can assure you it is the only chance for cases such as these. Troublesome injuries that simply won't get better and so drastic measures are essential.'

He ordered one of the grooms to hobble the animal's back legs. 'Mr Whelan, are we ready?'

'Yes, sir. I'm just letting it cool off as it has to be just right. Now gentlemen, please stand to one side of the forge. I wouldn't want you trampled. The best way to do this is quickly. You don't get a second chance at it. As you'll see, I'll be placing the iron lightly on his leg, like this.'

He had the hot iron with its wooden handle in his hand and made a deft, sweeping movement in the air. How simple and harmless it looked. The horse was approached with confidence, the iron kept out of sight. The animal tensed but not badly. His ears cocked and he would have turned his head but for the twitch holding him still. The groom stood before him with his legs apart, braced.

I prayed it would be quick and found myself holding my breath.

Edmund was next to me. 'How can this help?' he asked.

'It can't. Surely.'

'Don't look,' he said.

I turned to him. His lips were tight. His eyes were lowered.

'I have to. I have to look.'

I had never heard a horse scream before.

Whelan was right. You don't get a second chance. They should have hobbled the front legs too. The horse struck out and felled the groom. He was suddenly free but unable to move, save for his head and front legs. The twitch fell from his lip to the ground, his eyes were huge. They scanned the crowd as if accusing us. His leg was an ugly, burnt mess.

The smell of it was sickening. He wouldn't let anyone near. The injured groom staggered out of the way. Another groom grabbed the rope attached to the halter.

There was a bucket of water by the forge ready to cool the newly-made shoes. I picked it up. I got as near to the horse as I could and threw water on his leg.

# CHAPTER 21

It was the day before our exams. My room was stifling and it was hard to concentrate. I sat at my table in my shirt sleeves, the window was pushed up but the still air refused to come in. I was studying some illustrations of the horse's foot and reading some notes I had made from one of St Bel's lectures about founder. It was a difficult condition to treat and time was running out for one particular animal in our stables. The trouble was deep in the foot, there was little external to see or to treat. Sometimes, if you picked up the foot, you could see a groove where the wall and the sole were separating, but it was often hidden by the shoe.

I was powerless to do much. Firefly's stall was kept deep with straw and she was rested since leading her out only made her more uncomfortable but it was impossible to still my disquiet about the Grasshoppers. Christina was in my thoughts and I wondered what she knew since her brother would not spare her feelings. I called at their house but each time Mary blushed and worried at the sight of me. She told me Miss Coleman had gone down with a cold and kept to her bed. She never again led me up the stairs but I could hardly blame her since it was a risk I wasn't eager to repeat.

I moved from my little table and stared blankly at the stable yard where six or seven horses were tied up ready to go home. A fly buzzed around me and settled on my hand, too idle to be afraid. It was rubbing its legs together, making itself at home and checking out the taste of me.

'Yes, you would live off mankind, won't you? But fortunately for you we haven't found work for you to do. You would limp then, my friend.'

The horse with the flaxen mane and tail was among those going home, his injured leg evident even from this distance. He was led slowly and awkwardly to a hitching rail by one of the grooms and I could hear the Professor claiming credit for his likely recovery. There was a man with him who wasn't one of our subscribers. Judging by his clothes he was a working man, stocky and short and hot. He was wiping his forehead with a red handkerchief and spoke in a gruff voice. I remembered who it was once I picked up one or two words.

Hurriedly, I got on my best clothes, combed my hair and felt in my pockets for some coins. The corridor was empty and I was glad that the heat and the exams were making their mark and the students were studying quietly in their rooms. A few more days and we would be leaving here with or without a piece of paper qualifying us as vets so a feeling of nervousness was inevitable but I doubted our examiners would produce many failures. Why would they? Any of us would be better than nothing. That was Coleman's guiding principal and I decided to embrace it.

I waited near the stable yard for Professor Coleman and his visitor to finish their business. Their voices floated in the still air but I couldn't make out their conversation any more than I could understand the drone of the insects that were drawn to this place. Finally, the Professor shook the stocky man's hand with a dainty grip and watched idly as he got on his horse and rode away. The horse ambled out of the wicket gate and I was thankful for the beast's lack of speed as I ran through the college fields and saw him ahead of me in the lane.

'Mr Cross,' I called.

The knackerman pulled up his horse and waited for me to catch up. I glanced towards the college, an almost windowless building, and knew I couldn't be seen unless someone had followed me.

'You won't remember me, sir. I'm one of the students.'

'Oh, I know ye,' he said, without a hint of a smile.

'You do?'

'Aye. You're the one that wasn't squeamish. I'll not forget that in a hurry. The Frenchman wanted a body to cut up and it was a memorable day when I delivered it here.'

'You're right but post mortems are something we've all got used to.'

'Don't remember your name though, lad.'

'Bracy Clark, sir.'

'And what can I do for ye, Bracy Clark?'

'I wanted some information, if you were willing to share it.'

He gazed at the church spire in the distance, folded his arms and sucked his teeth thoughtfully. He dealt in meat, bones and bodies, not many people sought him out for such a rare thing and he appeared at a loss.

'You mean a price list, lad?'

'No, Mr Cross I need to know about the horses Professor Coleman wants you to slaughter. I presume that was the reason for your visit. I know there must be quite a few who won't recover in spite of all our efforts and…well, I know he calls you in to do the deed.'

'Aye, no one does it quicker.'

'Or so painlessly.'

'Aye.'

'That's important to you, I know. But if there was a chance of saving one of the horses, if we could get it better you wouldn't be averse to er…I don't know. Helping it, I suppose.'

'How can I do that? If the veterinary college with all its modern thinking can't do the trick I don't know what you expect me to do. I'm a knackerman, lad.'

'I think I can help it myself but I need time and I need you to help me.'

He looked as though I was some sharp pulling a pack of

cards from my pocket and indeed my hands were hidden, fiddling with the coins.

'You won't buy me with what's in there,' he grumbled. 'My business with the Professor is lucrative. If you think Richard Cross would put that at risk you must be touched in yer upper works. Why, Professor Coleman pays me well for each carcass I bring him and then he pays me for the slaughtering.'

He woke his dozing horse with a kick in its ribs and set off up the lane. I kept pace with them but thought I might have lost his attention.

'I wasn't seeking to persuade you with money, Mr Cross.' He grunted. 'And I didn't wish to offend you.'

His gaze was fixed on the horizon but I put on speed and got in front of his horse, walking backwards so I could look him in the face.

'I know you care about the horses. Not many people realise it. They think you're the knacker from Camden with no more thought about the animals than a butcher has for a piece of meat. But I know differently.'

He laughed and nodded his head. 'What makes you say that?'

We were leaving the lane, joining a road where wooden scaffolding was sprouting on either side and houses were growing like children at different stages of development. A wagon carrying bricks passed us; another bearing wood was being unloaded. The area was gripped with the industry of building, making the few patches of grass and weeds appear in retreat.

I knew nothing of the sort. It was a wild guess but it was my last chance. 'The way you ride that horse and the way he is with you. There's trust there.' He didn't interrupt me so I became loquacious. 'I've learnt a lot since being at the college but mostly I've come to know that most horses are destroyed before half their natural life is expended. You've known it for a long time...and it troubles you. You see, the owner parts with the lame horse but the horse cannot part with his diseases.

Each time he changes hands he falls into more base and distressing service until finally he comes to you. The blood horses suffer the most, don't they, sir?'

He sighed and pulled over near a builder's shed where two lads were working on a window frame. There was a lot of shouting, a man was carrying a long piece of timber but Mr Cross's horse wasn't skittish and ignored the lot.

'Aye, they do. They're started so young, is my thought. When they're babies, they're saddled and raced so a lot of them are wasted.'

'They're shod then too. When their feet aren't fully grown. It must be harmful.'

'You're right, I hadn't thought of that.'

'Their bodies keep growing but their feet can't, not with an iron ring nailed to them. I question whether they ever recover from it.'

'You planning on putting me out of business, lad? I wouldn't want you curing every ill that afflicts the horse, you know.'

'I wish it were possible but I suspect you're quite safe.'

He laughed and patted his horse robustly on the neck. 'Which one are you interested in?'

'The chestnut mare.'

'The high-bred one?'

I nodded.

'That's the Professor's horse.'

'His sister's.'

'It's badly lame.'

'I know. With founder.'

'And you think you can cure it?'

'I do.'

'Well, blow me.'

'How long has she got, sir? I might have to move swiftly.'

'She's on the list for early next week. Unless there's some improvement. Professor Coleman doubts she'll make it. Says there a weakness in the foot that is congenital and no amount of doctoring will help. Why that one?'

'I've got to like the horse, she has an amazing spirit and well…I believe founder could be linked to the shoes. I'm afraid the Professor won't listen to me, he won't try her without them.'

'You think it's as simple as that? Take off the shoes and away she goes?' he laughed.

Yes, it did sound foolish. I had seen enough animals stagger around the yard between shoeings to know that none would manage on their own feet. Not once they had been compromised by years of hammering and butchery from the farrier with his nails and his hot metal.

'No, sir…but given time and the right treatment I might be able to reverse the condition. I want to try.'

'And what do you expect me to do?'

'Well, I was hoping you could insist that the slaughtering is done on Tuesday…very early.'

# CHAPTER 22

The day of the exams was an anti climax; all those weeks and months, all our studying brought us before a group of surgeons who knew less of the horse than Professor Coleman. It would have been appropriate had I asked them a question or two to judge their suitability but I doubted many of them had ever saddled a horse before let alone found their way around its anatomy. They had their list of questions and could put a tick in a box and that was enough. I knew I had passed and it would take more time than I had available to find a student with the gall to fail.

I was preoccupied, not just about the fate of one horse but all the animals I would be leaving in a few days time. They would be in the Professor's care with the help of his new students and I made it my business to leave detailed notes for each case I'd worked on.

Part of me didn't want to leave this place. This tiny room had been home for more than two years and I knew every draught and every creak of the floorboards. It was stifling in the summer making it impossible to remember how cold it could be in the winter but already it was someone else's abode. Their unseen clothes might even now be pushing mine from the cupboard, my books were stacked in a trunk and my thoughts were of departure. This would be their window to gaze at the stable yard, to see the new patients arriving and feel the pleasure of them returning home, hopefully in a better state. In spite of the Professor's blunders, even with his greedy palm, our profession had made an impact. Now it was to face its greatest test as the first vets were to leave its sanctuary, it wouldn't be long before they found whether the world was happy to receive them.

It was a daunting prospect but I was ready to face it. I was to go to my brother's house and from there I would find some premises in the city of London and set up my practice. I had already seen a property in Smithfield but my work here wasn't quite finished. There was one task I had yet to complete but I would need a lot of luck and help if I was to succeed. Some divine intervention wouldn't go amiss either. I was glad the exams were finished so I was free from the Professor's jurisdiction. In two days I would be gone and hopefully, my departure would remain unremarkable.

I desperately wanted to see Christina and, even though I couldn't confide my plans, I hoped she might trust me to do something. She must know Firefly was terribly lame but did she know the animal was to be slaughtered? Perhaps her brother would lie and protect her but after hearing their conversation in her bedchamber I feared he would tell her the worst.

I saw them both on Monday when I was checking the soundness of one of the patients. They arrived in a gig and the Professor was wreathed in benevolent smiles thanks, no doubt, to the results which were predictably excellent and a testament to his regime. Rightly or wrongly, I felt to blame for the early exams so my relief was palpable. He left Christina in the gig while he shook my hand with great warmth and said sweetly that it had been an honour to know me. Goodness, he must have been glad I was leaving. The other graduates on the yard were given the same treatment, he couldn't have been happier.

Christina stared in front of her with her head slightly bowed as the Professor went to congratulate William and confirm his appointment. William was thanking him in a muddled way, saying his success was entirely down to the Professor.

'Miss Coleman,' I said. 'I trust you are better.'

'Thank you. I am.' She kept her face averted and spoke quietly with great effort.

'Why has he brought you here? You shouldn't have come.'

Her fingers fiddled with the ribbon of her straw bonnet. Her hands were white with cold even though the day was fine and her shoulders were curled as if her body wanted to shield her heart.

'I have to see,' she said, after some moments.

'Do you? It's quite unnecessary, surely. There's very little change in Firefly's condition. Why should you see her suffer? There's nothing you can do.'

'I must, that's all. I must see what I have done. It's all about responsibility, don't you see?' She turned to me, brimming with tears.

Oh, God. I wouldn't be able to unravel this suffering in these few minutes so I prayed Edmund would keep the Professor talking. Thankfully, he led the man to one side and became more loquacious than I had ever seen him. Fred joined them and was shaking the Professor's hand, making sure the man's back was towards me.

I estimated I had about three minutes and grabbed Christina's hand in both of mine. 'Sweetheart, it's not your fault. Please trust me. You did not hurt that horse, you did not ride her too fast and you didn't take her on ground that was too hard. The fault lies elsewhere.'

She seemed not to hear me, gathered the reserves of her strength and wittered on about water colour painting saying she was determined to improve her skills. 'I've neglected everything else, you know, and so I have very few accomplishments. Who wants to talk to a woman about horse riding? Or science? It was rather silly of me to be distracted. I need to do other things.'

'This is madness; you don't know what you're saying.

Let me take you home. There's nothing he can do to me now and in front of all these people he wouldn't dare say a thing.'

'No! Oh, I know you are trying to be kind and you think he's making me come but it's not as simple as that. I would like to see her, Bracy. For myself. I must. I know time is running out.'

I resigned myself. 'Very well.'

I offered her my hand and she got awkwardly down from the gig. I slid her hand through my arm and we made our way slowly to the stables. She moved more stiffly than she had before and I asked whether the accident had hurt her leg.

'No,' she said. 'I've had too many days in bed. The less I do the worse I get. I'll be fine; it's not me that we have to worry about.'

We reached Firefly's stall and Christina stiffened at the sight of the mare whose head was so low it looked heavy. She was sleepy but stirred at our approach. Christina stroked her and rubbed her neck.

'I was expecting her to look even worse. Are you sure she has founder?'

'She has all the symptoms of it. The pulse and the lameness. She stands typically too, trying to get the weight off her toes.'

Christina hitched up her skirts and went into the stall, crouching onto the straw to feel for the pulse at the back of the mare's fetlock. 'Where is it? I can't feel it,' she said anxiously.

I pressed her finger into the spot where a pounding beat of blood told us something was wrong. 'There.'

Christina looked at me angrily. 'And because of this she has to die? Why can't you get the better of this? You are meant to be vets and yet you seem to have done nothing for her. What's the point of all that studying if you can't remedy something like this?'

'She's been rested and she's been given a deep bed of straw.' Ridiculously, I was defending the Professor's treatment, conscious of my own plans that I couldn't reveal. 'It's hard to see with the shoes but there's this separation. She is still very lame.'

'So would you be if you sat around all day after an injury.'

'Your brother has done everything in his power. He's been very busy but in spite of that he made sure Firefly got his personal attention. It's a condition that we know so little about. I'm sorry. I promise you she hasn't been neglected.'

She stood up and leant against the horse, her head rested on Firefly's mane. 'I don't understand how she can have got so bad so quickly. She was fine only a few weeks ago and I was even jumping her. Don't you remember how good she was? There was nothing wrong with her feet then. There was no pain. Why, she took every jump as though she wanted more. Do you really think it's the shoes?'

'I do.'

'Have you said anything to him?' She spoke in a whisper and there was confusion on her face.

'I have.' I picked up the mare's left forefoot even though she struggled, not wanting to put additional weight on the other. 'I'm afraid he laughed at me. He's not a man who welcomes criticism and naturally that's how it sounded. He said I was making him weary and he actually begged me to spare him the details of his wrong doing. Like you, he thought I was making the allegation from malice.'

'I didn't say that.'

'Something like it. You thought I was driven by animosity towards him.' I let Firefly's foot down, not relishing the task I had set myself for later that night. 'I've ridden more horses with his Grasshopper shoes than anyone here and I know the design is at fault.'

'If that was the case she would have gone lame earlier. What you're saying doesn't make sense. She had the shoes on for at least a week before the accident. Edward said they would improve her going and I remember being excited about them. I'm sorry, Bracy, I don't believe it. I know you are sincere but it can't be true because he wouldn't put shoes on her that would hurt her. I think you forget that mostly, he's a very kind man. Oh, he's difficult and domineering and…'

'…and he locks you in your room.'

'Only for my own good…he's knows I would have got up much earlier. Mostly, he's been very good to me and where would I be without him?'

It always came back to that. She was so grateful to him that it skewed her vision. Why she should thank him for doing what was right for a sister was beyond me. What I failed to realise was how vulnerable a woman in her situation was. She was wholly dependent on her brother for everything from the roof over her head to the boots on her feet. There wasn't much she could do without his permission and the independence she achieved was hewn as if from stone.

It was cool in the stables and slightly dim apart from the shafts of sunlight coming through the windows. Everything was well ordered and spotless although no one could control the motes of dust that eddied about in the air or the insects that droned relentlessly. There were bursts of noise from the horses; a whinny from a new arrival who was unsettled and the steady munch of hay from those who had accepted their lot.

'Shall I leave you with her?' I asked Christina.

She nodded, her head was bent with emotion and I almost forgot my resolve to tell her nothing. I wanted to shout that she shouldn't worry, that I would make this horse better whatever the cost. I hoped I would succeed but it was better she was kept in the dark. I squeezed her hand and left her to say goodbye.

# CHAPTER 23

I was glad Edmund and Fred insisted on helping me that night for I never would have managed on my own. It must have been nearly midnight which, although not late by town standards, was a time of quiet at the college. The students slept, exhausted from the last few days and the unrelenting needs of the animals in their care, and the stable lads were off duty until the morning. A couple of them slept in the hay loft which meant we had to take care but I knew from past experience that they were ineffectual guards. You couldn't rouse them from their slumbers without an almighty din.

We might have provided it when Fred dropped the tools he had borrowed from the forge. They clattered on the cobbles and made us stop in our tracks. I picked them up since Fred was immobilised with worry.

'Is this horse thieving?' he asked. 'Only I don't fancy being transported.'

'How can it be stealing?' I said. 'The horse is due to be dispatched tomorrow. No make that today and anyway, you will be back in your bed by the time it gets exciting. Don't worry, my friend.'

'Oh, please! Keep your voices down,' Edmund whispered. 'We don't want to be discovered before we've even begun.'

We crept into the stables thankful there was a full moon since we would need its light. Horses only sleep for minutes at a time so we were met by wakefulness and stomachs already thinking about breakfast. One or two of them whickered in anticipation but the thought was quelled as we made our way purposefully to Firefly's stall.

'Do you think he'll kick up a fuss?' Fred rubbed his neck as if there was pain. His breathing was rapid. 'He was angry enough that you helped his sister. I'm not sure he's got over it even now but if you save the horse from slaughter he'll likely kill you. At the very least he'll report you for stealing it.'

'He'll never know about this night's work,' I said quietly and with more calm than I felt. 'Mr Cross is to make sure of it.'

'But if he does?'

'He won't find out. Not ever. And he would hardly complain publicly when all I am trying to do is cure a horse he plans to have killed.'

'If you think that, you don't know the man,' Fred muttered. 'He'd want to silence you more than ever. Don't you see? This will make him look cruel and incompetent and he won't rest until he has you locked up. Oh, Christ! How the hell am I going to do this in the pitch dark?'

We had agreed that Fred was the quickest out of all of us. I had seen him get a horse free of its shoes within minutes but he turned to me in frustration.

'There's not enough light, I won't be able to see the nails,' he said. 'We'll have to lead her outside. Quickly, I want to get this done.'

I grabbed a halter from one of the pegs. I had hoped to lead her out without the noise from her shoes but we had to take the risk. In spite of her lameness she followed me eagerly possibly because she had been confined for so long but it was almost as if she knew what tomorrow had in store and she was willing to flee whatever the cost. The pain in her feet was obvious but somehow she didn't seem like an animal ready for death. There was too much life in her, she shuffled along but nudged me in the ribs as if she couldn't wait to escape.

There was enough light outside thanks to the moon for Fred to work. The job was desperately difficult. He began with the backs and his speed gave me hope that she would cooperate with the fronts. I was wrong. She couldn't stand with one forefoot off the ground for as much as a minute.

We led her onto some grass where she was in less pain and easier to handle. Fred threw off his jacket as he had broken out in a sweat and I could hear his internal curses as he battled with the mare. She fell to the ground while he held the final foot and we kept her there, panting and alarmed, as Fred got the last one free.

'Yes!' he muttered under his breath as he joined her on the ground. Then he turned to her. 'I might be small but you'll not win an argument with me, you silly mare. You should know I'm only trying to help you. At least you didn't kick me.'

'She didn't have the strength,' I said.

'Want me to keep these for you, Bracy?' Ed asked, waving the shoes as the mare got to her feet.

I nodded. Then I noticed the light from a lantern in the distance, near to the Turnpike road. The college had watchmen who patrolled but I hadn't expected to see any abroad this late at night. They had been issued with muskets after one of the governors was held up by footpads but were lousy shots and more at risk from injuring each other. That didn't make our situation easier. I did not want to meet any of them as I walked from the college with a horse I didn't own.

'Now, we're for it. Damn,' Fred whispered. 'We've got to get out of here. Get her into the dark by that tree. Come on.'

The light came closer and we could hear voices. We must have disturbed an owl as it flew from the oak with a screech that unsettled the horse. She was too lame to do more than one sideways step but she relieved herself in another way and I hoped the smell would not drift to the two men approaching.

We began to hear snatches of their conversation. 'Thank you for your escort. Much appreciated. I shall mention you to the Professor. He'll be…um…as we all are, naturally. Grateful. Very.'

'I'll see you to the college before I'm off, sir. Fancy your meeting taking this long.'

'Yes, much later than I…I thought it would be doing.'

The watchman talked about the wisdom of getting indoors at a godly hour and William Sewell peppered his replies with frequent mention of the Professor, his appointment and his eternal gratitude. I started to laugh but only when it was safe and we saw the watchman's lantern heading down College Lane.

'Meeting? With a barrel of ale by the sound,' I said.

Fred and Edmund shook my hand warmly. I thanked them again and again.

'It will take you an hour to do that ten-minute walk leading this poor thing,' said Edmund. 'It had better be worth it. You have to cure her.'

'Of course he'll sort her,' Fred cried. 'Then I'd like to see the Professor's face. If only you could tell him. It will be a shame to keep it a secret.'

My destination was the Elephant and Castle Inn. My good friend, Mr Wrench, was expecting me and promised to have a stable ready for Firefly. She was to stay for a couple of days and then I hoped to move in easy stages until I got her to London but getting her to the Inn made the removal of her painful shoes seem easy. She walked reluctantly and at one point refused to move. I had to find the softest route across the fields; it took longer but avoided the stony track. Foolishly, I had hoped that removing her shoes would give her instant relief but she walked with such difficultly that I prayed the harm was not permanent.

By the time we were in Mr Wrench's hospitable hands Firefly was covered in sweat and my voice was hoarse from issuing commands and encouragement. The hardest part was the last few yards when we had to cross the Inn's yard. The sight of Mr Wrench with a bucket of feed made the final hurdle possible. I was never more grateful to hand over a horse to someone else for a few minutes and surprised myself by drinking a tankard of ale. We rubbed her down between us and I was thankful the stable was roomy as the mare lay down and rolled with a groan of relief.

Half an hour later, I was back at the college and climbing through the window of my room, exhausted and unlikely to sleep since so much was dependant on the morning. I thought endlessly about Mr Cross, the knackerman, who seemed such a straight forward and honest man. I hoped I could rely on him but questioned how could I put my trust in someone who did so much business with Professor Coleman. Surely, he would betray me.

I snatched a couple of hours sleep in spite of the turmoil that plagued my mind. By day break, there was enough adrenalin pumping through me to make me forget I was tired. I met Mr Cross in College Lane while it was still dark. He was driving a massive cart pulled by two dray horses and I opened the gate to let them in. I was relieved that the stable yard was deserted as he brought his team to a stop and leapt down. His assistant followed him coiling a great length of rope on his arm.

Before I knew it, he had gone to the side of his wagon with a long-bladed knife in one hand and a bucket containing some blood. He poured a small amount on the ground. The sun was creeping slowly upwards revealing silhouetted trees and the spire of St Pancras Church, inky black in the distance. It was still and quiet, giving the promise of a warm, sunny day although a bit of noise from a strong wind would have been more helpful to my enterprise.

'We've got about five minutes,' I warned them, thinking about the stable lads who would be rushing to lend assistance once they knew he was here. Fortunately, he was early.

Mr Cross and his nimble, but ox-like helper, worked quickly. They got ropes onto a chestnut mare that was already lying in the cart and made as if to winch her a few feet further inside. Firefly's substitute had died a few hours earlier although in this light it was impossible to tell the difference and I doubted anyone would take a close look.

Two stable lads joined us with their slow, early-morning rhythm and didn't question Mr Cross's eager start or my attendance. A lame chestnut mare had been dispatched and the corpse was already loaded without any exertion on their part so they didn't complain. The Professor was journeying to London today for a meeting with the government and was unlikely to be on the yard before he set off. So far, everything was going smoothly.

Then I saw John Bale, the stableman, running towards us, pushing his arms into a jacket, shouting and gesticulating. I hurried towards him. It was getting lighter and I had to steer him away from the back of the wagon.

'It's not like Cross to begin without me,' he complained. 'Why is he so early? I've not even had my breakfast yet...and where are the stable lads?'

Thankfully, he didn't ask what I was doing there. 'He needs to get back, so he said. He does seem in a terrible hurry but it's a job best done with speed, I suppose. The lads are getting the next one.'

'Are they now? It had better be the right one.' He nodded his head towards the cart. 'That Miss Coleman's horse? She was ailing that one. If the founder didn't kill her something else would. Hardly touched her hay last night, you know.'

'Really?'

'But why has he loaded her?'

Mr Cross appeared from the back of the wagon and was momentarily halted by the sight of the stableman, his fingers fidgeting on the handle of his knife. With every passing minute, the sun conspired against me and light filtered into the clouds. Dampness on the grass was being exposed and would soon be dried.

'Good day to you, Mr Bale,' the knackerman said, shaking the stableman's hand. He leant one meaty arm on the side of the wagon, blocking the path to the back and would have appeared nonchalant if he hadn't been sucking at his teeth. 'It'll be fine later, you mark my words.'

'I believe you are right, sir, but I didn't expect you this early. There's six to do today, I believe. Three are for the dissecting table, so the Professor told me.' He slapped the side of the wagon with his hand. 'This should have been one of them but you've loaded her already. You wasn't hoping to take more than agreed, I hope.'

Mr Bale spoke to the knackerman as though he was trying to pull a fast one. The carcasses had a high value and there was a danger the two of them might argue like surgeons over a human corpse.

'I wouldn't do that, thank you, Mr Bale. But I know my business and I'll load the first three that come. You wouldn't want a pile of bodies on the ground, would you? The lads wouldn't get the next ones out of their stables with that sight before them.'

'But surely, the Professor wanted to have a close look at Miss Coleman's horse? It had founder and I was sure he wanted her for the dissecting table tomorrow. How far have you pulled her on?'

He walked swiftly round the knackerman to the back of the wagon where the assistant was coiling ropes. My breathing halted while he peered inside. I stood behind him while Fate played this game with us. Mr Bale seemed to consider his chances of climbing on board. He seemed to be weighing up whether the knackerman and his assistant would be willing to heave the body out again. He looked towards Mr Cross expectantly.

I wanted to speak. To tell him he was mistaken. The Professor didn't want to cut up the mare. Not his sister's horse. He cared for it too much. Miss Coleman would be too upset if she knew. Mr Cross signalled me to shut my mouth before I said something stupid.

'You want me to pull her off the cart? When there's another horse on its way?' He tutted and raised his eyes to the heavens. 'Chaos. Get some more lads then to lend us a hand.'

'No wait,' said Mr Bale. 'You're right.'

We could hear Mr Cross's next customer on the cobbles

and I found myself breathing again. The poor animal's life was about to end but he had done much to lengthen mine.

I had an urge to slip away but knew I must see this thing through. The chestnut was soon joined by two others and I forced myself to watch. All were quickly and efficiently dispatched but the smell of fear was increasing and Mr Cross's customers were agitated. They were no longer easy targets for his knife.

With the use of some pulleys and a ramp they were able to get the corpses onto the back of the cart. It was a grisly sight but something every vet should see for this is the price of his failure. We had so much to learn. These servants of man had barely reached maturity and yet they were used up, all of them slaughtered before they were ten years old. Did we give them such a life of drudgery?

Once Mr Cross was finished I was left with a strange admiration for his skill. He gave them release, I suppose, and he made it swift and as kind as was humanly possible. We barely spoke but his eyes met mine in shared relief once the chestnut's body was hidden by others. I allowed myself a smile. We had done it. We'd got Firefly away from under the Professor's nose and, while she was alive, there was still hope. No one would be looking for her; she wasn't missing although there was still evidence of her time beneath the oak tree so I told one of the lads to clear up the dung before the Professor saw it. My request was heeded with alacrity. I must take up crime if I'm to be this good at it.

It was still early morning when the knackerman was ready to leave. He asked me to ride with them a while so I could open the gate which always dragged on the ground. I was happy to oblige as I wanted to thank him. Once we were out of sight, he shook my hand; it made me feel warm that he shared my excitement in cheating death that day.

'Yer a cool customer, Mr Clark.' He let out an almighty breath. 'I'll give thee yer due. A mighty cool one - apart from that one moment. And the mare? You got her away with no trouble?'

'I did but I'll not pretend it was easy and of course getting her away from here is only the beginning. I have much to do for her.'

'Let me know if you have need of my services.'

'I trust I won't.'

'You won't cure all of 'em, young man. You'll remember me, I hope.'

'Indeed, I will.'

'Now, about today's bit of work. I think you'll find this here bill is all in order.' He handed me a stained piece of paper with a flourish and a laugh. His head was nodding as though I was amusing him. 'I kept it to the minimum and there's no charge for the risk I was taking. Not seeing as how it was entertaining like. I don't always enjoy my work, much as I take pride in it, but this morning was a new departure, you might say.'

He took me by surprise and I apologised for not having any money on me. He didn't seem troubled, said I could pay him later and talked as though our working relationship might prosper for years to come. For a moment, I thought he was hinting that his silence might come at a price and I looked at his modest bill in some confusion.

Mr Cross laughed heartily and patted my shoulder. 'Like I said, you won't cure all of 'em…and there's none better than me to help 'em when you can't.'

# CHAPTER 24

Needless to say I was determined that Firefly and Mr Cross would not become better acquainted. She was hidden at the Elephant and Castle for now but it was too dangerous to move her. I was imposing on Mr Wrench but couldn't do much else since I had to stabilise her condition and trim her feet before she set forth on another journey. It was too risky to ask any of the local smiths to take on the task because of the threat of discovery and so I borrowed a rasp from the college forge and did it myself. I had trimmed a horse many times and never found it a problem but this was the first time I had tackled a horse in so much pain. Her feet stank but I could put up with that. Unfortunately, she couldn't stand on the remaining three for longer than a few minutes before she was snatching her foot away from me or falling on the stable floor.

She was housed at the back of the Inn away from the other horses. Mr Wrench wisely reckoned it was our best chance of avoiding discovery since the place was popular among the students and I was anxious she might be recognised. My fear was disproportionate since they were lured by Mr Wrench's excellent ale and his skittle ground but the gravity of what I had done weighed on my conscience. I feared to read the newspaper in the days that followed; the bleak news of men and women transported or hung for lesser crimes than mine was more than I could bear. Dreamless sleep was a distant memory and Mrs Wrench was threatening to dose me with strong liquor if the shadows beneath my eyes got any worse. Professor Coleman was a tireless adversary who would happily accuse me of stealing, cruelty and downright trickery. My attempt to cure a horse he had written off would be seen as yet another attempt to denounce him.

Of that I was innocent. It's true that to steal a horse in the dead of night, to substitute another in the knackerman's cart and embark on a secret attempt to cure her was way beyond the vet's usual brief but I had good medical reasons for this gross interference.

Firefly could get better. She had been fit and well a week before those Grasshopper shoes were fitted and it shouldn't be beyond the skills of a good vet to return her to soundness. I was qualified. I wanted to help this horse more than any other. Was that so very wrong? Professor Coleman accused me of many things in the years that followed. Never to my face and never in writing. What slanders I faced. So much that I questioned my own motives but in truth I hardly thought of the man as I tended that animal. Her feet were long, they were damaged and they were sore but, as the sweat built on my forehead, Coleman's animosity became irrelevant. I only wanted to avoid his notice and get the horse well enough to leave this cursed area. Revenge? What would a man like me want with such a thing?

No, my motives were pure even if I couldn't speak the whole truth. Well, I could hardly bring her name into the equation. To Mr Cross and Mr Wrench I was driven by a desire to save a horse from slaughter. I was a young vet full of enthusiasm, lacking patients but eager to test my theories. If they knew what a love sick fool I was, they didn't say. Not even my friends knew that I did it for her or, if they did, they never spoke of it.

Of course, Christina knew nothing of this and I couldn't confide especially while the animal's life hung in the balance. I could have faced an accusation of theft, I would have done so had the Professor discovered us and been brave enough to bring charges against me but I dreaded that anyone might think me cruel. As I watched Firefly paddling with her painful feet or shuffling awkwardly when I took her for a walk in the dead of night I had to fight against those whispering doubts. Was it cruel to keep her alive with this much pain? I prayed that she would be relieved soon, that her recovery would justify my decision to make the attempt.

I took hope from the tiniest signals since her progress was slow. For the first few days she spent a lot of time lying down. I took to crouching beside her and talking. She proved a reasonable listener.

'I wish I could tell her you're alive but thank goodness she can't see you like this,' I said. 'She wouldn't think well of me if she thought you were suffering. Not that I'm doing it for her thanks. I don't seek her gratitude; you know that, don't you?'

Firefly sighed wearily, as though I was being a bit of a bore, and then stretched out until I had to move over. Her tail brushed languidly across her flank, the steady summer rhythm that a horse will follow in its sleep so long as there are flies about. I stroked her neck absentmindedly and watched the dust motes being stirred in the air.

'She really did love riding you, didn't she? She said you were special and maybe she was right. No other horse will do, no other animal will give her what you did. I can't picture life for her without you. She'll not be allowed to go anywhere. God, I hope he's letting her out of that house. Don't you see? That's why we've got to do this thing and I promise you won't suffer; you won't be in pain for long. But I can see I'm keeping you up when you'd rather be asleep.'

Firefly rubbed her head in the straw, enjoying the luxury of the space she had gained since leaving the veterinary college. Seeing her flat out like this it was possible to forget that she knew any discomfort. There was no tension in her nostrils, her breathing was good and I was pleased at the improved shape of her feet although there was still much to do. I checked the pulse at her fetlocks but nothing there gave me any relief.

'I have this theory, Firefly.'

The horse sighed.

'About the shoes.'

There, I had her attention. She raised her head and her eyes were open.

'Not just the Grasshoppers. All of them.'

She stuck out her front feet as horses do when considering whether to get up. She stayed there for some time obviously in two minds; she could have been offering me her feet for inspection, asking me what her chances were.

'Think about it. The foot is not a block of wood. Some evil must arise from shoeing the tender feet of a young horse. Firefly, those shoes are bonds of iron. It must disfigure the feet, surely. Yours are giving you pain and I hoped, foolishly I suppose, that removing the shoes would give you relief.'

Firefly decided that this discussion shouldn't be taken lying down and I leapt to get out of her way. She stood and shook herself and then nudged me with her head.

'Yes, you must be impatient with my lack of progress but won't you help me prove what an evil they are? It could be the reason we lose so many of you when you are still young. I've always thought it was a black day for the horse when he gets his first set of shoes. The compromise he makes to his natural movement.' Firefly wasn't listening, her ears were pricked and she was alert to something outside. 'If only I had scientific evidence.'

I could hear Mr Wrench singing as he came round the side of the stable. He had a deep bass voice that could have graced Drury Lane so the appearance of his diminutive figure seemed out of step with the promise of his hearty song. He walked into the stable and shut the door, whispering as though Firefly might be a sleeping patient rather than a horse eager for the hay in his arms.

'How is she, then?' he asked.

She greeted him warmly and took eager steps towards

the hay. It was the soundest movement I had seen from her since her arrival.

'She's better than I thought. I was worried about how much she's been lying down but she must have needed it.' He put the hay in the rack and patted her neck. 'Mr Wrench, I need to find some alternative to the nailed shoe. What benefit is there in proving it's ruinous if I don't have something to replace it with?'

Mr Wrench sucked on his thumb thoughtfully as if it harboured the answer and then looked at me as though he had misheard.

'They're not all bad, young sir. I thought it was only Professor Coleman's that was doing any mischief. The horse won't manage without something on its feet, surely.'

'I'm sure you are right but we need to devise something that lives up to the name. Whoever described them as shoes must have been mad. And yes, I fear they all do some harm although the Professor's are the worst.'

'Mayhap he wants them horses sick. That way he can cure them when he's ready. I always said there was some witchcraft going on with that man.'

'Incompetence rather than witchcraft. If you remember, Mr Wrench, you thought me very suspicious when I attended your old fellow but we are taught science at the college, not spells.'

'So what happened to this one, then?' he said, nodding towards the chestnut mare. 'She was fine the week before, I saw Miss Coleman riding her. Why would she suddenly be struck down? Founder you call it. Well I have another name for it. It's evil and it makes a man shudder to think of it so I only hope you can get the better of it for it might take more than your science.'

'Would you have me boiling up some potion and saying some magic words?' I laughed.

He seemed alarmed and gripped my forearm with his bony hand. 'No, I'd have none of that here, if you please. She was bad when she came here and she's little better now. It's our prayers that she needs and a bit more of your science wouldn't go amiss, either.'

We left Firefly to her hay and walked into the sunshine. The air was heavy with heat and the grass had lost its spring vigour and reached middle age. Mr Wrench wanted to linger and I was in no hurry so we enjoyed the sanctuary the spot afforded us – away from the Inn's tap room with its wide open, oak door.

He was in a loquacious mood and I had the impression he had something to tell me. My apprehension increased for I was sure he must want us gone from here since we could bring him little income.

'I saw her this morning, you know,' he said.

'Who?'

He sighed. No, he grunted. 'Who else would I be talking to you about? Miss Coleman, young sir. It near broke my heart. To see her looking so sad.'

'You didn't tell her, did you?'

'Wanted to. No, of course I didn't. I haven't met a woman yet who could keep a secret like that to herself. She'd have told that brother of hers within the hour and why shouldn't she? She trusts him, it's only natural.'

'Indeed, I suppose you are right.'

'Besides, she was with him.'

No one of intelligence could rightly trust Professor Coleman. My future depended on destroying something between that brother and sister and the thought gave me a frisson of pleasure, another burden for my conscience to deal with. We sat on a couple of logs next to a stack that was growing in preparation for a winter that was impossible to imagine. There was an axe leaning against the wall and a broken cart which was unlikely to be brought back into service. Next to it were a few wooden cart wheels and other spare parts that were kept because they were too good to burn. They were covered in a layer of dust and growing through with nettles as if they would be reclaimed by the earth before their usefulness was remembered.

'How was she?' I asked.

'Over that troublesome chill but she didn't look comfortable.' He worried at a large stone with his foot until his strong shoes were covered in dust. 'They were walking along St Pancras Way, gone to see the new houses and she was going much slower than usual. She acted cheerful, like she always does, not that she fooled me and she asked after Mrs Wrench. You should have seen the look of distaste on that man's face.'

'I know it well.'

'It was like I was a bad smell. He was polite enough but...'

'You are beneath him, I fear. Your ale is better than anything they serve at Old Mother Red Cap's but you lack power and influence.'

He shuddered at the mention of the infamous Inn. 'Don't talk to me of that wicked place. I don't have power and I don't need it. It's customers that keep me happy, that's why I'm smiling. It saddened me to see her putting on such a brave face and to see her walking so bad. Much worse than I've ever seen her.'

Few people had seen Christina in the last few days but it wasn't surprising that walking would trouble her since she had taken a nasty fall.

'Mr Wrench, I wonder if I might ask something of you. I have to leave my room at the college now that I have graduated and I can't move the mare, possibly for a few weeks. I'd like to stay close until I've got her well enough to walk to the next stage.'

'Stay as long as you like.'

'A barn will do...and somewhere to put my things so long as I can stay out of sight.'

'It's yours. But you must promise me one thing. You have to cure that horse. I'll not be able to face Miss Coleman if you fail.'

'You have my promise, sir.'

# CHAPTER 25

It was a strange, rootless period in my life. I was waiting for a horse to heal and I was looking for somewhere for my practice. I had my eye on Giltspur Street. It was perfect but not fashionable. Smithfield was very unprepossessing but it was in the heart of the city and that's where I was needed. The place abounded in heavy horses and other working animals and I often asked myself whether the modern family would eat without them. Dray horses were the lifeblood of the breweries and the warehouses while others brought us meat from Smithfield market and produce from all the gardens that surrounded the capital. If food had to be carried by hand our nation would probably starve.

Number 17 Giltspur Street was available, admittedly in a sad state, but I could make some repairs and it was cheap. The agent showed me around and I confess I barely looked at the accommodation the house offered since I was so struck by the spacious yard, the counting house and the stabling. The gates to the cobbled yard were hanging from their hinges but I could see them painted green with my sign picked out in black. There was stabling for at least six horses which was promising and a store for hay in a loft above. It was a serious prospect.

I stood outside the gates with my brother, Henry. I hadn't signed the lease but he knew my eagerness to do so.

The uneven street was muddy from yesterday's heavy downpour and two women rushed to get out of the way as a heavy wagon rolled past with a screech of its iron wheels. A flock of disgruntled geese was driven past us, flapping their wings and honking as if we were intruders.

The spires from St Bartholomew's and St Sepulchre's were visible and on the corner with Cock Lane was the famous inn, The Fortune of War. It was the very spot where the Great Fire of London was stopped and was marked outside the Inn by the statue of the Golden Boy of Pie Corner. Henry thought me foolish but it seemed fortuitous - this was a place where good things could happen. The notorious compter was a few yards down on the other side. The proximity didn't trouble me but I knew Henry would have words to say on the subject. Why set up shop so near a debtors' goal? Newgate Prison and the Old Bailey were also close by but so far there were too many faults to find with the property for him to notice the neighbours.

'Look at this pavement,' he grumbled. 'And you'll be lucky if these gates ever close.'

'They can be mended, brother.'

'More expense. The house is big, that I'll grant you.'

It was a three storey building that would once have been elegant; it would be more than adequate for my needs and the location was ideal.

'Is it worth the money, Henry?' I asked.

I was seeking his advice as well as his permission. He had been in business manufacturing biscuits for many years and knew more of London property prices than I ever would. My small inheritance from our mother would be insufficient to set me up because I had made such dents in it during my years at college and Henry's investment would make up the shortfall. What Smithfield lacked in charm it gained in affordability.

'It is…,' he said, taking off his hat and peering at the roof top. 'But that doesn't mean we can't negotiate. We'll get the price down.'

I signed the agreement the following week. I was in

business.

True, I had no patients. Well, I had one who was never far from my thoughts and I returned to Camden hastily before I became embroiled in the serious business of establishing myself. I walked from Henry's house in Holborn which was nearer than Giltspur Street hoping all the time that Firefly would be fit enough to make the journey. My plan was to stay at the Elephant and Castle's barn for a few more days so that I could trim her feet once again and gradually increase the length of our walks at night. So far, she was managing the fields well but I feared the cobbles of the city would cripple her. Once I took possession of my new premises she would come with me there.

Mr Wrench met me in the Inn yard. His little face was smug as he took me round the large store room to the tumble down stabling at the back that had the useful appearance of decay. Firefly was tied up, basking in the sunshine and cropping some nearby cow parsley while her stable was being swept clean.

'What do you think?' Mr Wrench asked. 'Notice anything different?'

The chestnut turned at our approach and pawed the ground. She seemed eager as if she was anticipating a walk; her desire to get away from the stable was evident.

'She's stopped paddling,' I said.

The foundered look had gone and she was fidgeting in a way I remembered when she was ridden, a horse in a hurry. She was no longer shifting her weight from one foot to the other, no longer getting the weight off her toes desperately searching for relief. She was the most comfortable I had seen her for a long time.

I examined her feet, pleased to find them warm rather than hot. Her pulse was calm and, most tellingly, she let me pick up each foot and clean it with my knife. She was reluctant with the left fore so I concluded there was some residual pain in the right.

'Remarkable,' I said. 'I'll walk her later and see what

she's like on rough ground.'

Mr Wrench shook my hand and I reminded him that there was still much to do.

'And you didn't use witchcraft,' he laughed. 'If anyone asks me I can vouch for that. I've kept my eye on this here horse and there's been no funny business. I don't know how you've cured her but there must have been something evil about those shoes. That I do know. Make sure you throw them away, won't you. There's no knowing what harm they might do if they're left in someone's stable.'

'Mr Wrench, they are only damaging if they're nailed onto the foot. I promise you.'

'Well, you mark my words. I'll not have them under my roof, nor in my shed.'

Mr Wrench became one of my early supporters. Sadly, I was right when I told him he had little influence, in the veterinary world he had none. If only Lord Northumberland had seen the difference in this horse once she was freed of her thin Grasshopper shoes. He was president of the College, he probably dined with the Prime Minister and he was certainly a good friend of Professor Coleman. One day, I promised myself, even he would listen to me.

I stayed with the horse, grooming her and filing her feet with my newly-purchased rasp. It was an easier job than last time but I was hot by the time I had finished and washed my hands and face in a bucket of cold water. I retied my hair and brushed the dust and dirt from my breeches, conscious that my day's work was too marked upon my person.

In need of some refreshment, I poked my head around the store to the yard. It was deserted save for Mrs Wrench's fowl who were scratching in the dirt and a dappled grey cob harnessed to a gig. I recognised the animal from the college and thought the stableman, John Bale, was likely on an errand. I kept to the shadows and inched my way backwards. My thirst would have to wait until he'd gone; it was foolish of me to walk about so boldly when any number of students could have come on foot from the college.

A voice I recognised drifted towards me. It belonged to the person I most wanted to see in the world who had now become someone I dreaded to meet. I knew she mustn't see me. How would I lie to her? And although I had a story at the ready she was the one person who shouldn't hear it.

I was hidden by the stone wall and its shadow. My mind knew we couldn't meet but my eyes wanted to feast on her. It would do no harm to look, to see how she was moving and how well she had recovered from the fall. I had promised to write to her but had neglected to do so. This wasn't laziness but my life had been consumed by the horse she thought was dead and I was damned if I would write to her about anything else. My stolen glances might have to last me a little while and I wouldn't give them up.

She emerged from the building and held onto the side of the door. She was wearing a pale yellow dress and a white shawl that was more decorative than practical. Her straw bonnet had a matching yellow ribbon and her hair was thick with curls. She looked just as I remembered but a little vacant, perhaps. Yes, she was staring through a gap in the buildings to the fields where cows were cropping the lush grass. Even with a mind drifting off to some better place she struck me as resolute and a little cross. She was too belligerent to be considered typically feminine but, to my mind, she was incredible. She hadn't let go of the door and her head turned as if she was waiting for someone.

William Sewell joined her and offered her his arm. She smiled and thanked him. I leaned back against the wall and closed my eyes. There was no escaping that image. I told myself he was merely currying favour with the Professor, that Christina was being nothing more than polite. Why shouldn't she smile? Did I really think I had a right to all her gratitude? Jealousy did me no favours and prompted me to take steps I should have avoided.

I should have listened more closely to their conversation. William hadn't changed and it was foolish of me to think of him as a rival. They were walking slowly towards the gig. Christina was talking softly and I couldn't hear her. William's voice carried.

'Why don't you wait in the gig? Rest here, that's the thing,' he said. 'Must be painful for you, undoubtedly uncomfortable. Very awkward.'

She said something and he looked taken aback.

'Heavens, I don't mind the speed. We can go…well, as slow as you like. You just tell me where you want to go. Happy to oblige.' He looked in my direction and I stayed close to the wall. 'We can walk there, if you insist. There's only a few tumble-down buildings and broken carts. Hardly the place but happy to play my part.'

I rushed to Firefly's stable. It was nicely shaded but we'd become lax and the top half of the door was open and the mare's sleepy head was lolling contentedly out. I pushed gently on her nose and told her to step back while I closed it.

'Come on. She mustn't see you, neither of them must. I could end up transported and you'll be food for the dogs and a pot of glue.' The mare objected to my harsh treatment. She nudged me back, not wanting to lose her place in the fresh air. 'Quick!' I insisted. 'If they come round that corner we're done for.'

I grabbed the top door and she finally shifted at the threat to her nose. Then I put some distance between us by resuming my position at the corner. To my relief William was nowhere to be seen and Christina was standing alone by the gig. She was fidgeting; her fingers were tapping the wooden seat while she idly watched the hens' lazy, scratching ritual. I should have stayed where I was, where I could delight my eyes, but the temptation was too strong. The thought of talking to her was so appealing that I forgot how duplicitous I might appear.

'Christina!' I whispered as I approached.

I startled her but her sweet face made me bold; her smile assured me I was welcome.

'Bracy,' she said, loudly. 'What are you doing here?'

There! I was already in trouble. My lies had to start.

197

Only they caught in my throat. 'I…I…wanted to see you,' I stammered. 'I had to.'

'And now you have. You could have called in St Pancras Way. Why would you not do so? Would you really have gone back to London without coming to see me?'

'I could hardly do so when he's told me not to?'

'Ah, but that was when you were one of his students. He could command you then but not now,' she said, putting her hand tentatively in mine. 'He wouldn't say that to a qualified vet, surely.'

'I expect he would but no doubt you are a better judge. Perhaps you are right.'

She took in my dusty, working clothes and reached the obvious conclusion. 'Have you come to see Mr Wrench's horse? You look hot. I know you've been working. He thinks very highly of you, he was saying so only the other day. Your first customer.'

'Yes,' I said, hastily kissing her hand.

'Which one? The grey?'

Mr Wrench was the proud owner of two animals having bought a useful hack last month. I nodded towards the stables. 'Yes, he wanted me to check him.'

'But Bracy. He's in the field.'

'Is he?'

'Yes! At least I think so. He wasn't in the stable. Did you examine him in the field? And now you look so confused? You've gone quite red. Don't worry, I won't tell Edward. It's nothing to do with him anymore where you check your patients.'

'They must have turned him out,' I mumbled. 'Have you come to see Mrs Wrench?'

'Yes, William was coming this way on an errand for Edward but she's not at home.' The familiar use of Sewell's first name made me bristle. 'I thought we might go for a walk but...' She laughed as though I might share the joke. 'The prospect made him trip over his words more than I trip over my feet. Oh, Bracy. I have an idea,' she said, gripping my hand.

'You can take me. No one will let me go anywhere now unless it's towards a sofa. I can't tell you how bored I've been. Everyone fussing over me but not letting me do a thing. Fine! I don't have to ride, I know it's dangerous and everyone worries. But I can walk. And now you, of all people, look alarmed.'

'No, no. Of course I'm not,' I protested.

'No? You suddenly seemed frightened. I saw it in your face. It dropped. If you will only let me lean on your arm a little, I've got a little worse since the accident but if we don't rush I can manage perfectly well. We can go towards the fields. You can show me what's wrong with Mr Wrench's grey.'

'No…no, we can't do that,' I said. 'It wouldn't do at all.'

She was moving towards the back of the Inn where Firefly was hidden. Her hand was resting on my arm but my body tightened. My refusal told its own story and she flinched.

'Nothing would give me greater pleasure but you must excuse me,' I said. 'I really haven't the time. I've hardly had a moment to myself since qualifying you must understand.' I was grabbing at excuses, anything that came into my head. 'My situation is very different.'

'And not just your situation,' she said, archly.

'What do you mean?'

'Very different. In fact you are not the man I know.' Her hand slid from my arm and she took a step back. She seemed confused and viewed me with ill disguised disappointment. 'Your situation has changed and so have you. I never thought to see your face like that. You've joined them, haven't you?' Her cheeks were an angry red but her lips were creased with tension.

'Joined who?'

'All the people who think I should sit down and stay at home. Oh, they may not say it to my face but I'm not stupid.'

'I never thought you were.'

'But I know what they are thinking. They would like me to spare their anguish, they don't want to see me wriggling around the lanes or stumbling over my own feet. It pains them to see me get out of breath when I've hardly gone any distance.

If I stay at home they can forget that I make such a mess of something they can do without giving a moment's thought to the matter.' She sighed and focused on the fields beyond the Inn. 'Ah, but on a horse I was better than all of them. How funny is that?'

'I know you were…and will be again.' She snorted as if she didn't believe me. 'If you doubt me then you malign me. Your brother, on the other hand, is someone who would rather you stayed indoors.'

'Yes, but at least he suggested I came with William today.'

I bet he did, he probably sees Sewell as a means of marrying her off. Getting her off his hands. 'Did he really?' I asked. 'And is he encouraging you to ride again?'

'He would hardly do that when I'm still getting over the accident. He's cautious and protective, nothing more. It's understandable, I suppose, when you think that I am all he's got.'

I thought back to the Professor's disparaging comments about Christina. He'd said she was wilful and difficult to control. Not only had he thought it unhealthy for her to ride, he also considered it unseemly and an embarrassment.

'He never wanted you to ride,' I said.

'That's not true. Bracy, I wish you would stop hating him. You have graduated now. Isn't it time you let it go? You forget that it was Edward who bought me Firefly and even though I have lost her, she's not forgotten. He couldn't have given me a greater gift.'

'He regretted it.'

'Oh, many times but he never took her away, did he?'

Ah, but he did, I told myself. Why can't you see through him? I might absolve him of a deliberate, callous act, but he got rid of Firefly as surely as if he was holding the knife. He crippled her and in so doing he has crippled you, my darling.

'Believe me, Christina, he was responsible for her lameness. Perhaps he wanted to stop you riding more than I realised. Perhaps he didn't know he was doing it but he might as well have plotted that animal's downfall.'

'Oh, really?' she said with a look of horror. 'This is the head of the veterinary college you are accusing. My brother. He took great care of Firefly; you wouldn't say this had you seen his worried face in the evenings. He did not ruin my horse. I did that myself.'

'Oh, spare me.'

'I rode her too fast.'

'He desperately wanted you to stop riding.'

'Nonsense.'

'He told me himself. In his consulting room that day. I remember his very words. Christina is not like other women, Clark. She walks with great difficulty, she tires easily and I have the devil's own job to stop her from exhausting herself.' She looked at me sceptically. 'Those were his words.'

'Quite possibly.'

'He said you were wilful.'

'I am.'

'She even insists on riding every day saying it's good for her.' I mimicked the languorous voice I knew so well.

She laughed. 'Well, I did, if you remember.'

'How can all that jolting on the back of a horse help a limb that's already in such a mess? She doesn't care what the weather is doing; she'll even go out in the rain and it's my opinion that the damp won't help her either. There now, you must believe me.'

'I know all this. He worries about me. That's all.'

'It's not all.'

'Well, I don't want to hear any more. You're saying this because you hate him. You are a scientist; you should be above such pettiness.'

'How can you call me petty? This is your life we are talking about.'

'And now you are being hateful.'

'Please listen to me.' I held her arm because she looked as though she wanted to get away, not that she could go anywhere very fast. 'He complained that you wouldn't listen to the doctors and he fervently wished you would stay at home. He hated you riding. Careering about the countryside, he called it.'

'And in the end it seems he was right,' she said, fighting the tears in her eyes. 'It's too dangerous for me. The things I did, all the risks I took. He didn't know about half of them, thank goodness. Why, I even thought I could jump her. How ridiculous I was to even attempt it. I should remember that I'm a cripple.'

'Don't use that hateful word.'

'Cripple? Don't be silly.' She turned away from me and wiped one eye. 'I won't ride anymore.'

'You must!' I growled.

'And now you are being angry at me. It's nothing to do with you.'

My temper was rising, pushing aside all thoughts of holding her. I should have been a comfort to her, she'd had an accident and lost her horse but the tension of the past weeks was playing havoc with my reason.

'Of course it's my concern.'

'The trouble with you is that you want to cure everything. Including me.'

'Is that so very bad?'

'Yes! It is. Sometimes we have to accept loss.'

'But not a half life.'

'My life is very full…but I have to accept that it's changed and very soon it won't seem boring. You never got over that mare, the one who died from gripes. Then you thought you could get Firefly better and, frankly, your interference only made it harder to bear. Edward was right to end her suffering quickly. He saved both of us a lot of pain.'

'Well, I'm sorry if you found my foolish attempts…'

'I didn't say you were foolish…but you need to know when to let go.'

'And is that what I should do with you? Is that what you want? To leave you where you feel safe and unchallenged? With him?'

She looked shocked. She'd seen me this angry before. Our first meeting was coloured by my tirade against her brother but now the full force of my frustration was directed at her and she didn't answer me. Later, I realised I had gone too far. She had only ever seen kindness from me. Sweet words and gentle encouragement had taken her from the innocence of childhood into my arms and now she was feeling the sharp reality of their tight grip.

Thankfully, we were interrupted before I could say more. William came out of the Inn with Mr Wrench beside him. What a strange pair they made; one tall and pale, the other wiry and short. William was surprised to see me but greeted me affably, mumbling that the Inn was to host an anniversary dinner for the college that he hoped I would attend. I nodded and said I would be delighted.

'By the way, Wrench,' William said. 'You've a horse round the back there, shut in. With its door closed.'

'Have I? Oh, yes…of course I have.'

'I'm glad Professor Coleman hasn't seen it. He'd have some things to…to say about fresh air. Very good for the respiratory system. Isn't that right, Bracy?'

'It's not been well, though.' Mr Wrench's eyes darted about giving him the looked of a worried rabbit. 'Mr Clark advised keeping it calm like.'

'With no fresh air!' Christina was outraged. 'The horse will get ill, surely. What's the matter with it?'

'A minor injury,' I said. 'But the door's only to be kept shut while the horse eats.'

'That's right. Never finishes otherwise,' Mr Wrench confirmed.

'Well, I've opened it. Seemed the only thing to do. Pretty thing.'

There was silence for a few minutes while I, and no doubt Mr Wrench, waited to see if the Professor's assistant would say more. He'd seen Firefly many times but he hadn't recognised her. I couldn't believe my luck, or my stupidity in leaving her this long in a place where she could be spotted. I could swear Christina was bursting to go and see the animal; had our conversation been more amicable I'm certain she would have asked me or eagerly discussed its care in depth. She was the picture of irritation and turned to go. I was spared but I wouldn't rest until I had moved the mare to another place.

# CHAPTER 26

'You can leave those things here,' Mr Wrench said, surveying the barn with a worried eye. 'You'll need to travel light but here's my advice. Put a saddle and bridle on her. That way it will look as though the horse has gone lame and you're walking it home. You don't want to look as though you're leading a horse you've just stolen so put on your smartest clothes. On second thoughts, you don't want to look wealthy and attract the footpads.'

I laughed and said there was no danger of that. 'I don't have her saddle and bridle. They are at the college, no doubt, where they will have to stay.'

'I can lend you something but it worries me that you're doing this walk at night. It's not safe even for someone of your size, if you'll pardon me saying. You must take a knife with you and keep to the fields where you can. Trouble's best avoided is my motto. Dick Turpin might have gone to the gallows long ago but there's plenty who have taken his place and because you're strong you seem to think the world will do you no harm. You're too trusting by half.'

I wasn't worried about footpads but I would keep well away from the Turnpike and use my sense of direction to cross fields and woods to make sure I stayed unnoticed until I'd put this area behind me. I had no idea how long it would take to

205

get to the capital as we would have all the speed of a heavy wagon in deep mud. My plan was to find soft ground and hope I could get to Giltspur Street in one night. It was three miles, an easy ride on a sound horse but with Firefly still limping it was impossible to say how long it would take.

Mr Wrench stood with his hands on his hips and kicked at a pile of old hay sending up enough dust to look like the smoke of a lit fire. The sun was making itself felt today, sending bands of light to the floor through the wooden walls and heating the interior of the barn until it was almost airless. Most of my books had already gone to Henry's but my clothes were here and looked a sorry burden. I didn't amount to much; I wasn't even much of a prospect. Most of the populace hadn't heard of veterinary surgeons and although I might think of myself as a liberator I was acting like a horse thief stealing away under cover of darkness. My actions were not likely to recommend me.

'Shouldn't you stay a few more nights?' he said. 'That mare is still sore on those feet and you know it. She'll make very slow work and if there's trouble you'll hardly be galloping away. I'd rest easier if you left at daybreak. There's no sense courting trouble.'

'If I'm seen in the daytime the journey could be over before it's hardly begun. Having William see her was a close call and I'll not take the risk again. Thank goodness he didn't recognise her. We have imposed on you long enough.'

I put a change of clothes into a knapsack. I had offered Mr Wrench money for our accommodation but he'd looked offended and refused to take so much as a penny. I hoped one day I would be able to repay his kindness for he'd taken a huge risk harbouring such fugitives.

We left his care that night but not before both of us were fed and watered. Mrs Wrench packed me some bread and cheese and there were some oats for Firefly stowed in one of the saddle bags. It was good to see the mare saddled and bridled since it made her look like a quality riding horse again although it was a pity she was so distinctive. Had she been a serviceable cob with a heavy head she'd hardly draw attention to herself but there was no disguising the quality of her bloodlines.

Thanks to the riding I had done while I was at the college I had no trouble finding a route across the fields. Many of them had been cut for hay and gave off a sweet smell as we kept to the edges, listening for danger in every thicket. I hadn't been worried about footpads, not while I'd been reassuring Mr Wrench, but now his words hit home and I found myself tense. The noises of animals scurrying were enough to give me pause but the mare was calmer than I could have hoped for. She was alert but not skittish and didn't falter even when an owl broke cover with a screech that forced the air from my lungs.

I kept telling myself that I wasn't stealing; this was an act of mercy even if it had been undertaken in the most suspicious circumstances but guilt plagued me once my fear of thieves receded. Well, I had to think of something, I suppose, since the horse wasn't a talkative companion.

I was looking for a gate at the end of one of the fields that would lead me to another ripening with corn. There was enough light from a three-quarters moon for me to see the hedgerows but for a while I thought I might have missed the opening. I hadn't factored the steadiness of our progress in the equation. Finally, I found the place, opened the gate and led the mare through, closing and retying it again after us. The corn field was bordered by a row of poplar trees which rustled in the soft breeze like the sound of running water and then I remembered there was a little brook further on and thought that would be a good place to rest if only for a few minutes. It felt like an achievement when we got there. Firefly appreciated the reward of some grass under the trees, apparently there's nothing better after a diet of hay, and she wanted to drink. She pulled me towards the water and sighed once her feet were in the soft mud of the stream.

It seemed the cooling effect of the water was soothing. Horses often know what's good for them and we humans need to take note. I let her enjoy herself, taking a drink myself a little way upstream so that I would conserve my own water supply. Then she started pawing at the water, splashing it playfully, soaking herself and giving me a wetting. She snorted as though it was a job well done.

'You don't want to leave here, do you?' I said, giving her a few more minutes. 'You see, life is worth living, Firefly. Aren't you glad you did not give up?' She butted me forcefully with her head and there was no knowing whether that was a sign of agreement or not. 'You do realise that I am risking my future for you, you ungrateful mare? So, don't push me into the stream, if you please.'

She took another drink and settled peacefully. I knew I might have trouble moving her on again and finally persuaded her to leave with the offer of some oats. She was limping slightly but horses bear pain well and to be honest she got used to it and so did I. She was happy to follow me and indeed there were times when her walk improved and she took the lead.

It proved more difficult on less familiar territory. I was blundering through the fields not knowing where the gates were, having to turn back, searching for gaps in hedges that were hard to find once clouds obscured the moon. We skirted around the grounds of the three-storey smallpox hospital at Battle Bridge. I could see the imposing edifice against the moonlit sky looking peaceful amid its tree-filled gardens. Further on were some market gardens where Firefly could graze and rest. She was too busy to steal my bread and cheese and so we ate companionably, enjoying the solitude. This place would be buzzing with activity in a few hours and some of the gardeners might be known to me so I couldn't linger.

Eventually, there was little soft ground for the horse and the roadways of London welcomed us. It would have been a cheering sight but an animal that struggled across a field was suddenly made worse for the uneven, hard cobbles. She kept stopping as though she couldn't believe I could ask her to cover such ground. The granite slabs of the pavements were a little easier and she would take a few steps only to come to another sudden halt. She didn't seek to go backwards and I didn't know which way to turn.

I let her rest again, not that I had much choice, and questioned my wisdom in trying to cure this horse. I should have found a field for her and undertaken this journey in six month's time but she would have been too near to Camden. We had to keep going for both our sakes but I was riddled with doubts for making her suffer. I didn't become a veterinarian to inflict this pain and I felt I was little better than the master who used whips and spurs to beat his horse. Oh, look around you; every day you see horses straining to pull loads that should be given to an elephant. They are forced and beaten until they are fit for nothing and yet they bear it with such fortitude.

Firefly was well treated next to those poor creatures but I would have to get tough if we were to finish the journey because I couldn't risk staying at an inn or a livery stables. How suspicious we would look. A poorly dressed, young man with a lame horse of quality, one that would have been ridden by a lady. I would be forced to tell all sorts of lies and most likely wouldn't be believed. Giltspur Street had never seemed so far away.

I detached one rein from her bridle so that I had enough length to form a whip. Swinging it in the air made her stir but wasn't enough to make her move. She had to feel it on her rump before she lurched into action once more. After that I only had to swing the rein behind her to keep up her lumbering movement.

London was never deserted but at least anyone abroad had little desire for conversation and passed us with heads down and eyes averted. The night soil men ignored us and carried on their work although their horse gave Firefly an appreciative glance.

There were a few hackney cabs about and by now it was impossible to say whether they were finishing work late or starting early. Their horses' shoes clattered loudly on the cobbles so that we could hear them coming two streets away whereas Firefly was a stealthy individual. She padded rather than struck the ground but by the time we were walking down Grays Inn Road she was tiring again and I gave her a few oats to keep her spirits up while we watched the beginnings of the day. The dark was becoming fainter and deliveries were being made. There was a coal cart with its sulphur smell and countless wagons bringing food to this place that couldn't feed itself. There were two men herding some cows, no doubt trying to get to a slaughterhouse before the streets became crowded.

As we drew further into the city there were more people about - an amorous couple in a doorway and under a tree there was someone asleep in a pile of rags; not one of the fashionable areas, I gathered. I was approached by a woman who called me *love* and stroked my face. Her plumpness was on full display and she had the reddest cheeks I'd ever seen but she laughed when I told her it wasn't safe for her to be out so late. She tried to detain me by grabbing my hand, saying I was a fine gentleman and wouldn't I like to go with her and buy her some gin.

Then I realised her motivation and gave her some pennies. It was all I could spare but they didn't make her smile and I left her full of abuse towards me. I was looking for Lincoln's Inn Fields thinking it would be a good place to rest. I had a country boy's excitement at being here and realised it was such a different place at night. The sounds were softer and it was possible to hear echoes and footsteps that would have drowned in the cacophony of the day. I was losing track of time until I heard the first bird song. It was like a revelation because I hadn't thought you would hear such a glorious thing in a city like this but of course there were birds here too and they woke up with the same joy as if they remembered fields and hedgerows.

I began to think I was being followed but couldn't say whether it was shadows from the tall buildings or the unfamiliar noises of the town that were tormenting me. The horse wasn't alarmed, or was past caring, but whenever I stopped so too did the sound of another footfall.

I took the mare into a side street and waited to see if anyone would appear. They did. Two of them. They can't have been older than teenagers and the sight of them in their ragged clothes forced a laugh into my throat since one of my arms was probably thicker than any of their legs. I was about to tell them to get off home when I saw one had a knife.

'Don't be so daft,' I cried. 'Do you really think to take me on? Even with a knife we are a little ill matched, don't you think?'

I stared at them, my hands on my hips, and felt like cuffing them around their heads. I would have done were it not for their ridiculous weapon. One of them was taunting me, waving it towards me but I wouldn't move backwards and was ready with my booted feet.

'You're outnumbered,' he said.

He seemed to think the knife made his threats worth listening to. The other one was anxiously telling him to hurry up, to get it done.

'Listen, you two...'

'Three!' the nervous one muttered, nodding towards a spot behind me.

I finally gave them the respect they deserved but it was time to relieve them of their weapon so I kicked out and had the satisfaction of hearing the clattering of steel.

'Now we are equal,' I said. 'Don't think about picking it up.'

The nervous one looked towards it, uncertain, while the other scoffed. I could sense the approach of the third. The horse was getting tense and began shifting her feet as though she'd like to be gone and then she struck out with both back legs. There was a cry of alarm as the lad was thrown to the ground. The others weren't sure whether to risk going past the mare to see to him and stayed where they were in spite of his groans.

'You've killed him,' one of them complained.

'Hardly,' I said. 'Sadly, I think he will live long enough to learn not to approach a strange horse from behind.' I picked up the knife and held it by the blade. 'Oh, I'm not going to use it on you, never fear. What did you hope to achieve apart from some broken bones? I have nothing on me apart from the remains of my bread and cheese which you could have had for the asking.'

They eyed the mare and looked at me in disbelief. Ah, so they had thought to rob me of my horse or she had given them the impression I was worth closer inspection. I sent them on their way, minus their weapon with some worldly advice about honest toil but doubted they heard me.

We rested a while at Lincoln's Inn Fields where we were joined by more cattle and a man with a pig. Having floored a thief, Firefly surprisingly took exception to the pig and decided it was time to leave such a dreadful place. The pain in her front feet was forgotten in her rush to be away. All I had to do was follow and keep our direction easterly, towards the River and St Paul's.

The sun was soon pricking the sky and making the streets seem misty. How grey and milky it all was, shadowy and rather lovely. The houses became crowded. They were squat and less imposing before giving way to warehouses and industry. I could smell the stench of the River and the tanneries and breweries were not far away. It was a rich mixture of smells and it was no wonder they were not allowed near St James. I had forgotten how much dirt, rubbish and other unmentionable things littered the streets. I picked my way carefully and then I saw it.

St Paul's.

I was too close, I must have taken a wrong turn but it didn't matter. Its domed roof dominated the sky and left me awestruck. I leant my back against a wall and simply gazed at it. We would have to turn north again to find Giltspur Street but I knew it wasn't far now. I don't know how many hours it had taken us but we had made it.

# CHAPTER 27

Number 17 was mine and I had the key in my pocket. I no longer felt like a thief as I led the mare through its gates and found a place for her in its stables. For myself, there was a crudely furnished bedchamber and, in spite of my euphoria, I let oblivion claim me.

Those early days in my own premises were strange but exciting. I longed to tell Christina what I had achieved, even though the mare wasn't cured, but I couldn't. Not yet. So, I contented myself with writing to say that I was here, that I was thinking of her and longed to see her. I even took a risk and referred to that day we'd met at the Elephant and Castle saying there were reasons it had been so awkward and one day I would be able to confide in her. I hoped it would be enough. I felt the horse was keeping something alive between us only Christina didn't know it. How awful she must be feeling. She had lost her horse, her brother wasn't the kindest keeper and now she thought I had joined those who wanted her to live her days quietly and unnoticed. My letter would put things right. She would read between the lines and know I cared.

I promised myself that I would see her again in a few weeks but, if there was to be a future for us, I had to first establish my practice. That meant overcoming all the suspicion and distrust I knew to be out there and it meant taking lucrative business from the farriers.

My brother, Henry, was a successful businessman and proved a good mentor. He told me to have cards made and to visit all the warehouses and livery yards I could find.

'On foot?' I cried.

'No, that would look highly unfavourable. Why would they trust a poor man? Can't you use the mare?'

'Not yet.'

'Hire something until she's ready. It's worth the investment.'

So I did, although I doubt the lustreless hack would have impressed any potential customers. He was a brown gelding with hocks that turned inwards and made him seem a strange creature. He came on the rounds with me and seemed grateful for the rest every time we stopped.

My cards were taken willingly but I suspected many were thrown into the fire grate. Veterinary Surgeon - in bold, italic script. I lost count of the times I had to explain what it meant. One burly man who owned a coal yard on Newgate Street scoffed but at least he was honest.

'A surgeon! For a horse! I can hardly afford a surgeon for myself. Too expensive. Sorry, governor.'

'I would not charge a lot, sir,' I said. 'Please call on me if you have need. You have three horses at this yard, I believe, and I could keep them on the road for you better than any farrier. I'm in Giltspur Street.'

He laughed but tucked the card in his pocket. I should have toured the area on foot but I got back on the hack, refusing to be put off. There were thousands of horses in London. They thronged the streets, bringing food and goods into the capital and taking waste out again. Livery yards were on virtually every street, animals crammed into every mews. They were expensive to buy and maintain and businesses would fold without them. If horses were cheap and expendable my cause would be hopeless but I reasoned it was only a matter of time; they needed me.

There was a scene of chaos when I visited one of the

large timber merchants on Skinner Street. Men were shouting and running about and there was the sound of screaming from inside the workshop. I told a man on the periphery that I was a veterinary surgeon, new to the area.

'A surgeon,' he said, grabbing my arm and pulling me into the workshop. 'It's the youngster. Stupid lad fell in the fire.'

I was about to correct him when I saw the boy writhing in pain while someone attempted to bandage his leg. They were surrounded by people offering advice, telling him to keep still. He was badly burned; his face was almost as red as the wound he was fearfully trying to grip with his hands.

The bandaging ceased. Fortunately, so did his screaming and everyone moved back as I knelt down beside him and touched his shoulder gently.

'What is your name?' I asked.

'Tom,' he said, choking on the word.

'Well, Tom, I am not going to touch your hurt, do you see?' I said, lifting my hands. 'Will you show it to me?' Cautiously, his trembling hands released the limb and he looked at me in trepidation. I turned to one of the men looking on. 'Do you have a water trough for the horses?'

'In the yard.'

'Stand back, then,' I ordered.

I picked the boy up quickly, before anyone knew what I was about. He was thin but muscular and weighed as little as a coil of wire. I got hold of him without touching his injury and carried him out.

'No, I don't want to,' he wailed.

I thought he might start screaming or that the men might stop me so I moved hastily, hardly aware that I was followed by a crowd.

'The hurting will stop very soon, Tom,' I told him. 'Hush.'

I moved purposefully across the yard and placed him gently in the trough. His legs were in although his hold around my neck didn't slacken. Tears were streaming down his face and he gasped at the coldness of the water. He whimpered but he didn't yell. Gradually, the shock waned and relief took its place.

'That's put the fire out now, hasn't it? Stay there half an hour and then your wound can be treated with some salve and bandaged. A blanket might be helpful.'

Someone fetched a horse blanket which was placed around his shoulders and his audience looked on in relief and wonderment. I have often found that cold water can help a burn, especially if it can be applied early enough but the men looked at me as though I had performed some conjuring trick. I was thanked; I was treated with respect and someone commented that I must be an excellent surgeon. A man who appeared to be the governor shook my hand and told some of the others to get back to work.

'Thanks for that. His screaming was enough to drive my customers away all morning. Not that I blame the boy but, honestly, falling in the fire. You'd think I'd have enough to do without that.'

He looked at the sorry-looking lad with some affection so that I knew he held no grudge for the loss of potential business, a subject he turned to once he had got his appreciation out of the way. He asked how he could help me and promised a cut-price deal by way of thanks.

'I'm sorry to disappoint you,' I said. 'It's not timber I'm after although once I'm more established a new set of gates to my premises might be in order. I'm a veterinary surgeon who's new to the area and thought to introduce myself.'

The man, middle aged and fiercely strong, took on the blank look I was becoming familiar with.

'A doctor for the horse,' I explained. 'Fully trained in all the veterinary sciences. I can tend cuts and injuries, heal lameness and remedy most of the common ailments.'

'How did you know what to do for the boy? Did they teach you that at your school?'

'No, I apprenticed with a surgeon before attending the veterinary college but the remedy for burns was of my own discovery. I have some salve for him if you need it.'

'Horse salve?' he said, suspiciously.

'It works for both.'

'You gave up being a surgeon to doctor the horse?' he chuckled, touching his head, giving me the impression that there might be something amiss with my own.

I tried not to bristle. 'Your own business would sink without them. Look at the timber on that wagon. How would you deliver it without the dray? They're expensive to replace if they become broken down as so many are before they are even ten years old. With my help you will keep them healthy for a lot longer.'

He looked at me, ignoring the boy who was splashing in the trough as though he was playing in a stream with his friends. 'Think you can cure the gripes?'

'Not always. I'm working on a new medicine.'

'At least you are honest. What about canker? Thrush? Founder?'

'The first two are easy. Founder is difficult but given time I hope to understand the condition better. I have a mare with it and she is very nearly better. I hope to use her on my rounds in a couple of weeks.'

In truth, I didn't have *rounds* to go on but my emerging business sense told me to keep quiet about that.

'Alright. How will I find you if I need to?'

So I gave him my direction and while I didn't wish his horses to suffer any complaint or injury, I looked forward to the day I might get to know them better.

I shook his hand. 'Bracy Clark.'

'Wally Glossop. Tom's father. Thank you for helping him. You've spared me his mother's wrath and for that I'll give you a chance.'

I departed Glossop's yard with my spirits lifted. It had been a busy morning. I hadn't earned one penny but I had made an impression and word began to spread. My business cards were largely superfluous since most of my potential customers were poor readers if not illiterate. But they impressed the bigger merchants and I soon found that the city of London was a small, tight-knit community and once you won the trust of a few you were on the road to acceptance.

There had been no word from Christina. I was disappointed but not surprised since it might be hard for her to get a letter sent. Every week I sent her word of my progress. A full report was devoted to poor Tom Glossop especially as the lad helped me when I visited Calvert's Brewery the very next day. I asked for the head stableman and Hugh Duggan looked me over as though I might be a horse for sale; he didn't smile but took my proffered hand, assessing the strength.

He spoke in a slow, thoughtful way. 'Water? Nothing more?'

Being familiar with the speed of gossip, I knew he was asking about yesterday's events. 'Water took the heat from the burn, certainly. Some salve and bandaging were applied later.'

'I heard you were at the place out in Camden that some Frenchman opened. Do you really expect me to trust that?'

'Being a man of sense I think you would especially as you have the care of some of the finest horses in the city. I can see at a glance how well you look after them. Why shouldn't you benefit from the scientific discoveries that are helping medicine?'

'And what does your learning tell you about this one?' he said, leading me along a line of empty stalls until we reached a dark bay Shire who looked the picture of health.

A test!

I asked for the horse to be brought out of the stall. He wasn't lame and Mr Duggan didn't favour me with the nature of the animal's complaint. I had to find it for myself. I had devised a series of checks that would assess a horse being considered for purchase and made use of that same routine. So, I looked at his teeth, felt all his legs, his feet – looking for pain or heat. I knew he hadn't lost his appetite because he had been eating hay but something had to be hurting for him to be idle and off work.

It was the point of the shoulder. Pressure from my

fingers caused the animal to flinch.

'I'd like to see him with a collar, please,' I told one of the grooms. This was put on with some fussing from the horse. 'It's a common injury for a harnessed horse. Bruising and sometimes sores caused by the collar and the harness. Fortunately, you've stopped him working before any real harm's been done. I would advise using him lightly from a breast plate until this has healed. I can give you something for it. The collar doesn't fit very well, I'm afraid.'

Mr Duggan was a man of few words but he told me I was hired. It took me two pages to tell Christina of my happiness at this outcome. Such a customer! And so soon.

Two weeks later I put a sign with a picture of a horse on my newly mended gates and returned to my stables where Firefly was the lone resident. The hired hack had been returned to the livery yard and the mare came with me on my rounds, saddled but not ridden. She was bearing her solitude well and it was my practice to give her the run of the yard when I was at home. Her feet were improving and now that our daily walks were on the uneven cobbles they were toughening up. I was big for her but felt confident that soon she might carry me for part of the day.

I wondered what I could tell her rightful owner, whether the time had come to confide but Christina's silence made me hesitate. Surely, she could have got word to me by now but there was a risk that someone else might open my letters and I knew I had to remain quiet a little longer.

The weeks turned to months and my patience was at breaking point as there was still no letter from Camden. I thought of returning there for why shouldn't I simply knock on the door and ask to see her? But my possession of her stolen mare made me reluctant. We'd had an understanding though; she'd told me she'd wait for me and in spite of her silence I had no reason to fear she had changed her mind. I was disappointed, I missed her but we had a future together...once my practice had grown everything would be fine.

Both Fred and Edmund urged me to say nothing, fearing an accusation of theft. I had involved them in my *crime* and allowed myself to be influenced. Edmund made himself particularly nervous by reading the Newgate Calendar with its ghoulish accounts of the latest crimes and their punishments. They had set themselves up in practices a couple of miles away and we kept in touch especially once we began publishing *The Veterinarian*. It was good to be able to get my findings down on paper and share my research with others. The evils of shoeing were my greatest worry, fearing it was responsible for many of the horses' ills but we covered so many topics that would interest owners and grooms responsible for their care.

While I was busy, so too was Professor Coleman. He was slowly filling the capital with his three-month pupils and I could picture the day when there would be one of his so-called vets on every street corner.

I met one attending a horse with gripes at a cramped livery yard in Brook Mews. I watched him battling to get a dose down the animal's throat but I could see from the bottle that his medicine would be ineffectual. It was yet another of Professor Coleman's patented brews and consisted of turpentine and water – nothing else.

The horse's discomfort abated as it often does in these attacks only to return with more vigour an hour hence. The vet hurriedly presented his bill to the stableman who introduced us with red-faced embarrassment. It was a large livery yard and no single vet had secured the patronage of those owners who had turned their backs on the farriers for doctoring. We greeted each other in a friendly manner but my colleague started when he heard my name. His eyes fell to the ground and he was guarded when I asked about his gripe mixture and its ingredients. I was determined to draw him out so I complimented him on his handling of the horse.

'It will help you a lot.' Thinking of William Sewell, I told him, 'One of my fellow students was so nervous of horses that I was sure he made them ill. He certainly couldn't cure them.'

'Is that so?' he said, with much hostility.

'Yes, I remember him examining a horse with worms. He didn't spot the trouble and was convinced there was something wrong with his teeth.'

'Hmmm…I expect we all make mistakes in the beginning. We do our best for them but there's always some that think they know better.'

He could have been talking about Professor Coleman but I was the more likely target. Perhaps he'd been conscious of me watching him work and feared I wanted to encroach. He turned away and began packing up his black leather bag.

'Indeed, we never stop learning,' I said. 'But you have such a head start thanks to your natural ability with the animal. To my mind, it's something that can't be taught. At least, he never learnt the skill.'

'I'm sure he got by. He'd be better for them than the farriers, you forget that.'

'Believe me there's not a day that I don't remember.'

'We're an awful lot better than nothing.'

'Very true.'

'And the college is making its mark.'

'It will. It will.'

Given time and a new professor at its head. He faced me. His body was tense as if he feared my reaction and then spoke quietly. 'He says you were a lot of trouble.'

'The Professor and I didn't always see eye to eye.'

'And he says you're still causing a lot of fuss even now.'

'Really? I don't see why he would say such a thing.'

He viewed me suspiciously. 'At least, I think it was you. Said you were in practice in the city.'

'I am but…'

'It sounded as though you were mighty eccentric and yet you seem pretty level headed to me. It's your articles on shoeing that are making people laugh at you.'

My discomfort was gaining pace. 'I don't think I have written anything amusing.'

'Well, don't take offence but it's the daftest thing wanting the horse to go around on its bare feet. Some would say it was cruel and I don't suppose you'd go without your own shoes, now would you? And to make out that Professor's Coleman's shoes are even worse. Well!'

'My attack on shoeing was not personal and I wasn't suggesting that horses go barefoot; most of them wouldn't cope on the cobbles. If you read the piece you'd know I was suggesting a flexible shoe but the Professor is too busy making money from all his nailed-on versions.'

He grunted and began to move away from me but I needed to forget my own chagrin and find a way to keep him here. It wouldn't be long before his patient showed signs of renewed distress by my reckoning. My smiles grew in spite of his cool demeanour and I returned to my tale of William Sewell and how he'd once been unable to diagnose a horse with diarrhoea until he'd slipped in the mess.

The man laughed and, for the first time, looked at me honestly and without embarrassment. I continued in this vein until he began to tell me of his own time at the college and how dear Professor Coleman had secured places for so many of them with the cavalry regiments. His name was Robert Brough and he'd chosen to set up practice near home as he had a wife and three children. He must have been older than me by a few years and was delighted to be earning more money as a vet than he had as a linen draper.

No wonder these people were so in awe of a professor who had made them into quacks and given them financial security. My colleague's reticence was finally abandoned and he talked about some of the larks they'd got up to in Camden.

Then he turned to me; his face quivering. 'Miss Coleman keeps herself away from the students, not like in your time, Mr Clark.'

'Indeed?'

'Well, I probably only saw her twice in all the time I was there. Dreadfully shy, I'd have called her but they do say she didn't used to be. Shame about her really, terrible for the Professor, her being crippled.' He ran on in spite of my look of discomfort. 'He never said much himself although he always looked pained any time she was mentioned. It was his assistant who told me.'

I swallowed what felt like a stone. 'Told you what?'

'About you chasing after her. Arranging to go riding with her, that sort of thing. I didn't credit half of it because I've seen her try to walk so she'd hardly be dashing about the fields on the back of a horse, would she?'

'It's hard to believe, certainly.'

'Of course now that I've met you I can see that none of it's true. Why would a personable fellow like yourself trouble a girl like that? Really, I didn't know where to look when I saw her moving.'

'I hope I wouldn't trouble any woman,' I said, stretching to my full height.

'No?' he laughed. 'The funniest thing is he said you had plagued her with letters every week and the poor thing had to throw them on the fire. Don't worry, I know it's nonsense. Mr Sewell has the liveliest imagination.'

'He can add it to his accomplishments.'

Why? Why would she throw my letters on the fire? I couldn't believe it. Surely, she would never be so heartless. There were shouts from the stables that curtailed my wanderings. I prodded my friend into action.

'You're needed,' I warned him coldly, nodding towards his distressed patient.

He appeared surprised and worried, saying he had run out of gripe mixture and what was he to do.

'Here, take some of mine,' I fetched my bag and shoved a bottle into his hand.

'What's in it?' he said suspiciously.

'Pimento berry, mainly. It's a warm stimulant and will help to restore the digestive process. I have found it very effective.'

He took the bottle from me and was gone.

# CHAPTER 28

His words lingered. And, like a scattering of seeds, they took root.

So, she had received my letters...and she hadn't welcomed them but had put them on the fire. It was hardly surprising then that she had not replied. Well, she should have penned me one line telling me to cease so I could have saved myself such effort...let alone the paper and the ink which everyone knows to be costly. It wasn't long before I found myself glad that she had set light to my words for at least no one else would read of my foolishness. For weeks, may be more, I stayed away from the coffee house where I met my friends. I carried on with my work, I went on my rounds and cared for my patients but I didn't want anyone to see me in this sorry state. We'd had an understanding and yet she could treat me like this without one word of explanation, without reading my letters. Did she have no interest in me at all? I forced myself to believe it but...

I left that livery yard with my mind in uproar. There was an embarrassing mist in front of my eyes and, although I could remember the next horse I had been commissioned to tend, the name of its owner was beyond me. There was a good chance I might have lost his patronage but fate was kind because I forgot to present him with my bill so no doubt he forgave my churlishness.

The happiness of my friends required all my patience in the months that followed. Edmund was courting but Fred was better company since he appeared to enjoy a multitude of women, none of which distracted him from his writing.

My brother, Henry, was the only one who saw past my assumed contentment although he never alluded to it. Instead, he took action – at least, I assumed it was his doing when I joined him and his wife, Anne, one evening.

'Oh, Bracy.' Anne dabbed her mouth with a napkin and pushed her plate to one side. 'I met Isabella Penfold's sister at last. I've forgotten her name. But never mind, you'd like her, you have so much in common.'

'Oh? What is she like?'

We were lingering at the dinner table; the dark oak had such a deep shine that it reflected the candelabra with its expensive wax candles. There was red wine in our glasses, an unusual occurrence since we weren't enthusiastic drinkers, but it was a special night and we wanted to mark it.

Anne fingered her dark brown hair which was seeping out of a lace cap. 'Well,' she hesitated. 'It's just that she's a very comfortable person. Her father is a pharmacist and so she would understand that your duties might call you from home at odd hours. She would make the perfect wife for a surgeon…or even a veterinary surgeon.'

I kept my dismay in check. 'Comfortable? You make her sound like a cushion?'

Henry eyed me with irritation; he'd put Anne up to this so he'd have to settle for my teasing.

She was quick with a superficial laugh. 'Oh, Bracy, you are funny. I didn't mean in that way; she's quite a thin girl, if anything, but very pretty. Now, why can't I remember her name?'

'You know, I wasn't thinking of marrying for a while.'

Henry rested his hand on Anne's and fingered her wedding ring. 'By the time you are much older you won't want to stay a bachelor. Being a married man has many advantages, you know.'

This was their wedding anniversary and there were cosy smiles that excluded me but didn't make me uncomfortable. Neither did they inspire me to set up near Green Park merely to snare a wife. The investment would cripple me and there were enough horses in the city to keep me in funds. I reasoned that I had more chance of buying Stubbs' portrait of Eclipse than winning a wife who interested me.

I had told them about Christina Coleman and they had smiled about my calf love as they called it. Neither of them was disparaging about her disability but neither did they take my fascination with her seriously. Perhaps it was the scientist in me that had been drawn to her. I had wanted to see how she wrung every ounce of joy from her narrow life. I came to wonder if my meddling with her horse was a way of getting close enough to cure Christina herself. She had accused me of it as though it was a crime and perhaps she was right.

Curiosity still had its hold on me. I often met some of Professor Coleman's dupes and would enquire about the man's family. He married a few months back and his sister resided with them. Sometimes, she was mentioned and I would feign some slight interest, not too much, I couldn't allow the pain she caused me to filter to the surface. It had been a year now since I last saw her, may be more. Enough…I should be myself by this time. I comforted myself with the thought that she had been a professional challenge so that the scientist was frustrated but the man was left untouched. If only the man could find other things to interest him, as the scientist had.

Perhaps I would turn to the likes of Miss Penfold for comfort. There was not a house in the city that would not welcome me as a suitor by now. I was the owner of two very fine coats, my breeches fitted me nicely, William Sewell might even acknowledge the precision of my neck cloth and my boots were polished. Even in these dark colours I felt like a peacock. Oh, I was not so fine a catch as a surgeon. They laughed at us still; looking down from their lofty rung of the ladder. But Edward Coleman and his ilk would open their arms. There it was again. A note of bitterness that I could do without.

'You look troubled, brother,' Henry said, breaking into my thoughts.

'He's lonely,' Anne said. 'He's a young man and he lives overlooking that stable yard of his. There are umpteen empty rooms and the only people he sees all day have four legs.'

They laughed. Quite heartily. 'I see my friends. My customers. There's my stableman.'

Anne took a minute to compose herself. 'And they no doubt talk about their friends who also have four legs. There's a danger that the horse will take over your life if you're not careful.'

'My dear, you are too harsh on the boy,' Henry intervened, a smirk on his face. 'I hope you are not trying to say he's becoming a bit of a bore. It's true that he spends all his waking hours pondering the ills of the poor animal...and his nights, too, by the look of his weary face but I'll not have you say my brother is too single minded.'

'No, no...I wouldn't dream,' she chuckled.

'Wasn't it only the other day that he delighted us with his opinion on the cause of cholera? Most of the time the horse dominates but sometimes mankind is given his attention. Have you never regretted giving up surgery, Bracy?'

'There have been times when your words have haunted me, brother, but not anymore. It's behind me now.'

Henry's mouth twitched on one side; the movement suppressed. 'It could be worse, Anne dear. It used to be insects. I would far rather hear about horses and their ills and why they don't need bits or shoes. You must remember him talking about the disastrous effects of shoeing and how it was making the foot shrink.'

'I'm going to prove it, too,' I said, latching onto the conversation with interest. 'One of my clients has a mare that's never been shod. He's letting me run an experiment with her and very soon I will be able to publish my findings. The veterinary college will have to take an interest. I must talk to them on the subject.'

Henry patted me on the shoulder. He was seven years my senior and apparently becoming more and more like our father who died when I was only two. He dressed soberly, which added to the impression, and his hair was prematurely thinning. It provided a dark, worn covering for his rather full, round head which was punctuated by soft, brown eyes. He was shorter than me; a fact which irked him, especially when he took it upon himself to influence my life.

'I'm sorry if I've been somewhat obsessed lately,' I said, a sigh escaping me.

Henry coughed. 'Not at all.'

'It's been an exciting time, you know.'

'We understand.'

'And I like to tell you what I've been doing.'

'We like to hear, I promise,' Anne said, with a smile. 'But we worry about you. We want you to be happy.'

'I am.'

'Happier then. Won't you meet Miss Penfold? I'm certain you would like her. You are established now; you could move your practice anywhere in London. She's such a sweet girl, I'm sure she would be happy near any of the parks.'

'Don't rush away with the idea, I haven't met her yet.'

'But you will! Oh, that's excellent. I shall arrange it. We'll have some of those cinnamon buns for tea.'

Sarah Penfold was perfectly sweet but I was determined to find her dull because my relatives were pushing her towards me with too much enthusiasm. I began to regret my lack of effort in cultivating connections of my own making for now I had to perform under scrutiny.

She was pretty but rather pale and thin and made me seem like a stupid prize fighter because I had so little refinement. Her fair hair was almost colourless as though the sun had caused it to fade and her eyes were big but watery. Her eyebrows were so pale they were impossible to see and I found myself staring at her as if I wanted to paint in her features with a small brush. She was a good match for the weather with its milky, grey clouds and bitter cold that made us think spring would never come.

We were neatly arranged one Sunday in the sitting room which faced the front of the house overlooking a square. Plane trees swayed in the light breeze reminding me of the earth's rhythm and I could hear the sound of people, horses and carriages obliterating any bird song. Most of the time I was too busy to miss the sounds of the countryside but now I longed to hear the call of a ploughman with his Shire or a lad scaring the crows.

Miss Penfold had come with her sister to tea and sat back in the chair by the fire as if she meant to stay. The room was warm, almost overheated, and the servant had taken coats and gloves before being dispatched for the tea things.

'Have you been to Ranelagh Gardens, Mr Clark?' Miss Penfold asked me once Anne had engineered me into the seat next to her.

I'd gone to the pleasure gardens at Ranelagh with some boisterous friends I'd known at school. They introduced me to too much wine and it wasn't my finest hour but it was an elegant place and I could picture Miss Penfold there.

'No, I've heard it's charming,' I said.

Henry, who remembered the state I was in on my return, overheard me and spluttered on his tea. Neither of us had been brought up accustomed to drink, our mother had frowned on it, the Quaker school had forbidden it and I had vowed never to sample so much ever again.

'It is absolutely delightful. Do you know, they have so many lights there…and the ham. It tastes like honey,' she said, with a weak smile and a wave of one tender hand.

How could Anne picture me married to this girl? What would we talk about? Although I hadn't known many women, I had gained enough experience to know what would be required of me since not all of my information had been gleaned from the farm yard. This girl would snap.

I felt my face redden. It was difficult to look at her once my thoughts turned to the onerous task of bedding her. Her lack of breasts was putting me off, there was no soft curve around her hips and although she was nicely dressed in a green, woollen gown I couldn't imagine ever wanting to see her without it. Why was it never like that with Christina? Images of Christina had always intruded when I least expected them. Even now. It was wrong to compare them but Christina had been so strong, so vibrant. A sigh escaped me, fortunately no one noticed. What a moment for the longing to return.

'I was wondering when you decided to become a veterinarian.' Miss Penfold repeated the question I hadn't heard. 'I'm sure it must be fascinating even though many people are suspicious of it.'

So I told her about the Frenchman and the post mortem of Eclipse. After five minutes she seemed rather breathless and I realised that even pharmacists fail to bring up robust daughters. I had achieved the impossible for now her lips matched her skin.

She rallied bravely however and asked, 'What made him die?'

'A simple attack of the gripes.' She looked confused so I explained. 'Stomach ache.'

'And that killed him! You'd think such a famous racehorse would have a more flamboyant end. How dull.'

'At least his life never had a dull moment; he was a very popular stud horse. In fact…'

Anne overheard me and was sadly familiar with the story that was on the tip of my tongue. I resolved to find another tale to entice young ladies; my social skills were wanting and my head was bereft of suitable topics. Anne called Miss Penfold over to her with the onerous burden of bringing me more cake; I wouldn't be able to say anything regrettable if I was chewing.

'Do you ride, Sarah?' Anne said, breaking into my meditative study of the carved oak sideboard. 'You must ask Bracy about the new horse he's thinking of getting. One of Lord Heathfield's, isn't it?'

'Oh, really?' Miss Penfold gasped in rapture. 'I love to

230

ride although I'm not sure I'm very good. They are such big animals and I'm afraid I bounce terribly when they run.'

'Bracy can teach you,' Anne laughed. 'He's quite an expert and he might have something in his stables that you can use. Such a pity you are in Giltspur Street but you could still bring a couple of the horses over here for the day. You would be able to get to Hyde Park in no time at all.'

Miss Penfold was agog at the prospect. Her wan face was suffused with colour, for the first time she appeared healthy and quite pretty. Anne was right; I was lonely but Firefly was Christina's horse. Surely, I couldn't give her to another woman to ride. It seemed such a betrayal.

'I would be delighted to take you riding, Miss Penfold. But the little mare I rode today is very lively, I'm afraid.'

'She's never seemed lively to me,' Henry muttered with a hint of a challenge. 'I've never seen a horse that was better behaved. I'd have thought her the perfect mount.'

'No, Henry, not for a beginner.'

Miss Penfold stepped between us with perfect adroitness by asking about the horse I hoped to purchase at Tattersall's next week. It was a stallion who had been backed and ridden but whose life had been predominantly serving mares. So, what was I to tell the delicate creature beside me? How quickly could I make her blush? I had a foolish urge to test her. Suddenly, the boredom left me. If she could cope with the conversation, perhaps she wouldn't be such tedious company and I might even take her riding.

'He would be a good buy because of the life he's led, he hasn't been ruined. His legs are good and he hasn't worn shoes for too long.'

'Why hasn't he?'

'So that he doesn't hurt the mares, you see.'

She didn't. There was a blank look that would have been charming had I been a man of delicacy and tact. Anne was distracted, talking to her friend, and Henry had left the room so there was no one to stop me talking openly and honestly.

'Why would he want to hurt them?' she laughed. 'You

231

wouldn't want to buy an aggressive animal, I'm sure. My father used to say to look for a soft, open eye in a horse. Never buy one that shows the whites of his eye but I'm sure you know all that.'

'Indeed. No, he's not an aggressive horse as far as I know but he's entire so naturally he needs to be handled with care.'

'Entire? I've never known that type before.'

'Not a type, Miss Penfold.'

Her questioning face turned to me. I bent closer to her ear until I could smell the sweet scent of her hair. 'He's a stallion. It's usual to keep them without shoes while they are at stud so they don't injure the brood mares.'

'Oh, I see.' She turned a healthy shade of pink and averted her eyes. 'I'm not sure you should…'

'Speak to you of it. You are probably right but being a woman of intelligence you asked me so many questions and it would have been ridiculous to fabricate nonsensical answers. Anne fears that I spend so much time treating horses that I might lose the ability to converse with humans. She might be right, I'm afraid; perhaps you could teach me if I took you riding.'

'Teach you to converse?' she laughed. 'Mr Clark, I fear you are teasing me.'

'Not at all. I have lost the art and would value your input. I would ask you to talk to me of the things that interest you – the latest news, books, fashions - and you must chide me every time I venture on another story about my wretched patients. Dead or otherwise.'

She simpered and nodded. 'Very well. You would need to find me a very slow horse, though. It was not false modesty on my part when I said I'm not a good rider. I hope you won't expect to go too fast with me.'

I could have told her there was little danger of me pushing her anywhere in a hurry. Then I remembered we were referring to horse riding and assured her that I was happy to keep to the pace she set herself. Miss Penfold would have an additional task, one she wasn't aware of. She could help me forget the memories that refused to shift; she could give my mind another feminine voice to latch onto.

There was an amateur portrait of our parents that hung in Henry's sitting room. I had no memory of Father and my young Mother was equally unfamiliar but I often turned to it when I was unsure of myself. They looked stern, as people do for portraits, and it seemed their frowns might have been aimed at me.

# CHAPTER 29

I had a perfectly suitable mare in my stables for Miss Penfold to ride but I was troubled. I couldn't return Firefly to Christina without confessing a serious crime but how could I hand her to another woman to ride?

Firefly had very little work to do once I bought the young stallion I was after. I named him Heathfield after his illustrious former owner and increasingly used him to visit my patients. Speed was in his blood and he was so eager to get out of the gates in the morning that I barely had time to get my feet in the stirrups but he was better than fine tailoring in my line of business. He gave my clients confidence and it wasn't long before I had earned his purchase price in fees.

So, in spite of my misgivings, Miss Penfold and I made Hyde Park a favourite destination. I did everything I could to improve her skills but there was only so much I could achieve with a rigid spine. Miss Penfold had no springs but she peppered me with questions.

'What will happen if those horses run past us?'

I reassured her that nothing would happen.

'How do I stop her going after them?'

'She won't. She'll stay with Heathfield. The lightest feel on the reins will stop her in any event.'

'Oh, we don't have to go as fast as they are, I hope?'

She saw another rider trot along one of the tree-lined avenues and her hands tightened on the reins until I was obliged to take them away from her, leading her from Heathfield as you would a child. It was a struggle to focus my mind and to stop myself thinking back to the time I had enjoyed the company of another rider, one who was filled with joy rather than fear. How easy it had been to talk to Christina. There had been no searching for suitable topics, no empty head to plough through. I forced a smile to my lips; I tried to enjoy the park.

It was at its best. The first decent day of spring saw the trees straining from their bark. The grass was muddy in places but new shoots were invading its dullness. We kept to the paths which meant we had to contend with more traffic but at least it was slow. It wasn't until our third excursion to the park that Miss Penfold fulfilled her part of the bargain by talking to me of something other than horses.

She was enchanted by the Royal Family and was relaxed enough to close her eyes a moment and say that the King and Queen didn't fall in love and get married, they married and fell in love. An enormous sigh escaped her and she glanced at me dreamily. I asked her quickly about some of the Royal children and she entertained me with the latest excesses of the Prince of Wales.

Of course, it being Sunday, there were no lords or princes to be seen. This day was for ordinary folk enjoying their one day of rest and putting off the beau monde who paraded there for the rest of the week. I saw one or two acquaintances – some were clients – and then we encountered my friend, Edmund.

I introduced them and Edmund grinned happily. 'Still no recurrence of the founder? You are to be congratulated. It's nice to see her ridden by a lady again.'

Miss Penfold was delighted, as if I was being praised for securing her company. Judging by Edmund's lop-sided smile his remarks could have been interpreted either way.

'Have you had her a long time then, Mr Clark? Even

though she's been unwell?' she said.

Edmund took up the story and gave it far too much embellishment. 'This horse is very lucky to be alive, Miss Penfold,' he said in conclusion. 'She had been ill treated and was due to be destroyed because she was so badly lame. Bracy took her on at great risk to himself.'

'What sort of risk! Was she dangerous?' she said, with a dreadful return of anxiety.

'No, no, nothing like that,' I said, signalling Edmund to cease singing my praises. 'It was very early in my career and there was always the danger that I would damage my reputation if I didn't cure her.'

'Oh, that's wonderful,' she said, relaxing her grip on Firefly's mane. 'I shall make sure everyone hears of it. So many people discard their horses when they become lame. It's quite dreadful.'

For the rest of our ride she related Firefly's history whenever she could. There was enough vanity in me to let her and so many people asked for my card that I was extremely pleased by the time I took her home to Park Street. Seconded by her father who stood smiling warmly at the door, she invited me to take tea with them. I could hardly refuse but when I saw the richness of the fruit cake being served it dawned on me that I was stirring parental expectations. Their treatment of me was in such contrast to my memory of Professor Coleman that my pride grasped their interest like dry skin would soak up oil. I had enough sense to be careful, reminding them that I was obliged to Miss Penfold for giving the horse some exercise.

'Such a treat for Sarah,' said Mrs Penfold. 'And such a beautiful horse, too. The perfect hack for a lady. Even Sarah, who the world knows is no rider, looked wonderful on her.'

Miss Penfold was serving tea to her father with all the gracefulness that escaped her on horseback. 'Mr Clark saved her from slaughter, Mama. She had a terrible illness in her feet and couldn't walk but he made it better. She was still limping when she came to London, you know, and he had to walk all the way with her. It took him four days.'

You see where embellishment leads. Four days! Very soon I would hear that I had swum across oceans with the poor mare. It would have been rude to correct her so I sat back as she related the story.

'Gracious, where did you bring her from?' Mrs Penfold asked.

'She was housed at one of the inns near Camden as a matter of fact,' I said.

'Oh, near the veterinary school?' Mr Penfold asked.

'Um…yes, that's right.'

'So many houses have been built there that I wouldn't recognise it, I don't suppose,' he said. 'I'd imagine the owner didn't want the mare if she was that lame. Still, their loss is your gain, wouldn't you say? You could always sell her if you have no use for her especially if they never paid for all the treatment you gave her. You know, I might even be interested in that horse myself.'

'I'm sorry, sir. I couldn't part with her.'

'You see, father. Mr Clark is sentimental as well as modest. She was one of his first cases and he will probably keep her until the day she dies. That way he knows no harm will ever come to her.'

'You mistake me, Miss Penfold. I don't feel as though she is mine to sell.'

'There's no room for sentimentality in a medical man,' said her father. 'Leastways, not if you're a surgeon but mayhap you vets are different. But if she's not yours to sell, how can you justify keeping her?'

'You're right. I don't know that I can,' I said. 'I happen to know that the owner can't look after her so I hold her in trust. One day it would be my greatest pleasure to give her back.'

'Well, I don't think you should,' Miss Penfold said. 'The owner left her at that horrid inn. You have to keep her and perhaps one day I will be a good enough rider to hold the reins myself. It's very good of you to put up with me; I must be quite a trial to you.' She sat next to me on a small sofa and could whisper discreetly enough for her parents to pretend not to hear. 'Sack of potatoes, Mr Clark?'

'You are far too petite for me to describe you as that,' I said, nearly choking on my cake.

She stared at me admiringly. 'Your tolerance knows no bounds.'

I hoped I could keep expectations at bay even though we were becoming a familiar sight on a Sunday afternoon. Sadly, we became talked about. There were many knowing smiles and indulgent looks. We were often stopped and asked about the horse, about Miss Penfold's riding progress and told how enchanting we looked. It was becoming time to declare myself or pull back.

It had done me good to leave the narrow confines of my life for a few hours but whether Miss Penfold derived the same benefit is doubtful; she never learnt to hold the reins lightly and her association with me can't have been useful. Not in view of what happened.

# CHAPTER 30

I ignored the doubts building in my mind and buried myself in my work. I became obsessed with it because I had made the most alarming discovery. For hundreds of years man had been nailing shoes onto the feet of the horse and it was killing them. The blood horses suffered the most because they were shod and raced before they were fully grown. The animal's body continued to develop but the foot was encased in iron and became deformed. We were so used to seeing the mutilated feet of these noble servants that we no longer knew how a natural foot appeared. I would anger the farriers with this revelation; but the veterinarians would listen to me. Even Professor Coleman would take me seriously, for once.

Thanks to a customer of mine I had the proof I needed. He had a very rare commodity – a mare who had never been shod and he allowed me to run an experiment with her. We had a plaster cast taken of her feet and then fitted her with shoes. After a year we took another cast and the results were shocking. Her feet had shrunk. I had engravings made from the plaster casts and now I could show what harm those shoes had done. I was going to write a book so that everyone could see the damage we were causing.

Once it was published I was so excited that I determined to see Professor Coleman. It was two years since I had graduated and I imagined him curious rather than cynical. He might have been flawed but he was the head of the college, the most important man in our field, and I needed his support if my research was to be recognised. In spite of some misgivings, I wrote to him and enclosed a copy of my book. I no longer cared if he found out about Firefly because what did one horse matter when we were butchering and nailing the entire equine population on a daily basis? Our appointment was for three o'clock and had taken enormous patience to arrange since our correspondence was business like on my side, charming but lacking in commitment on his.

Apprehension was inevitable that day and I resolved to answer him with honesty if he asked me about the mare. We would settle this. I would pay him, if necessary, although what value you would put on a horse about to be slaughtered I had no idea. If the man would help me find a remedy for the evil I had discovered, there would be no need for harsh words or legal battles. We would work together towards enlightenment and end this so-called shoeing that had tortured horses for hundreds of years.

I rode Heathfield on a long, light rein. His neck was stained with sweat more due to the heat of the day than exertion. The soft smell of the horse filled my nostrils as we paused beneath a crab apple tree where he ate fruit that was beginning to drop like hard pebbles to the ground. The Turnpike road had taken me past the burial ground at Islington and now I was heading towards Camden alongside open fields flanked by foaming cow parsley. I could see St. Pancras Church, the Elephant and Castle Inn and beyond it a glimpse of the unimpressive college.

How strange it was to return to this place that I had known so well. Withered hazelnuts seemed to be jittering around inside me and there was a pulse beating beneath my ears. The nearer I got to the college the more my doubts crowded out all optimism. Such a low, bleak building – more barracks than a seat of learning – it faced me like a tired mother with no remnants of youth or beauty. But far larger than I remembered.

I nudged the horse into a brisk trot to close the final mile and as I reached the familiar wicket gate I could see there were new stable blocks around a central garden. Professor Coleman had forced his troubled institution onto a firmer footing and I was impressed in spite of my unwillingness to credit the man with achievement.

Heathfield was taken by one of the students and I found the Professor in his consulting room. In spite of the open window, the air was stifling and the man seated at the large desk appeared over-warm and uncomfortable.

He didn't look up. 'Apologies, I won't keep you above a moment.' He carried on scribbling awkwardly, apparently finding his quill something of a trial. It made a mess of his page and ink stained his fingers, marring the beauty of an emerald ring. 'I must get this done although, I must say, it's a task I have never relished. Give me a surgeon's knife any time, eh?'

The Professor's deftness with surgical instruments had been impressive. I remembered him dissecting with confidence, his hands mapping a lifeless corpse, feeling for the cause of death as a groom will offer comfort to living flesh that needs calming. I looked at the bowed head of my former teacher and saw that marriage and time had been a benign influence. There were the first hints of grey in his dark hair which was swept elegantly from his face but there were no lines about his eyes and the set of his mouth was relaxed and soft. He leant back in his chair, stretching his arms across the desk to ease the tension of writing and looked at me thoughtfully.

'Should I be fearful? Oh, do stop hovering and sit down. You mustn't expect me to crane my neck. I hear you have established an enviable practice, you are to be congratulated. And now you have come to accuse me of something. What could it be, I wonder?'

I laughed politely at the teasing note. 'I thought we might rise above our differences for once, sir. For the good of the horse.' I sat opposite him and put my saddle bag on the floor.

'Such nobility, dear boy. I'm profoundly impressed. Your way with words was always excellent. I flatter myself that I am able to match you, however. You very kindly sent me a little book you have published. It sits by my favourite chair waiting for a moment of idleness in which I might indulge myself.'

'You haven't read it, I take it.'

'That doesn't mean I won't and I am honoured that you have remembered to send me a copy but I hope you haven't come all the way from the city to check on my reading habits. My dear Mr Clark, we will have to find you some more customers if you have time for such an excursion.'

'Thank you, Professor, but I have enough for my needs. Indeed, it is difficult to find time for them all.'

'Good.'

He waited with hands steepled beneath his chin.

'It's about the book...,' I mumbled.

'Yes?'

'It's very good of you to see me...'

'Yes, it is...in view of everything.'

If he was alluding to anything I ignored him. 'You see, I have made the most alarming discovery.'

'I see.'

'About the horse.'

'I assumed that much.'

'Sir, I wish you had read the book for it is far more eloquent than I am.' I pulled a copy from my saddle bag and turned to the page I needed. 'If you will look at these illustrations you will understand my concern.'

He did as I asked and peered at the page as though he might have some trouble seeing clearly.

'Do you see how the foot has shrunk? And this is after only a year of shoeing. Is it any wonder they have such lameness given that their feet are so deformed?'

Professor Coleman grunted and turned a few pages. The noises he made were not encouraging but at least he hadn't thrown the book in my face.

He smiled and I felt hopeful. 'This is fascinating, Mr Clark.'

'I hoped you would be interested, sir.' I pulled up closer and sat on the edge of my chair. 'You see, it's killing them. Slowly and surely. But of course we are so used to seeing their ruined feet that we hardly know how they should look in nature.' I stood and pointed out one of the engravings. 'Do you see that frog, there? It has withered to half its size. And think of the accidents they have.'

'How do you mean?'

'Most accidents happen to the horse when he is about four or five...soon after first being shod. I had never questioned it before but now it is so obvious why.'

'Really?'

'It would be better if we put off their shoeing as late as we can,' I said with enthusiasm. 'Oh, somehow we need to help their limbs withstand the violence. When you think of the service they give us, they should be treated with mercy and indulgence. Not this life of abject servitude.'

'And what do you propose? That they wear nothing on their feet?'

I sighed because the remedy eluded me. 'I'm attempting to develop a less harmful shoe, something that is flexible.'

'Indeed! Will you patent it?'

'I hadn't thought to. The money doesn't interest me. In fact, I would love others to copy me. Why not? If it will help end this slow slaughter.'

'People will only take you seriously if you protect your design. The world won't understand you. Your generosity of spirit will be mistaken for a lack of competence and you risk being ignored. Well, I wish you luck. Naturally, I can advise you on patenting should you reconsider. If you get that far, of course.' He seemed to doubt such a thing was possible. 'Now, you must allow me to give you a tour of our new facilities since you have come all this way.'

He rose from his seat as if he was ending the interview but I wasn't quite finished. 'Will you allow me to present my findings to the college, Professor? I had hoped, at the very least, to discuss my research. You do see how important it is? For centuries mankind has shod horses through ignorance but now that can change.'

'Can it? When your research is so ill formed? You have raised only questions and you should speak to me in a few years when you know the answers. Remember, we are in the business of teaching students how to heal these animals. What is the use of worrying about something that even you are unable to solve? Come, I think the new stable block will impress you. Security has certainly been improved since your day.'

'But Professor...'

He silenced me with one hand. 'Enough. Do you really expect me to lend you a platform?' he said, bitterly. 'After the despicable thing you have done? No, we will not speak of it. We will not tire ourselves with heated words. Your motivation was to ruin me, had you been driven by something noble...or even romantic, you would have returned the animal.'

'The mare?' I hesitated and turned away from him, it was enough to hear the accusation. 'You know then?'

'Of course, I know! I do not fear you. Years ago you were no threat to me and you have not improved your position with that disgraceful piece of foolery.'

I had been prepared for this confrontation but it came with a horrible sense of inevitability. I felt like a mere observer struggling to breathe in the wind while Professor Coleman decided whether to blow away my future. 'I would happily return the mare if I knew she would not be made lame again,' I said, rather weakly.

'And how would we achieve that?' he said, glaring up at me. 'Barefooted? What cruelty!'

One of us was certainly cruel but I could absolve myself of that crime at least. 'She is barefoot now and coping very well,' I said, biting my lip.

'Yes, because she only has to walk around Hyde Park once a week. Given an appropriate amount of work no horse will cope without shoes. There's the dilemma. If we want them to work, they need shoes. You need to toughen up, my boy, it is not our job to make them live happily and forever.' Then he chuckled almost to himself. 'You will be against whips and spurs next, I suppose. Or perhaps the bit will not find favour with you.'

'Well, yes,' I said, letting the thought give me strength. I straightened and looked at the contempt in his face. 'It is my belief that a horse that is free of pain has no need of any of the cruelties and restraints we impose upon them. They will lead from the thinnest piece of string if they are happy.'

'I thought as much. You are a dreamer. An idealist who is so far removed from the real world that you are beyond belief. But returning to the issue between us, not that I have any desire to discuss it. I don't know how you achieved that ridiculous farce or what others you embroiled but it was not me that you wronged. I might well have been your target but you had no right to do that to my sister.'

I could never harm Christina or her horse. It's true that I'd been secretive but for the first time I realised that my *crime* didn't amount to much. I had stolen a doomed horse. It was hardly a crime at all even though I'd risked transportation.

'Sir! I didn't steal the horse.' I turned to the Professor as a great burden left me. 'I bought her in good faith from Richard Cross, the knackerman. You sold her, if you remember.'

I might have crept out with the mare in the dead of night like a low thief but as soon as the deal was sealed with Mr Cross she became legally mine. Why hadn't it occurred to me before? I could have walked with her openly to London but we would have looked a sorry sight. It was better to have maintained a low profile while the outcome was so uncertain.

'I sold the man a carcass,' the Professor said, between tight lips. 'Or so I believed. He was to have slaughtered her and ended her suffering and that would have been the kindest action.'

'How can you say that? She is free of pain and you should be asking me how I cured her. She was crippled with founder and it's gone. She would be ridden more if I wasn't too big for her but you don't care for that, do you? It is of no interest to you.'

'There are thousands of horses in the capital and very little room for one that does no work. How long did it take you? Months? A year? No owner can house an animal or pay for that much treatment. Your theories are unsound and uneconomic.'

'It always comes down to money with you. Tell me, does Miss Coleman know? I have written to her, you see, but never received a reply.'

'Of course not. That period in her life is best forgotten.'

'Does she still reside with you?'

'Yes, but she keeps to her rooms where she is quite content. I hope you are not thinking of favouring her with a visit. Once a week my wife takes her to see a friend in Kentish Town. Thankfully, they are there today.'

'A pity. I would like to pay my respects. Perhaps I should write to her again.'

'I think not.'

'I always considered I was holding the mare in trust for her. That when she took up riding again she might like to make use of her.'

He laughed and leant on the back of a chair for support. 'Riding! Are you serious? My sister does not ride, damn it. That worry is behind me and it's a relief that she keeps herself still these days. She has had the good sense to understand her limitations and live accordingly. Why she should have pushed herself to those extremes I shall never know. Christina is barely able to move. That accident took its toll on her and weakened what was already a fragile frame. She was a cripple then; I'm not sure what one would call her now.'

Prisoner seemed a possible candidate. I forgot the anger and disappointment that Christina had caused me. I longed to see her and thought I would call at the house before I returned. The Professor could be lying or she might have returned from her visit and be happy to see me. It was a remote chance since she hadn't written but if I could see how she was or persuade her against this restricted regime she was enduring. If I could only talk to her for a minute. Or touch her. He had called her a cripple, not for the first time. How ridiculous to call a woman like Christina such a thing. It was a word that put up insurmountable obstacles. It brought an army of difficulties and acceptance was the greatest of them. How many people had told her – *don't?*

Society, with her brother at its vanguard, had frowned on her interest in science and laughed at the forceful way she expressed herself. Why had no one celebrated her achievements? Her limitations meant her abilities were all the more remarkable. I decided to walk to St Pancras Way after my chilly parting from the Professor. I was brooding on Christina's plight.

Mary, their maid, opened the door at my knock and recognised me instantly. I asked for Miss Coleman but was told in stumbling accents that she was not *at home*. That can mean anything and the maid had the manner of someone who had been instructed poorly and couldn't remember her lines.

I felt Christina was in there. Don't ask me how I knew. Perhaps it was the maid's face, her slight blush, her stammering lies. The house she was guarding didn't seem empty. I don't say I could sense Christina's presence but I could picture her confined to her room, resting rather than living. There was a hat of hers placed carelessly on a hall table that I thought I recognised. Sounds reached me from the kitchen and then someone called the maid, told her to bring Miss Coleman's tray. Well, that didn't mean much since it could have been an empty tray but I had the feeling that the woman I sought was waiting for her tea.

'Mary, please! Will you not give her a message for me? I know she's in there. The Professor won't be home for hours so you need have no fear on that account.'

The maid looked frightened. Mostly, of me, I have to admit. I suppose she feared I might force my way into the house since my foot was in the door but I hadn't seen Christina for two years and would hardly rush up the stairs to her bedchamber. What purpose would it serve? Perhaps I hoped to rekindle the feelings we'd shared but mostly I wanted assurance that she wasn't being basely treated. It was ironic that I had rescued her horse from the Professor's care and in doing so had left the woman behind to endure it. Our difficulties stemmed from that chance meeting at the Elephant and Castle when I couldn't be honest with her. She'd been fully aware of my awkwardness but misinterpreted it. Surely, she would forgive me if she knew.

Mary looked over her shoulder and spoke in an undertone. 'He told me not to this morning. He knew you would come. He knows everything and I mustn't go against him, sir, it would only make it the worse for her, don't you see?'

I had withdrawn my foot and these last worrying words were offered through a crack in the door. Christina's situation must be uncomfortable if a visit from me could make it worse. Once again, I had to walk away from her. Oh, the powerlessness. I wanted to force open her window and break into that house in the dead of night. I wanted to make her talk to me but most of all I wanted to free her of this nonsense. I suspected she was kept to her room against her will. At the very least she was so worn down with his concerns that she allowed those walls to become the limit of her world.

I turned back to the college to retrieve my horse. There was a very fine carriage being cleaned before it was put away, its yellow wheels looked splendid against the black of the coachwork. It was recently purchased by the Professor, I learnt. How elegant he must have looked in it.

The light was fading but that journey home must have been one of the slowest of Heathfield's career. It was hard to rush when I didn't want to leave. A feeling of responsibility claimed me. It ate at my insides because my failure, my inadequacy, was tormenting me. My horse stopped once Camden was behind us, an unusual occurrence since it was not one of his favourite paces, and I turned in the saddle. The college and the new houses were shrouded in dark trees. The church spire was just visible. I sighed, knowing it was useless to turn back. There was nothing I could do unless I was willing to kidnap the woman in the middle of the night. I was sorely tempted.

# CHAPTER 31

'I wonder how long he's known about the mare,' Edmund said later in the week when we gathered at Fred's lodgings to discuss our periodical. 'And you say he had no idea how we did it?'

'None. I told him it wasn't theft which of course it wasn't since I bought her from Cross that very day. I have his bill somewhere.'

'I'll be able to rest easier now I know you won't be deported.' He slumped in a wing-backed chair and nodded his head at my stupidity. 'Had you imparted that important bit of information at the time I would have explained the definition of theft to you, my brilliant one.'

'Don't worry about the mare, not when there are thousands suffering,' Fred argued as he looked up from the papers on his desk. 'The big issue for us is his refusal to let Bracy present his findings to the college. He's trying to silence you, don't you see?'

'Surely I can get this information out into the world without his support.' I smiled but doubts were lurking. 'There's the book.'

'I'm sorry,' Fred muttered. 'Who will read it? You need to influence the profession, not a few of your supporters. His refusal is a blow. I thought he might rise above your petty differences.'

'Our differences are vast. They always have been. Goodness, he must look very fine in that new carriage.'

I sighed and sat heavily into a chair opposite Fred's desk. His little study was lined with books and the room was dim in spite of the bright sunshine outside. The dark, elm floorboards were dusty and his desk was littered with cups and glasses. He was so at home amid the clutter, enveloped in the chair that seemed about to swallow him. On the wall was his certificate qualifying him as a veterinarian and a framed print that looked to be by Gillray depicting the ignorant blunderings of a farrier. It was a measure of how far we had come to see the satirist devote a work to such a subject.

'Carriage! What carriage?' Edmund asked.

'The Professor's. The upholstery was a Burgundy red, it looked very comfortable.' My fingers played with the worn arm of Fred's furniture, tucking back some padding that was trying to escape. 'I wish the head of the college would devote more of his energies to learning.'

'That would be a departure, my friend,' Edmund laughed.

'I know. Not one paper has come out of that place in all this time.'

'There never will be any papers with Coleman in charge of the place.'

Edmund was right but it was hard for me to concentrate on papers or carriages or anything other than the woman I'd left behind. I longed to confide in them but they thought me happy and I didn't like to bring them more bad news. If only I knew she was content but was she even safe? With no word from her, no glimpse, my imagination began to fear the worst.

'Coleman's corrupt.' Fred slammed one fist on his desk until it shook. The noise made me start. 'You've always known it, Bracy. And now the college is one of the most rotten public institutions in the country.'

'But I couldn't prove it.'

'Not then but now it seems our Professor is getting

careless if he's buying himself such finery. Do you have any idea how much a carriage like that costs?'

'A lot.'

'Exactly! And he's buying it on a salary of two hundred a year! We have to oust him. There's no other way.'

'How?' Edmund looked shocked. 'By suggesting it in *The Veterinarian*?'

Fred got up and paced about the room. 'We'll launch a campaign. Don't look so doubtful, it's for the good of the profession.'

'Really? It sounds like the opening volley in a battle to me,' Edmund muttered.

'Take heart,' Fred cried, cheerfully. 'We will win...because every attack will be justified.'

'I could try to persuade him one more time, I suppose,' I said. 'But I doubt he will see me again. It took long enough to get an appointment the first time.'

'You would need to spend years toadying to him like William Sewell.' Fred rolled up his sleeves, dipped his pen in the pewter standish and began taking notes. 'Instead, you've continued to humiliate him.'

'Have I?'

'Yes, you have. You've cured that mare. Can you imagine the shame for the head of the veterinary college? A horse he was sending to slaughter now to be seen trotting about the park.'

'Trotting! I wish.'

'And to make it worse you can prove beyond question that horse shoes are harmful. I've lost count of the number of shoes he's patented. The last thing he wants is you emptying his pockets. He's never forgiven you the misdeeds of your youth.'

'What do you mean?'

'The shocking way you chased after his sister,' Fred said with a beaming smile. 'Pretty woman. He didn't like you bringing her home in a state of semi consciousness, it was never going to win you favour. Bracy's courtship is gentler these days, isn't it? The woman gets to stay on the horse and comes home in one piece.'

'I am not courting,' I said quietly, not that they heard.

'Sadly, Fred's right. You won't change his mind, Bracy.' Edmund looked dismayed that we were considering this step. 'We have to go on the attack, I suppose. It can be your revenge.'

Revenge! Was that what gripped me? I might have had cause but I never thought to lower myself to its spell. I looked at my two friends and it dawned on me how crucial Professor Coleman was to my life. Then and now. How different it would have been had the Frenchman lived. He would have discussed my findings and we would have found a solution together. Coleman not only wanted to keep me out of his sister's life, he wanted to suppress my work. How to help Christina eluded me but I would not let him silence me.

'Can a man seek revenge unknowingly?' I said.

'Why not?' Fred muttered, his brows knitted in a deep frown.

'Then I've been hurtling towards it for months, perhaps even years, and it seems I am the last to realise. When I set out on this journey my motives were entirely honest. I wanted to save that horse more than any of the others. Oh, you know why. But also I was sick of the numbers we were losing at the college. There were too many and damn him, he had no interest in finding the cause.'

So our little periodical went on the attack. An article on the leaders of the college was cushioned nicely between one of my recipes for worm balls and advice on finding a respectable forge in a city that had one on virtually every street corner. We didn't name them but anyone close to the profession would know we were targeting Professor Coleman and his worthy assistant.

Coleman was the most curious opponent. He remained silent. Oh, we had merely prodded him deftly in the side but there was no defence from Camden where he remained supreme. Gradually, we went further and we complained of corruption. No letter, no rebuttal. I couldn't understand it but we continued the onslaught, hoping the mud would stick if we threw enough of it.

I was in the coffee house one evening with Fred, Edmund and a young surgeon. A couple of other vets came in but ignored us pointedly. I lie. I could hear them talking about me and my views on shoeing in voices designed to carry. One of them had a copy of *The Veterinarian* and was pointing at it and laughing. I was getting used to such mockery but wondered how they could describe themselves as scientists. How could they dismiss my research so easily? They wouldn't intimidate me with their snorts of disfavour. I sat back in my chair and stared at them until they turned away.

Fred looked at me with one eyebrow raised. 'Are you really going to let that go?'

'Would you have me pick a fight?' I shrugged but the humiliation stung. 'They can't help their ignorance; they've been taught rather poorly.'

It was raining heavily and the windows were steamed up, closing us in and making the air damp and full. I was devilishly hungry but conscious all the time of my opponents in the other corner. The tea with bread and muffins was very good value at this place and helped to distract me while the others made plans for our first public lecture. They had a mind to use my premises since the yard was big enough to accommodate a crowd. They were assuming we would attract a good number and I didn't like to contradict them, not while there was butter to spread. A second plate of muffins was placed on the table without me asking; no wonder I liked coming here.

No matter how low my spirits I was always able to eat. For that reason it was hard for my friends to sense anything was wrong. I had such trouble sleeping and when I did fall into a fitful doze my thoughts turned to Professor Coleman and how I could liberate his sister. Coleman's slanders would now be added to my list of worries.

Robert Brough, the vet I had met in Brook Mews, came in and hesitated when he saw us. It surprised me when he came near our table but he wanted to thank me for the use of my gripe mixture and pressed some coins awkwardly into my hand. I introduced him to the rest of the table but he appeared uncomfortable in our company and said he wouldn't stay long.

'I wanted to warn you, Mr Clark,' he said in an undertone. 'I was talking to Mr Sewell the other day.'

This news produced a series of snorts and much mirth as Brough anxiously rubbed warmth into his hands.

'Did you understand a word he said?' asked Fred.

'Well, I know what you mean…but I got the gist of it…you see, he said…'

Fred leant back in his chair and, ignoring the fact that the man had something important to tell me, launched into an amusing anecdote about one of William's lectures.

Brough laughed but still hadn't sat down. 'He does wander a bit but he's mighty fair about it and says anyone who hasn't been able to follow him can have their money back. He had to in my view because so many were grumbling but he's a good man.'

I looked at him in surprise. 'They're charging for lectures?'

'That's new,' Fred muttered, getting out a notebook and pencil. 'On top of the fees for the course?'

'How much?' asked Edmund.

Our surgeon friend was more worldly wise and argued it was customary for medical men to charge for lectures. They debated this for another ten minutes but I was composing a letter to Christina in my mind, one I was unlikely to post, and hardly followed them.

Brough sat down next to me and shook my arm. 'Listen to me,' he said. 'There's talk of suing you. Mr Sewell was telling me. He can't have known that I had met you and anyway he said to keep it to myself. It's something about a horse you've got that you shouldn't have. He said it wasn't yours and that…well, I could hardly believe it…he said you had stolen the animal.'

'The Professor is welcome to sue me,' I said. 'But I don't think he will.'

I must have spoken forcefully. Fred halted in the middle of an attack on resurrection men who dug up corpses to sell to supposedly respectable surgeons.

'Really?' he said. 'I never thought Professor Coleman would be brave enough. Hah! No, he'd have to be mad. The whole story would come out and he would be ruined. He won't sue.'

'Is it true about the horse, then?' asked Brough. I told him a little of Firefly's history and his mouth hung slightly open. 'Miss Coleman rode it, you say?'

'She did. Remarkably well.'

'But she can hardly walk,' he said in astonishment.

'After her accident she got a little worse but she was remarkably strong on a horse. She was an excellent rider.'

He looked at me, his brow creased. He hadn't credited the stories of my pursuit of Christina; so many people never imagined that someone so flawed should experience something as normal as a man's admiration…or even his love.

I sometimes wondered if she had been aware of it. Even if I hadn't expressed it well or often she must have known my feelings or did she assume I was taking advantage of her physical weakness? Perhaps, like this man before me, she thought I was only toying with her; that she wasn't worthy of something more and yet the opposite was true. It had gone so wrong on that day at the Inn; she knew something wasn't right and she misread me. Oh, I didn't want to revisit those days. The intensity of them was still strong and could even now goad me into a sharp retort. Brough's look of disbelief was making the muscles in my hands clench and my tongue was ready to do battle.

Whatever he was thinking he let it go and we returned to the question at hand. Would the Professor dare to involve the authorities? Would I be charged with theft? The bill from Richard Cross mentioned services rather than the sale of a horse but I was confident he would speak in my favour.

The Professor was a worthy opponent. His whisper campaign made me extremely uncomfortable but in the end he did something much worse.

# CHAPTER 32

There was never an open attack against *The Veterinarian* but I was the target of much slander. He was filling the capital with his three-month pupils and the few that were willing to talk to me told the same tale. I was an enemy of the college and I was a laughing stock for my views on shoeing. It had taken an enormous effort to get Robert Brough to talk to me at our first meeting and even now he was embarrassed to be seen with me. I was vastly uncomfortable when backs were turned at my approach and this was all down to Coleman's remarks which were never to my face. Had he accused me in an open, manly way, I could have defended myself but each day he seemed to make dents in my reputation. Sales of my books were good but how much better they would have been had these vets, these people with influence, understood my work. I had to fight against this suppression but there were times when I felt like David next to Goliath. It didn't matter for myself, but how was I to help the horse if my own profession was against me? Oh, I had expected no mercy from the smiths since we were all a threat to their business but to be isolated and ridiculed by my peers was no easy thing.

We had relentless rain for more than a week and I began to think we would have to cancel our plans for a public lecture. I couldn't imagine even the keenest horseman sitting through a deluge for a talk about the animal and its ailing feet. My house was now fitted up and repaired and had a perfectly respectable sitting room which might have accommodated twenty people if we moved out all the furniture. Fred was overly optimistic in my view and thought we would attract double that number.

I needn't have worried for there wasn't a cloud to mar the sky that morning and it looked set to stay fair and warm into the evening. The yard was swept and seating had been borrowed from the Fortune of War and my neighbours. I allowed myself a measure of pride as I stood at the entrance and surveyed the premises which were respectable and workmanlike. Beyond my walls were the sounds of the busy thoroughfares and the cries from the men as goods were unloaded into the warehouses. I could smell roasting barley wafting from the brewery and, if the wind was in the right direction, the stench of the Thames hung over us like a soiled blanket. I had a feeling of peace here, an oasis amid London's core. We had only three patients in residence plus my own horses so there was no reason for the place to look anything but calm. Thankfully, the muck was collected yesterday and the predominant smell was from the hay store but with all the thousands of horses in the capital you were never far from their excrement.

Much to my surprise Miss Penfold and her mother offered to help us with the event. They ordered the arrangement of the chairs, chivvied my one servant into a thorough cleaning of the kitchen and parlour and set up a table for selling my books.

I was putting the books out when Miss Penfold came next to me and sighed. I mostly saw her in a serviceable riding habit and now she was wrapped in muslin and lace. Her complexion was no longer pallid and her hair was lifted high with one or two pale ringlets tumbling down her neck. I searched for a compliment but, as ever, was too slow with this sort of thing.

'It's such a lovely book,' she declared with one hand touching her heart.

'Thank you, Sarah,' I said, relieved to be on such safe ground. 'I didn't know you had read it.'

'Oh, yes!' she said, breathily. 'Well, the first few pages. How clever you are.'

She ran a hand across one of the pages like a caress and I felt my skin contract and form gooseflesh.

'Aahh,' I said, looking towards the stables rather than her face. 'It's kind of you to have tried.'

She would have said more but Fred joined us, insisting I used the mare during the talk.

'Don't back down now,' he argued. 'People want to see her for themselves and you will only disappoint them if you keep her hidden. You can't be worried about Coleman, surely. He's a coward and he wouldn't dare go to the authorities. You, on the other hand, are not. Yes, I think you should use her; you let Miss Penfold ride her so what is the difference?'

Miss Penfold didn't know the full story and looked confused. 'Did this Mr Coleman own her?' she asked. 'The head of the college?'

'No, he didn't…his sister did.'

'The crippled one! Rather a waste to have such a lovely horse pull a gig and then to treat the animal so badly. Well, I'm very glad you took Firefly from such horrid people and if I saw them I would tell them so. Not that they would dare show their faces here but I see no reason for you to protect them. You haven't done anything wrong, after all. Have you?'

'No, but it was all very clandestine. I had to get her out under cover of darkness and fake her death the next morning. Thanks to Mr Cross, the knackerman, we got away with it.'

'Did you really? That's wonderful, you are so modest. I thought you found her at that inn and took her on; I had no idea that you actually rescued her. Wait until I tell Mama. She loves you already but when she hears this…'

Miss Penfold dashed off to the kitchen where her kind parent was organising the refreshments.

'What am I going to do, Fred?' I felt startled and worried but it had nothing to do with the lecture I was fast forgetting.

Fred was rearranging the books and laughing quietly. 'It looks as though you will shortly be able to do anything and everything you want. I can't believe you haven't regaled her with the dramatic rescue story before now. You could tell half the women in London about it and have them falling at your feet, sighing dreamily. If it was me, I'd use it. What a waste of all that goodness if you don't tell them about it.'

He was smirking but I was unsure whether he was in earnest. 'Only a rogue would exploit it, surely. I can't believe you are suggesting that I...well...what? Seduce women with such a tale? Besides, Miss Penfold is not that sort...and I would hardly...really, I couldn't.'

'Well quite. But one can't help wondering when you're going to do the honourable thing.'

Oh, no, what had I done? I crushed my notes and stuffed them in my pocket, heading to the stables to find a moment of solitude. I had worried that Mr and Mrs Penfold might have expectations of me but hadn't thought their daughter would misunderstand my feelings. Not one word of endearment, not one touch, had I given her. Did she, did Fred, really think there was anything between us? I had only wanted Christina's mare ridden, nothing more. Was that so extraordinary?

Peter Logan, my stableman, was giving Firefly a professional shine. He coughed and I realised he'd asked me a question which he had to repeat.

'Yes, saddle her,' I said.

'Oil on her feet? We want her to look her best.'

'No, I might want to pick them up. Sorry.'

He looked disappointed. 'You have to pretend it's only me you're telling, sir. It's not so worrying then.'

'Do I look that nervous?'

'Afraid so.'

I began to have some sympathy with William Sewell who gave the most confusing lectures in the short history of veterinary science but then banished the thought. He reportedly hosted a lavish dinner at the Pulteney Hotel for a dozen or more people last month. Yes, on an assistant's salary.

'But as soon as I look at the audience I might come apart. That's if anyone turns up, of course,' I said. 'I hope they fall asleep and spare me. If you hear snores please don't wake anyone up.'

'Don't you worry; you'll be fine once you get in your stride. This might help.'

He pulled a silver flask from his jacket pocket, handed it to me and bade me drink. The strong taste of brandy made me cough.

'Has no one ever mentioned the war with France to you, Peter?' I laughed, taking another sip.

'Yes, but it doesn't stop trade now. Go on…one more.'

The French liquor eased my jagged breathing but didn't prepare me for the large crowd that had gathered in the yard when I walked out to take my place at the front. There must have been nearly fifty people and the sight of them slowly cheered me. A glance told me that Coleman's dupes had stayed away but if I couldn't address my own profession I might be able to influence the public. The talking died to a murmur as I set my eyes to a point over their heads. I knew there would be friends among them – Fred, Edmund, the Penfolds and my brother, Henry and his wife, Anne, but I would have to acknowledge them later. I might get through this ordeal but not if I allowed myself to be distracted.

I glanced at my notes and made a shaky start by thanking everyone for coming. Three times. After a few minutes, I talked about the horse's foot and its elastic properties. And I was getting in my stride by the time I expounded on the contraction caused by shoeing as illustrated by my experiments. My audience listened politely but I hadn't gripped them.

'We are killing these noble servants,' I warned. 'And it's a black day for the horse when he begins his first lesson and shoes are nailed to his feet.'

There was no outcry among my listeners. I was

accustomed to the reaction. Exposing the evil of shoeing was all very well but where was the cure? How many horses would be able to go barefoot as some of mine did? It was hardly a practice I could promote. I persevered and told them about my journey to Bath on a horse without shoes. How the animal had made good going once past the cobbled streets of the capital, how we had galloped across the fields and made the distance in three days.

There was a murmur of interest and much scraping of chairs. I was aware of a conversation being conducted at the back and too much attention focused on the refreshments on offer later. People who were accustomed to lecturing told me this was perfectly normal and that a quiet, rapt audience was a rarity.

I raised my voice and embarked on Firefly's story. 'She would have been a casualty of shoeing. She had founder and was due for slaughter. I thought she deserved another chance.'

Peter, who had been biding his time, led her towards me. There were cries and a murmur of protest as Firefly danced about with impressive ease on her unshod feet.

'Yes, it would have been a shocking waste of a good animal wouldn't it, ladies and gentlemen? This mare was crippled and miserable. Her feet were ruined by the effects of injurious shoeing and I had the devil's own job getting her here, I can tell you.'

Now I had them spellbound as I gave them an edited version of Firefly's story. The mare trotted in a circle around Peter, tossing her head impatiently.

'I don't believe it. That horse never had founder,' shouted a gentlemen from the back. 'And walked all those miles to London?' He had the audience with him. It seemed I was a charlatan. 'All the vets would be curing them if that was true.'

The issue was debated and I was forgotten. I could hear Fred shouting that I spoke the truth; that he had taken her shoes off himself. Glasses of ale were being passed around at the back and, since it was impossible for me to be heard, I tried to compose myself by looking down at my feet. My first foray into public lecturing could have gone better.

Sadly, it got worse. I called for quiet; I tried to get people to listen but it was to no avail. Everyone had an opinion and no one believed my story of Firefly's recovery. If only I had some independent witnesses to vouch for me.

There were a few women in the audience and I stupidly thought their presence would help to keep the crowd in better order. Mrs Penfold and Sarah began serving tea and thankfully Ed managed to stop a tussle between two lads who would have been more at home watching a cock fight. Suddenly, a hush descended. At last, some respect! But not for me. An elderly lady was given room when she got up to leave and I thought others might follow. She used her stick to force a way out but instead of leaving she headed towards me and although she wasn't frail she was painfully slow. She was enveloped in a velvet cloak in spite of the warm evening with the hood covering most of her face. Now that it was quiet it was possible to hear the swish of her silk as she moved. Her head was a little bent and there was an atmosphere of expectation. I felt it myself as if I foolishly hoped she might prove my case or, at least, get my audience back in their seats.

By the time she was a few feet away she stopped and leaned on her stick. I moved towards her offering my arm even though I had no clue whether she wanted to stay or go but the slightest angry nod kept me in my place. I was not her focus. As she got nearer the horse she straightened a little, almost as if her body uncurled. And then she stood completely still and watched Firefly in her restless walk around her handler.

Three more times round my stableman and the mare came to a halt with her feet splayed out and her head up, ears pricked. Firefly quietly whinnied. Then she rushed towards the old woman and began sniffing her face. I was worried she would be knocked over as Peter was struggling to hold the mare so I came forward and gripped the woman's arm whether she wanted help or not.

She felt surprisingly warm and muscular. I understood

why when she lifted her chin and turned to me.

Christina registered my look of shock and dismay. Her own face was filled with contempt.

'How could you do this?' she hissed.

# CHAPTER 33

The silence was uncomfortable. Mine wasn't the only face suffused with shock. She only revealed herself once she had the full attention of the audience and yet she looked at me alone. Waiting.

I spoke quietly, fearing my every word was being lapped up at last. 'I couldn't do anything else, would you rather I let her die?'

'Of course not…but to say nothing. Not one word…for two years.' She seemed close to tears but rallied and spoke almost to herself. 'Why did he send me here? It doesn't make sense.'

'I'm afraid it does,' I said, my voice audible over the hush. 'Your brother doesn't wish to accuse me himself and so he's sent you in his place. How clever. You are the only one who could injure me. If he'd come himself I'd have made *him* a laughing stock but this was a brilliant move…'

'Accuse you? Of what?'

I hesitated to say the word. 'Theft!'

There was a rumble as the scent of a crime wafted over fifty people. 'You haven't stolen her, though. She was dead; I thought she was dead.'

'He might call it theft because I made off with her after buying her from the knackerman. I couldn't tell you but I wrote to you.' My fingers itched to wipe a tear that bubbled in one of her eyes.

'Did you really?' She might as well have called me a liar, she was so full of disbelief.

'Yes, I did. I lost count of the times but you never replied so I could hardly tell you the truth. I had no idea who was reading those letters.'

Perhaps she hadn't burnt them; she might never have received them. So many stories emanated from Camden and I knew many of them to be false. Oh, I should have forced myself past their front door and found out the truth. My audience was rapt for the first time that night. The tension in front of them was like a play just before the final curtain. Even the mare stood patiently while Christina stroked her neck.

Finally, we became aware of another presence. Miss Penfold came beside us, her eyes darting about trying to make sense of what was happening.

'Is this your mare?' she cried.

'She was.'

'And was she lame, miss?' a man in the front row demanded. 'Like he said. Is it true?'

'Yes, every word of it. It's incredible. I don't know how he cured her but all this time I thought...no, I knew...she was dead.' She turned to me, ignoring the excited audience. 'How?'

'Did you ride her?' Miss Penfold asked, mesmerised by the sight of Christina who was standing unsteadily on her tired limbs, dabbing her eyes which were stinging with red.

'Yes!' She faltered a moment. 'Yes, I did. Every day. She was my joy, she kept me alive.'

'How could you? How could you treat her like that?' Sarah bit out. 'You reduced her to a cripple...just like...just like...'

'You misunderstand, Sarah,' I said, before she could say more.

She had embellished the story in her head and turned it into a lurid novel. I had been at fault in not correcting her belief that Firefly had been treated cruelly. Without the detail

267

she mistakenly thought the fragile woman in front of her was to blame. The brother who had ordered her destruction was nowhere to be seen.

Christina was accustomed to the censure of the world and took such disapproval in good part. 'Shocking, isn't it?' she said, sarcastically. 'Riding should only be for those with two good legs. That's the common view, certainly. But it wasn't my disability that caused the harm. I had a love of speed and I'm told I rode her too hard.'

'On the wrong shoes,' I corrected her.

Miss Penfold wasn't finished. 'How dreadful of you to treat such a nice horse like that. You should be thankful to Mr Clark for saving her but I hope he doesn't give her back. You don't deserve her and you'd probably make her ill again.'

'Sarah, please. It wasn't Miss Coleman who did the harm.'

'No? She said herself she rode her too hard. It's impossible to imagine, I know, but if she'd cared for the horse it wouldn't have happened. When I ride her I'm very careful. Mr Clark takes me out on her on Sundays to the park and I would never make her lame. I wouldn't even know how to. There, you see, Bracy, you mustn't feel obliged to give her back.'

She turned away with a look of disgust before either I or Christina could respond. By this time we had a crowd around us examining Firefly and asking questions. It was hardly the lecture of my dreams but the story and all its ramifications was dragged from me. The head of the veterinary college had ordered the destruction of a horse that I had cured. He had refused to listen to me, prevented me revealing my research to the students…in other words, he had silenced me. There was an outcry. Edward Coleman's name swam around the yard and I heard more than one person demand that he should be thrown out of the college.

I lost count of the hands that slapped me on the back, the congratulations washed over me but the words I had longed to hear did nothing to lift my miserable heart. What an empty victory. We ran out of refreshments. More importantly my books sold out within minutes and I had a list of people who desired my services. The evening was a success, Fred assured me, running a hand through his hair excitedly. Even Edmund was impressed. He arrived in time to see my shaky start and confessed he had been worried about me.

'Well done,' he said.

'It was a circus!' I replied, testily. 'A ridiculous show.'

'It's what they wanted, it made them listen. People love a good story and you gave it to them.'

'Where is she?' I asked. The yard was nearly empty by this time. There was the light from a lantern in the stables where Peter was finishing with the horses.

'Mrs Penfold took her into the parlour. She seemed very tired and distraught.'

'I'm not surprised. I never thought Miss Penfold would confront her like that so publicly. I must see her. I just hope she will listen to me for more than two minutes. I knew she would be angry.'

'She has no right to be angry. How can she be annoyed with you for saving her horse?'

'I think it's the subterfuge that makes it so difficult. And the fact that I kept it hidden for years.'

'More that you've publicly trounced her wonderful brother and made him look a fool. I'm surprised she came here.'

The parlour was empty but I could see Christina had been there. There was an empty cup on the table and there were cushions nestled on one of the chairs to make someone comfortable. Miss Penfold bustled in from the kitchen and eyed me suspiciously.

'Have you seen...?' I faltered. 'Sarah, have you seen Miss Coleman?'

'Oh, gone, thank goodness. But not before I gave her my opinion. Well, really. How dare she turn up here where no one wanted her?'

With the greatest effort I hid my irritation. 'Gone?

When? I didn't see her go.'

Miss Penfold waved one hand negligently. 'Oh, I didn't notice. Five minutes, may be.'

I looked about the room and my anxiety must have been evident. I picked up the cup and held it. 'I wanted...I had hoped to see her...'

Her eyes widened. 'I see.'

'I wish you hadn't said those hurtful things. Don't you realise she has enough to cope with in life without that?'

'Well, I didn't mean to be unkind but...you'll have to forgive me, I was thinking of poor Firefly.'

'Oh, don't worry about her. She was rescued whereas Miss Coleman was left behind. Oh, God! What a mess.'

'So it would seem.'

'You don't understand. She's had a difficult life; she's a very brave woman.'

'I hadn't realised...but I'm beginning to.'

She fiddled with the carving on an oak settle before her hand became a rigid grip. Her eyes were blinking and her lip was trembling. Her breathing was the only noise until she said faintly, 'Oh, dear.' There was a pause and a deep intake of air. 'Mama will be wanting to go, you'll have to forgive us not staying longer but Father will be coming for us soon.'

'I'm sorry. I didn't mean to...um...'

'No, I know,' she whimpered. 'It's my own stupid fault. It's just that...oh...'

She started to cry. I should have seen it coming, perhaps I could have prevented it but all I could do was try to stem the flow with a handkerchief. I wanted her to stop, I wanted to find Christina, check the horses, anything but comfort this woman I had caused such pain.

'Don't cry, Sarah. I'm not worth it, believe me.'

'It's just that....' There was more crying and then, 'I've been so happy. And I thought, I thought you were too.'

'No, I mean, yes, of course.' How could I tell her that the woman who could make me happy had just left and that I desperately wanted to chase after her before it was too late? 'I

270

was happy. It was very enjoyable.'

'I don't understand. My sister said...oh, never mind. She was wrong...but it's been every Sunday for so long.'

'I'm sorry. The horse needed to be ridden. It was never anything more.'

'I thought it would have been more but you were too busy.'

'Well, I was but...I told myself that you understood.'

My arms around her only seemed to increase her sobs. So I stepped back, pressed the handkerchief into her hands and apologised repeatedly. I was a rogue. I couldn't offer her my time even now and suggested she find her mother, that she'd be fine by the morning after a good night's sleep. There were more tears and then finally, the sight of her retreating back.

The desire to find Christina propelled me from the room but guilt came with me. I was so stupid, so tactless. I hadn't meant anything; I hadn't promised anything but I should have stopped long ago.

I found Christina in the stables. I watched her from the double doors and my body felt as though I'd been running. I couldn't speak and couldn't move towards her. I worried my tension might frighten her or that she'd flee if I spoke. Guilt still claimed me and I didn't want it to seep out and contaminate this moment. Christina was standing at Firefly's head, not touching but simply staring at her with the light of a lantern. I could hear Peter with one of our patients and then he called out that he was heading for home. Christina and I were alone for the first time in two years and I felt all the constraint that uncertainty brings.

If only she would smile. Or reach out instead of accusing me. There had been a time when I could touch her as if I had the right. I would have promised her the world then but she would have laughed at me. There was little laughter in her now although I could sense the belligerence that was so familiar. Had I passed her in the street I would hardly have

271

recognised her. She had lost weight and her vibrancy was replaced with weariness.

I had been impatient to share my triumphs with her and now this tired, wan creature was here in her place with the same voice but giving the impression that talking might extract the last ounce of strength. Standing was making her tired but to offer her a chair would be a mistake, judging by the rigidity of her back.

'What happened to you, Christina?'

My frankness made her turn. 'What do you mean?'

She rested one hand on the side of the stall and I winced because she was blushing and it was my fault. My eyes travelled over her thin face, the stick she carried was resting in one corner and anger rose up inside me. How could she have allowed this to happen? Why hadn't she fought this crippling decline? The Christina I knew would never have given in so easily.

'I'm sorry,' I said. 'That was rude of me, you are not well but it is such a shock for me to see you like this.'

'Is it? Oh, I forget. You are mistaken, though. I am perfectly well.'

'You can hardly walk!'

'That is not an illness…and it is something I have lived with for a long time.'

'You didn't used to carry a stick.'

'I should have done, it might have saved me from a couple of falls. How foolish I was then. Perhaps, I had too much pride and didn't accept the inevitable. I'm sorry. It makes you uncomfortable, doesn't it?'

'No, of course not…'

'Don't lie to me, Mr Clark,' she scoffed.

'I'm not uncomfortable if you need a stick but you are very changed. You didn't used to have one. And you would try anything when I knew you. Don't you remember?'

'It was stupid of me although I don't regret it. You don't expect me to be doing those mad things now, I hope.'

'Why not?' We could have been talking about the wild

way she rode her horse but my thoughts turned to some of the other things we got up to when we were on the ground. She might have read my thoughts for her skin lost some of its pallor and her eyes turned downwards. 'Why have you stopped riding? You said it was good for you and you were right. It kept you strong. It's ridiculous that you let one accident stop you.'

'Not really. There was little else I could do. If you recall, I no longer had a horse to ride and unless my brother found me a suitable replacement I had no means of getting one for myself. Your friend, Miss Penfold, was right, I didn't deserve another one.'

'I'm sorry she said those things, she didn't understand.'

'No, she only spoke the truth. No doubt she's a very able bodied rider and it's nice that you've found someone else. To make use of the horse, I mean.'

She sounded resentful. Her skin looked cold and her manner was sour. She must hate me for what I had done. Instead of helping her, I had betrayed her. I had taken away the animal that gave her movement, cured her and given her to another.

'Do you really think I should have sent her back to you?'

'Perhaps. You can hardly justify keeping her here all this time. You are an honest man. What do you think?'

'Christina, I promise you that I was very uncomfortable about it. I was worried but didn't know what to do. If I returned her, he would have made her lame again. No, I couldn't do it…but I wanted you to have her. I wrote to you, I even visited but was turned from the door. Why did you come here, Christina?'

'You were trying to ruin him, so he said. There were so many rumours, you see, and Edward was getting very angry. His temper isn't always very good. I know he doesn't mean half the things he says but he found me reading your book and well, I'm afraid he threw it on the fire. We had the most almighty row and he said you were parading a horse that looked like Firefly simply to humiliate him.'

'And now you know it was Firefly.'

'He didn't know that. He thought you were using a horse that looked the same.'

'He did know; we spoke of it when I came to the college last month.'

'Oh, are you sure? Well, he planned to have you silenced one way or another. I didn't believe him so he told me to come here tonight. Well, I knew you would say some dreadful things about him but I doubted you would go so far as to get a horse that looked like mine just for the purpose of blackening his character. It never occurred to me...I never thought I would see Firefly. She was dead; when I saw her tonight I couldn't understand.  If only you had told me it wouldn't have been such a shock.'

'I tried to.'

'Well, I never saw your letters.'

'Mary wouldn't let me see you.'

'That must have been Edward's doing. I hardly went out for a year.' She spoke softly as if she was thinking back on someone else's life for she seemed not to recognise it.

'Why ever not?' I cried, not giving her time to answer. 'Cruel, cruel man. He has done this to you. He always wanted to restrict you and that stupid little accident gave him the excuse he was looking for.'

'It was hardly a little accident. I was concussed and quite unwell.'

'Only for a few days, he had no reason to imprison you for a year.'

'I wasn't imprisoned. Oh, don't be vexed with me, it wasn't like that.'

'He didn't allow you out; he locked you in your room for some of it. What else would you call it? And of course, getting rid of Firefly was an important part of the story. Your one chance of freedom...never has a horse's lameness been so convenient. No wonder he wouldn't listen to me. He didn't want her to recover; you can see that now, can't you?'

She nodded and her fingers grasped her mouth to hold

the bitter words inside. I paced about the small stable coming to rest with one hand on Firefly's flank.

'If only I had done more,' I said. 'I should have persisted or pushed Mary out of the way. Do you know, I thought about climbing up to your window? I wanted to see you so desperately but something stopped me. I saved your horse but I let him crush you. I can't believe how foolish I was. Oh, it's...it's unforgivable.'

My anguish must have upset her. At least, something made her soften because she touched my arm. 'There was nothing you could have done. It was not your fault. Edward learnt to be even more protective, that's all. Most brothers would do the same. I'm sure they would if they were given such a burden so young. He needed to keep me safe.'

'But he hasn't kept you safe. Look at you. I'm sorry but you were never frail. Never like...like this.'

She sighed and defeat clung to her like smoke to a battle. 'It was too much. Fighting all the time, arguing with Edward. I got so weary of it and, for once, just wanted a quiet life. It was so much easier to accept what God had given me.' She slapped her leg in irritation and the focus of it seemed to help her. 'It could have been worse, it could have been both legs and I had my hands. I could paint and sketch. I even became quite good at it and it was so much more sensible than trying to ride a horse with the encumbrance of this stupid thing.' She saw me looking at her stick as though I wanted to snap it in two, which I did. 'I walk more elegantly with it. It's no good struggling for breath and squirming around. I look idiotic.'

'You did not. Not to me. I should have married you. This wouldn't have happened had I got you away from him but I stupidly thought I had to wait until I had established myself. I couldn't ask you to take the risk and foolishly thought you were better off with your brother. If I could turn the clock back I would have carried *you* from Camden in the dead of night. Not your horse.'

'What arrogance! You would have ordered me not to

sink into a decline. Prevented it with the gift of great happiness. How would I have managed with everything that marriage entails? Or have you forgotten that? Why, I do believe you've aged a great deal yourself; you are not as sharp as I remember. And you are forgetting another thing. You never asked, not formally. And I never accepted. It's rather presumptuous of you to assume that I would have happily done your bidding and married you.'

'You will have to forgive me,' I said, sounding peeved. 'I thought we had an understanding. You never seemed immune to me.'

The memory of some encounter we had shared made me smile in spite of my annoyance. Her leg never stopped her riding hell for leather and it didn't prevent her kissing me back with all the ardour any man could wish for but I had nothing to smile about. The love of my life was here in shadow form, like a half remembered dream. She was so familiar and yet so different. Her voice was strong and resolute and her mannerisms were the same. The way she touched her leg impatiently, that hadn't changed. That limb was like a piece of unwanted shopping picked up at the butcher's, something she hadn't ordered and had no need of. Then she'd recall that she was stuck with it and struggle on, at speed if she had to.

'I was never immune to you but marriage is another matter,' she said.

So now we were both smiling. Hers turned to laughter which lit her face and made it come alive for me. She asked me how I got Firefly from the college and was astonished at the lengths I had gone to in order to cover our tracks. The knackerman's involvement shocked her since he was risking his business with her brother. It shocked her still more that Firefly had been at the Elephant and Castle Inn on the day I'd met her there.

'What will you do now? Will you confront him?' I asked.
'Oh, yes. Eventually. I can hardly do anything else.'
'Eventually?'
'I'm not going back to Camden for a few weeks. Do you

remember my friend Suzanna Goodall?' I nodded at some vague recollection. 'She married a banker and is called Mrs Phillips now. They live not far from here in Aldersgate Street. I'm staying with them.' Christina leant back against the stable wall and stared at the horse, there were tears in her eyes. 'I'm so glad she's alive. I've missed her. Thank you for saving her.'

She spoke quietly and looked so awkward, stroking the horse, that I knew it cost her a great deal to say those words. She thought herself responsible for Firefly's lameness but she had no cause to thank me. I could have told her that keeping the horse from slaughter was reward in itself. Then it occurred to me that Firefly had been a substitute for Christina, a connection to her that could always be mine. My urge to cure the woman in front of me was overwhelming. It was there at the beginning and it burned a path through my mind now. Was this the lover or the scientist in me? I couldn't tell.

'You don't need to thank me…but I would ask one thing of you, Christina.'

'Of course. What is it?'

'Get back on her.'

'Don't be absurd! You don't mean now, I hope. Well, of all the nonsensical ideas. There isn't a doctor in London who would recommend it and here you are with your veterinary training suggesting I leap onto a horse when I can hardly walk as far as the next street.'

I let her carry on saying what a fool I was, how I would risk her one good leg with the attempt and how I was so stubborn that I couldn't accept what was in front of my eyes.

'Tomorrow,' I said.

'It must be getting late,' she said, ignoring me. 'I really must be going.'

'Or if not tomorrow…then soon.'

'I wonder if I could prevail upon you to escort me.'

'I'll hold her, she'll behave perfectly. All you have to do is sit on her and I will walk you around the yard.'

'I sent Suzanna's manservant away two hours ago but he hasn't returned. What he's thinking of, I don't know.'

'You'll enjoy it. You know you will. You know you want to.'

'Mr Clark? Please.'

'Of course I will escort you…when you've agreed to my terms.'

# CHAPTER 34

Christina laughed every time I proposed getting her back in the saddle. Her friend lived five minutes away but the walk took an age, we took frequent rests and I was worried it was too much for her. My suggested ride began to seem ludicrous and I wished I had harnessed one of the horses to take her back.

'We came in the gig; it hadn't seemed so far away. I shouldn't have…but then, I wanted to come; I wouldn't have missed it.'

Her confession was mixed with apology. Her embarrassment was evident. She was a little breathless and she was covering up the pain her leg was giving her. I tucked her hand through my arm and we took slow steps over the uneven walkway. It was dark and moonless but easy to navigate thanks to light spilling from some of the houses and a noisy tavern that I wanted to steer her past as quickly as I could. No one troubled us and the singing from inside was a comfort of sorts. Our destination was only two more streets away but Christina seemed uncertain of the way. I was not so hampered since I worked in the district and knew virtually every livery stable and every mews.

I was relieved to see the lights of a hackney coming to a stop some yards behind us and disgorging its two passengers.

The driver would be equally pleased to get another fare in this quiet part of town so I hailed him and helped Christina inside.

'Aldersgate Street,' I said, as I followed her.

'It's just round the corner, sir,' he complained.

'I know, take your time. In fact, go round the block.'

It was two days before I saw her again. I had pushed her to the back of my mind thinking she wasn't going to come when I heard her voice. She told me Suzanna's husband had dropped her on his way to an appointment and would collect her in a few hours if that was convenient. It was. I had finished my rounds and had only to tend the resident patients this evening but my confidence had fled thanks to our walk the other night. Her brother was wrong to confine her but, perhaps for the first time, responsibility touched me. If Christina was hurt, the fault would be mine.

She was wearing a serviceable brown riding habit that she had borrowed from her friend and a straw bonnet decorated with flowers. She seemed younger somehow as though her riding clothes reminded me of happier days. For a few minutes I found the excuse of a patient very convenient. A dressing needed changing. It couldn't wait. The sound of her uneven tread, the click of her walking stick on the cobbles reminded me what was at stake. How could she seem so light with so much risk before her? It was as if her reticence had fled in a night of dreams.

She went into Firefly's stable and began brushing her coat. She was singing. My heart dropped. I had taken the mare on the rounds for these last two days to ensure she wasn't fresh but I was all too conscious that she was a lively ride and prone to excitement.

'Are you nervous, Christina?' I asked, coming to join her at last.

'A little,' she admitted, staring at me with a puzzled frown. 'But not as much as you. Second thoughts?'

'Well…it's just that…you don't have to do this. I put too much pressure on you and that was hardly fair.'

'Come on. Saddle her up. The more you think about things the less you do. And it won't do to think. You do have a side saddle, I hope.'

I went to fetch it. 'I didn't think you would come. I'm very pleased you did.'

'You don't sound it.'

'You can always change your mind,' I said. 'It seemed such a good idea at the time…'

'But now, in the cold light of day…'

Firefly began fidgeting as soon as the saddle was on her back. I bridled her and led her to the yard. Christina was chatting inconsequentially about the weather, the district and her friend's home which was delightful. She was more worried than she led me to believe for she hardly took breath. She had left her stick in the stables and walked with an uneven stride, clutching my arm in a pincer grip.

'Christina, I only suggested this so that I could see you again,' I admitted. 'I had to find a way to keep you coming and it was the only thing I could think of.'

'Now you are being absurd. I hope you are not trying to stop me.'

'I'm beginning to think another horse might be better. The mare is so lively. Heavens, how did you ever ride her?'

'Through sheer stupidity and stubbornness. It took a serious fall and her lameness to make me stop. No, let's be honest…it took her apparent death. Oh, goodness, Edward is going to kill you when he finds out how you did that.'

'He already knows most of it.'

'Well, if you get me riding again he will probably manage to kill you twice. Are you really willing to take such a risk?'

She was laughing almost hysterically at the mention of her brother. We hardly spoke of him the other night although he must have been in both our thoughts. He always resented me challenging him, forgetting that I was motivated by a precocious quest for understanding rather than malice. His corruption was another matter entirely. I had put my accusations into print but he remained silent.

'Your brother doesn't frighten me but getting you to do something risky is making me slightly nervous.'

I led the horse to a mounting block but Christina stopped dead with her hands on her hips. 'I'm not sure how we are going to manage this.'

Her face was suffused with red and I realised the steps of the block were a serious obstacle. I tightened Firefly's girth and looped her reins over my arm so that both my hands were free. Fortunately, the horse ceased her relentless fidgeting at the sound of my impatient voice.

'It won't be the first time. Come on, I'll lift you on. Face me. Tell me if I hurt you.'

I didn't give her enough time to hesitate or even to warn me against the idea. I gripped her around the waist as gently as I could and lifted her into the saddle. There was a trace of shock but it quickly disappeared. Her legs dangled motionless on one side and she gripped my hand.

'Have you got her,' she said, under her breath. 'Don't let her move, not yet.'

'She's not going anywhere, she's waiting for you. What an intelligent horse.' I tried to sound reassuring and hoped Christina didn't notice the tremor in my voice. She let out a breath and let go my hand then lifted her right leg into position over the pommel. 'You've done it! You're there! Are you ready?'

She nodded and I led the mare round the yard. I wanted to hold Christina by the leg to keep her steady but contented myself by walking backward so that I could be sure she was managing. She was.

'Are you comfortable?'

'I'm fine.'

'Does it hurt?'

'Not as much as I thought it would.'

'So it does hurt. You must tell me.'

'Bracy, stop fussing and watch where you're going. You'll walk into that gig if you are not careful.'

I turned to face forward and a feeling of elation hit me.

She was here, she was riding and she wasn't calling me *Mr Clark* any more. Everything was going to be alright. We walked for twenty minutes, maybe more, keeping to the confines of the yard knowing the noises of the street would be too challenging. She didn't complain of discomfort and I stopped asking if she was happy since she looked as if she could be singing. For anyone who takes their two legs for granted, it might seem that being led on a horse was no achievement at all. Christina had given up on the skill. She might never regain her true ability but she had made a start and seemed fascinated at the thought of doing more.

I helped her down and she was a little unsteady. Perhaps it was wrong of me to turn such a situation to my advantage but I couldn't help cradling her in my arms. The warmth of her made me hot. And quite joyous.

'We shouldn't be doing this,' she said, although her face was pressed into my chest and it was hard to glean any conviction.

'We're not doing anything. I want to hold you; that's all. You are amazing. You did it, Christina. You are so brave.'

'Foolish more than brave.'

'Don't argue. Not about this. If you can do that, you can do anything, but I'll not have you disagree every time I make you a compliment. Christina, don't you see?'

'What?'

'You will ride again.'

'Indeed…with you leading me. Don't get too excited.'

'No, by yourself. We'll ride every day. I'll lead you at first until you get your strength back and then you'll be able to do it on your own. It will be like before, I know it will. I didn't put all this work into Firefly so that you could spend your days sitting on a sofa painting some wretched picture. Why are you laughing?'

'Because it's funny. You've seen me walk. My performance on the ground is rather laughable and I no longer look like a cracking rider. I know I never did but I've got worse and you have to be realistic. No one who sees me walk would think I should even be on a horse. Most of them think I should stay indoors and be taken in the gig if I need to go anywhere.'

'What fun is there in that? Such a boring life, for someone like you. You want to do it again. Admit it.'

She looked up at me through her lashes. There was something flirtatious about the glance and she burrowed her face into my jacket knowing I saw into her heart. She fidgeted and I lifted her into me until her feet came off the ground. I kissed the side of her face and then tangled my hands into her hair. She was surprised for a minute and she was saying my name repeatedly as though she was delighted or slightly horrified.

'It was fun, wasn't it?' I said again, kissing her neck, her forehead, anything I could reach. She wriggled but her hands came around me and she clung to me tight. 'Tomorrow?'

Her laughing stopped. 'Very well. Tomorrow.'

I couldn't credit that I was going to see her again, that this horse I had nurtured would finally help Christina walk without stumbling or being limited by pain. Was it a foolish dream? Were we blind? We couldn't see the dangers or the difficulties, only the promise of a better life. With five good legs, instead of one.

I sealed the bargain with a kiss. How light and warm she felt, her old self, bubbling with life. She seemed like a moth trapped in a jar able to flutter around seeking the outside world which was tantalisingly out of reach. If only someone would lift off the lid.

Christina was to come at twelve the next day and I was rushing to tend a patient staying with me. The mare had a troubling infection in her hock following a road accident. Her owner was anxious since he was unable to deliver to his customers without her and this was the first day I was able to give him any sign of a hopeful outcome.

'Thank goodness,' he managed, shuffling on his feet instead of taking himself off, much to my irritation. Frankly, he would only have been in my way even without the added complication of Christina's riding session.

It was a cloudy day with a brisk wind and the mare's owner finally took the hint and headed back to his office remembering that he had paperwork to do and a rare chance to attend to it.

For once, I was alone on the yard as I'd sent Peter on an errand. I didn't anticipate him making things awkward but wanted Christina to face the challenge unwatched. Our difficulties came from another quarter entirely. She arrived in a gig and was handed down by a middle aged man dressed smartly in a black coat with a tall hat set squarely on his head. His long side whiskers and stern features reminded me of the elderly surgeon who had apprenticed me all those years ago. It was a useful look if you wanted a patient to keep still while you bled them.

I shook his hand undaunted and ran a professional eye over the black gelding which stood placidly between the shafts of the gig.

'Mr Clark, your reputation precedes you,' he said with cold precision. 'I can't envisage ever needing your services, they are simple creatures when all's told and I have never had cause to doubt the wisdom of my farrier. Veterinary science seems to be the new fashion though and for your sake I hope it lasts.'

He nodded his head doubtfully and took me to one side after Christina left us to see her horse.

'Does Professor Coleman know of this ill advised scheme of yours?' he asked. 'I thought not. She's old enough to know her own mind but as she's staying at my house I feel some responsibility for her. I can't say I approve.'

'You surprise me,' I said. 'You must know that exercise will be of great benefit to Miss Coleman.'

'I might agree with you if it was exercise we were talking about. But riding a horse is dangerous and a fall for that girl could have very serious consequences. I'm not her doctor and I'm not her brother so I have no right to tell her what she should do but you must know that neither of them would sanction this folly. Tell me this, what is the purpose of it? It's pointless and what's more it's giving her false notions.'

I doubted he would dare say this in front of Christina. She had lost much of her strength in the last couple of years but her belligerence was beautifully intact and she would have put this fellow in his place.

'False notions! To rekindle a skill she was so formidably good at? Had you seen her natural ability on a horse, as I have done, you wouldn't decry her. Believe me, sir, she was a better horsewoman than anyone I have ever seen. She loved it but it was torn from her all because of some stupid belief that she would be better off doing nothing. And what has that produced? A woman who has such trouble walking that she's in danger of seizing up and spending the rest of her life in a chair.'

'And you expect me to say nothing of this to the Professor?' he said, scornfully. 'What dreadful conceit to assume that her treatment is ill advised? Very well, you leave me no choice. See if you can keep her in one piece in the meantime.'

Christina was humming *The Lass of Richmond Hill* when I joined her in Firefly's stall. I didn't want to mar such happiness.

'Oh, goodness, what did he say to you?' she asked once she saw my face.

'He was concerned that you shouldn't fall off, I suppose. Not much else.'

'He's a dry old stick, isn't he? Like toast. I've yet to see him smile even when I told him about my finding Firefly and riding her. How could he not be happy that the horse I lost has been restored to me, thanks to you? I suppose he thinks I'm riding her properly. If he could have stayed he would see there's nothing to worry about. It's the easiest thing to sit on a horse while someone leads her round. If it was another horse it might be different and you are hardly going to let me tumble off.'

'No, but I can't promise you are perfectly safe.'

'I know there's a danger but there is crossing the road.

Or even getting out of bed. Especially for someone like me.'
She laughed and shook her head. 'I'm an accident waiting to
happen, I make people nervous. Why, I even gave Mr Phillips
indigestion yesterday when he saw me going up the stairs. He
wasn't sure whether to run away or to carry me the rest of the
way.'

'Which did he choose?'

'Oh, he took the middle road and followed me,
coughing at a safe distance. I think he hoped to catch me if I
fell.'

'But you didn't.'

'No, of course not. I only looked as if I might. Why is it
that you never found me embarrassing? My wretched leg was
invisible to you; it's funny that you were able to make me
forget about it too. Sometimes people don't even look at my
face. They stare because I'm not standing straight or they
remark how badly I walk. I used to think they were quite rude.
I used to get angry about it. Did you know that?'

'Yes, and I don't blame you.'

'But you were different. You saw *me*. You saw my
strengths and not my weaknesses. How?'

'It wasn't difficult, Christina. Almost as soon as I met
you I knew you were a remarkable woman. You were bold and
belligerent. I loved that about you. The way you stood up to
your brother.'

'Only sometimes.'

I nodded because there were times when his
oppressiveness was too much for her but she was older now,
surely she had the right to dictate her own life and her
disability shouldn't take that from her. Why should her brother
stop her riding if she wanted to? There was more to this
argument though. She had the right to be loved and his denial
of her true place in life disgusted me. It always had but, now
that we might be getting a second chance, the threat of his
interference was even more worrying. I knew how effective it
could be.

Thanks to my conversation with Mr Phillips I knew we

didn't have long. Would she oppose her brother? She was financially dependent on him so there was only one way that I could change her situation. I estimated I had only a few days to convince her. I had no time to consider my own doubts; I was under so much pressure I didn't even know if they existed.

It was easier getting Christina onto the horse this time. She'd thrown her nervousness away since it was of no use to her and let me lift her on with all the softness of acceptance. I stopped comparing her in my mind to how she used to be and only saw how much better she was than yesterday. She picked up the reins and settled into the saddle with all the confidence of her former self even though her body was having trouble keeping up with the challenge. I held the horse lightly on one rein as the rider appeared to have taken control.

'You look as though you never stopped riding,' I said.

'Thank you but you exaggerate. I wish I hadn't, for now I find myself worrying what will happen if she goes faster. I'm not sure I will stay on. How awful to bounce all over the place, like a beginner. Bracy, do you think we could try it?'

I had to laugh. She was so determined to conquer this that she would take a risk.

'Why not?' I said. 'Just a few paces and I'll have a hold of her and make sure she doesn't get ideas above her station.'

So Firefly went into trot and Christina broke into giggles of excitement. She held onto the horse's mane to steady herself but managed to acquit herself pretty well.

'That wasn't too good,' she confessed. 'I'll do better next time.' She grabbed the front of the saddle and took a breath. 'Keep going for longer otherwise I won't get into the swing of it.'

I lost count of the times I trotted her in that yard. Her hair was in disarray and her face was as hot as mine once we finished, but she was elated.

'We should go for a proper ride on Sunday, come with me, the streets will be quieter and we should be quite safe,' I said.

'We'll see, although I will probably be aching by

tomorrow.'

'The more you do the better you will feel so you had better come again tomorrow.' I helped her down and held her in my arms. 'How long are you staying with your friend?'

'Three weeks.'

'Come every day that you can. Promise me.'

The years flew from us like migrating birds. I found myself saying her name, breathing in the scent of her and running my fingers in her hair. I kissed her cheek and her forehead until she was laughing and gasping. For a moment I could pretend that everything would be alright, that her brother could do nothing to stop us. I only had to convince Christina that this future I had mapped out for us was the way forward. I would work on her slowly, capturing portions of her day to claim for my own. She was trembling and rightly or wrongly I interpreted it as encouraging. I took her hand and told her that we would put Firefly back in her stall together. My eyes never left hers; they must have been full of meaning, fuelled by my hidden agenda, because she stopped smiling and squeezed my hand. More encouragement? I was relying on the tiniest unspoken messages.

I ran a finger under my neck cloth and tried to steady my breathing. The last thing I wanted was to frighten her and unless I could get myself under control there was a danger of rushing instead of cajoling. I unsaddled the horse and got some hay, a job that was impossible to do and remain tidy.

Christina broke into a peal of laughter and began picking bits of hay out of my hair while I brushed at my clothes. 'Anyone would think you had taken a tumble in the hay loft,' she said. 'There's more on you than there is in the rack.'

She was so close to me that I could feel the warmth of her breath on my skin. She had to stretch to reach the top of my head and grabbed my arm to steady herself. Her body was pressed against me, blissful and soft. I wanted to turn my hand and cup her breast but I didn't touch her, not yet. She was so close but I wanted to pull her closer still as if my thoughts would find a way in if only I could envelop her and hold her painfully tight.

'Bend your head a little,' she said.

She was struggling with her balance but at no time did she ask for the stick that I had carefully concealed in a corner of Firefly's stall. I did as she bid me and she worked cheerfully through my hair, remarking how thick it was, shorter than before but the most beautiful colour. I was basking in the attention, a cat rolling at her feet.

'Will I do?' I asked.

She wobbled, laughed and fell against me once more. She had lost weight but not as much as I'd thought. Her movement was less confident and her body more fragile but I couldn't connect her with the impression she had given me at my lecture. I had seen the stick and the hesitant walk and assumed she was an elderly woman. The back of my hand was telling me she was in her prime. My body was urging me to turn my hand, to feel her. But I was frozen.

I melted when she looked at me. There was no hiding my thoughts, not even had I closed my eyes. She read everything in an instant. She seemed alarmed and took a step back.

'Perhaps I could come tomorrow,' she said. Her face reddened and she was staring at the floor. 'It was nice.'

'Nice?'

'Yes, indeed.'

'It was nice! Is that all you can say?'

She began walking away from Firefly's stall but I was one step behind her and she knew it.

'I'm sorry,' she said. 'That wasn't terribly gracious. It was very kind of you to take the time, I know you must be very busy and I shouldn't take up any more of your day. Thank you for letting me ride her. There, is that better?' She gave a nervous laugh and avoided my eye. 'I left my stick somewhere. I never used to do that, I must be getting forgetful.'

'It's not better.'

'Where have you put my stick?'

'Don't worry about that ridiculous thing. You don't need it.'

'If I'm to walk back I do. Will you come with me?'

'You've been walking all morning without it because your mind has been so busy on other things and I've just followed you as you've marched from one end of this stable to the other. Perhaps we should make a habit of me chasing you. Christina, you don't need the bloody thing.'

'Don't be silly.'

'And it's not better. It won't do saying it was *nice*, it was kind of me. That's an insult.'

'What do you mean? What sort of gratitude are you after?'

That made me smile. 'It would be an interesting trade, would it not? I think you should acknowledge that you are regaining skills that you lost and that it was wonderful. It was joyful…that it gave you a taste of freedom that you haven't felt for two miserable years. You should be throwing your arms in the air and jumping.'

She tutted as if I should know that jumping was beyond her. 'I am. I am overjoyed.' She didn't seem in the least happy, she was close to tears. 'And my life isn't miserable. It has limitations but I make the best of things. That's why it's very difficult for the people close to me, who care for me.'

'Forgive me. I didn't realise. I thought the last two years might have been as miserable for you as they have for me.'

'Oh, Bracy! How can you say such a thing? You have your practice, you are successful and so many people are talking about you. You will make your mark on the world as I said you would. Yes, you are very lucky.'

'I've never felt so. I'm single, remember?'

'You could marry. Why, you could have your pick of women.'

'Is that right?'

'Yes, naturally. You've always been striking, I suppose, and now you are very presentable, you know. Quite the smart, young man about town. You have a book that will have so much influence and I know lots of people who say you are one of the best vets in London.'

'Is that all? Don't stop, you are doing so well.'

'You are joking with me but you have become a very nice looking man. Perhaps you are a trifle shy…and bookish…but that shouldn't hinder you. And you have many friends who will introduce you to…um, why are you laughing?'

'Did you say I could have my pick of women?' She nodded but looked startled. 'You relieve my mind. I hadn't thought it would be so easy. How foolish of me to imagine that I might have to spend hours, no days, persuading you.'

'Persuading me of what?'

'That we should be together.'

'Oh…but how?'

'Christina, sweetheart, come here.' She took two steps nearer, her movement was awkward and stiff and her eyes were narrowed as if she was worried I might pounce. 'I can't imagine a future without you.' I took her hand and drew her towards me for the last few steps. She nestled in my arms with her head lowered.

'It's not possible.'

'Give me one good reason. We love each other…or have I misunderstood?' She sighed, she nodded but she didn't look up. 'I feel as though I've been waiting for you for years.'

'Oh, why would you wait for me? I would not make you a good wife. I wouldn't manage, not with everything you would want from me. You don't understand.'

'I think I do. At least I know what you are referring to but we would be fine. We would be gentle with each other. I promise. You should talk to your friend Suzanna about it as she may be able to ease your mind in a way that…well, it's not for me to explain, but it doesn't have to be at all brutal.'

She blushed quite stunningly. 'It's not…it's not just that. You will want children.'

'And you think you wouldn't be able? Or that giving birth might be too hazardous? Have you asked a doctor for an opinion?'

'No I've never needed to.'

'Perhaps now would be a good time. But whatever the doctor says, we would manage. We don't have to have children; there are ways of stopping that happening. Christina, I still want you. Will you have me?'

# CHAPTER 35

It's strange that sounds rush towards silence like a river in full flood. We didn't speak. All we did was to stare at each other in awe. I could hear the thump of my heart and the rumble of my stomach which the tightening of my muscles did nothing to deter. Then there was my breathing. It reminded me of a tired dog and I made sure my mouth was shut in case my tongue decided to loll out. Christina put the knuckles of one hand to her mouth. She seemed to want to stem her words until she'd rehearsed them enough. The horses were chomping on hay and filling the quiet with the stamp of their feet. The massive oak doors to the yard were wide open and the wind brushed the cobbles with feathery hands. The city began on the other side of the wall, a place teeming with trade and activity. We were on one of the routes favoured by farmers bringing cows to Smithfield's Market and I could hear men calling and struggling to keep their herd together.

You could always tell when one got separated. There is a particular sound from a cow that's bucking and rushing between the crowds, alarming the hackney horses and leaping onto the walkway. I would normally go and help if I could but not this time. I thought I had run out of words but surprised myself.

'At least you haven't run out the door,' I said. 'There are

some advantages to that leg of yours.'

That made her start, checking to see that I was joking. She came towards me and her arms were around my waist. 'I don't know what to do,' she said.

I clung to her but her timidity was palpable. It reminded me too much of her fragility, something within her that was always present. I've ignored it or wished it away many times in the past for it made me impatient and irritable. I struggled to accept it was part of her, part of the equation she would bring to our marriage. She used to laugh at my continual efforts to find a cure for her weak leg. Even now I was getting her to fight her condition and regain her riding skills. No wonder she feared I would be unhappy since I was forever trying to change her.

She hadn't left me with many choices. If she was going to be this close my body was going to do everything in its power to convince her. Besides, I could feel her willingness and had no thought to hold back.

So I kissed her, relishing the warmth and welcome of her mouth. I was reminded of our first fumbling attempts since we were so careful of each other. But I was no longer a brash youth cautious of the passion lurking inside us. I wanted to find it again knowing it was my ally. Reasoning with her hadn't yielded the results I hoped for so I would kiss her into acceptance if I could. Although she was kissing me back with satisfying enthusiasm her arms were wooden. She was too controlled for my liking, she hadn't voiced her refusal but I felt it on her lips.

I pulled back to see her face was full of sympathy.

'Why not?' I asked.

'I don't know...I'm frightened.'

'Of me...but I love you.'

'Not of you.'

'Is it the marriage bed? Do you think I would be rough or that I would make demands that would hurt you?'

She wouldn't look at me so I had my answer. I understood her fear. Any woman would feel nervous of such an unknown thing and Christina had more reason than most to feel trepidation. When she spoke she surprised me.

'We would have to try first,' she said, walking around the stable and turning her limp into mere unevenness thanks to her determination.

'Christina! You can't be serious.' She seemed to be inventing some sort of performance trial. I must have misunderstood.

'Why not? You nearly seduced me once; perhaps if you try again I won't stop you. Not that I would have stopped you then but you called a halt. Bracy, you will hardly be ruining me. I don't have suitors lining up at my door. Your own enthusiasm is very singular, you know. Yes, it's the only way. If I can manage without my leg falling off I will know what to do. Oh, but wait! What will we do about Edward?'

'I'm hardly going to announce to the Professor that I've become your lover. Really, I don't think I could face him. I never thought you could be so calculating about this, I don't know what to say.'

She laughed. More sympathy that I didn't appreciate danced across her features. What an outrageous imp she was.

'No, of course we wouldn't tell him anything about that. But if I were to marry you he would have a fit. You've spent the last few years trying to discredit him.'

'I have only told the truth. I'm sorry if it has been painful for you.'

'It hasn't affected me at all. It's hardly affected him either but you know that. He has a lot of support and his students are very fond of him. The governors think he is wonderful, it's only you and your friends who seem to take pleasure in criticising him. You won't topple him. He's too powerful.'

'Christina, I don't feel like talking about your cursed brother right now. I have other things on my mind.' I stood in front of her to stop her pacing; her face was puzzled and calculating. We could have been talking about the delivery of a joint of lamb rather than me showering her with love and affection. 'Your suggestion is not very romantic. You've um…well, you've surprised me.'

'Oh, dear. I expect you are quite disgusted with me but I have to be practical, you see. We might not have very much time. It's Mr Phillips. He's written to Edward about us. And Edward will read too much into things and it wouldn't surprise me if he takes me home.' She was tapping her leg and her eyes were closed. She was finding it difficult to talk. 'I can already hear him prosing on about my riding. How dangerous it is. How I should rest.'

I estimated I had a few days in which to convince her not to return with him. I didn't know what sort of deal we had struck or indeed whether we had made one at all. I had never had a woman offer herself to me so coldly and the effect was not helpful. The desire that gripped me while I was kissing her had dissipated and I was left like a forge that hadn't been tended for a week.

'Oh, I didn't want to talk about him,' she said. 'He comes between us even when he's not here and I wanted to forget about him just for a morning. Just the sound of his voice does something to the muscles in my stomach. All the time it's *don't do this, don't do that*. Well, I'm sick of it. You're right, I want to be able to fall over again.'

She frantically began searching the stables, looking for something. In the end she found it in the straw at Firefly's feet. Her stick.

'Break it for me.'

Her eyes were wide, she was agitated and feverish. It was a stout, masculine stick with a rounded top but no adornment or carving. She thrust it into my hands and took a step back, waiting. Firefly turned her head in alarm but then relaxed. Outside, the wind picked up and rattled the branches of a tree that grew weakly against the side of the building, hitting the pane like a whip.

'You might need it. You don't need to ruin it,' I said, offering it back to her.

'I don't want it, it's got to go.'

She rubbed at her arms, occupying her hands so there was no possibility of me giving it back.

'Christina, I'm sorry I was so angry about the stick. If I've made you embarrassed about it, I regret it, but don't get rid of something you need. It's wrong of me to be always pushing you and trying to make you something you can't be. I don't think any the less of you because you walk with the aid of a stick. I still love you.'

'I know but you don't understand.'

'Then explain to me. Why should I break this thing?'

'He bought it for me. He made me carry it. When I didn't want to, don't you see? It was a couple of months after the accident and I was trying to get out a bit more. I was walking a lot to get my strength up since there was no chance that I would be allowed to ride a horse. And it was working, I'm sure I was getting better but he hated me going on my own in case anything happened and if he came with me he always cut the walk short. I'm sure I embarrassed him. I know this might seem silly but, if I need a stick, I will buy one.'

'I will make you one!'

'And I will cover it with ribbons and bells like a Morris dancer,' she cried, smiling.

'It's still not right that *I* destroy this thing. You have to do it yourself if you want to be free of what that stick represents.'

'Have you seen how thick it is?'

She took it from me and assessed its strength between her hands. She was grumbling and hitting it against the big oak doors of the stables with something akin to petulance. My, she was getting angry with it…and possibly with me.

'I'll probably injure myself in the attempt,' she muttered.

In one corner of the building there were racks for the harness and saddles. Beneath them was a bench which was covered in an assortment of rope, pieces of leather and tools, some of which needed repair. Her hands landed on an old pruning saw which was a little rusty but light enough to manage. Without turning to me she leant the stick on the bench and gripped it tightly. There was a moment's hesitation and then she scored the surface. Finally, she gained some momentum and the saw was embedded in the stick. The wood wasn't giving up the fight easily; it was closing on the saw and making it jar in her hand. Wisely, she turned the stick over and began on the other side. Yes, it was a stout piece of craftsmanship and she was tiring. In a fit of anger she threw the lot into a corner and saw the stick shatter into two.

# CHAPTER 36

She left me with the task of arranging our tryst even though I was plagued by doubts on every possible level. My own performance was the least of my worries and thankfully her expectations were unlikely to be high. She explained to me with horrifying sangfroid that she only needed to know that she was capable of the act. Her pleasure didn't form part of the equation. I didn't anticipate any either and thought it would have been better had we been consumed by passion and tumbled onto a convenient pile of hay.

She agreed with me but didn't waver from her plan. 'That's exactly the point. You can't tumble me anywhere. All my movements require a degree of planning and it's only fair that you find out what you would be taking on. Imagine how I would feel if we married and you were disappointed.'

I tried telling her there was no chance of that happening but she stopped me with a shake of her head. I had taken her to my study so that she could sit down. My desk was covered in papers, articles for *The Veterinarian* and illustrations for my next book which I pushed to one side. She took a glass of water and looked at me kindly while I cradled my head in my hands.

'Does it not occur to you that it's wrong?' I complained. 'That I might be taking advantage of you?'

She laughed and put one hand on my arm. 'I wouldn't accuse you of that. You never took advantage of me before and you wouldn't be now. Don't people call it anticipating their vows? That's all I'm suggesting…and it's my idea so no one would blame you. Beside, who will know? I won't brag about it.'

'Are you sure about this?'

'The bragging?'

'No, I trust you not to do that,' I said, smiling. 'Is this really what you want?'

'Yes…yes, I'm sure.'

'Then if you've rested enough, come here and sit on my lap.'

How sweet and trusting she looked as she got up slowly from the chair. I had to focus on her beautiful face to keep my doubts at bay. Her eyes were downcast and it worried me that she might be having second thoughts. I took her hand to steady her and gave it a squeeze. She landed awkwardly on my knees and I pulled her onto my lap until she was resting against my chest.

'Kiss me,' I told her.

'I don't think I remember how.'

'You managed very well yesterday but it's like riding a horse, you never quite forget.'

I waited for her. It was important that she made the first move. She took a deep breath and held my face in her hands, feeling the roughness of my cheeks and the outline of my lips. I wanted to respond but bided my time, longing to take the initiative and wondering what she would do next. I expected her to dab me with a swift touch of her lips but she surprised me with her open mouth. There was nothing shy or tentative about Christina. If she was going to try something she did it wholeheartedly. My arms came around her, wanting to crush her against me. How easy it all seemed. Worry fled and in its place came breathless anticipation. I wanted to touch her lovely body and realised with a jolt that I had permission to follow every instinct, every dream. She seemed content to keep kissing and wriggling on my lap while I fondled her breasts. This was no place to undress her and I had to be satisfied with the feel of her through layers of fabric until I had the happy realisation that her skirts were already half way up her calves.

My hand rested on her leg and very soon it was her knee I was caressing. A few more inches and I had my first taste of bare flesh. How sensual it was to stroke the silk of her thighs after the roughness of cloth. She was gasping and breathless and I knew we would be fine. Had she clamped her legs tight or stopped me with a cold rebuke my doubts might have got the upper hand but she was so natural and frankly quite open to everything I had in mind.

It would have been the simplest thing to give this woman her first moment of pleasure and I convinced myself she had the right to the experience as she was teetering on the brink of release judging by her flushed face. She sighed as my hand delved further. Instead of tensing when I touched her she shifted in my lap as if she was struggling to draw me in but didn't know how.

I helped her move her right leg as she seemed light headed and didn't open her eyes. I could picture her, naked, on my bed and it was all I could do to ignore the erection that was pressing into her bottom.

She was crying out by now but I was determined to tease her. Just a bit. There was a look of mild shock on her features by the time I had finished with her. She'd had no notion of what to expect and it must have taken her by surprise. Her neck was flushed with warmth and she stared at me in awe.

'Did you know that was going to happen?' she asked once she had recovered herself. She was out of breath as though she'd been running.

'I wasn't sure.'

'It was the strangest thing. I don't know what to say. I'm all tingling, I'll probably never walk again.' She looked…well, she looked very happy and excited. I straightened her clothes as best I could and kissed her. She responded with all the fervour of the enlightened. 'So that's how normal women feel.'

'Sometimes. Maybe...I don't know.'

'When can we do more?' she said with enthusiasm. 'We need to find an excuse for me being here in the evening when there's no chance of someone coming to consult you. I feel so lovely. I never thought I would feel like this. Ever.'

But gradually her smile crumbled and emotion was popping out of her like fireworks.

'Don't cry, darling.' I dried her eyes with a handkerchief and held her against me. 'We're going to be fine. You are everything I could possibly want.'

'Really? Oh, I do love you. Hold me tight.' I obliged but didn't stop her ragged breathing. 'It seems so...well, unfair to you. Why would you want someone like me?'

'Now you are fishing for compliments. I want you because I love you and can't live happily without you. I should know that by now as we've been kept apart for two long years. I don't want you away from me for another five minutes, do you hear me? So no more doubts. I want you and I'll not let anyone...not even your damn brother, come between us.'

With that I stood up slowly and set her upon her feet. There were noises in the yard and I knew we would soon be interrupted. A horse was being led in and from the conversation I could overhear the poor thing had been involved in a carriage accident.

Peter popped his head around the door with an apologetic smile. 'Found them struggling with the animal in the street so I told them to bring him here. Oh, pardon me, Mr Clark. I didn't know you were busy.'

He hadn't seen Christina at first since I was blocking his view but he didn't seem surprised and might have been suppressing a grin.

'Miss Coleman is going to help me with my accounts and invoices,' I explained hastily. 'The business will flounder if we don't get those payments in.'

I didn't look at Christina but heard her murmur in agreement. 'Perfect.'

'Let me see to this patient and then I'll take you back home,' I said to her quietly. As I closed the door she was already looking through my papers which were in dire need of sorting. It seemed I had found the perfect excuse for her to visit me tonight.

# CHAPTER 37

I don't have live-in domestic servants. A daily woman takes care of the house and leaves me a meal for the evening unless I'm going out to meet friends at a coffee house. Peter takes good care of the stables so it's rare for me to spend an evening at home once I've eaten. It's far too big a house for a bachelor and at times I feel as though I'm rattling around in it like a dried pea in a pod. Peter and I worked late on the injured horse. Its bandages needed changing and I applied some more salve before settling it for the night. The streets were getting so busy around here. Every day there was some accident or other, people knocked over, carriages entangled and horses injured or frightened.

I arranged to pick Christina up in the gig that evening. Thankfully, her friends didn't treat her as an ordinary woman and assumed men would have no designs on her. If she said she was helping me with my accounts the last place they thought she would be heading was my bed. I could have been taking their elderly aunt for a sedate drive, they had no suspicion and, thankfully, Christina played out the deception beautifully, exaggerating her infirmity as she ambled awkwardly towards me.

'Are you sure you have enough ink, Bracy?' asked the woman who was so enamoured with bookkeeping.

Her friend, Suzanna, was waiting at the door, ready to search for more.

'Plenty of ink. Paper too,' I shouted and then added quietly. 'Laying it on a bit thick, aren't you, darling? You will delay us and I won't keep up the charade much longer.'

With that she waved to her friend and put her hand in mine. 'Don't wait up for me, Suzanna. I've got my key.'

I carried her to my bedchamber feeling less nervous than anticipated. Two hours earlier I was a basket of worry attempting to bring order to a part of the house that was my domain alone. I was in the habit of bringing work here and so there were as many papers on the table by the window as there were in my study. At least the laundry was out of sight, put away in my dressing room or bagged up for washing. I had allowed my standards to slide and the prospect of entertaining a woman made me see the room through ashamed eyes. By the time I was done I had to rush my evening check of the horses and give myself a thorough wash in cold water rather than hot.

Setting Christina on the floor I went to check the stove. The nights were getting colder and I had lit the fire earlier. I opened the stove door and glowing coals lit the room.

'You made this yourself, didn't you?' She came behind me and touched my back.

'Yes, I have another in the sitting room. In winter, I run them all the time and so it's always warm here.'

Her keen interest in science meant we spent at least ten minutes while I explained the superior operation of the stove over an open fire place. Then there was the view from the window to discuss in depth. I closed the curtains but she opened them again, peering into the dark to see what the prospect would be like in the daytime.

'Can you see some of the horses from here?'

I sat by the fire and opened a bottle of wine knowing we needed something to calm our nerves. 'I can...although sometimes in winter the fog is so thick it's like looking out onto a cloud.'

'Can you see Firefly?'

'If she puts her head out.'

'You are so lucky.'

I was but not because I could see her horse from my bedchamber window. My thoughts were turning to other things but I let her bustle about the room with no mind to rush her.

'Do you think we should do some work on the accounts first just so that I can talk about it tomorrow?' she asked when she saw my newly ordered table.

'No, Christina, I don't. I am convinced you will be able to talk your way through that one without any trouble at all. You put on a very good act in front of Suzanna; you should go on the stage. Come and sit here. You look cold.'

I gave her the only chair – I was such a confirmed bachelor because it hadn't occurred to me to get a second – then I poured her a glass of wine. She took a few sips but was agitated. I hadn't expected her to fall into my arms as soon as we got into the room but thought she might have been bolder since it was her suggestion.

I sat at her feet and proposed a toast. 'To you.'

'To us.'

I could have told her we didn't have to do this, that I would take her home but she was never going to falter. I had seen that familiar look of determination so many times but wished that going to bed with me wasn't being faced in the same way she would approach adversity. Christina was ready for pain and discomfort. She might have been thinking of humiliation and failure for all I knew and I wanted to take the pressure from her shoulders.

Taking her hand and raising it to my lips I sought to reassure her with my love. It wasn't enough. I topped up her glass but she didn't have much enthusiasm so I took it away from her and clasped her to me.

'We need to get used to each other,' I whispered. 'Perhaps I should let you play around with me and leave it at that.'

'No, Bracy.'

'You don't want to?'

'No, you know what I mean. I need to know. What I'm capable of…and so do you. We've been through this.'

'Oh, dear. Yes, we have. Christina, I might well have some training as a surgeon but you are looking at me as though I'm about to carry out an operation. This is not some medical procedure; it should be an act of love.'

'Don't be angry with me.'

'I'm not, darling, but if you've changed your mind.'

'I haven't but it was easier this afternoon. I wasn't expecting anything to happen so it didn't occur to me to get nervous. I'm sorry, I'm ruining it.'

'You are not ruining anything. We have all our lives before us but you are treating this one night as though your fate depends upon it. That's bound to make things very dull. Never have there been two lovers so disinclined to make love. To my mind, we are going about this the wrong way and it's no wonder we are stumbling.'

'What do you mean?'

'Well, you fear that your brother is coming for you soon. Maybe next week.' She nodded. 'And that means we have very little time to find out whether you are willing to marry me. You have set me this test.'

'I didn't mean it to feel like that. Not a test! That would be awful.'

'Well, it is. I feel as though you will be marking my performance and declining my offer if I don't please you. Unless I am a brilliant lover I will be kicked out the door never to be allowed beneath your chemise ever again.'

She started laughing, knowing that I was teasing and exaggerating. 'I would never treat you like that but I see what you mean. I'll put the score sheet away, shall I? So, now what shall we do?'

'We should have a glass of wine and then you can tell me what you've been doing for the last two years.' She gave me a strange look and I realised she was still a woman in a hurry. 'We have time, darling. I used to know you so well and now I don't, not so much. Humour me.' I stretched out my legs, trying to get comfortable. 'Do you mind if we sit on the bed, though? It's pretty uncomfortable on the floor and there's only one chair, I've never needed another in here, you know.'

'Yes, let's. We can turn it into a sofa if we prop the pillows up against the headboard. It's a magnificent bed.'

It was fashioned out of oak with an ornately carved headboard and posts, a discard from some aristocratic family who were upgrading, no doubt. Very English in style and so sadly out of vogue, it was a little overstated for a property in Giltspur Street but I hadn't worried about that when I bought it. It was large and being aged oak would never suffer from woodworm; that was all that mattered.

We pulled off our shoes and got comfortable. I proposed another toast. 'God bless this bed and all who sleep in her.'

Christina looked at me with a warm smile. That was better. I hated it when her eyes were downcast. We touched glasses. We drank. I put my arm around her shoulders and pulled her close.

'You took up painting,' I said.

'There wasn't much else I could think of to do. My embroidery, I should warn you, is very poor and I once stitched a sampler onto my dress by mistake. It took me ages to unpick and some of the threads had to be cut. At least the dress wasn't damaged. Mind you, I've been messy with a paintbrush too. I've learned to wear an apron.'

'What do you like to paint?'

'The Fleet River.'

I was expecting her to say more but she fell silent. 'Anything else?'

'No, that's it. I paint the river. I've got quite good at it although the water gives me trouble so I don't know why I bother. With watercolours you have to plan ahead and not paint any bits you want to be white. I usually forget.'

'I can picture you out there with your easel and a large brimmed hat, painting in the sunshine surrounded by birds and animals.'

'Then you have a very good imagination because I paint from memory. I have a little studio at home, it's my domain and sometimes I don't come out for days at a time. Don't look so troubled. It's my choice.'

'No wonder you look pale. Why don't you go outside to paint? Your leg is not so bad that you have to stay indoors.'

'It was for a while and the stairs became a problem. It worries Edward to see me trying to get about and he'd go with me to make sure I was alright. He didn't have time to be chaperoning me on painting expeditions. He said he would let me out on my own if I used the stick.'

'You don't like to be coerced, do you? Did you argue with him when he locked you in your room?'

'Yes, not that it made any difference. I don't like to think about that time.' She was staring at the stove which hissed like a pot put onto boil and straining at its lid. 'We've put it behind us.'

'Nevertheless I think you should tell me about it. If you don't mind. I need to know what I'm dealing with and if he turns up here in search of you it would be better if I have all the facts.'

I kissed the top of her head then on the cheek, wanting to reassure her.

'It was after the accident,' she said.

'Surely not. I saw you after the accident. More than once. You were hurt but recovering.'

'I know but I had another fall a few weeks later. Coming down the stairs. That was the final straw for my brother. He said he couldn't stand the constant worry and he gave me a choice.'

'Go on.'

'If I was to stay with him I had to abide by his rules and that meant staying in my room unless someone accompanied me. If I didn't agree he would find somewhere else for me. Bracy, don't doubt me. There are places, I've heard of them. People who will house cripples like me in exchange for some filthy bit of money. Not everyone wants their embarrassing relatives at home and these places exist, so I'm told. The thought of it frightened me and I decided I would do anything he said to stay where I was. At least it was my home and I had a lot of freedom. Compared to the other option. My room was only locked because of the stairs. He worried in case I got up in the night and was confused. In the day it was mostly unlocked. Now, of course, I dutifully use my stick. Well, I did until you got me smashing it to pieces. I've never been very interested in clothes and fashions and my dressing room made the perfect place for a studio. I was happy there, in my own world.

'So, I accepted the inevitable and began painting. I'm no George Stubbs and much as I would have liked to paint horses my amateur attempts were abysmal and I stuck with landscapes. Places I had ridden to were my favourites and then I settled on the Fleet River. It gives us so much trouble, flooding in the winter and seeming so benign in the summer that I wanted to capture it and one day I will succeed.'

'Do you never go and look at it anymore?'

'Yes, occasionally in the summer if someone will take me there.'

There was a lump in my throat that wouldn't shift no matter how many times I swallowed and my eyes smarted and threatened to betray me. I told her she was the bravest and the most beautiful woman I had ever met. She amazed me. There was so little bitterness in her and yet she had carved a life for herself using fingernails into granite.

I had enough animosity towards her brother on my own account and now there was an added burden. Not that I considered Christina a burden, she was a joy. Thoughts of revenge flickered on the edges of my mind until I realised that I had what I wanted. Christina was lying next to me. Our bodies were relaxed with the closeness and she was very nearly mine. I turned onto my side and propped my head up in one hand so I could study her at my leisure while she talked about her painting. She said she wasn't proficient but she was most likely hard on herself.

Very soon I lost focus on her story. Her voice became a soft murmur with rhythm and tone but little meaning. She was light and easy to move in spite of the awkwardness of her leg and I pulled her gently onto her side so that she couldn't avoid my gaze. I stroked her face and pushed a tendril of her hair behind her ear. She was wearing it in a coil on top of her head and my fingers alighted on the pins, pulling them out one by one and throwing them onto the nightstand. With each tiny clatter of metal against wood something changed. Her hair fell around her shoulders and tumbled about her arms. It was the opening bars in this symphony we were composing.

The talking stopped. Her eyes were wide and her breathing became a series of soft sighs. My hands met skin that was warm and welcoming. She smiled when I set to work on the buttons of her dress and she laughed when I helped her struggle out of the thing. She leant a hand with her stays for which I was glad as my own hands were not so adept. We sat up, it was easier. Her stockings slipped off and soon she looked like a nymph in her chemise. It was hard for me to continue. I wanted to feed on the sight of her. She was so much more substantial reclining on the bed, in command of her body…and mine. She didn't have to move about; this dance was far more subtle. How could she fear being at a disadvantage?

Her hands fell onto the buttons of my shirt, shakily undoing them, ripping one. Christina was getting nervous again…or impatient. She pulled it up my body and I threw it over my head.

'Oh,' she said, faintly.

'We look very different, don't we?'

I had always thought myself clumsily built. My height was partly to blame but my physique was muscular and I thought it might disturb her. Then again it might have been the hair. She ran her fingers over my chest in a tentative exploration. My confidence grew thanks to the look on her face. It seemed that I pleased her.

We kissed but soon it wasn't enough. The rest of our clothes were quickly dispensed with and we clung together under the covers, feeling our way. She was like a diminutive piece of fruit that I feared to squash but I shouldn't have worried. Christina was far bolder and more agile than either of us expected. Sadly, she wanted to rush and get it over with. I was having none of it. Being stronger it was easy for me to have my way. So I laid her on her back seeking to satisfy her first since the act of consummation was less likely to give her pleasure. She knew what I was about this time and when she cried out it took all my control not to follow her into languorous oblivion. From the light of the candle on the nightstand I could see her skin was flushed and drenched with moisture. It was almost enough to satisfy me.

'Will you not do more?' she asked.

Her eyes were wide once more and the sight of me seemed to impress and worry in equal measure. I played with her a bit more not wanting to mention the pain I might give her and my reasons for stretching and pressing on her maidenhead with my fingers. Get into a scientific discussion with Christina and you risked an unwelcome distraction. I had joked while we sat by the stove about her testing my skills but the thought returned to haunt me when I eased myself slowly but rather too eagerly inside her. I was met by her cry of wonder and a slight whimper of pain that drove me on and impeded me at the same time. I had been right to satisfy her first for this was not the time. This was consummation. I was claiming her...and now she was mine.

# CHAPTER 38

Christina came to help me with the accounts every night after that. We became quite skilled in a language we developed for these visits. Columns, entries and addition took on humorous meanings while my accounts book acquired a layer of dust from the London air.

She was particularly adept at finding new phrases to describe my prowess and I found it almost alarming that after only these few nights she was able to discuss double entry bookkeeping with a knowing smirk.

We laughed at the most ridiculous things, feeling protected by the high walls surrounding 17 Giltspur Street and the lock on the gates which was secured at night. My bedchamber was being filled nightly with happy memories and rewarding discoveries. It amazed me how much we confided and discussed. I told her about my work, the struggle to set up my practice – all the things I had written to her about. She was dismayed that her brother had shown so little interest in my research.

'That was to my face, Christina. Behind my back he's done everything in his power to make me a laughing stock,' I told her. 'It's such an important discovery and yet he wants to suppress it but I won't rest, not while I've got strength. I will be heard.'

'Your books are selling so you will achieve that without his help.'

'It seems I will have to.'

'Bracy, you will think me seditious! But it's all about freedom, don't you see? All of us need to escape the things that bind us.' She sat up in bed and stared at me closely amid the shadows. 'You need the freedom to speak, to tell the world about your research. You always wondered what your purpose was and now you've found it.' She laughed and had trouble continuing until eventually she said: 'I want be to free to stumble about in my own way and in my own time without being mocked or made to sit down. And Firefly...'

'Oh, yes! What does she need?'

'You know that more than any of us. Freedom from the iron shoe. She's walking very well on her own feet and I want to be just like her.'

'I think you are right, my little radical.'

I took her back to the Phillips' house dutifully by eleven o'clock. Our lingering looks were never questioned and it seemed no one noticed the change in Christina. She'd always had an air of confidence so perhaps I alone saw the added note of serenity. You will forgive the pun, I'm sure, when I confide that her riding also became much more proficient.

There was only one subject that dented her happiness. Our marriage. She talked as though it was some distant dream and if she talked of her future it was always as a single woman without children of her own. She was defensive when I pointed this out to her.

'I've been resigned to being a spinster for so long,' she explained. 'It's enough that you've given me this time. It's been special.'

'What! You must be joking. We had a bargain, remember? Am I to take it that you are reneging on your promise?' We were lying in bed and the window was open, letting in the smell of the city and its inhabitants. We were hot from our exertions and I turned her to face me. 'Damn it, I've become your lover. You can't turn around and tell me that you no longer want me. I suppose I'm not good enough. Is that it?'

'No, that's not it at all. But I will probably be going home in a couple of days…how can we make it happen? It's not going to be possible but I thought I might try and visit Suzanna again soon. I'll let Edward have his say and then perhaps he will calm down and forget about it. I have a way of managing him. I was better at it when I was younger but now I find it's best to ignore what he says and work my way round it. He will be cross about the stick, though. I'm not sure he'll forgive that so quickly.'

'Why will he worry about the stick when he finds out the rest? You think he'll be happy that we've become lovers?'

'I wasn't planning on telling him. I don't see that it's any of his business. He must know that I've seen you and that I've been riding Firefly so he won't be in the best of moods. He never liked it when you humiliated him. He's going to be furious.'

'Christina, if we wait for him to be happy before we tell him of our plans we might never marry. I thought you might feel the same impatience.'

'I do,' she cried.

She looked sincere but she was causing me such pain. 'Darling, we have to stand up to him. We will do it together. There's no way you should handle him on your own and then I think we should ask your friend Suzanna if you can stay with her until we are married. I don't like the thought of you going back to Camden. Somehow I fear I'll never see you again once he's shut you in your artist's garret.

'If you like, we can be married at St Sepulchre Church. I'll get a licence and we can be married in three weeks…if you want to, that is.' She nodded, saying she would be happy to. She threw her arms around me begging my forgiveness for ever doubting I could contrive it. 'You must talk to Suzanna in the morning, we are going to need her help.'

We began making arrangements for our wedding and our lives. I wanted to know what help she might need in the house and what changes she might like to make but, other than an extra chair in the bedroom, she didn't seem to care.

Her brother was always in the back of my mind. The thought of Christina having to face him alone worried me. She used to stand up to him but he'd used her falls to control her, disguising it as love and care, until she was meek and biddable. She hid it well but she was frightened of him and frightened of life without him. I wished we had more time.

On Saturday I got back from my rounds feeling particularly tired. The worry was starting to tell on me and I had to stifle a yawn when Peter took Heathfield from me.

'You have a visitor, Mr Clark,' he said. 'I showed him into the study as I didn't know where else to put him. He seemed a bit too inclined to take a look at your dispensary cupboards, if you ask me.'

'Did he have a name?'

'None that he volunteered. He said he was a vet but I've never seen one that dressed quite like that. Fit for the King he is.'

In spite of a sense of foreboding I gave Peter instructions about a patient due to arrive that afternoon with recurrent lameness. I wanted the animal on a deep bed of straw and the largest stable we had so that he moved as much as possible. Peter untacked Heathfield and I made my way slowly indoors where I came face to face with William Sewell. I was surprised to see him, we had never been friends and now we were enemies thanks to my public attacks on him and his benefactor.

'William! How good to see you,' I said with all the urbanity I could muster.

'Bracy,' he said with a condescending drawl. 'The pleasure is all mine.'

We shook hands and I bade him sit and offered him tea which I was glad he declined. He hadn't changed much but his clothes were finer. He was wearing a poppy-red waistcoat with buff pantaloons and a dark blue jacket that fitted to perfection. His neck cloth was intricately arranged and sported a gaudy pin in its lavish folds. He was pale still and his chin had the makings of a soft, downy beard. Only his eyes showed signs of maturity. There were dark shadows beneath them, faint lines at their corners and the unmistakable evidence of a nervous tic. He was finding it hard to sit still and his gaze was locked on the door as if he would rush out given the chance.

'I hear good reports of your gripe mixture,' he ventured after a few awkward starts. 'I thought to ask you about it…just in case…might be useful, if it works.'

I would have been flattered had anyone else asked me for the recipe. Had I been in his shoes I would be asking for proof of the accusations made in print. I would be throwing punches in all probability but this fellow was as guilty as Professor Coleman. He wasn't here to defend himself or demand recompense.

'It does work,' I said, playing along with him. 'But surely you didn't come all this way to talk to me about one of my cures. We are a long way from Camden. You are still at the college, I presume?'

'Naturally, I'm still there. Did you think? But no matter. It's no distance, not to me…for such an important reason. I'm giving a lecture about the gripes and wanted to investigate all the latest findings.'

He stared at his hands during this speech and I had the feeling he wasn't telling me the truth but I couldn't fathom what other reason he might have for calling on me. I got a bottle of my mixture from the cupboard and handed it to him. I even told him the ingredients which he scribbled on a notepad that he took from his pocket.

'You don't wish to protect the discovery? I think I would. If it was…if I had made it.'

'No, unlike the Professor I don't see the need for patents. I'm happy to share my knowledge.'

'Really?'

'What use is it if the only animals that benefit from my discovery are my own patients? I would be delighted if this remedy was used at the college to help as many horses as possible.'

'B...but you could sell it, man. Don't you see? If it works, if it cures the horse you could be rich.'

'I would far rather be happy.' I gazed at him with a measure of disgust. My sober approach to life had always irritated him and we couldn't understand one another.

'Well, I wish you luck. But tell me, what made you think of using pimento?'

'It's a mild relaxant. The aim is to soothe the gut.'

'And that must be helpful, I suppose.' He seemed puzzled and rattled on at unusual speed about a case they'd had at the college that had stumped them all. He asked for my opinion. Mine!

'It's always difficult to say without seeing the animal. But come now, William, what really brings you to my door? There must be something else on your mind other than this interesting discussion.'

I would have felt for him had he not been a toadying fool who was using his elevated position to acquire wealth rather than enrich understanding. He sat before me, dissembling. I was losing patience and stood to leave. He got up and his face was suffused with red. Embarrassment? Why?

'Did you ride here?' I asked, for the first time noticing the empty yard. 'I see you didn't drive.'

'Er...no. I came with...I was brought here.'

Now I was truly alarmed. 'Who by?'

He didn't seem inclined to answer me and his excuses turned into a cough. I whipped round to stare at him as realisation dawned. I shoved him hard against the door. He was tall but a lightweight and it would have been a minute's work to throw him onto the muck heap. But I wanted answers.

'Who brought you?' I shouted. 'Was it the Professor? Answer me, damn you.' I had him by the throat so now he had two reasons for having trouble with his words. 'Is he really worth a broken nose?'

I raised my fist and I would have struck him. I heard Peter rush from the stables but he took in the situation and left me to it. William nodded and I released the pressure.

'He's gone to fetch her, hasn't he?' He nodded again. 'And you were sent here to make sure of my whereabouts. You only needed to keep me here a few minutes, just enough to make sure he got her away. You filthy toad.'

'Filthy? Me?' He regained his voice and his composure as I pushed him away. 'That's a bit rich coming from you. Ruining that poor, crippled creature.'

That was it. I couldn't help myself. I punched him in the jaw and watched in satisfaction as he landed awkwardly on the ground, wriggling like an overturned beetle. Then I rushed to the stables where I found Peter putting a side saddle onto Firefly – she wasn't the speediest choice but, if I had some persuading to do, she would be my best asset. The saddle was designed for a woman wearing a riding habit but I managed to perch on the thing astride.

Firefly was good on the cobbles, no stumbling, no slipping and she was nimble enough to weave through the congestion. It was no distance to Suzanna's house but I was thwarted along Newgate Street by one of the brewery wagons which had shed its load. The street was covered in barrels and confusion, people shouting and trying to get through and there was a carriage that didn't have space to turn. I doubled back and turned at the next junction, Firefly getting into a brisk trot now we had some room. I saw them as I turned the corner with too much speed. Christina was in an open carriage covered in enough shawls and blankets for an influenza patient. Her brother was swinging up beside her and Suzanna was standing on the pavement with a handkerchief in one hand, her face blotched with red. Christina looked up when she heard me approach and I stood Firefly in front of the Professor's horse to make sure he couldn't move. I didn't dismount.

'We had better go inside to talk about this,' I said. He ignored me. His face seemed drained of emotion although I suspected he never felt such a thing in his life. 'You're not taking her, Professor. You have no right to.'

He took up his whip and pursed his lips. 'Get out of my way.'

'No, I'll move when I'm ready. She doesn't want to go with you and you can't take her against her will. She's not a minor.'

Christina appeared glassy eyed. She didn't seem to care what was happening. It was worrying me that she wasn't able to do battle with him as I could hardly force her to stay. Our raised voices were causing a stir and a crowd was gathering around us. One woman asked Suzanna what was happening. Suzanna fell on her shoulder and burst into tears drawing more onlookers towards us.

'She's not well,' The Professor said loudly. 'She needs care night and day and it is my duty to make sure she is safe. I have done so for many years and I will continue, preferably without your interference.'

'You exaggerate. She is not ill. Tell him, Christina. You want to keep her locked up, that's not safe. That's a living death.'

There were cries of *shame* among the crowd which agitated him. He was hemmed in on all sides by now and couldn't move unless this lot dispersed or he drove over them.

'Mr Clark, she is a cripple and you want her to run about until she kills herself. You might have mesmerised her for a few days, got her hopes up and made her pretend that she can live a normal life but, like all good things, it must come to an end.'

There was enough of a crowd for me to safely ride to the side of the carriage so I could speak to Christina. I leant down and Firefly nudged her in the shoulder.

'You have the right to leave him, Christina.'

'Do I?' she whispered. 'Even normal women have very little say.'

There were tears puddling her eyes and for the first time I noticed a red mark on her face and wondered if he had struck her. My jaw clenched.

'As a single woman you can choose whether you live

under your brother's protection…or you can marry me. If you don't want to do either I can help you find another way. He can't force you to do this. You can be free of him.'

My call for Christina's freedom struck a chord with the crowd. Shouting and debate rippled through them and it struck me that we could be viewed as a seditious gathering since the authorities were highly nervous after the revolution in France. There were shouts of *let her go free*, some people were jostling and at one point I thought she might be pulled from the gig. A seller of apple pies shouted about his lovely wares and a singer with a scrawny dog struck up a song. The crowd was my ally but the connection was fraught as I had no control over them. Professor Coleman sought to enlist their help.

'My friends,' he said, his tone affable and assured. 'My sister is very weak, please let us pass as I need to take her home. She has great trouble walking, she relies heavily on a stick and this dreadful scene must be exhausting and humiliating for her. I beg you to do what's right for her and disperse.'

Christina stirred as though she'd taken a dip in cold water. She looked at her brother with her brows tightly drawn so that she gave the impression of seeing him in a new light.

'But Edward,' she cried, happily, 'I can!'

He sighed and closed his eyes. 'You can what, my dear?'

'I can walk. Without the stick,' she laughed and looked at the crowd as if the people were her friends.

A man with only one leg leant on his crutch and bobbed awkwardly up the pavement shouting gleefully. 'Yeah, we can walk. Look at me!'

There was singing and people began to dance reminding me of some impromptu celebration.

'Christina, you can hobble. That is hardly walking and you know how often you fall down. It's ridiculous not to take care.'

Firefly whickered at Christina and gave her another nudge. Christina rubbed the mare's head and threw the blankets from her lap. 'Look, I'll show you. Watch me walk without the stick. You see, there's a lot I can do if I practice. Sitting down is the worst thing for me, that's what you forget, Edward.'

She got down from the carriage. She did it backwards and it wasn't the most elegant exit but she achieved it unaided. The crowd parted and a hush descended. The man with the crutch ceased his own antics and watched her, spellbound. And then she did it. She walked. Not terribly well. She limped but gave a respectable performance. Suzanna gave her an enormous hug and another woman patted her affectionately on the back and told her in a loud voice to, 'Follow yer heart, luv.'

She walked to the horse and stood beside me. 'Get off her would you, Bracy. There's something I have to do.' I slid off and handed her the reins, thinking she might lead the horse back to Giltspur Street. It wasn't too far and she was quite capable of it if we didn't rush. 'Help me to mount.'

I hesitated. Well, I had no idea what she had in mind and didn't want anything to go wrong. 'You want to get on here? But...there's a crowd...she won't keep still...'

'Never mind. Come on, we've done it so many times now. I have to show everyone, you must see that.'

I cupped my hands reluctantly and threw her onto the saddle. She sat there like a queen with her blue, silk skirts flowing over the mare's side. She was wearing a straw hat decorated with blue ribbons and her hair was loose and tumbling down her back. She took up the reins like the capable rider I had always known.

She turned the horse in a circle and gave me a slight nod, telling me to keep away. She didn't need any help.

Her brother's face was white. 'Christina! Mr Clark! Get her down. Are you both mad?'

'Not mad, just in love. You see, Edward, the stories you heard about a chestnut horse that looked like Firefly were not quite true. It was her all the time. Alive and well and living in London. Can you believe it?' Christina walked the mare up and down, the crowd giving her room while she spoke. 'You know, I have much in common with this horse. We've both been lame and written off. And we're both going to be as well as we can be.'

'I'm telling you for the last time. Get down from there.' He turned to me. 'You are responsible for this. If she gets hurt it will be your fault.'

Christina controlled Firefly's urge to trot down the road, brought her to a halt and faced her brother. 'No, Edward. I am responsible for myself. I know I'm not safe but at least I am alive. That's the difference...and you must let me live. Yes, you must let me be happy.' She turned the horse expertly and briefly looked up at the sky. 'I'm probably much safer here than I am on the ground.'

The Professor's face was like a boiled pudding about to burst. He sat motionless and for once without power.

Christina sent Firefly up the road away from him, nodding to me to follow and shouting behind her. 'By the way, Edward, did I tell you I'm getting married? We'll invite you to the wedding.'

She waved and I caught up with her as the hoots from the gathering around Professor Coleman's carriage faded into the distance.

'Do I take it, Miss Coleman, that you've accepted my proposal?'

There was an impish light in her eyes when she looked down at me. 'Only if you let me walk up the aisle all by myself.'

THE END

# THE PEOPLE BEHIND THE BOOK

Bracy Clark was the gifted son of a Quaker but gave up his surgeon's apprenticeship to be one of the first pupils at the Veterinary College when it opened in 1792. Unlike some, he was able to cope with the strict rules against strong liquor and ran the dispensary following the sudden death of Charles Vial de St Bel, the college's professor. Clark set up a successful practice in Giltspur Street, London. He exposed the harm of shoeing horses and went on some long distance journeys on a barefoot horse but worried that he had discovered an evil for which there was no remedy. He was mocked by the veterinary establishment who wouldn't allow him to sell his books to the students. Clark spoke out against the shortened veterinary course and the practice of taking any student for the sake of the fee. He accused Professor Edward Coleman and his assistant, William Sewell, of corruption.

Edward Coleman, a surgeon, became professor of the college a few months after the death of St Bel and remained at the helm for 45 years. On his death, it is said he had amassed a fortune of £47,000. He shortened the training course and placed many of his vets in the cavalry regiments, thereby securing funding from the government. It is recognised that he held back the profession, resisting attempts for it to gain a Royal Charter. One historian described him as an 'unmitigated evil', questioning his appointment when he knew nothing of the horse. He patented the Grasshopper and the Spitbar shoes, which Clark complained had crippled countless horses.

William Sewell was Professor Coleman's assistant from the age of 15 and succeeded him as professor in 1839. He had a reputation for giving the most confusing lectures and famously offered students their money back if they were unable to understand him. He was a pupil at the college after Bracy Clark and was later charged with maintaining discipline. Clark accused him of corruption, complaining that he was credited and paid for discoveries that he hadn't made.

Charles Benoit Vial de St Bel was a French émigré who established the college with the support of the Odiham Agricultural Society. Their stated aim was to improve farriery and they recruited subscribers who paid to have their horses treated.

Edmund Bond attended, with Bracy Clark, the post mortem of Eclipse carried out by St Bel in 1789. He was given the skeleton which his widow later gave to Clark in order to repay a loan.

F.C. Cherry was involved with Clark in the publication of The Veterinarian and The Farrier and Naturalist which attacked the regime at the college.

Granville Penn was one of the founders of the college.

Eclipse was the most famous racehorse of his day. Unbeaten, he retired to stud and sired hundreds of winners. He is said to be the ancestor of many horses racing today. Bracy Clark owned his skeleton which he stored in a cupboard in his study. Shortly before his death he sold it to the Veterinary College in Edinburgh for 100 guineas. It now resides at the Royal Veterinary College.

Heathfield was the son of Waxy, a grandson of Eclipse. Bracy Clark purchased him as a three-year-old stallion from Tattersalls and used him on his veterinary rounds.

Richard Cross was the knacker from Camden who supplied the college with horses and mules for dissection.

Mr Wrench ran the Elephant and Castle Inn in the early 19th century. It was popular among veterinary students.

Christina Coleman is a figment of my imagination! She was drawn from all the wonderful riders I saw at the Paralympics in Greenwich – all of whom were far better equestrians than me.

# 18<sup>TH</sup> CENTURY VETERINARY TERMS

Founder : laminitis. Today's vets still refer to a horse that has foundered – a case of laminitis that is so severe that the pedal bone has detached and is pushing against, or through, the sole of the foot.

Gripes: colic, stomach pain.

Firing: Bracy Clark abhorred the practice of firing a lame horse in which a hot iron is applied to the leg in order to affect a cure. Firing is still carried out in some parts of the world today.

Read the first chapter of Linda Chamberlain's lighthearted account of her battle to give horse shoes the boot.

# MY BAREFOOT JOURNEY

I've made it a policy to avoid arguing with well muscled men wielding a hammer and nails. I'm not a tall woman, more a lightweight who can be pushed over easily but my stand off with the farrier that day required me to get in touch with my masculine side. Quickly.

You see, my requirements were simple; I wanted the shoes off my two horses and it was not a job I could do myself. He shouldn't have started a fight over it but he was jangling a set of new shoes in his hand and he wanted to fit them. I wanted him to put them in the back of his van and drive off – once he'd taken the old set off, of course. He was a nice guy – young, lovely smile and the well-defined muscles of his trade but he had a natural desire to keep hold of his business. Even in the face of some daft woman who had read a tiny but controversial book about riding barefoot horses. That book had shocked me and I couldn't forget its dire warning that nailing shoes onto the hoof was slowly killing the animals we loved.

'They won't manage without them,' he said, rubbing his chin and eyeing the sad state of Barnaby's feet.

My daughter's pony made him sigh but he wrenched the old and worn shoes from her feet, gave her a trim and was ready to smooth her hooves with the heavy rasp that he could wield as if it was my nail file. He straightened his back, swept his hair from his head with one easy swipe and came to a decision without meeting my eye.

'We'll put shoes on their fronts; that's the answer.'

I liked this guy, he was one of the nicest farriers I had used and we had shared a few hours over the years chatting about horses and drinking tea. He had been a competitive rider when he was younger and handled the animals with sympathy and understanding. But I was a coward and couldn't find the words to tell him that farriers had become second to undertakers on my people-to-avoid-while-alive list. If only they would retrain and become barefoot trimmers, I thought.

He grabbed the tray of tools from the back of his blue van without waiting for my answer and was about to start up the furnace of his mobile forge. Years ago, I used to ride for miles to take my horse to the blacksmith but now the old forges have become bijoux dwellings and farriers drive these vans with a little gas furnace in the back so they can hot shoe horses in their own homes. The smell of burnt hoof follows them like an invisible mist.

'Oh, dear. No, I'd rather keep them all off, if you don't mind,' I said.

My voice was a bit too high pitched to be taken seriously. It needed measured base tones for men to know I meant business. So the first attempt didn't quell the gas flame.

I needed to try harder since he wasn't listening. I wanted my horses to be barefoot. We were only riding on Ashdown Forest, hardly any road work, so surely they didn't need metal wrapped around their feet.

'Nah, his feet will crumble. Look at that crack all the way up his foot! White feet; they're all the same. Weak and useless. He'll never go barefoot.'

I took a look at the horse that had carted me around for the last five years. He was as strong as an ox and pulled like a tank; he had given me so many reasons to seek out good osteopaths who bemoaned the state of my weary and pulled shoulders. Every farrier that came within two yards of him warned me his feet were his only weak point. They cracked, they didn't grow quickly enough and so they were full of nail holes with nowhere to fix a new shoe.

His feet were in a sorry state even though I had done everything conventional wisdom had advised. Dutiful and regular shoeing every six weeks. It didn't seem to be working, his feet were getting worse and he was unlikely to make it into old age as a ridden horse. Barefoot was being mooted as more than an alternative…it was a cure. That crack on my cob's near hind was caused by shoeing. I knew that from my reading and I knew that his feet were destined to get worse the longer he walked on metal instead of padding on his own feet.

It might have been the hammer that did it; then again the sight of the nails goaded me. Sharp and shining. Lined up neatly in their trays ready to be driven into Barnaby's feet if this man had his way - consigned to the history books if I had mine.

One word was all it needed. A two-lettered one.

'No.'

I explained again. 'We don't ride them very much. We don't compete, you know, so I really think they'll be fine. I don't want the shoes on.'

Frankly, I would have chosen not to ride if it meant driving nails into their feet every few weeks. I was full of my new-found cause and brimming with facts like a cynic who'd found God on Facebook. This is the crux of it – the hoof is a moving part of the horse. It is not a block of wood. In its natural state, the hoof acts as a shock absorber by flexing on landing, it supports the heart by pumping blood back around the body and it can't work with a metal shoe. Nailing metal onto a moving part of a horse causes injuries, shrinks their feet and gives them life-threatening diseases but we've been doing it for so long we're blind to the harm.

The trouble is that the hoof appears immobile to the human eye. It appears as unmoving as a pair of coconut shells that we slap together to mimic the sound of a horse trotting. But if you ever get a chance, grab a barefoot horse by the leg and give his foot a squeeze. Or get someone like me to do it for you. There's a central groove on the underside of the hoof and if you press hard on the sides you can see it crease.

Better still, go on the internet and watch the films of barefoot horses in motion and see how the foot spreads when it lands, how the sole descends, how the part called the frog touches the ground.

If only the horse had a repertoire of facial expressions like a dog. Don't forget that the metal shoe is nailed on when his foot is lifted from the ground so it is not weight bearing. It is at its narrowest. If only the horse could frown. Or wince. Or shake his foot as though his trainers were too tight. He doesn't do any of those things but he walks in a new way that people become accustomed to. His feet are heavier and as I said, they can't flex. The only warnings for a rider who isn't listening or watching for the changes are the potential health problems further down the line.

One lone vet from Germany, Hiltrud Strasser, was swimming against the tide and saying their lives were being shortened dramatically by the practice of shoeing. She had warned that the average age of a euthanized horse was about eight years old so my two had already passed their sell-by date. Most horses that are put to sleep are lost through lameness and according to Strasser, most lameness is caused by shoeing.

I was upset and deeply moved when I read her book. First of all I had to deal with the guilt. I had owned horses since I was fifteen. My first horse had been with me for twenty years and naturally she was shod. Had I harmed her?

Yes, I had.

She'd suffered from painful foot problems and had been put to sleep at the age of twenty six. It was considered a good age but with hindsight she would have been more comfortable without landing on metal with every step. We might even have found cure and enabled her to live for longer. I couldn't turn the clock back but I could change the future for the two I had now. I vowed they wouldn't suffer this acceptable cruelty. Although, I didn't expect them to live forever, I was going to give it my best shot.

But I didn't like to hurt my farrier's feelings by repeating these revolutionary thoughts and I hated confrontation.

'Well, what am *I* going to do?' he asked.

He seemed shaken with annoyance but he was only losing two horses from his list; he wouldn't miss them, would he? I mean, *I* liked them, but surely he hadn't got attached on such a short acquaintance. His face was tight as if he needed to hold onto his teeth. Embarrassment crept inside me.

'What do you mean?' I said.

'I lose the business then, do I?'

'Perhaps you could still trim them for me,' I suggested, apologetically.

This was nearly fifteen years ago. A set of shoes cost about £45 and I have no idea what that has risen to now. I was offering him a job that would yield him £10 or £20 per horse every six weeks at the most. It wasn't much and he knew it. These horses would need trimming but his business was shoeing. To his mind, it was better for the horse to wear metal shoes since the perceived wisdom was, and still is in conventional circles, that they protect the foot. It was also better for his pay packet.

The little veterinary book that had set me on this journey had warned me against getting the farrier to trim their feet. They trim the feet, it said, to fit a horse shoe rather than to set a horse up for his barefoot life. But, there weren't many specialist barefoot trimmers in Britain at that time – I had heard of only one and she lived more than a hundred miles away – so who else would look after their feet?

It was looking more and more likely that this guy wouldn't be coming back for my measly few pounds.

He flung the rasp to the ground. He wouldn't look at me and turned away with a hunch of his shoulders. I wasn't as daft as he thought because I understood and I sympathised but I was too English, too polite to tell him what I really thought of shoeing. Perhaps we both knew that I would be the first of many owners who would take this step. Neither of us could have envisaged that we were witnessing one of the first cracks in a tradition of metal shoeing that has held sway for a thousand years; a crack that would grow, with or without my contribution, into a worldwide movement affecting thousands of horses. There would be prosecutions, vilification and plenty of hatred. But there would be no stopping the change that was coming.

Horse shoeing. My farrier thought it was essential. I thought it was killing the animals in our care. The middle ground argued it was a necessary evil.

We stood eyeing each other. I kept hold of my thoughts and waited. I had the upper hand. He *had* to do the job I was asking. Take off the shoes and trim their feet. Nothing more. Or someone else would do it.

So, of course he did and he left me with promises of a return visit that was never to happen. My horses – Barnaby, a black and white 10-year-old cob, and the small-but-perfectly-formed pony, Girlie - were barefoot. And I was on my own.

8415075R00201

Printed in Great Britain
by Amazon.co.uk, Ltd.,
Marston Gate.